CLARECE

THE QUEEN OF SLAVES

BOOK 2

THE CASSICAN CHRONICLES

MARTHA J. VAUGHT

Cassican Press, LLC

United States of America

Cassican Press, LLC
USA

Clarece: The Queen of Slaves
Book II
The Cassican Chronicles

Cover illustration by Danny O'Leary, www.Illustrationweb.com
Interior design by Jon Marken, www.lamppostpublicity.com

First printing 2020

Printed in the United States of America

Clarece: The Queen of Slaves/Martha J. Vaught
Library of Congress Control Number: 2019921251

ISBN 978-1-7321107-2-4 (pbk)
ISBN 978-1-7321107-3-1 (ebook)

Contact:
www.Cassicanpress.com
email: Martha@cassicanpress.com
Martha J. Vaught, Facebook

The use of paragraph dialogue format is intentional. – The Author

For Kyle,

You heard every word, first

The Edict of Byzanthia

...and as for the rebellious land, Heaven,
itself, will mark your subjugation.

A daughter of Cassica will be born on the same date as the last son of Byzanthia. Before her seventeenth birthday, Cassica must surrender her daughter, as tribute, to Byzanthia's son, presented as the prisoner of war she is. And the son may ransom or kill The Tribute as he desires.

And so shall the terms of The Edict be, forever, satisfied....

I

The guard slouched, bored. Scads, what a dull, dull day was this. He could be outside now, out with his fellows, talking, drinking, guarding some gate or wall. But no. He had stupidly volunteered for this watch, hoping to impress his superior, whom he was certain he hadn't impressed, hoping to impress his peers by covering for an injured comrade. *Blast, fool!* he thought. He'd been with the guards three months now and still had not learned the iron rule: volunteer for nothing. Well, at least he was warm, there was that, even if he would rather be with his squad than, here, in this silent, empty place.

Of course, it wasn't entirely empty nor entirely silent. There had been much yelling in the chamber near him until finally, it regurgitated one small slave girl. The guard remembered, smirking. The little waif nearly fell trying to kneel to him as she carried a large laundry basket. Stupid slaves. They must breed stupid. His rank didn't require a full kneel; a half would do. But he was certain the tiny slave would have knelt to a lamppost, so rattled she looked. The teary face that glanced at him was swollen from a beating. Thank the gods he wasn't born damned, like a slave. He would have killed himself from shame.

A figure moved to his left. The numbed man glanced to inspect it. "*Oh, yes*!" he exclaimed, internally. This was not a lost watch after all! His fellows would be jealous, for there she was: the striking form of the insulit approached him from the far end of the east wing. The guard didn't even pretend to hide his stare. He stalked her every step. God, could she walk! Everything of her body moved in a deeply pleasing way, like beer foaming at the head. The woman kept her gaze forward, acknowledging neither man nor leer. It didn't matter; it wasn't her attention he wanted.

"God's Beauty," he announced, as she passed him, "on your way to service, are we? You could save *my* soul...." She gave no response, though certainly she had heard.

Scads, the woman oozed desire like a sweet sweat. His eyes caressed her retreating form. How he wished for more than a caressing of the eye. A wave of desire washed over him. He reveled in the surge. There was much to occupy his mind now. How much could it cost, to rent her a half-hour? Maybe if he and his friends pooled their resources. *Oh, well,* he smiled, *it costs nothing to fantasize.*

The guard stood more satisfied now, his mind happily engaged with the beauty of God. Such a spiritual experience it was, this private reverie of bodily worship. He barely even noticed the little slave returning several hours later. She had completed her task of washing her owner's clothes and had set them out for the sun to do its work. She knelt humbly to the guard before entering her mistra's chamber. How she wished to be invisible. Muriel was in a frightening mood, beating her for nothing. She had been a good slave today, dropped nothing. Did nothing wrong and still her mistra glared at her with blood in her eye.

The guard had just flipped a page in his liturgy, anticipating the high act of communion, when a muffled explosion disrupted his service. He searched for the source of the noise. A door, the little slave's door, burst open, revealing an angry, crazed royal.

"Guard!" the woman yelled. "Get this shoat from my room—immediately!" *Scads!* he cursed. The woman looked as though to pummel him. "Y—yes, my lady," he stammered, jogging to the chamber. He entered the room. His gaze arrested from the furnishings to focus on a tiny, fallen form.

The little slave lay face down on a rich tapestried carpet, a shattered, crystal vase lying near her body. A small hand twitched but as he watched, even this movement stilled. Blood oozed from the left side of the head and out the left ear. All was still and silent. He heard nothing but his quickened breathing and pounding heart.

"Don't just stand there, gawking!" the angry voice spoke from behind. "Tis staining my carpet. Get it out of here!" The guard bowed to the royal. "Yes, my lady. Where do you wish me take her?" "I don't care!" she snarled contemptuously. "Just get rid of it!"

The guard studied the body for a moment. He'd never touched a slave in all his life. How was he to accomplish this task? He resorted to skills he knew and lifted the light burden under his arm like a log. It didn't weigh as much as a log. Her blood left a trail as he exited the room. It dripped as he paused in the empty hall, weighing his options. Scads, where should he dump this carcass?

His eyes spotted a dark opening. He had seen slaves come and go through that doorway. Surely one would discover her, eventually, and do whatever is done with dead slaves. He walked into the darkness and dropped his load. It fell with a soft thud. He returned to his post and only then noticed the blood on his sleeve. It was still warm. The young man cringed, feeling somewhat nauseous. He eyed the blood on the floor, his appetite for worship, lost.

It was less a half-hour later when he noticed the familiar form. The insulit was returning from her service. Her face bore a sullen and defiant look. *Blast*, thought Asla. The morning was repulsive enough. All she wished was to bathe and hide in her stall until the evening services, but here was this asinine manchild of a guard. She should have taken a back route to the pen.

"Insulit!" the guard whispered, loudly. She passed, silently conducting him to hell. "Insulit!" he screamed quietly, frantic. The blonde woman spun, enraged. "You can't afford me," she spat, "but fantasy is on the house!" She turned to resume her way.

"No, wait!" the guard called after her. "A slave...." Asla spun again, concerned. "What slave?" she asked suspiciously. "The girl slave, the little one. You know...." "What of her?" Asla asked, approaching the guard, wary; this could be a trap. Her eyes scanned the hall, glanced at the floor. It was then she saw it. A puddle of blood. *Raina!* her mind gasped. "Where is she?!" she demanded. The frightened guard pointed to the recess in the wall. "She's there. I put her in there. She's...she's dead."

Asla turned cold. She ran to the slave's passage and peered inside. Enough light from the hall reached a still form, revealing two little boots, green socks showing above them. "Oh, no," the young woman cried, "no...." She stood for a time at the sight, then slowly knelt beside the broken child. Raina lay face up, and from that position, Asla could see the blood on her head, in her ear. Tentatively, the woman reached for the still face.

An observer would have thought her hesitant to touch a corpse. She wasn't. The insulit was well-acquainted with death. It was another fear she fought, the same fear that kept her from the cathedral and religious books.

In all her life, Asla had never touched a slave – except Clarece. But with Clarece, she had permission, granted initially by the desperation of pain. The insulit had no right to touch this girl now, but she must. And, half-expecting to be burned, she did, tenderly turning the head. The neck wasn't broken. "Raina?" she asked quietly. She moved her hand to the girl's throat and felt. Nothing. Asla shook her head, despairing, then carefully placed her ear over the little heart. It beat. Raina's heart beat still.

"Raina!" she repeated, relieved. "Don't you die. Not yet!" She wrapped her left arm over the waif's legs and, placing her right arm under the bleeding head, cradled the child to her breasts and stood. Her gymnast's arms found the weight easily borne. She must hurry to Casica. She jogged carefully down the passage unto the main slave corridor, wishing Raina life as she went. She fairly ran down the pen stairs and up again to the princess' chamber. She stepped, breathless, into the doorway and looked about. The room was empty. Empty.

"For gods' sakes! Where are you?!" she declared, confused. It was tea time; she should be here. They were always here, and now that she needed her, the healer was gone. It never occurred to the frightened woman to look outside the window. Had she done so, she would have seen Casica sipping her tea in the garden, listening with rapt attention as Clarece paced the picnic table, delivering a tutorial on arboreal specimens in the region.

"Help me!" Asla cried, not knowing to whom she called. She looked at the pale face in her arms. She turned and carried the girl to her stall, carefully laying her down. There was the donkey book, awaiting its reader. Raina did not own a pillow; her mistra provided her nothing.

Asla ran to her stall and gathered her cloak and her and Clarece's pillows. She took some blouses and a pair of trousers and placed the pile of fabric under the bleeding head. She must have it raised, she knew. She then retrieved her red cape and placed it along with Raina's over the still body. Finally, as an afterthought, she ran up the stairs and scribbled a note on some of the princess' drawing parchment. "Come to Raina's stall. Now.," she wrote and placed the note on the dining table.

Below in the pen, Asla examined Raina's scalp. She took a clean cloth and held it against the open wound, but not too tightly. Perhaps she could staunch the blood. There. There was nothing more she could do. She could not pray. She could not heal. She could do nothing except sit helplessly and wish to the little girl, "Live, Raina. Live."

II

Casica entered the chamber, laughing. What a delightful afternoon it had been. Clarece was in fine form. The princess took their cups and placed them on the table, noticing the paper as she did. Her mind winced. "Clarece! My satchel!" she ordered, bolting from the room into the darkness below. Clarece glanced at the note, confused. *Oh, God!* she breathed. She found her mistra's bag in its usual resting place: the sitting area. Gathering it, she flew down the familiar stairs and ran to the little girl's stall. There, stood her owner and friend hovering over a small, still body.

"Raina!" the slave whispered, lowering the leather satchel absently. Her worried friend looked to her, shaking her head. Casica's eyes were closed. Her shalonn blazed as she kneeled beside the body, one hand on Raina's heart, the other placed directly upon the bleeding wound. Clarece stood, stunned, disbelieving what she saw.

"What happened?" she asked quietly. "I don't know," Asla whispered. "The guard told me where she was...but I don't know what happened or when." "Dear God," breathed Clarece. She looked at her mistra. The brown eyes were open now. "Mistra, how is she?"

Casica shook her head. "Alive...." She studied the injured skull. The little girl should be dead. "You slaves have the hardest heads I've ever met," she observed, numbly.

Clarece remembered the satchel at her feet. "Do you need anything from your bag?" "No," the healer replied, shaking her head.

"Not yet. The bleeding has stopped. I need keep it from clotting. To ease the swelling." Casica studied the bloodied ear, nervously. It could be bleeding from the brain, but she didn't think so. More likely it was the child's ear. She would know soon enough.

Clarece stood for several minutes before remembering herself. Pony, she needed to cover Raina. "I need to go to Muriel's and cover Raina," she told herself aloud. Asla stared at her, unbelievingly. "You're going to slave for that witch?" "I must," Clarece explained apologetically. "I'm the chief slaveswoman. Tis my duty to cover a fallen slave—no matter who their owner." The senior slave stared at the floor, angry. And very, very shamed. No decent woman would serve such a monster. No free woman would have to. But she wasn't free. She was slave and must do what slaves do.

Casica looked up, sensing her friend's discomfort. "Clarece...." The slave struggled to meet her owner's eyes. "I understand. Tis your duty. But you be careful. You do what you must then come back. Yes?" "Yes, my lady," the slave bowed. Asla chaffed under her earlier response. This was no time for Clarece to leave the little slave. "I'll go, Rece," she offered. "You should stay here with Raina. She'll need you." Clarece shook her head. "No. Tis my place. You stay with Raina, As. She's your friend."

Asla winced at the word. It was true. The scamp *was* her friend. She thumbed her palm anxiously. What was an insulit like her doing having friends? "As you wish, Rece," she bowed. "I'll stay and help Casica." The senior slave placed a mittened hand on a thin, covered leg. Her heart felt strangely at peace. "Live," she prayed silently. Turning, she walked the pen, taking the slaves' stairs to the wing above. Behind her, Casica asked Asla to fetch her cloak.

The guard watched as another slave, a tall one, approached the chamber. "Scads, what is this?" he asked himself, noticing the mittened hands. This must be the chief slaveswoman he had heard about. The somber slave offered him a half-kneel before knocking on the heavy door. It took its time opening.

"My lady," Clarece kneeled, fully, acknowledging Muriel's presence. "What do you want, slave?" was the guarded question. Clarece's response was as respectful as it was distant. "It seems misfortune has befallen your slave, my lady. I come to cover her.

Is there anything you need?" Muriel considered the chief slave suspiciously. "Yes," she answered finally. "I need my laundry and for this mess to be cleaned." Clarece bowed, humbly. "As you wish, my lady." "Clean the mess first," Muriel ordered.

Clarece bowed before entering the chamber. Nothing had been touched. A vase, the replacement for the one Raina had broken weeks before, lay on the floor, shattered. A pool of blood dried near the glass. Blood trailed over the rug and out the door. She would let the other slaves tend the hall; cleaning the carpet would take time enough.

Muriel disappeared into her bedchamber. Clarece found soap, water, and cloth and began the grisly work of washing her young charge's blood. The task was time-consuming and difficult for her maimed hands, but eventually all evidence of Muriel's evil was wiped and cleaned away. The senior slave left to gather the royal's clothes.

Once outside, Clarece deliberately turned her back on the chamber. She scraped her feet as a dog does over its dung, displaying a slave's ultimate gesture of disgust and contempt. She was the chief slaveswoman. She would do as she must, but her feet gave her final word on the matter.

Casica placed her hand on her blue cloak and smiled. It was like another pair of hands, keeping Raina at a good temperature. The healer turned her head slowly, bidding her shoulders relax. She dropped her head and listened to the activity outside the drawn curtain. It was supper and the pen filled with the voices of slaves, hungry and happy at the day's drawing to a close. The voices were quieter than usual, respecting the littlest slave's condition. Every slave knew it could easily be them clinging to life. What happened to Raina was unremarkable; harm was common among their lot. But it did serve to make the meal tastier than usual. To eat you had to be alive.

Clarece returned from delivering Muriel's dinner, relieved at the end of her service. She was excused for the evening. Muriel had no desire, she said, to see a slave again this day. Her own mistra wanted no dinner. The chief slave took her place at the slaves' table. It had been a long day. It would be a busy evening. She was hungry. She must regain her composure.

Having done all she could for Raina's head, Casica concentrated on her ear. An ear is fragile; the blow to Raina's head had injured hers. It was certain she had lost her hearing. The josquin sighed, saddened by the thought. She had never healed an ear and doubted her ability to do so completely. She rested her head in her hand, wondering as she did, how long it would be before Raina regained consciousness—*if* she regained consciousness. A familiar voice interrupted her thoughts.

"May I join you?" Asla asked, self-consciously. "Of course," the princess replied, surprised. Asla sat on the other side of Raina, supper in her hands. "Tis guild meeting tonight," she explained in g'Helderleicht. The insulit lowered her eyes, embarrassed. "My presence is not allowed."

Casica shook her head. *This woman saved this girl's life, protected her and has helped only God and Clarece know how many guild members, and still they ostracize her. What madness.* She turned to the insulit. Asla ate her food hungrily, happy for the princess' company. Usually on guild night, she would take her food to her stall and eat alone.

"You did well, Asla." The young woman looked up, a spoonful of porridge in her mouth. "What's that?" "You saved Raina's life today." The slave glanced down, uncomfortable. Saving lives was not what insulit did. "*You* saved her life, Casica," she mumbled, "not me." "No," the healer countered. "Had you not found and treated her as you did, I doubt she would have lived long enough for me to help."

Asla glanced at the princess' eyes, unconvinced. The Cassican was just being kind. "Thank you," she said simply. She looked at her bowl. It was almost empty, and she hadn't offered any to the woman. Just like a whore. Thinking only of herself. "Would you... would you like some bread?" she asked, shyly. No one but Clarece would accept such an offer.

Casica smiled. "Yes." "You would?" Asla replied, surprised. She broke off a small piece for herself and handed the rest to Casica. It was received gratefully. "Thank you, Asla," the princess nodded, taking a hungry bite. The insulit watched for a minute then offered the woman some mead. She should pour it in another glass, she thought, but the princess took her cup and drank well. Casica sighed. "This is so good," she declared, returning the drink to its owner. "Thank you." Asla smiled. It *was* good. It was good to share with another.

The sound of a heavy wooden spoon beating on an empty pot drew the women's attention to beyond the curtain. "Good evening, esteemed colleagues!" Clarece announced, officially. "The meeting of the Guild of the East Wing is now called to order...." The chief slaveswoman waited patiently. The talking quieted as slave men and women turned to face their leader, expectant.

"Our first order of business is Raina," Clarece began. "You all know she was hurt." "Will she live?" a voice interrupted. The leader's answer was immediate. "Yes. She will live," Clarece declared, willing the words to somehow empower her desire. "But we'll need to cover her, and I don't know for how long." A murmur trickled along the table. "I will cover her this week," Clarece explained, "and I'll let you know from there....

"On a happy note, Solange is still bedded with her baby. Both are well." Approval filled the pen. Clarece continued. "Crockett slaves on a hunting trip, Puris is breeding..." (male hoots rose at this announcement), "and Jonas—I don't know. Does anyone know where Jonas is?" Her tone was anxious. Jonas' absences always frightened her. Heads shook. "Tarrant," she requested respectfully, "will you, please, check on him, make sure he's alright?" "Yes, my lady," came a deep reply. "Thank you," Clarece bowed, grateful, to her loyal friend.

"The rest of you are well, I trust?" Nods greeted her. "Good!" she smiled. It *was* good. "Now for this week's chores. None of the regular duties have changed except that, gentlemen, tis your turn to clean the wing's hall." She glanced at the masculine side of the table. No mutiny to this announcement, thank God. "As for supper, the chore of providing food this week is...mine."

Clarece paused as laughter rippled across the table. The slaves loved this part. "Now...for the clock," she began, preparing for her role as a fool. "Who will volunteer to wind the clock for me this week?" A sea of smiles all but drowned her. Scads, they did this every time. "Anyone? Is there no one who will graciously serve their humble leader and gain, in return, prayers to Heaven on your behalf?"

Casica looked to Asla. The g'Helderleit had joined her laughter with the slaves'. "They love doing this to her," she whispered, explaining. "Tis the responsibility of whoever serves food to wind the clock. Rece can't wind the clock." "What about you?" Casica whispered back. Asla shrugged. "They won't let me touch it."

The senior slave sighed deeply, shaking her head. "Alright," she conceded. "What do you want?" *Now* she was talking. "Your bread!" someone yelled. "What?! You would want that I give you my bread for the week? I starve like the rest of you. You don't know a Cassican's belly."

Casica glanced at the curtain, shocked. What did she mean by that? She'd been leaving scraps for weeks!

"Surely someone has a better offer." "Your spoon!" came the answer. The table laughed in response. Clarece shook her head, good-naturedly. This was a rough crowd tonight. "Never!" she declared. "A glass of wine!" offered a male voice. "A glass of wine?" she echoed, hopeful. "Yes," the man answered, "and not mead. Tis the real thing I want. Your mistra's wine!"

Clarece sat on the offer. This was doable. Just a pity it was being done in the hearing of her mistra. "You would have me thieve, Cullis?" she replied, shocked. "You wish me steal from my generous and kind and forgiving mistra?" "Yes!" he challenged. The senior slave considered for a minute. It was highly unlikely this mob would offer a better deal. "One glass...only one for the entire week. Agreed?" "Agreed," Cullis nodded. "Then you've a deal." The table clapped.

Casica looked at the grinning Asla. "Does this happen all the time, that owners are plundered?" The blonde woman laughed. "I'm not sure about all the time. A slave does what a slave must, my lady." The meeting continued.

"Are there any other matters?" the guild's leader asked, knowing quite well there was one other matter. One that had been tabled the meeting before. One that could not be tabled tonight. A single hand rose. It was Marjan's. Clarece looked right through it. "No other matters?" "Uh-hum!" cleared a rugged voice. "Well, if there are no other matters...."

"I have a matter, great guild leader," Marjan announced loudly. The slaves hooted in anticipation. Clarece lowered her head. Here it came. "The guild leader recognizes the great slave

Marjan—however reluctantly. What is your matter?" The lusty slave stood on his bench. "I wonder if the great guild leader has come to a decision concerning my offer for her to...."

The revered Princess of Cassica was, at this very moment, drinking water, water which, instantly, she spewed, ignominiously, across the injured girl. The insulit fell from her stool in a spasm of laughter. From within the closed curtain of Raina's stall was heard a fit of choking. The slaves turned to look, somewhat concerned.

It was through heroic effort that Clarece maintained her composure. "The guild leader has considered your offer, great Marjan," she began, returning the slaves' attention to the table, "and while she is flattered at the generous proposition, believes that to accommodate your request would be to bestow an unwitting favoritism, one which might serve to disrupt the tranquility of our esteemed guild. The guild leader is reluctant to be shown such favor from one man. She must, therefore, with great regret, decline your offer." Marjan was not dissuaded.

"I appreciate the great leader's wisdom in this matter. I, too, would not wish my brothers to suffer any disrespect. It is, therefore, my offer, on behalf of my brother slaves, for you to accommodate each and every one of we humble guildsmen."

The table, both male and female, exploded with laughter. Clarece marinated in the mockery, pursing her lips. What she wouldn't do for a timely reply, but the mental image of her complying with Marjan's request rendered her speechless. She looked down at her mittens, struggling desperately not to laugh. She waited as the din quieted.

"The guild leader requests that your magnanimous offer be tabled until our next meeting for the purpose of consideration," she announced. Marjan smiled. "As it pleases your great Leadership."

Clarece bowed humbly. She glanced at the clock. "Now, *if* there are no other matters *(thank God)*, we still have some time. As it pleases *you*," she asked, presenting her mittened claws, "we may continue with our story."

The roomful of slaves voiced their happy approval. This was their favorite part. "Very well," the leader smiled. "When last we left our story, the ogre met the defenseless prince on a parapet of the deserted castle." The room silenced as she began, "'The ogre lifted his club with deadly intention. This time, the prince he would render ox fodder....'" She continued the story, weaving her audience into its world with a trained and gifted touch.

Casica observed her companion. Asla sat, listening through the curtain, captivated. The cloth might keep her from the guild but not from her enjoyment. The princess smiled. The story, she knew. Clarece was reading it when she first came to Byzanthia. That was months ago; yet, here was the chief slave, reciting it from memory. The josquin glanced from the happy insulit to the broken girl before her. What a crazy world these slaves lived in, she thought, smiling wanly at the meeting she had just witnessed. Clarece truly did rule in this slavish realm. She would make a good queen.

Princess Casica stroked the blue cloak. In the presence of these people it was she who felt, strangely, the subordinate. How strong these people must be. She studied the little girl. How strong they are. They receive the blows of a free world and yet stand and laugh and love—and live to slave another day.

Josquin caressed the tender, pale face. Raina's breath was shallow but steady. The dark hand rested on her brow. Raina: "queen." As she poured healing into her body, the healer spoke silently to the sleeping girl. "You, dear child, are a member of what may be the noblest people I have ever known...."

III

Quite the colorful court, Your Majesty...."

Clarece glanced up sheepishly. Asla had left for a service; the senior slave took her place as Raina's watcher. The pen was quiet now. Night had stilled it with a cold touch. The heavy door separating the slave men and women was locked. All around them slept. Only the princess and her charge remained awake. Their voices were as soft as the candlelight gracing Raina's still face. "And what exactly *is* Marjan's request?" the princess continued, quietly. "Is it anything akin to royal access?"

Even in the dim light, Casica could see her friend's face redden. Clarece looked down, embarrassed, before conjuring a reply. "Tis very much like it, yes," she said, dryly. "Both being equally improbable." Casica concealed her smile. "I look forward to learning the outcome of this request," she observed, seriously. "As do I, my lady. For years, the guild's esteemed leader has fended off Marjan's proposals. She can only wonder—with dread—what level of tastelessness remains on his platter."

Casica reached for her healer's satchel, purposely avoiding her friend's eyes. "I can only imagine," she ventured, "but I shouldn't," she concluded to herself in Cassican. She searched her satchel and from it produced a razor. Rarely had she used the implement, but the time had come. Raina had not regained consciousness, and while she continued to breathe and live on her own, the healer grew in her concern for the child's brain. She needed to see what harm was done, needed to determine when to begin healing the injured skull.

Very carefully Josquin shaved the area around the wound. Her heart ached at the sight of Raina's long, reddish hair fall. For a woman—even a child—to have her hair cut was disgraceful. Something of the sight repulsed Casica more than the gash it revealed.

Clarece moved to sit beside her owner. The little slave's scalp was sliced, marred by a jagged gash a stite and some in length. The wound yawned hideously, revealing a dark, bloody swell of flesh. Casica took a vial from her bag and put two drops of its contents into the wash basin. She waited while the solution blended into the water. "What's that?" Clarece inquired. "A purifying ointment. Tis used to cleanse water. I can treat infection, but I'd rather prevent it."

Casica opened a small pouch in her satchel and from it removed a two-pronged object. She soaked its tips in the water before using it to gently, expertly, open the wound further. The healer grinned at the sight: while the child's skull was injured in this place, the fluid that stained it was not of the brain. She sat back and sighed, relieved. "Her brain is not struck," she informed her questioning companion. "Tis injured from the blow, but not directly."

Clarece asked what she still dreaded. "Will she live?" Her owner looked away to the girl. Raina was so very young and weak. The fact she had not yet wakened boded unwell; still, the little slave had lived thus far when she shouldn't have lived at all. "I believe she will," Casica answered finally. "I don't know how it will be with her when she wakes. Tis certain her ear is injured. A child's ear is vulnerable to harm—tis not fully grown. And I'm concerned about her mind, how she will be. We can't know until she comes to herself."

The princess returned the pronged instrument to the water, propping it against the basin to soak. She watched its shadow dance against the wall, flickering with the candle. Her emotions flickered with a similar movement. It had been a long day, and her resolve to surrender vengeance waned. She took a deep breath, fighting against a rising surge of rage. This was no time to indulge that emotion. She needed her mind clear, needed it ready for the moment when she *could* do something to help the broken girl. The temptation to repay Muriel for her savagery she must not, could not, entertain.

A calm voice interrupted her battle. "How did you learn to heal, Mistra?" Casica turned to her companion, considering the question. How *had* she learned to heal? It was like trying to remember how she'd learned to talk. She had always known how to heal, or so it felt.

"Well, healing is born into a josquin—it's who we are. But we *are* trained how to use our gifts, either through lessons or, more effectively, through experience." "You had a tutor?" "Yes. Maman and Berea were my primary teachers. Berea more...though I'd have preferred my mother's tutelage," she confessed, grinning. "Berea is a demanding teacher," she explained to Clarece's inquisitive look. "Very strict and unforgiving." "How do you mean?"

"Well...," Casica searched among the many scenes availing themselves to her. "For instance, josquins don't get sick. We can get hurt and we die but not through illness. Berea decided I needed to know how it felt to be sick and took it upon herself to give me the experience. So she concocted some disease and made me so ill, I thought I *would* die. I *wanted* to die." The woman shook her head at the memory.

"Kai. I hurt so much. I'll *never* forget how it felt. When Maman found out, she was outraged. She and Berea got into quite the row, but the end result was that I became very patient with hurting people."

The josquin placed her palm on the open wound. She glanced down at her memories and laughed lightly. "Of course, I had a knack for discovering painful lessons all by myself." The senior slave pulled her cloak more securely about her. "What do you mean?" she asked. She knew so little of her owner's childhood.

The healer shook her head, remembering. *God. What a nightmare.* "Twas a terrible day...," she began. "Actually, it began the day before. I grew up with a cousin who lived with me at the palace. When this happened, I was about six; he was a few years older." She smiled at the boyish face. "We were like brother and sister, he and I. Best friends, worst enemies. Always playing, always competing." Asla's friend nodded. She knew what that was like.

"Anyway, one day we had this archery contest. I beat him by doing something *he* thought was cheating. Well, to me, just because I could do it and he couldn't, didn't mean it was cheating, so we got into this huge fight." She smiled, mischievously. "My cousin was *livid*...didn't speak to me for the rest of the day.

"Well, the next afternoon we had made up—or so I thought. He asked if I wanted to go riding. It looked to storm any minute, but I didn't want to say no and rile him again, so I went. We had ridden a couple hours from home when my cousin, he challenges me to a race—to settle the argument from the day before. I accepted, of course, in defense of my good name." Casica paused. Defending her good name had gotten her into more trouble than it was worth.

"Anyway, we take off. I was in a dead run, *flying,* when all a sudden, my saddle slips. Just slides under my horse with me on it: my cousin had loosened my cinch." Clarece stared in disbelief. Who would do such a thing to a little girl—and a princess at that? How cruel that boy must have been. Casica saw her thoughts. "He wasn't a bad boy, Clarece," she defended, "just...a boy and very, very angry at being beaten by a girl." Clarece wasn't convinced. *What kind of man would such a boy become?* she wondered.

"Well, I slipped from the saddle and, to put it mildly, had a very bad fall. I landed against a boulder." Chills crossed her flesh at the memory. "When I came to, my cousin was standing there, staring at me. I didn't know what was wrong till I looked down. There it was. My left forearm was broken, bones sticking out, muscle, blood—it was grisly. I was examining my arm when the next thing I knew, my cousin faints from the sight. Plunk! And strikes his head on the same boulder."

Casica shook her head. It didn't get any better after this. "Here we were," she continued, "out in the middle of nowhere with my cousin knocked out and me with my arm and bleeding inside. I didn't know what to do. I just sat there thinking, *'Oh, my God, he's hurt!'* It never occurred to me to get his horse.

"I finally managed to get up and then it happened. *Bam!* Lightning—you know the kind where the light and thunder meet, like cymbals?" Clarece nodded. "It was like that. My cousin's horse bolts. My horse is long gone. I'm standing there watching our transport run for its life, thinking, 'this can't get worse,' when it starts to pour. I mean a deluge. My cloak is on my horse, my cousin's on his face, and my arm's sticking out of my flesh. I just stood there and cried...." The storyteller shook her head again.

"I don't know how, but I popped my arm back in place and healed it as best I could. I picked up my cousin and walked to some trees to try to get out of the rain. I brought him to and healed him. He and I decided the only thing to do was to walk home. We were terrified. It was getting dark, and God only knew what people would think when our horses reached the palace without us. We had walked maybe an hour when here comes my father. He hadn't sent a guard to find us; he came himself."

Casica closed her eyes. "God help us. Let me tell, you, Clarece, the wrath of a king is a fearsome thing—especially when he's your father. I will *never* forget Baba's face. It was *white* with fear and rage." Casica sighed. "I don't remember much of what happened on the way home, just alot of cursing and threats against my cousin.

"When we reached the palace, Berea met us. She was pale, too. You see, in Cassica it's required by law for a josquin to be present in the palace at all times. My mother was gone to one of her cities and Berea was there covering her. Rea takes one look at me and my cousin. Me she orders to my room to heal myself. My cousin, she heals and bathes and tucks into bed while I spend the night trying to figure out how to mend my liver...." Casica frowned, still hurt by her mentor's treatment. "Well, just when we thought everything had settled, a few days later? Mother comes home and it's all a-storm again."

The princess gave her head a final shake. "Goodness, what a mess. But...because of what happened that day, I can heal bones and livers like nobody's business." Casica rested a moment before concluding, "The best kind of healings come from injuries—if we survive them." She considered her most recent injury. She would never have asked to be harmed as she was coming to Byzanthia. But if she ever faced a bleeding injury, she was prepared to heal it as never before. "God is always bringing good out of harm," she reminded herself, aloud, adjusting her healing into the little girl's body.

"Scads, Mistra," Clarece remarked finally. "What a hellish experience." She was answered with a nod. "I'd no idea royal children knew such days. It sounds like the kind of day a slave would have." The women considered the small, still form. A day like Raina's.

The senior slave scanned the story. It filled her with questions, but her body was too tired to entertain all. She settled for two. "I'm surprised at how you describe the woman Berea, Mistra," she began. "Such wasn't my impression on...." She couldn't bring herself to say *the day you were tortured,* so she said, "the day I met her." Casica looked at her, intrigued. "What do you mean?"

"Well, she was so tender with you—protective. So filled with compassion. I thought she was your mother at first, so loving was she." *"Really?"* the healer asked, surprised. "Well, yes, my lady. She never left your side. The only time the great lady seemed to jest at all was when she removed your necklace."

"She took my shalonn?!" Casica interrupted, shocked. "Well, yes, Mistra, but only to save you," Clarece defended. "And she didn't do so lightly. She said you wouldn't appreciate it."

"Berea took my shalonn," Casica repeated, incredulous. Clarece cringed. *Scads.* She'd opened a can of Cassican worms. "She did, Princess," she moved quickly to explain, "but she put her own about you in its place." "She gave me hers? What did she do with mine?" "She...she gave it to me. To wash," Clarece answered, countering the princess' shocked expression. "It needed it, Mistra," she added, glancing away from the memory. What an awful, awful day that was. "Blood?" Casica asked quietly. Her charge nodded, looking down. Her eyes teared at the memory.

Casica studied her friend's pained expression and, for the first time, contemplated what horror Clarece must have known that day; she hadn't been the only person to suffer. All Josquin's indignation melted in the face of gratitude. The Byzanthian continued.

"And then the lady took your necklace and put it around *her* neck—to fill the stones with color again." She looked into her owner's eyes. "You should have seen your teacher, Mistra; she was so gentle. Her love for you is manifest." The next thought brought to her lips a smile. "She kept calling you a kind name, I think: 'M'Yat'."

Casica sat silently, listening to Raina's soft draws, lost in the scene Clarece had painted. So Berea was gentle with her; gave her own shalonn—endangered her own life—to save her. It wasn't that Casica didn't know the esteemed josquin loved her, but tenderness was not a facet she'd experienced in their relationship. It surprised her, like learning her shalonn contained a color she hadn't known was there. A grateful smile graced her as she breathed to herself, *"M'Yat."*

"My lady?" Casica returned to the present. "'M'Yat.' It is a name?" The Cassican nodded, smiling still. "Yes. Tis...you might call it a pet name. It means 'night light'." She grinned at her friend's reaction. "I think that's why I enjoy your name so much. You're the morning light. I'm the night's." Clarece smiled at the connection. "So M'Yat is what your people in Cassica call you."

"No," Casica corrected kindly. "Tis not a public name. Only those most intimate with me would know, much less address me so." "Oh, I see," Clarece nodded. And she did. She saw much. The image, however, was framed in confusion.

Her owner's voice broke into her troubled thoughts. "Clarece," the princess invited, "why don't you go to bed. There's nothing more you can do. You need sleep." The chief slaveswoman sighed. She was so very tired, yet afraid to leave her little charge. "I'll be with her," Casica assured. "I'll wake you if anything changes."

Clarece nodded. The morning was coming quickly and with it, a repulsive duty. "With your permission, Mistra, I need slave for Muriel tomorrow, to cover Raina." Her eyes hardened at the prospect. There were many things she'd like to do to that royal; slaving for her was not one of them. The princess wavered. While she understood Clarece's role, she recoiled at the thought of entrusting her to so dangerous a woman.

"I don't know, Clarece. What would keep Muriel from hurting you?" "You would," came the simple reply. "Her fear of you—and my standing. I'm not a child she can abuse without consequence. Tis strictly forbidden to touch another's slave." Casica nodded, finally, giving her approval. "Alright. You may serve her, but if she threatens you in any way, leave. I'll not have you harmed."

Clarece looked up, grateful. How blessed she was to be owned by one who loved her. If only Raina had such a mistra. "Yes, my lady," she sighed, staring at her boots, weary. Weary of the day. Weary of harm—both threatened and delivered. The focus was not lost on the princess. "Before you go...," Josquin began.

The senior slave watched as her owner kneeled at her feet and unlaced her worn boots. Clarece squirmed, uncomfortable with the humble ministry, yet relieved; it would have taken her forever to do that simple thing. God, how inadequate she was.

She couldn't care for herself, how much less for her people. She looked at the still, small form of Raina. She had failed miserably at protecting her. Clarece bowed her head and wept quietly, ever mindful of the stall beside her. *"Please, God,"* she whispered, *"forgive me. Let her live."*

The healer reached for her defeated friend and raised her into an embrace. "Peace, Clarece," she wished. "You're a good leader. You haven't failed. Raina belongs to God." Clarece rested in the familiar warmth, wondering how on earth Casica could possibly know her haunted thoughts. Eventually, she surrendered even this musing. She was growing sleepy, whether through the healer or her own body's urging, she didn't know. But first she must ask; otherwise, the nagging question would hold all sleep ransom.

"Mistra? What became of your cousin?" The princess blinked, surprised. With all that troubled her, why would Clarece care? "Oh, him. He regained my father's favor—eventually. He lives away from the throne now, serving in a different capacity." "Oh," the groggy woman managed. She nodded in understanding.

Within minutes, she nodded in sleep. Her last waking glimpse was of the Byzanthian sergeant of the guard. Kneeling on the floor. Poul whispering to the broken girl from Cassica, *'M'Yat'*....

IV

Breath. What a comforting sound, thought the healer, observing the small slave's chest rise and fall with a steady rhythm. Raina remained, still, in the world of the unconscious, a world which not even a josquin could comprehend. Casica touched the quiet face. Warm. The girl was growing warmer, her breaths deepening. Every sign pointed to a return to this world.

The princess smiled. Raina's healing progressed, though very slowly, as it must. Never should an injury of this sort be hurried, she knew. The key to successful healing was to work with God and nature, to assist what already was being accomplished. Patience. Casica smiled again, this time at herself. She wasn't known for patience, at least not with normal activity, but in the realm of healing she was, indeed, a very patient subject. She reached for her breakfast plate and took a final bite of bread, pleased with herself. Pleased with her work. "Thank You," she prayed softly over the little body. "Thank You for healing...for letting me be a part of Your kindness."

Her prayer was interrupted by another facilitator of the transcendent. Asla poked her head around the curtain, mouthing, "May I?" "Of course," Josquin answered aloud in g'Helderleicht. The pen was empty now. There was no need for whispering.

The insulit took her seat opposite Casica, placing her red cape beside her. "How is she?" she asked softly, studying the little girl anxiously. "Improving," the princess smiled, nodding. "I don't know where the sleeping go, but I think she's making her return to our world."

Asla was not smiling. While she certainly hoped for Raina's life, she didn't anticipate what awaited her homecoming. "'Twill be good for us to have her back, but I don't know about good for her," the g'Helderleit offered, bitter. "That devil Muriel will kill her yet. There's nothing to be done to stop it."

Casica's eyes lowered. She had been entertaining the same thoughts during the night. What would keep Raina's owner from destroying her? It was clear the little girl needed a different owner. Herself, perhaps. "I've been thinking similarly, Asla. I wonder, do you think Muriel might consider selling Raina to another royal?" The insulit turned her attention to the Cassican.

"You? Don't, Casica." "Why not?" "For Raina's sake. I'm not saying you wouldn't be a perfect mistra for the girl, but Muriel excels in hatred. Why she hates Raina, I haven't a clue, but her disdain for foreigners is legend. Cassicans especially. She placed a bet on your death. 'Lost a fist of gold." She looked at the small child. "I think for you to show interest in Raina at all would seal her doom."

Casica gaped, incredulous. People were wagering upon her death? *That's* what Jonas had meant that night! God, how she hated her role in this land. Here she was, a healer, a life giver, and this woman who should know, was saying that mere association with her could endanger another's life. "That's not a comforting thought, Asla, to think that association with me is so dangerous, so defiling."

Asla regretted her words at once. She knew how it felt to live as a stain, to be so evil that light could not dwell in her presence. Never would she aim to cast that shadow on any soul, much less this kind, pure woman. "Forgive me, Casica," she began. "I didn't mean to suggest you're soiled or dangerous...." *Like me,* she thought. "I...I only meant that Muriel is wicked, and your interest for Raina might give her wickedness a quarry. Please, I...."

She averted her gaze, ashamed and confused. Her thumb found her left palm. Gods, what was she doing here? She wanted to help. Wanted to see Raina better, wanted to encourage the healer, but no. Everything she did was evil. A sigh punctuated her thoughts. It may all end soon enough. Edsner had made a change this morning in her schedule. Three days. The Baron Millient in the city for three days. He never took her in the city and never had her for more than a night. Why the city? Why so much time? *It must be a front. I'm being fronted but for whom and why?* Casica watched as the young woman gouged herself with her thumb.

"Asla, what's wrong?" The voice broke into a yawning terror. Asla jerked up. She found Casica studying her anxiously. "What's wrong?" Josquin asked again. Asla fronted herself, presenting her best fake smile. "Nothing," she lied. "Tis nothing. I only came to wish Raina well and to ask you to tell Clarece goodbye for me. I'm going away." "Where to?" "The city. For three days."

Casica frowned. Something was terribly wrong. The fear Asla stored so neatly was seeping into those ethereal eyes. The insulit answered her thoughts with a wan smile.

"Don't worry, Princess. I'll be alright. I...you just take care of Raina, will you?" Casica was shaking her head. "Tis not for Raina I fear. Something's horribly wrong, isn't it?" God's Beauty let out a short laugh. "Yes. *Me*. I am horribly wrong. But...," she nodded, determinedly, "all may soon be righted."

Asla avoided the princess' gaze and turned, instead, to one who could not see her. "Goodbye, Scamp. You get well, you hear?" The smile on her face was genuine. It was the closest thing to a prayer she could offer. Instinctively, Asla reached out to touch her friend's cheek, but in the instant before she did, she remembered herself. With a jolt, she drew back. *Dear gods in Hades, what am I doing—and in the presence of the souled?*

Casica misinterpreted the scene completely. "Tis alright, Asla," she encouraged. "You won't hurt her. You can touch her." Asla secured her hand against her chest like a weapon. "No," she said, emphatically shaking her head. "I can't. I haven't her permission." She looked down. Casica watched the thumb return to her palm. "Insulit can't touch the souled without you granting us the right. Tis forbidden."

The princess thought back to that first night she met Asla. The night of the bath. "I am Asla. I am insulit. May I touch you?" Never had the words registered until now. She watched as the lonely woman wiped silent tears, hurt and ashamed. "That's a wicked law of man, Asla," Josquin offered gently. "Not God's. A higher law allows you access to life."

"'A higher law,'" the insulit echoed. Her laugh was bitter. "Oh, Casica...what you don't know." "What, Asla? What don't I know?"

the princess asked, feeling all the world as though she did know nothing, so bizarre was this interlude with her friend.

Asla paused, sensing herself creep towards the edge of a deep, black chasm; voices from within screamed for her to flee...flee for her life. But what of her life? It was ending soon. She should leave behind a memento. The truth, perhaps. One cry of truth amidst all the damnable lies. Curse the voices! Curse them all as they had her. In her mind, the hollow one glanced about. If she were to do this, she must hurry. Hurry before it came for her.

"The insulit, Casica. We are few. How do you think we come into our slavery? When we are infants, who brokers us?" The princess frowned. She had never considered the question. "I don't know," she confessed, shaking her head.

Tears, bitter and raging, burst through the insulit's veil of secrecy. "*God* does," she spat. "His 'holy' church. His 'holy' priests. His 'higher law' took me from the assembly of the souled and made me what I am. You see? We aren't born hollow...."

From somewhere, deep within her spirit, was heard the clang of a heavy metal door. It was released. They had heard and now it was coming for her.... "Whatever do you mean?" Josquin asked, shocked. She wasn't answered. Asla was listening to something else: the approaching howl of darkness.

Casica watched, horrified, as the young woman gasped for breath, trying desperately to speak before it smothered her. "I had light," she managed. "I had *light*. But they took my candle and...." The words caught in her throat. Before her rose a face of hell. *"Forbidden!"* it screamed, *"To speak is forbidden!"* The deafening roar stole Asla's breath and with it, her voice. *"No!"* she screamed silently, clutching her heart in a futile attempt to protect her flame.

She couldn't. Her light was captured, extinguished by a crimson wave. She cringed as the candle dropped into a pool of red and in her terror, stood to flee the sight. The dancer took one step and toppled, plunging helplessly to the floor. She never reached it. Casica caught her and even now held the woman in her arms. "Asla! *Dear, God!* Help her!"

Twas God's name, not her own, that snatched the suffocating woman back into the breath of life. Asla opened her eyes. The healer's shalonn was on fire, blazing with a pure, white light.

Instinctively, the insulit reached for the necklace. Its light seized her.

Casica held the trembling woman in a tight, protective embrace, her own heart pounding as quickly as her friend's. Her mind spun in a blur of confusion. She hadn't a clue what to do. So she did what all josquins do when they don't know what to do: she prayed. For what she prayed, she didn't know. But at some point, all began to quiet both within and without.

It was gone. The crimson was gone. The darkness, gone. Asla slowly returned to herself. Only now did she realize she still clutched the glowing stones about Casica's neck. She went cold. It was forbidden even to touch the souled; and here she was gripping the princess' very heart. Asla allowed herself a continued gaze into the light, then slowly began unlatching her fingers from the shalonn.

"Forgive me," she whispered. A dark hand covered her own, inviting it to stay. "Asla, what was that?" Slowly, the blonde woman shook her head, calmed but resolved. "No. I have spoken too much. Tis forbidden," she said simply and ended the matter.

She released the light and stepped back. "I must go," she told herself. "No, Asla," Casica pleaded. "You needn't leave. Stay." The slave let out a short, tired laugh. "I can't avoid my life, Casica," she smiled weakly. *Or my death,* she thought. "Tis who I am."

In this moment, Josquin came as close as she ever had to violating a human's will. It took all within her not to pour Asla into sleep. The force that restrained her was the knowledge that, eventually, her friend must wake. Awake and enter whatever life held for her. As much as she desired, Josquin could not protect this precious woman.

The insulit moved to gather her cape. Casica stopped her. "Wait. If you won't stay," she began, gently taking her rich cloak from Raina, "then, please, wear my mantle. To remind you you're not alone." Asla smiled sadly. "You may never get it back," she whispered, her voice breaking. The princess took the garment and wrapped her friend within it. "I don't care about the cloak," she answered. "Tis you I want back." She reached around the woman and pulled the little tassels. The cloak's hem rose obediently.

"Thank you," Asla breathed, grateful. "Tell Raina I say to get well." "You'll tell her, yourself." Casica closed her eyes and embraced her friend tightly. "God be with you, Asla of g'Helderlend. I'll place a candle in the window for you." A nod moved against her shoulder. A candle. Casica always kept a candle burning to welcome her home. A candle....

The insulit held the healer only a breath longer. If she didn't leave now, she never would. Asla surrendered her hold and turned away. Without looking back, she walked towards the princess' stairs.

Casica watched until the woman left her sight in the dark passageway. And even then, her gaze continued.

V

Clarece jogged lightly along the slave passage. She must hurry if she hoped to visit with Casica before procuring her and Muriel's lunches. The passage here was floored with wood, weaving in and out at the strangest angles, as a maze. At times, the tall slave ducked to pass through a doorless doorway or dodge peculiarly low ceilings. Along the way her steps orchestrated a strange cacophony of hollow and creaky notes. Often, the woman had considered the possibility that this portion of the corridor had been constructed by drunken workmen. In their inebriated state, perhaps all this cockeyed handiwork seemed plumb. She, herself, had (on a rare occasion) traversed them with a less than sober mind; the angles seemed perfectly fine then. She had just glided past a familiar windowed recess when an even more familiar voice hailed her.

"Rece!" The woman slid along the oiled wood, smoothed by countless footfalls. She spun, as a slave does, and stepped into the nook. A large form fairly filled the small place. "Tarrant," she smiled softly, extending her hands in greeting. Large hands took them into his own. "Clarece," he answered, his voice as warm as it was deep.

Clarece whispered though she needn't. This was the most private of slave nooks, leading as it did to nowhere except the strangely placed window. "She's getting stronger," she began, still holding the man's hands. "Casica thinks she may wake soon." The burly slave lowered his head in relief. "Thank God," he breathed to himself and Heaven. The grasp upon Clarece's mittens tightened.

"If she dies, I'll kill her." The slavewoman glanced around. There was no one nearby of course; even so, she moved the man towards the window, closer to the light.

"Tarrant, you mustn't even think that," she whispered, her soft voice drawing to it his face. The eyes that met hers shone moist with concern. The woman sighed. It had been so very long since she'd looked into that lush bluish green depth. "Casica is a powerful and skilled healer—truly. If anyone can help, she can." She released her grasp to place a hand tenderly upon his chest. "You must guard your heart, Tarrant. Keep it pure for prayer."

Tarrant's large hand swallowed hers on his chest. It felt good to have her touch. His heart always quieted in the presence of this woman but even so, his mind raged with vengeance. "I pray constantly for her, Clarece. But if her mistra hasn't killed her this time, she will the next. I can't stand by and allow that. I won't." His voice was flat and ominous.

The chief slave lowered her head. *The next time.* That was the issue. What haunted her throughout the morning, slaving as she did before Muriel. The woman was dangerous, of that there was no doubt. Worse. She was, herself, enslaved and the master she served was more treacherous than she. Already this day, Muriel had emptied two skins of wine. No wonder her treatment of Raina was mindless; the royal lived in a world outside reality.

Clarece searched the angry face. "I'm working on this, Tarrant." Her heart quickened with fear. She knew the passion of this man. "Please, give me time. Promise you won't do anything—nothing. I haven't the strength to worry about you both. I beg you. Please." The tense man stood back; he couldn't bear the look in her eyes. After all these years, she still had the power to undo him.

His fingers swept through a reddish shock of hair. "I don't know what I can promise you, Clarece. But I'll give you time. I know you're trying. I thank you. God...." He looked away trying to conceal his sorrow. "Tis agonizing. To be near her but never with her." He blinked, pushing away a tear. "Clarece," he asked finally. "Do you think I could visit her? Could I go be with her today? Just for a time, only a short time? I...I only wish to touch her. Just once to feel her." *Blast,* he thought. When Raina was whole, the possibility had never existed but now, now that she lay broken—perhaps.

Clarece studied her mittens. Casica. What would she tell Casica? "I think you can. I'm *sure* you can, Tarrant. Tis just...I don't know what to tell Casica." "Tell her anything you need. Everything if you must. Only let me be with her." The senior slave nodded. "Thank you," the man sighed, his mind easing from the vise that gripped it.

A leather mitten caressed Tarrant's arm. Its owner stood silently, looking about the small space, her eyes resting finally upon a place, there, under the window. "I know," he said, softly. "I've been remembering, too." Rough fingers tenderly brushed her face. *She looks so well,* he thought. There was a vitality about her; the color of life filled her cheeks. Clarece's heart ached at the familiarity of his touch. She looked into his eyes, now soft with memory.

"You are more beautiful than even then—if it be possible." Tarrant knew her heart belonged to the guard, but still she was as no other to him. He leaned his face against the woman's throat. Beginning at her shoulder, he passed his mouth lightly along the smooth neck, smelling her flesh as he did. At her ear, he stopped and breathed her in.

The woman closed her eyes as he scented her, then returned the gesture in kind as the two embraced silently, lost in a kaleidoscope of memory. "I must leave," the deep voice said finally. Clarece stepped back, nodding. "I'll tell Casica what—three?" "Yes." The man smiled, grateful. Grateful for many things. "Goodbye, Clarece," he wished, "Tis been wonderful." The tall slave nodded. "Goodbye, Tarrant. God be with you...."

He grinned and offered a boyish wink. Clarece laughed lightly, shaking her head as he turned and slipped out into the passage. She would see him, again, at supper as she did every night of her life.

The chief slaveswoman returned to the window. She rested her head against the cool glass. Her mitten picked a peeling place in the sill. "I'll never get back to Muriel's in time," she informed herself. There'd be hell to pay. She didn't care. Tender sunlight caressed the air about her. With Tarrant, it had been moonlight. A sigh closed her eyes in remembrance.

Moonlight. For years it danced upon their skin. The woman opened her mouth, breathing deeply as though to inhale the scenes that graced her. Her mouth smiled softly at the irony of life. Raina could have been her child....

Casica stared unseeingly at the still child, haunted by the events of the morning. Her gaze dropped to her necklace. Only now did her shalonn rest in its colors. Never had she witnessed its strange behavior, riling as it had of its own volition. The healer rubbed her chest. Three bloody scratch marks showed where Asla's desperation had met her flesh. The Church. *My, God,* she wondered, *what could Asla possibly have meant?* The g'Helderleit's terror clung to her like a nightmare.

So entrenched was she in her rumination, the princess never sensed Clarece's approach. Did not even hear it. "Mistra?" Casica jerked, startled by the voice. "Are you alright?" her charge asked, concerned at her owner's expression. "Yes, I'm fine...," the healer lied, "just thinking." "Oh...," Clarece replied, unsure. "And how is Raina?" Casica considered the little girl. Thank God she continued to improve. "Better. She moved her hand an hour ago. She may wake today." Clarece's smile was genuine. Thank God for good news.

"I came to tell you I'm running late with your meal and...to ask if Raina may have a visitor. A male visitor." The princess squinted, puzzled. The slave hurried to explain. "Tis the slave Tarrant d'Titus, my lady. You've not met. He's a giant of a man but gentle as he is giant. He would like a short visit with the girl." She struggled with her wording. "He...Tarrant has a kind interest in her. May he come?"

Casica sat, confused by the request. Confused by all that had transpired this day. She surrendered finally to trust. "Whatever you think best, Clarece," she voiced. Her slave sighed, grateful. "Thank you, my lady. He'll be here at three. I will be later with your food—if I may." "Of course." Clarece lingered only long enough to touch the little slave. Wishing the girl well, she kneeled to her mistra, then quickly went her way. Casica listened as her steps echoed through the empty pen.

The josquin stood. She stretched slowly and deliberately, inviting deep, refreshing air into her lungs. Perhaps now was a good time not to think so much, she thought. She leaned over the quiet girl. Color returned to the still face. Casica placed one palm on the child's brow, the other over her heart. She was coming; Raina was coming home. The healer closed her eyes and exchanged her thoughts for prayer. May it be a safe homecoming, she asked. May Raina return to find her house ready and filled with light.

Her thoughts traveled to another girl, one who would not return for days. Casica paused and prayed the same for her.

VI

At precisely three o'clock, she heard him. Heavy steps sounded in the pen as a presence Casica did not recognize approached her post. The steps paused a time outside the curtain. Finally, a deep voice asked, "Princess Casica? I am Tarrant d'Titus. May I enter?" "Yes," he was answered.

A hand moved aside the curtain as Tarrant stooped under the rod. Casica glanced up from her seat. The man was huge, a good five stites over four cubits. He filled the stall uncomfortably. She stood and found herself in the decidedly unnatural position of craning her gaze up.

"God's peace," she welcomed, extending her hand. Tarrant kneeled to one knee before receiving the gesture. He started at the sensation that filled him. This woman was warmth, itself. "Thank you for allowing me, Princess." "Of course," Casica answered, "but you may wish to return when Raina's awake so she might enjoy your company." "No," Tarrant replied, shaking his head. "Now is the only time."

He looked down at the little girl. She was so small, so fragile. Yet in the presence of her life, all the world stopped. How often had he watched her across the table, straining to hear her voice above the others, fretting over the small portions of food allotted her, agonizing over the bruises that marked her body. He remembered that first night, when she limped painfully to their table. Her first day at the palace. Muriel had beat her, welcoming the slave to her service. Clarece had treated her wounds; still blood stained her blouse, seeping into the thin cloth. The child struggled to sit upright. It was Penelope who fed her that night.

He was moved to pity. The girl bore upon her face the look of one who had never before been striped, that numbed expression of having had the fabric of security rent. He was staring intently, when, for some reason, the child looked up at him. Their eyes met and in that same instant, Penelope said, "Eat, Raina. You must eat." *Raina.* Name and eyes fell within him as a sword into a scabbard. Those were *his* eyes gazing into him. The girl turned to receive the porridge offered her. Never again had they met. And now here she was, lying quietly near him.

Tarrant reached tentatively for the smooth face. He stopped, suddenly aware of the royal. "May I touch her?" he asked, oblivious to the tears that streamed his face. Casica looked into the man's eyes; they wept with love, there was nothing else to call it. Silenced, she nodded. Tarrant reached towards the girl as though for the Holy. A rough hand met the smooth cheek. Tarrant gasped at the connection. His head bowed as in prayer. He lowered his face close to the child's. "Raina," he whispered, "I love you."

Casica watched, stunned, as the man brushed his mouth along the child's throat, looking for all the world as though he were smelling her. She had never seen such behavior and didn't know what to think. She averted her gaze and felt her face blush so intimate was the gesture. Only now did Tarrant seem to remember her.

"Princess…." Casica looked up. "Will she live?" "Yes. She will," Josquin answered, not knowing why she whispered. Tarrant smiled. "She's strong," he announced, proud. He looked again at the dark woman. Had it not been for Raina, the Cassican would have held all his interest. Never had he seen anything like her.

"Did Clarece tell you about me?" he asked. "She only said you had a kind interest in the child." Tarrant grinned. Just like Rece to reveal as little as necessary. "Your slave holds many secrets, Princess," he offered, looking again at the child's face. He turned back to the woman.

"Raina is my daughter," he shared, quietly. His confession was met with a look of shock. "I know it sounds impossible, but I'm sure of it. I bred a woman six years ago, here, in the city," he reasoned aloud. "I saw her four years past. It was the most queer event. I literally bumped into her in the market. She told me I'd bred a girl into her. She had heard that the slave broker had found an immediate buyer and that the child had weaned here, in Byzanthia. The buyer was an elderly woman of some standing but no heirs. Only animals. She bought the girl to care for them. She had named her 'Raina'." The man looked again at his child.

"Then one day, here comes this new little slave. To my pen. What a strange fate that brought her here. If you saw her mother," he continued, "you would know the face. Have you seen her eyes?" "No." The man smiled. "You wait till you do. You will see mine." His finger tips tenderly caressed the small nose, the chin. "She's beautiful is she not?" he said, declaring more than asking. "Yes," agreed Casica. "She will grow into a lovely woman. Tall, I think—especially now, having seen her father." Tarrant smiled at the title. "So you think she'll live into adulthood?" "Yes," the princess declared softly. Her expression comforted him.

Casica watched as the tender hand turned into a fist. Tarrant brought the fist to his mouth. "She might live if she had a mistra who allowed her life and not that accursed...." He repented, at once, his words, remembering his promise to Clarece. He turned to Casica. "An owner makes a slave, my lady. We become what we serve. Take *your* slave, for instance. Clarece blossoms under your care. I've never seen her so well. So happy. I thank you, Princess. I thank you for covering her so kindly. You return a good favor. Clarece, she is a woman above all women." Casica listened intently, wondering within herself how to judge his expression.

His attention returned to his child. "'Raina'. Tis a good name." "What is her mother's?" Tarrant shook his head. "I don't know. I only saw her twice. The day we bred and that day in the market. But I see her every day in Raina." His eyes suddenly saddened. "I see Raina every day of my life. This is the first...," he lowered his head, "I'm sure the only, time I will ever touch her. So close... always so close."

Silence filled the stall. Outside the curtain, the clock ticked conspicuously. Tarrant sighed. He should leave. "Will you tell her?" Casica asked. He shook his head. "No. 'Twould do no good and may do great harm. It would only confuse her life. I am slave. I can sire her, but I can never father her. Tis better she doesn't know." The clock chimed the half hour. He must leave. Yet, when would life ever afford him this opportunity?

"May I hold her?" he asked, hoping against hope. The healer debated only a moment. This man would handle Raina like a dream. "But of course." She looked into the father's face. Her heart ached at what she saw. This might be the only time he would have with his daughter. "I'll wait outside," she voiced, rising. "Spend all the time you wish." Tarrant rose, bowing humbly as she left him. She closed the curtain behind her.

Casica sat on the slave's supper table, away from Raina's stall. For a long time, she buried her face in her hands. Her mind was exhausted, she concluded. Then paused. *No.* It wasn't her mind. It was her heart. Her heart bled raw with emotion. What kind of world sent a woman to her death; kept a man from his child; chained people from their lives; brought children to their...?

Her head bobbed up. Tarrant was ending his visit. She watched as, carefully, he closed the curtain. He looked full into the royal's face, then kneeled on one knee. For the first time, Casica noticed that slavemen knelt on one knee. Slavewomen on both.

"I cannot thank you enough, my lady," he said. "I cannot pay you—with my life I could not—for saving her. For helping her. For letting me be with her. May God repay what I cannot." The princess bowed, humbled by the blessing. "You are welcome, Tarrant. I'm sure Clarece will keep you abreast of Raina's recovery." "Yes. I thank you again, Princess, for loving your slave. God has at last shown her mercy. With your permission...." The Princess of Cassica nodded.

Tarrant rose, turned, as a slave does, and walked quickly away. He disappeared through the doorway leading into the men's quarters. Josquin waited until she no longer heard his steps. She would sense if Raina needed her.

She lay back on the table and slept.

VII

She sensed her approach but only shortly before being awakened by the aroma. Dinner coming early or lunch very late, it didn't matter. She was hungry.

"My lady?" Clarece greeted quietly. Casica took one more deep breath before rising. Her shoulders felt slightly stiff from the hard table. The princess looked into her friend's sapphire eyes; anxiety filled them. "Are you alright, Mistra?" Her lady nodded. "Only dozing from Tarrant's visit." "So he came?" "Yes. He spent a goodly time with the child."

Casica studied Clarece's expression with interest. There was much between the powerful man and this woman, clearly. But only God knew what. Clarece interrupted her rumination. "Where do you wish eat, Princess? Here or above?" Casica glanced about the room. Though she missed sunlight, she should stay with her patient. "Here. Let's sit with Raina."

The slave waited for her owner to proceed, offering a half-kneel as she passed. As Casica took her place beside the sleeping girl, Clarece uncovered her meal and poured her wine, filling the little stall with the fragrance of food. In such proximity of sustenance, the slavewoman salivated. *Blast,* she thought, disgusted with herself. Just like a dog. She hungered more these days than ever before, before the Princess of Cassica came into her life.

This matter, the senior slave had puzzled over for some time, especially at night when she lay down after having her hands treated by the healer. Clarece had developed several theories explaining the mystery. Foremost was the fact she now enjoyed scraps. Her mistra left food at every meal, something heretofore unknown. And as she received the food gratefully, the morsels stirred desire, awakening her belly for more. A second explanation, Clarece reasoned, was that her life had grown in busyness with horse rides, walks and long conversation.

Thirdly (and this observation most intrigued her), as her hands improved so did her body increase in energy. The slave wasn't nearly as fatigued as before. It was as though all the energy—both physical and mental—which, for so many years, had been devoted to the bearing of pain was released now, having no tormentor to serve. In its liberated state, the strength roamed freely, channeling itself into countless affluents of life. Clarece sang more, laughed more, dreamed more. She *felt* more. And had she the language, the experiential knowledge necessary for understanding, the teacher would have derived through this realization the root of her increased hunger: Clarece d'Casica lived more. Something was springing to life in the enslaved woman, and from it flowed mysterious streams of desire.

It wasn't simply more food she wanted. It was everything. Clarece wanted more of all life possessed. And the fact that life's reserves could not accommodate her enslaved state mattered not. Her soulish appetite grew. Though she could not yet put words to this reality, her heart was being freed in ways her bound life could not satisfy.

For the moment, the senior slave tried distracting hunger with the scene about her. Nothing had changed except for the little slave's cover: the princess' blue cloak had been replaced by Asla's red one. "Where's your cloak, Mistra?" (Conversation could sometimes stave off hunger.)

Casica swallowed deeply of the wine. "With Asla," she replied, nonchalantly. "She's gone to the city for several days. She asked me to tell you." Clarece studied the cloak. The city for several days? That wasn't customary. "Did she say whom she serviced?" she asked, striving to quell the rising fear of her heart. Casica was cutting the roast on her plate into little pieces. "Some baron. Asla didn't say which one. She didn't seem concerned, however, only irritated at being gone so long." "Oh," Clarece nodded, obviously relieved.

Casica busied herself with the meat, avoiding her friend's eyes. May God forgive her lie, but she could see no good in telling the truth. Clarece was helpless to do anything for her stallmate, and Heaven knew she shouldered enough burden at this time.

"Here, chief slaveswoman," she invited. "Would you join me?" Clarece debated within herself, watching as her owner reached for a glass on Raina's stand. The princess poured wine into the cup and now offered it to her. To accept in this setting would be unseemly, she knew. Years of slavish breeding rebelled against the thought. Yet, she hungered. Heaven, how she hungered. Casica watched the silent battle in her charge. "Roast for you now in exchange for a bowl of the kingdom's finest this evening. Seems a fair trade, yes?" The slave grinned. "Yes," she agreed, capitulating to desire. "Thank you, Mistra," she bowed, receiving the glass.

Clarece drank well of the wine before retrieving her old tin spoon from her vest. The roast was delectable, forcing her to contain her eagerness. For all slaves, eating slowly was a losing fight. Nothing of their lives trained them for it. Their schedule allowed no time for relaxed dining. The food, tasteless in its monotony, certainly did not invite slow enjoyment. And hunger, that cruel master, drove them to consume whatever was available as quickly as possible to quiet the relentless voice of want. Clarece fought valiantly, however, and paced herself with the princess; for every bite Casica took, she would take one.

The healer occupied herself with Raina, inwardly shaking her head. Nothing as food exposed her selfishness, she thought, placing a hand on the little girl's throat. She watched Clarece from the corner of her eye; though she, herself, felt like she starved, her friend truly did. The slave waited patiently, however; it was Casica's turn. "Have the rest, please," the princess offered over her shoulder. "I shouldn't eat anymore until later. It makes for better healing."

The senior slave weighed the comment. Though she knew nothing of josquins or healing, it made no sense. "I can save it for you," she replied, feeling out her owner. The princess remained focused on Raina. "Thank you, but no. 'Twill be better for Raina if I wait." *Kai, I've lied more the past half-hour than I have in months,* confessed Casica toward Heaven. She hoped God would understand.

Her charge still tarried, examining the situation like it was bait. Bait. Even that was food. Still, she thought, her mistra wasn't accustomed to lying—at least not that she knew: only God knew the mind of a Cassican. She bit. "Thank you, Mistra. I serve this week. I'll see you have a full bowl tonight." Casica glanced at her, grinning. "Just make sure it doesn't contain your own allotment." "It won't." It would contain Raina's and Asla's. Asla. Days without her sala. How empty, how quiet would life be. Already Clarece's heart ached with missing her. "How long did Asla say she'd be gone?" "Three days," Casica answered, leaning back into her seat. Her mind raced. How could she discontinue this line of questioning?

"How is Muriel treating you, Clarece?" "She treats me well, my lady," the slave replied. Casica wasn't the only one lying this evening. The truth was, the wretched royal treated her like a brute. Under the pretense of punishment for delivering late her lunch, Muriel had forced Clarece to spend the entire afternoon kneeling at attention upon a graveled tile. The tile was made of broken shell, designed specifically for the purpose it served upon her tortured knees. The chief slaveswoman bore the torment in silence, bolstered by the knowledge of what Raina must bear at the hands of this sadistic owner. For her part, Muriel enjoyed the entertainment, thoroughly, losing herself in a drunken revelry. The memory was not something she wished discussed. How could she discontinue this line of questioning?

"And what did you think of the slave Tarrant?" Her owner chuckled. "I think he might be the biggest man I've ever met in my life. But as you said, he's as gentle as he is giant." Casica studied the child. "He told me his story," she shared quietly, returning to the sacred whisper his image evoked. Clarece glanced down at this knowledge, hoping he had not told *all* his story. "How long have you and Tarrant known each other?"

Clarece chewed her food, awash in a cascade of memory. "Many years, Mistra," she answered, softly. "He came to the pen four years after me. He is a good man, Tarrant." Casica contemplated the silent woman. Her expression filled the silence with meaning. Again the healer brought a hand to Raina's throat. The act reminded her of a puzzling one earlier in the day.

"Clarece," she asked, "Tarrant did something I've never witnessed. He ran his mouth from Raina's shoulder to her ear. It looked almost as though he were...smelling her. Do you know what this was?" The slave's hesitation was not lost on the josquin. "He *was* smelling her, my lady," she answered, uncomfortable. "He was...we slaves...it's called 'scenting'. Tis our way of...kissing," she explained, softly. "Friends, family (She spoke this word awkwardly; Tarrant was the only slave she'd ever known with family.), lovers. Tis not that we don't kiss as you free do, but... scenting is our way." The woman ducked her head. "I guess it seems brutish to you."

Casica shook her head slowly. "No. On the contrary, tis exquisitely intimate. Not that I've anything to compare it to, but...." It was the princess' turn to look down. Clarece stared a moment before asking a most inappropriate question. "Have you not kissed, my lady?" There were tears in the girl's eyes. "No," she whispered. "Not as a man and woman do." How strange she felt speaking this. How strange the entire day; her entire life.

Never had any man shown overt romantic interest in K'eran's daughter. This reality certainly wasn't due to a lack of physical attraction. And God knew, it wasn't for want of interest on her part. Berea's stories and her own experiences as a josquin (not to mention living in a josquin's body) had filled the Cassican princess with curiosity enough to last a lifetime. In her country, where she was widely popular, many young men gladly wished to entertain her questions, but none dared. For guarding the woman was a battalion of fate. Destiny had delivered her into the world betrothed. She was born another man's wife.

A fine riding boot scraped the granite floor, its owner's heart a mixture of sorrow and bitterness. "I'm sure your *'Lord Bastien'* has kissed many women," Casica spat. "That and much more." The words had no sooner left her, than the princess winced with regret. *God, what is wrong with me?* It must be the fatigue; must be her encounters with Asla and Tarrant; must be the dim environment of the pen, must be. Oh, whom was she fooling.

It was she. She had waited her entire life for this man. This man the king spirited away as soon as she recovered strength enough to sit. Casica's months in the palace had revealed many things, not the least of which was that Byzanthian men hadn't the principles of their Cassican counterparts. Purity meant nothing in this kingdom, it appeared. Perhaps among the women, yes, but certainly not the men. Still the woman's conscience pricked her.

She'd no right to say what she had. God, what a bizarre day it had been. Would it never end?

"Forgive me, Clarece," Casica apologized. "That was wicked of me. I don't even know your master, yet I defame him." Clarece was still pondering a woman her owner's age having never been kissed. It was only proper her lady were a virgin but to not be kissed? "You haven't defrauded him, my lady," she replied, attempting to comfort her mistra. "Only God knows what you think, coming from a land such as yours. I've read Cassican poetry; it appears as fiction compared to ours. To put it politely, fidelity is *not* particularly esteemed in Byzanthia." The slave glanced into her memory. "But I don't think my former mastra has been with a woman." The princess looked up, shocked. Clarece must be inventing this. For her part, the slave simply continued with her speculation.

"As for kissing, I know not. But I've slaved Prince Bastien since he was four. And a houseslave knows such things. To my knowledge, your husband has waited for you. I know his mother, may she rest, spoke with him about waiting for you."

She paused here, remembering the occasion. It was afternoon and she kneeled near their feet, scrubbing the boy's floor. The queen's voice was filled with urgency: "You're not like your brothers, Bastien," she was saying. "You may never have the throne, but fate has given you a greater inheritance. She awaits you and will be worth any indulgence you abdicate on her behalf." Clarece left the marble floor to return to her seat in Raina's stall.

"Here," she resumed, "when a boy turns thirteen, he's taken to a whore for a coming ceremony. I'm certain my master didn't participate in this. He and his brothers had an impressive—argument—in his room concerning it." *Fight would have been the truer word.* "As I remember, they took him out and got him quite drunk, instead."

Casica perched in a haze, astounded and embarrassed. She shouldn't be hearing any of this; still, she found Clarece's information healing. The resentment curdling within her dissolved. She felt grateful, as she did considering Bastien's thoughtfulness in constructing her room and wished anew for his presence in her life.

The senior slave still mused silently, shaking her head. She voiced, finally, her conclusion. "Tis time for your husband to return."

Time for her husband.... How much her charge knew of this man, thought the healer, following Raina's rising chest. How much she knew about everything compared to her. Casica scraped her boot again, wondering if she would ever be anything but ignorant in this land. Still, something nagged her. Clarece knew much of what the princess considered private affairs. How?

"Clarece, how is it you know all this about Bastien? I mean his mother's conversation and his brothers' fight? Servants are privy to most anything in a master's house, I realize, but still, my mother's intimate conversations with me, no servant would hear."

Clarece was listening to the activity beyond the curtain. Her people were coming in from delivering their owners' meals. Some of them took their seat at the great table. "Do you remember the prince's comparing me to a piece of furniture, my lady?" Casica rolled her eyes. How could she forget? "Well, that is your answer." Clarece glanced round the stall. "No one cares what a chair sees or hears...and that is what we are to our owners." She fiddled with her mittens, frustrated. "You forget we are the not-human. We are chattel. What a slave witnesses would shock you. But it doesn't matter. It doesn't matter what we see, for they don't see us. The unseen are invisible."

The chief slaveswoman stroked her collar absently. What an insulit lacked in soul, she decided, slaves lacked in presence. A voice filled her silence. "*I* see you, Clarece," the princess offered gently. Her slave nodded, a slight smile gracing her lips. Twas true. Her lady did see her. "Yes, you do," Clarece acknowledged, studying the floor intently. "You rather frighten me, at times, with your vision. Tis a fearsome thing to be seen. It requires much. It awakens much."

Hunger stirred, again, within the woman. She could smell the porridge, now by Tarrant's hands borne. For years he had covered her brokenness in this way. "I must go," Clarece ventured. But first she had a debt to pay. A sheepish grin accompanied her request: "May I've a draft of your libation, Mistra?"

Casica responded with a grin of her own. "Ah. The extortion payment." She poured a full glass of her dinner wine. "My compliments to Cullis," she quipped, presenting the drink to her friend. Clarece received the graft, gratefully. "Thank you, my lady. I will see *you* soon." She kneeled. "With your permission...."

The healer nodded, wondering how soon soon would be.

VIII

God, it was cold. From her seat in Raina's stall, Casica listened as the wind pummeled her chamber above. It was the windows rattling against the squall. There were no windows in the pen to buffet, but wind poured down the chimney, escaping the flue with a rush. Not that it disturbed the fire. It was long out. Hours earlier, Clarece had gathered just enough flame to light her little lamp. That was normally Asla's ritual, but tonight, the little pile of firesticks her stallmate kept on their nightstand remained untouched. The handless woman couldn't manage them.

Clarece had bid her owner goodnight with deep sorrow. It wasn't so much that she retired to an empty stall. Asla's schedule often kept her away at bedtime; rather, it was the haunting prospect of losing her friend for all nights. It was only a matter of time. The exhausted woman cried herself to sleep, grieving the knowledge that someday, she must live every minute of her life without the presence of her dearest friend.

Casica now pondered her charge's forlorn expression. Their hour of healing went well, but, clearly, her ministry had failed to touch Clarece's heart. Futility seemed her lot in this land. The discouraged healer sighed deeply, watching her breath steam in the cold. God, how did the slaves do it? Sleep in such cold? The chill made her think of the covers. Perhaps progress was made on that front; perhaps if she became free during the next day or so, she would call on Silian for a report. A sound beyond the curtain drew her attention. At least she could derive some comfort knowing that the occasional coughing she heard was from cold and not illness. Her presence in the palace accomplished its work.

A sudden movement startled her thoughts. She jumped, almost tripping onto Raina, when the dim stall muttered, "Meow." There, announcing himself with a deafening purr, was Soren, the palace cat. The tomcat offered the royal only passing acknowledgment before pussyfooting across the little girl to pause on her chest. From this vantage he gazed into the still face. Content with whatever he saw there, the king of cats lounged upon his human throne and proceeded to bathe, oblivious to fellow royalty or etiquette.

"Scads, Kitty!" the princess scolded quietly. "Don't you ever knock?" The orange tabby made no reply, being as he was, thoroughly engrossed with the fleshy area between his back toes. The inferior conscious life in the stall stroked him happily. It had been since Cassica that Josquin had been in the company of a cat; she loved cats. But this cat was obviously in a category by himself. Never had she seen such a scruffy specimen.

Soren was substantial, approaching two stone in mass. The tip of one ear had departed his furry person entirely, and the other looked none too long for this world. A big gash, the remnant of some past skirmish, cut a bald ridge under his right eye. Several patches of fur went missing along his hind quarters. And his nose, though most likely pink, looked gray so scarred with scratch marks it was. The healer frowned at the regal tail. It crooked at an unhealthy angle.

"Well, Sir Tom," she observed, "it appears you've a rough time establishing your kingdom. Makes one wonder what the pretenders look like." Tom had completed his short bath and now curled his domain into an awkward ball. Raina simply was not throne enough for his eminence. The princess took him into her own lap, half-fearing his weight may suffocate the ailing girl. 'Twould be criminal, having Raina live through all she had only to succumb to a furry crush. The big cat relaxed quickly enough.

Josquin massaged the sleeping animal, and as she did, released a particular kind of healing. One of the great mysteries of "josquinning" (as Clarece rendered the act) was that it helped not only humans but animals as well. Casica knew a josquin who could revive trees. The dilapidated animal on her lap suffered from not a few cuts and aches. He slept even more soundly as the healer administered her touch.

Casica sighed, thankful for the company. She leaned back in her chair and noticed, as she had before, the worn book propped against the back of her patient's nightstand. She reached now for it—carefully—as not to disturb his sleeping majesty.

The book's cover had shed its spine, leaving a blank yellowed page as its face. The healer opened the work at its center, as was her practice with all new reading. Her eyes scanned the large print. She gaped at what she read:

"A small, still sparrow sat by the shallow spring. A still smaller voice skipped over the water. 'How is it a donkey races with horses?' asked the small, still sparrow. 'A donkey is not a horse,' the sparrow spoke. 'How can you run with horses?'" The astonished reader turned the worn page, thinking to herself, *A donkey does run with horses. But he runs with horses as a donkey does....* "A donkey can run with horses," the page read. "But he must run with horses as a donkey does...."

"Crispus!" Casica exclaimed, softly. "Tis the donkey story!" This very same book sat on her shelf at home, home in Cassica where a small, still girl learned to read with the hero of this story. "Sir Tom, look! Tis just like home!" Soren raised his head. Unimpressed, he returned to his slumber. A story of his own developed, one involving a successful mouse hunt.

The princess brought the book to her nose. She breathed deeply of the parchment, smiling. It was as though she'd found a bottle in the sea with her name written on the note inside. She looked to the sleeping girl before turning to the story's beginning. She and Raina had more in common than ever she could have imagined.

Unbeknownst to the reader, in addition to hers and Soren's, a third story unfolded, a frightening, confused one. Raina was coming home, but she did so in a panicked rush. She was chasing her, the devil was, racing for her from the black of oblivion. The devil was a woman in her dream, conjured by the child's ghastly torment at the hands of her owner. And the devil was black, so dark that the desperate girl could see her in the thick darkness through which she now fled. And in the midst of all this horror was the wind, ringing in her ear. The child's heart raced with her in terror, and her breath, which for so long had come in slow, rhythmic draws, quickened in her chest.

"'What is this?' the head horse asked unkindly. 'What is a donkey doing, thinking he can run with runners such as I?'"

Casica lowered the book. Something was happening in Raina. The child's breathing quickened, her mouth opening to swallow more air. Tentatively, she leaned forward, prompting a vexed Soren to lumber off her lap. "Raina?" the woman asked, cautiously reaching for the child's arm.

At the connection, the little girl's eyes opened, focusing in a blurred fashion upon the Cassican's face. They widened in horror. *Tis the devil! The dark woman's caught me!* the confused mind cried. The child jerked painfully. In terror she realized she couldn't escape, couldn't move at all except to raise her hands before her, trembling. Casica sat back on her stool, raising her own hands in surrender. "Raina, you're alright! Tis me—Casica!" But the dazed girl hadn't a clue who she was. She had seen the dark woman only once before, months ago when Casica had come below.

The healer's mind reeled. She backed away and ducked quickly from the stall to Clarece. The chief slaveswoman slept soundly, warmed by her mistra's earlier touch. "Clarece! Help!" The words sounded as an alarm.

Clarece jumped from her sleep, reflexively grabbing her cloak from its place on the wall. She ran after her mistra and while Casica remained outside the curtain, entered Raina's stall. At the sight of the senior slave, the little girl quieted. It was Clarece. Her mind knew this woman well. She was the embodiment of all that was safe in her enslaved world.

"Raina," Clarece spoke comfortingly, reaching for the child's face. The little girl closed her eyes in relief. Already her breath slowed. The blue-green eyes opened to the familiar face of her leader. "Mistress?" she asked carefully. "Is she gone?" "Who's gone, Raina?" "The devil." Clarece nodded, having no idea what Raina meant. "Yes, little one. The devil's gone. You're safe." The wounded head nodded as much as it could. A sleepy Soren walked up to her. Raina smiled weakly in recognition. "Soren...," she whispered.

Clarece smiled, petting the ragged creature. You never knew when Soren would show. He might visit the pen for a week then disappear for months only to show in another place of the palace. This was his third pass to the pen in half a year. Raina remembered him from months earlier. "He came to welcome you," the chief observed.

Even as Clarece spoke, the child's smile fled her face. It was all coming back to her. Her mistra...the vase...the snapping sound in her head...the darkness. Clarece watched as the soft light of recognition in Raina's eyes dissolved. In its place rose a void, a frightening, familiar gaze of emptiness. "Raina? Look at me." The eyes turned slowly towards the voice. A dead glaze covered them. Clarece spoke over her shoulder, "Princess."

The healer entered tentatively, fearful of upsetting the child again. Blue-green eyes focused on her. Casica blinked. It was just as Tarrant had said. Those *were* his eyes looking at her. His eyes, except that they were missing something. She swallowed hard in concern. Something was terribly wrong here. "Raina, you remember my mistra?" Clarece was asking. "Yes." "You remember she's helping my hands?" "Yes." "She's been helping you, too. Is it alright if she touches you?"

The child studied the dark woman as closely as her confused thoughts would allow. This was not the devil. This was the healer, the one who loved Clarece. The reddish head offered a slight nod but her eyes squinted suspiciously. Casica sat opposite Clarece at Raina's right ear.

"Hello, Raina," she smiled. "How do you feel?" The child wept at the question. "Bad...." The healer nodded. "I can help that. I'm going to put my hand on your head. Is that alright?" *Her head.* Raina's breathing quickened. She didn't want her head hurt again. She glanced at Clarece. The chief woman was here. The chief would keep her safe. "Yes," she managed.

Very tenderly, Josquin placed her hand on the girl's brow. At the touch, Raina closed her eyes. Healing, as warm as light, flowed into her mind and body. The sensation made her sleepy, quieting the steady ringing in her left ear. All pain left her body, and in its place came a blessed comfort. Breath deepened as the girl fell into a normal sleep.

"She won't sleep long," Casica explained, turning to her friend. "I'm worried, though. Something's happened in her. I don't know what." Clarece nodded. She knew what. She had seen that empty gaze before. Had carried it in herself, once. She did not voice her fear though. Perhaps the look would fade.

The healer placed her hand over Raina's heart. She was so very weak. Clarece watched as her owner thought furiously. "I'm going to the kitchen," Casica determined. "I'll get her something to eat. She's in desperate need of strength. I'll be back as soon as I can." Casica glanced into Clarece's sapphire eyes. Something was wrong. "Clarece, are you alright?" "Yes, Mistra," the slave lied. "You're correct. She needs food."

Casica pondered Clarece's response, absently stroking Soren who now dozed at Raina's neck. She frowned in confusion. She would sort this out later, she decided, and stood to leave.

Clarece bowed as her mistra passed, then turned to the sleeping form. She closed her eyes and offered a silent prayer, "Please, God, make her try."

IX

The princess stood at her warm brazier, ladling hot soup into an earthen bowl. How comforting to be in her familiar chamber. It had taken quite some doing to accomplish her task, but she was pleased with the outcome. She and the kitchen maid may yet become friendly, if not friends. The rotund woman looked upon the Cassican with new-found respect, watching as she deftly prepared vegetables for her creation. In the end, the maid offered well wishes to accompany the meat she had added to the victuals.

Casica tasted her offering. Even at this strange hour the soup awakened her gnawing appetite. Hours of attending Raina, Clarece and Soren were beginning to take their toll. She glanced down to her shalonn. Several pobbles had lost their color. A healer's telltale sign of strain. She needed sleep, and soon. But for the time, Raina's needs took precedence.

Casica took the bowl and spoon. The pot she left near her brazier. She walked the stairway to the cold pen, pausing within the comforting perimeter of Clarece's lamp light. From there she continued to Raina's stall and peeked inside the curtain. Clarece's wool cloak was wrapped tightly about her. The senior slave smiled, more for Raina's benefit than her mistra's, in hope of encouraging the silent girl. Two hours before, Raina had wakened; yet she spoke not a word, simply lay still as death, gazing emptily before her. The only sound was that of Soren's occasional snore as he slept blissfully in his selective oblivion.

The healer approached tentatively. The heaviness that draped Raina was as thick as her soup. Josquin met her friend's gaze. Clarece shook her head. "Raina?" Casica asked quietly. "I brought you something to eat. Tis my own creation: Cassican stew. Tis guaranteed to make you feel better." The child looked at the bowl. Its steaming fragrance made her eyes brim. She closed them against her gnawing hunger and would have turned away her head except her neck, injured by the blow, prevented her.

Casica watched, confused. "Perhaps you'd prefer Clarece feed you," she ventured, offering the bowl to the chief slaveswoman. Clarece accepted the soup with a bow. She moved to sit upon Raina's cot, placing herself squarely in front of the child. With her maimed hand, she stirred the soup. It smelled delicious. She took a spoonful and grinned approvingly. "The princess makes a fine stew, Raina. Here, try some."

The girl looked at the spoon and for a moment, only a moment, considered acquiescing. But then loomed a symbol more powerful and basic than even food. Her mistra. Her mistra had tried to kill her. Her mistra, the very reason for her existence, wished her dead. She was a stupid slave. She was a wicked slave. Useless to her owner. Useless to life. Raina d'Muriel, barely five years old, understood completely her owner's power over her. Life was not a right. Life was an indulgence, a tenuous state that could, with a word, be obliterated. Her owner had spoken that word. The hand that held her life had struck to destroy her. And she had lived. She could not even die right. But she would. She would.

"Raina." The voice was that of her leader. "Eat. Please. Eat." The child stared into her with eyes the woman knew well. They sliced like knives. "No." The answer was as final as it was succinct. Clarece bowed her head. This was a battle she dreaded, but she must fight it. Fight it now before Raina's vow set like mortar; it was her only play.

"Raina." Tarrant's gaze met hers. "I am Clarece d'Casica. I am your leader. I am the chief slaveswoman of every slave in this wing. I order you...," she bit her lower lip. She could do this. "I command you: Eat."

For a long minute the two slaves gripped wills. The younger one wavered. Clarece was not only her leader. She was her center, the axis of all her small enslaved world. Yet she was not her sovereign. Whereas Clarece governed slavery, Muriel mastered life. The chief slaveswoman did not buckle. But her eyes glistened. She saw, clearly, to whom this battle went. Death. Raina had decided: she would fail the woman she admired and respected as none other. It mattered not. She failed at everything.

"No."

Clarece knelt. She lowered her face against the girl's and scented her tenderly. "Please, Raina," she breathed, "I love you. We all want you. I beg you, please, don't do this." *Don't do what?* wondered the princess. What in God's name happened here? As a door, Raina slammed shut her eyes, sealing in death, sealing out life. Clarece held her in this place for a long time, willing her return. She did not. She slept instead.

A hand closed softly upon the slave's shoulder. "Come," Casica mouthed. Outside the curtain, life stirred. All around, slavewomen busied themselves with morning chores. Concerned faces glanced at the chief slave and her mistra, but none breached the space about them. Casica led her friend to her stall. She sat on Asla's cot. "What in Heaven's name is happening here?"

Clarece gazed at the floor, shaking her head. "She's broken." "Broken?" "Yes," Clarece replied, looking now at her mistra. "Raina's broken," she repeated. That should be explanation enough. It was not for the confused Cassican.

"She'll improve, Clarece," Casica began. "Her injuries will heal with time. She's not permanently harmed." "That's not what I mean, Mistra. I mean Raina has lost her spirit." How could she explain this? "Her mistra wants her dead. She's tried to kill her and in doing so, she has. Tis as a command for Raina. For a slave...," she struggled to explain, "Muriel is as God for Raina. And God has damned her. Tis as if Muriel has excommunicated her."

"Excommunicated?!" Casica spat. "What is wrong with you people? Clarece, Muriel is *not* God! She hasn't the power—." "She *has*, Mistra!" Clarece countered. "Hers is the final word of life and death over this child!" The slave took a deep breath. She needed to regain composure. "Mistra, you keep thinking we're human. And I confess, you convince me we are. You persuade me I might...I may, perhaps, stand equally with you *before God.* But in *this* world, we are the not-human. We're property. Like a horse—*less* than a horse—especially a little slave like Raina.

She's no value, not to herself if not to her mistra. I have seen...," the images brought a mittened hand to her mouth, "I have seen grown slaves hang themselves over this," she whispered. "Raina will starve herself."

The healer sat, undone. The past two days had rent asunder her understanding of life. *This can't be happening,* she thought over and over. Little girls don't starve themselves. God forged people to live. The instinct to survive, He instilled in all. For some reason, her experience with Asla crawled over her, and for a moment, Casica truly felt she were going mad. She sprung from the cot.

"Nepa!" she cursed in Cassican. A flood of rage engulfed her. It pulsated in her being and channeled swiftly through her body into the stones about her throat. The shalonn burned in a most terrorized manner. Casica closed her eyes and yielded to the sheer impulse of hate, choosing as her target, Muriel, Baroness of Keltan.

The energy that flowed so powerfully in this woman pooled, gathering to leave her as it did often, attacking and destroying disease in the palace, in the city, in the region. As no josquin before her was she endowed with power. But this time, it was not Life Casica wielded.

Across the channel, Pelana, Queen of Cassica, awakened, terrified. Terror for her daughter's victim. Terror for her daughter. She had no power to stop Casica's intent, but across space and time she screamed, "Bai, M'Yat! Bai!" *Neverno, M'Yat! Neverno!*

Her mother's voice jolted Casica as from a trance. But too late. Her stones discharged her command. With a start, Josquin lunged for the deadly energy and with her will grasped it, straining against her own power to thrust it back into her being. Her body staggered at the effort.

The healer fell back and would have collapsed upon the floor had it not been for the Morning's Light. Clarece caught her and, sitting back onto the cot, enveloped her owner in a protective embrace.

X

She fingered the ivory contemplatively, breathing deeply with the pulse. The blows fell rhythmically against the ancient wood floor, filling the cathedral with a heavy, solid cadence. The canter glanced at her and nodded. The choir was at ready. She lowered her head and leaned into the maskil.

Music filled the sanctuary as she joined her instrument's voice with her friends, swept away into the beauty of creation. But in her mind, she could hear it. For some bizarre reason, the cantor's staff continued its beat, softly at first but now more loudly; building in dynamic until it drowned out her music, overwhelmed even the voices with his steady, strong pulse. How strange. Casica opened her mouth to inquire of his behavior when she realized it was no canter's pulse she heard at all. It was a human pulse, the steady throb of a beating heart. It was her own heart she heard. How strange it beat so loudly at concert. Playing usually quieted her.

The princess slept to the pulse only a few measures longer before waking to reality. Twas not her heart she heard but another's. Her head rested against Clarece's breast; it was her friend's steady, strong heartbeat that permeated her dreams.

The slave had not slept, nor moved, but held her owner tightly into the morning, bidding her recovery from whatever awful thing it was that happened. There was so much she did not understand about her mistra, so much unknown about the ways of josquins. But whatever transpired a few hours earlier had overcome her lady. Clarece's concern for Raina was supplanted by the needs of the young woman. Casica was her mistra, her primary responsibility. She would keep watch over her until she woke or whatever it was a josquin did.

Casica stirred in the slave's arms. She was waking, stretching in her sleep. Clarece eased her embrace tentatively, concerned the girl may faint yet. Brown eyes met her own. They were clear and alert. The slave smiled. "Good morning, Mistra. Did you rest?" The princess nodded sleepily. "I had the most wonderful dream. I was home, accompanying the school choir." Her eyes squinted in thought. "I can't remember what it was we performed." No matter. The dream comforted her. She noticed Clarece still wore her cloak. "Have you been with me all this time?" "Yes. You looked to faint. Are you well?"

Memory returned, bearing that distinct nauseous awareness of almost having committed an irreparable act. "Yes...I. I almost did the unthinkable last night." Could it truly have been her mother's voice in her mind? Josquin dropped her head in shame. And relief. She had not murdered Muriel. But what was happening to her? She desperately needed help. Cleansing. The comfort of a holy place.

Her charge watched anxiously. She didn't know what the unthinkable was, but clearly it rattled her owner. "Clarece, can you watch Raina for a few hours today? I need to attend confession." "Of course, my lady, but if you may, allow me time to feed Muriel breakfast first. I'll return before lunch." The princess nodded wearily. "Alright. 'Twill give me time to treat Raina."

With a bow, the slave stood to dress, slipping on her trousers. She turned away from the princess to exchange her night shirt for a day one. Casica lowered her eyes in modesty but not before seeing Clarece's body. Vicious stripes, scarred reminders of previous owners, wrapped her arms and back. The free woman studied her hands, uncomfortable. What had kept the slave Clarece from being broken? So she wondered but asked, aloud, another question.

"Where do I find the Cassican intern, Clarece? I'd rather confess in Cassican." The slave nodded as she buckled her belt. She had often wondered why her lady had not yet visited her countryman. "You can find him in the yard chapel...," she directed, turning around, "the one outside, where we slaves go. But you should break fast first, my lady. A full stomach serves to drain more effectively the stagnant waters of the soul." Casica smiled despite herself. *The stagnant waters of the soul,* indeed. There was nothing stagnant about Clarece's soul. "As you wish, Your Holiness," she replied.

Her eminence reached for her boots and stopped. *Scads.* No one was here to lace them. Casica observed the awkward situation only a moment. "May I?" she asked. The slave glanced at her, embarrassed. "Please." The princess squatted in front of her friend and shod her in leather, reminding herself to purchase Clarece new boots as she did so. Lacing, that purgatory of activity for the handless woman, the handed accomplished quickly. "Thank you, Mistra," Clarece offered. She stood before her owner and then kneeled, her knees smarting from Muriel's slate. "I will serve you directly. By your leave."

Casica nodded her assent and watched as Clarece rose and walked towards the slaves' passage. She stood and looked around the stall, arresting her gaze on Asla's schedule. The insulit served many men. Next to the schedule was an apple.

Where on earth did Asla get an apple this time of year? she wondered, taking the fruit and rubbing it in her hands. The green skin felt smooth to her touch. The healer held the treasure and bowed her head in prayer. She should wait till her soul were more fit to pray, she reasoned, but she would offer this one petition through grace. *Remember this woman, please,* she asked silently. *Bring her home safely and soon.* Her short supplication ended, the healer rose to visit her patient.

Raina dozed in her dark stall, Soren poured out against her side. Casica stroked the catatonic feline. She stretched her hand to Raina's left ear and snapped. No response. She moved closer and snapped again. Nothing. She snapped her fingers lightly at her right ear. The little face wakened. "Good morning, Raina," she greeted, kindly. "How do you feel this day?" The child said nothing, only looked at her with the bluish green gaze of her father. Dark lines shadowed her eyes. Her face looked sunken, ill. Casica laid her hand upon the girl's stomach. Perhaps this would help. She would make her feel ravenously hungry; surely, then Raina would eat.

"Raina?" The eyes watched her intently. "Do you remember me?" The head whispered a nod. "I see you're reading the donkey story. You know, I read that same book when I was young. The donkey is strong and stubborn—like you," she grinned. "You come from stubborn stock. So do I." The princess glanced away, playfully. "I have, on occasion, been accused of being rather... hardheaded."

She stopped and peered into the weakened face, all playfulness gone. "I am told you wish to die." A single tear fell from the left eye. "I wish you to live. God has made you to live and nothing, nothing that wicked Muriel says or does changes that, Raina. She hasn't more power than God." The healer scratched Soren's ear. The cat was positively snoring. "I can keep you alive for a *very* long time. I may not fare so well in the process, but I'm willing to chance that for you." She placed a hand on the girl's brow. Warmth and health flowed into her patient. "I care for you, Raina. So many people love you and want you to live. We're trying to find a way to get you away from Muriel. Please, give us the chance. Give Clarece a chance."

The child said nothing, made no response at all. The empty gaze continued. Josquin placed her hands on the young face and looked deeply within it, aching at the depths of pain and hopelessness there. Silently, she pulled Asla's rich, red cape around Raina's face. Its owner's scent reached the child's nose. Raina opened slightly her mouth to capture it more fully. The motion wasn't lost on the healer.

"You smell her? You smell Asla?" Raina blinked at the beautiful woman's name. "You know, Asla saved your life," Casica shared quietly. "Twas she who found you and brought you here. She stayed with you. Cared for you. She's gone to service for a couple days, but she'll be back. Before she left, she asked me to tell you to get well." A dark hand covered the small heart. "Asla loves you, Raina. We love you. You're like the donkey. You can win this race, because you're not alone." The child listened for two breaths more then closed her eyes and slept.

Clarece returned much more quickly than expected. A plate of warm food accompanied her. "I went to procure Muriel's breakfast, but a servant had come before me. Apparently, the wit—the baroness had a nightmare last night. She woke wanting no slave for now and got the broker to hire a servant for her." The chief slaveswoman placed Casica's meal beside her and set herself next to it.

"This is the time to arrange a new owner for Raina," she began, "now that her mistra has a servant. He won't stay long. She'll run him off." She chewed her mitten, anxious. "Tis a knotty vine, though. I know only two openings in the palace. One in the North, one in the West. God knows I don't want her in the West. But we *must* keep her in the palace." She reviewed her mental hand of cards. There remained one, an ace in the hole, but the timing was all wrong.

The senior slave continued to ruminate, only now registering the taste of bacon. She sat back, startled. A piece of meat was where her chewed mitten had been. "Here, chew on that instead, Chief," her mistra beckoned. Clarece blushed in embarrassment. Chewing one's mittens was poor form. Still she was not one to deny herself pork. "I hear and obey," she mumbled, but continued, more confident. "There *is* another possibility." "Whom?" Casica asked. "The Countess." "You mean Dolca?"

"Yes," Clarece injected between bites. "She would make a fine mistra for Raina, but the timing is all wrong. Lady Dolca still owns a slave and hasn't yet advertised for another. Also...," She fretted with her hooks. "The countess is renowned for her selectivity. Sometimes it takes weeks for her to settle on cloth." She lowered her voice to a whisper. "Raina would make a fine slave for her. I know it. But she's young and broken. She hasn't many selling points." Clarece looked tearfully at the pale girl. "Of course, all is moot if she chooses to die."

The princess nodded. With what she had done to Raina, the little girl should be awake now, begging for food. She felt starving, that was certain. But it wasn't her body that reigned now; it was her heart, as sickened by despair as it was void of hope. Raina's mind held no blank pages for the future.

Casica set her plate beside Clarece. It was time to pray. "Finish this for me, if you will. Stay with Raina. There's stew in my room. Try to have her drink water at least. Lack of water does more harm than food." She looked, gratefully, into sapphire eyes. How blessed she was to have Clarece. "I'll be gone for some time. I've much to confess." The slave smiled, kindly. "Enjoy your visit, Mistra. I'm certain God looks forward to being with you. You may take my cloak, if you wish. Tis lowly but warm."

It was Casica's turn to smile. The last time she had worn that cover it was pouring rain, and its owner was a stranger, cloaked in mystery. She stopped at Clarece's stall for the garment and then ascended to her own chamber. Light warmed the cool room. Outside the windows stood towering reminders for her to look up. How refreshing to be above ground again. Josquin paused for a deep breath. The act reminded her of something else; she hadn't bathed in days. She almost postponed her confession for a bodily rite but decided against it.

It wasn't her flesh that needed cleansing. It was her soul.

XI

Fresh air. Casica stretched on her landing. She took a deep breath. *Oh, Father,* she smiled, how good it was to be outside in light! Above ground, level with green life tossing about playfully in the wind. The breeze wasn't quite cold. Only chilly enough for Clarece's cloak to warm cozily. She turned from the breeze to the wool; never in life had she owned such a plain cover. Still, there was something regal about it; the heavy cloth, the long full arms, the hood she let fall back upon her shoulders. Josquin rubbed her hands. The wool scratched them, and she wondered how her friend bore the irritation before remembering Clarece could not feel it.

Clarece. The princess smiled in realization. That's why the garment felt regal. It felt so because it bore its owner's sense of presence. Increasingly, the Cassican princess sensed there was more than met the eye about her charge. She didn't yet know what, but surely, history had adorned her friend with something greater than a silver band.

A red bird stole her thoughts. Its song joined the wind in exhilaration, bidding her bless the day and the One who made it. A place in Josquin's heart rose to the occasion, only to run headlong into a wall of guilt. How close she had come to murder. How dare she rejoice? She thought back on her mother's belief that all God's children had the right to sing along in a funeral procession. Could it be she was allowed to sing on the way to confession, even a confession of such magnitude as hers?

Casica pondered the question as she stepped down the stone way. Never before had she even imagined killing someone with her shalonn. What had happened to her these past months to cause such a breach of heart? Worse, she reasoned under a canopy of green, what if nothing had happened? What if this desire to harm were simply conjured in this tormenting environment but had brewed within her soul from the moment of conception? What if she were nothing more than a murderess shrouded with a peculiar power to give life? What if everything she thought she was were a sham?

She paused her rumination to view the garden. Everything, it seemed, lay dormant, awaiting the kiss of spring. Kiss of spring. Kiss of death. *Kai, Cass!* she commanded herself. Don't think this way! Don't accept this darkness. She looked about searchingly. Byzanthia and Cassica were once one. Surely, something of her homeland must grow in this place. It was difficult to tell, now that all blooms and flowers slept.

A green entity snagged her sight. Ivy. A Spennel Ivy trekked the trunk of an ancient oak. She knew that plant. Scads! She knew that oak! Cassica lived all around her in the persons of these towering monoliths. And she had almost missed them in her determination to find some *little* thing. A sentry of these oaks guarded her palace at home, their ancient limbs caressing and snaking their way along the ground.

A particular tree came to mind. It was reputed to be five hundred years in age. Its limbs rested upon the earth, fifteen cubits at a stretch. But peculiar to the oak was the shape of its foliage. Only a few limbs grew to the east; almost all the rest fell toward the west giving the tree a strikingly unbalanced appearance. Her father speculated that in the past, some storm had wrenched from the oak its normal shape; and having never fully recovered, he explained, "the tree grew in perpetual obedience to a voice that no longer spoke."

"A voice that no longer spoke." Her father could wax poetic when he wished. Casica considered Baba's words. Surely, she had been wrenched from her normal state. *So whose voice do I obey now?* the woman wondered, resuming her trek. A voice from the day she was tortured? A voice sounding like Jonas? A voice from Ars sent on her sixteenth birthday demanding her delivery to his county? Her own voice speaking on the edge of the cliff or railing at the injustice of her being moved about history like some pawn on a chessboard?

In the young woman was embedded a vein of justice. More than once her passion for right had spurred her to hasty, ill-advised action. Usually her actions proved themselves wise or at least redeemable. But even then, the girl's impulsiveness brought upon her equally impassioned discipline. By her mother, especially. How often, after Casica had exhausted her defenses in the presence of this immovable maternal court, would her mother chastise her, warning her of herself.

"You haven't the luxury of impulsiveness, Casica!" Pelana would reprimand. "You don't know the power that dwells in you. Tis not as mine. Tis not as Berea's. Tis not as a dozen of us pooled together. I don't tell you to stifle your heart; tis good and filled with light. And I don't tell you to kill your emotion. Your passion is God's gift to you, Child. But you cannot, you mustn't, be swayed by your feelings—even correct and righteous feeling. The line between emotion and volition is yet too porous in you, zeal and rage mingle too easily. With a thought, you could kill a dozen. But to my knowledge, you cannot raise the dead. Consider that. Consider how carelessly you can do what cannot be undone."

Casica saw herself in this particular argument. She sprung from her bed and prowled the room, filling it with her rebuttal. "I never asked for this power! I never asked to be surrendered to some God-forsaken people! I never asked to *be* at all!"

The princess stopped the memory, blushing in shame. Twas the only time in her life she'd ever cursed her mother. "Blast you! Could you and Father not refrain? You speak of control. You hadn't self-control enough to wait a month to prevent a Delender birthday!" Tears coursed the girl's face, tears looking very much like those coursing her mother's at that moment. She would never forget the image of her Maman. Pelana, Her Royal Majesty, Queen of the Isle of Cassica, stood before her fourteen-year-old daughter, shamed and cut. Though her mother had never done so, Casica fully expected her to strike, rightfully, for her insolence, but even in this fear she stood her ground, defiant.

The queen's daughter watched anxiously as her mother waited. She could not see what Pelana saw, could not hear the agreement she and K'eran had made—to lay together not at all in the month of Mala for dread of delivering a daughter into the control of an ancient Byzanthian edict. She could not see the day that undid all their planning, that sun-drenched day in a wheat field as the young husband and wife walked joyously together. All the world was gold that day. The sun above, the field around, the bands on their fingers. "Tis like we're in a cathedral," Pelana observed, laughingly to her husband. Her face was radiant; she could feel it in her pulsing shalonn, could see it in her lover's eyes.

"If this is a cathedral, you are communion," K'eran cooed. "I would consume you and lose myself in your beauty." Pelana received his desire teasingly. "Only if you could catch me. This Host has legs!" She shoved him away and raced through the stalks.

She heard him laughing long before feeling his arms around her waist, pulling her playfully to the ground. There in the scent of hot grass, they drank deeply of their cup. For a moment, they halted, both aware of the month and the fearful possibility it held. Pelana looked up into the doorway of Heaven. It shone with light, a transcendent glory that filled now her very soul. Light. It penetrated the night of their greatest fear, the fear of creating life at the wrong time.

In their youthfulness, they did not know that life is never misplaced, never mistaken. Life holds all the world sway. It was the will of Life that this be so. This they didn't know; they knew only they loved and in this holy place, lost themselves in the glory of their King, offering Him the consummate gift of worship. It is written that in the presence of love, fear must flee. It did. And in its place was conceived Casica, the daughter they named "Life," the one they called Night's Light....

Pelana wept in pain and smiled in pleasure. She looked at the child of her love, the body that bore her eyes and her Love's dimples. "If only you knew the Glory that ruled your father and me that day, Casica, you would never question your being." The woman looked away at her memory. "Neither I nor your father has ever regretted our decision. Nor do I now."

And then she turned, as only a queen can, victorious in humiliation, to exit the room. Casica watched, confused and afraid. Afraid of abandonment. "Maman, please!" she cried. Pelana took two steps further and stopped. The grace it took for her response, her daughter would never know. The tall queen turned to face her child. "Forgive me," Casica cried, falling on her knees. "Please, for—."

She never finished. Pelana spanned the distance between them and raised Casica into an embrace. Both their shalonns glowed in response. "Sol kana shea," Pelana wept, repeatedly, as Casica clung to her. They held each other for how long, Casica didn't know. But she did remember asking her mother finally, "Nelada." Help me. And Pelana did. Then and many times afterwards. And again last night.

Casica looked into the sun. Her josquin eyes could bear much of its glory. She breathed deeply and asked, in anticipation of confession, "Forgive me. Please. Help me."

In the light of grace, guilt fades. For the time it did. And in its place came song, blazing the trail before her as she made her way to the holy place.

XII

The holy place, it turned out, was a solid stone structure, small in size but heavy in substance. Huge stones made its shell and rough hewn shingles its covering. A small cemetery made its yard. The princess walked along the markers. Most of them were wooden, their writing worn clean with the elements. Occasionally, stood a marble or granite gravestone with the names of several dead carved into it. All the names possessed the distinct "d'" of slavery. "Martain d'Lowen" this one said, followed by several names under it, all bearing the Lowen moniker. No dates of life were mentioned. Only names, and judging by their placement, the buried slaves lay together in the plot. Several stones revealed slaves of differing owners buried together.

"So this is a slave's cemetery," Casica observed to herself. "Clarece might rest here." At once, she dismissed the thought. It didn't feel possible. She could not imagine the woman who served and filled her life so richly being interred in such a place. Still, she considered, looking about, perhaps she could. The grounds were well-kempt, maintained by lawn slaves. Above towered oaks and full around was the serenity of rest. All these slaves, whose lives labor defined, now slept in the comfort of a holy house and living earth. Yes, there was something beautiful about this place. Even the slaves' being buried communally. The slaves' world functioned through camaraderie—like bees in a hive. When, at last they must be ushered from the colony, it was fitting they rest together.

A creaking sound crossed the yard. Casica glanced up, thinking it must be the trees but it wasn't. It was a shutter, waving slowly in the breeze, bidding her, Come! And so she did. She approached the side entrance but found it locked. As she made her way around to the front entrance she stopped, surprised by the striking musty smell of a cellar. But it wasn't a cellar, she observed, squatting at the foundation. It was a waterbreak; the building sat on small pylons covered by a siding of stone. Underneath, earthy air congregated in the darkness. The smell escaped through breaks in the masonry.

The princess tarried a minute, smelling the current of earth and wondering, absently, how old the air might be. At the chapel's front, she paused before two large doors—like barn doors, she thought. Above them stood a smaller door with the remnant of what appeared to be a ladder leading to it. One barn door was ajar and through this, she entered.

Inside, the building was furnished sparingly, dominated by a cool moist fragrance. Heavy pews formed two flanks, separated by a series of four, roughly hewn square columns. Four windows, two to either side, eyed the walls, their shutters heavy like everything else. Casica glanced up. Above was a ceiling, conspicuous in the vaulted roof. A few steps forward confirmed her suspicion. The ceiling was the floor of a balcony; the little door outside must be its entrance. There were no books in the pews and while there were kneeling bars, none were padded. To the right was set a small confessional and to the front a simple lectern raised three steps above the floor. Candles, about fifty, burned softly. Even from where she stood, the princess felt their warmth, so damp was the sanctuary. A lone worshiper sat in the front pew, his head shrouded with a black cowl. With his posture, he looked all the world as though he were warming himself with the candles.

Though Casica stepped quietly, her footfalls shattered the chamber's silence with hollow sound. The priest glanced back. It was a slave, of course, and judging by the cloak, it might be the one, Clarece. *God help me,* he thought wryly. That woman asked the most perplexing questions. He rose to meet her. Then froze.

The woman had pushed back her hood. There, revealed, was the Princess Casica, her faced lit by the soft light of her shalonn. She smiled at the wonderfully familiar face. The man she didn't know, but the dark complexion she did. Cassican. Thank God for a Cassican intern.

The young priest almost fell with shock, but caught himself in time to kneel before his sovereign. "No, no. Please," Casica invited, extending her hand. He accepted it with a gasp. In all his life, he had never touched a healer. Warmth and health flooded him. He'd been feeling somewhat ill all day. That feeling fled immediately at her touch.

"Sair," she bowed humbly. "I am Casica Elespoir. I come to confess." The man smiled at the Cassican word for his office, yet floundered in the moment, still reeling from her royal presence. "Yes, Your Highness. I mean my daughter," he fumbled. "I am Flautis. Please, we can go to the confessional." The woman glanced at the cold nook. Flautis didn't need to sit in that damp place.

"With your permission, Sair, our Cassican tongue would provide as much privacy as the booth. Might we sit here?" The man nodded, catching his breath. *God,* he thought, as he joined her on the pew, *how beautiful she is.* How marvelously familiar in this pale-peopled place.

"Sair Flautis," she was saying in Cassican, "you may wonder why I've not visited you sooner." "My lady," he stammered, "I am but an intern. What am I to you?" So Flautis said, but, in truth, he had often questioned his princess' absence. Certainly they would never have met in Cassica, but this was not Cassica. He may be no one in their land, but royal or not, wouldn't she have wished even to see a familiar complexion? He had no leave to enter the Byzanthian palace without invitation. The resentment he felt over this royal snub of him had, more than once, sent him to his own confessional.

"I beg you, don't think that way." Flautis winced. What way? Was she reading his thoughts? "You see," she continued, "I did not safely arrive here. My movements have been few and close. I rarely leave my chamber, much less the palace. Even so...." Her eyes turned away. "Even so there is danger. Not only for me, but I fear for anyone with whom I associate." Flautis grew warm with shame. He had heard of the princess' treatment but had not allowed himself to believe it. Clearly, the rumors were true.

"But beyond that," she was saying "there is my slave, Clarece. I overshadow everything of her life. I wished to leave her at least space with God without my intrusion. Tis a strange world in which I live," she said, as much to herself as him. "The very reason I came is gone. Prince Bastien and I, well...I don't know what I'm doing anywhere." She brightened suddenly, remembering her audience. "In any case, I do know why I'm *here*. What of you, Flautis? How long have you served?"

Flautis broke from his introspection. "Interminably," he quipped. "Tis been a desperately dark winter. I've been here nine months." "And how long is your assignment?" "Eighteen." "With no furlough?" The man shook his head. "None. No early release. Not even for good behavior." Flautis checked himself. Here he was serving as priest before his queen, and all he did thus far was whine.

"Forgive me, Highness. I forget myself. I shouldn't complain. I asked to be sent here. It was my choice. I thought it would be educational and it has been; tis just...." "Boring and isolated?" The two had more in common than either would have guessed.

The priest grinned, nodding his head. "I would think you haven't many parishioners here," she suggested. "More than you might think," he replied. "But they are all slaves. Tis not that I don't enjoy them, but they don't allow much discussion, except for one in particular. Yours." The princess laughed quietly. "I can imagine. She's filled with questions, that one. As many as she has answers." Josquin looked about the building. "Tis a lonely spot, yes. But houses a good spirit."

"Yes," agreed her priest. He had spent much time cleaning and polishing the ancient structure. "Tis said that this was one of the earliest chapels in Byzanthia." He directed her attention to the back. "The balcony held slaves. They entered from the outside. This place was built by them, as I guess was everything else. When the palace chapel was completed," he explained, "they exhumed all the free bodies and interred them in free cemeteries. The slaves they left. Apparently, no one wanted to touch their bodies, so the chapel fell to them."

Casica was nodding. "I see. Worse things could have befallen them. What of your fellow priests? Do you enjoy them?" Flautis' eyebrows rose. "You mean my Byzanthian compatriots? Only in passing. I am housed quite alone in a structure whose lineage is highly suspect. Smells like pig. You see, my lady, even in the

Faith, Cassicans are kept separate." "Hmmm," Casica replied, thinking of Asla's stories of the clergy. "That may be a blessing, I think. The clergy, here, are not as ours at home." "Indeed," the priest snorted. "Little here is as it is at home." "Yes," replied the woman, softly. "Except for sin. It followed me clear across the channel."

The priest looked into his queen's eyes. They were those of any woman, troubled at this time, anxious to share her heart. "How may I help you, daughter of God?" he inquired gently. Casica looked up to him, wiping her eyes on Clarece's cloak. "I'm a sinful woman, Sair," she began. "I am filled with hate and rage." She stopped to take a deep breath before continuing. "Last night, I came a sigh short of murdering the Baroness Muriel."

Flautis blinked. What could she possibly mean? "With my thoughts, Sair Flautis," she answered. "Oh...you mean you had murderous thoughts towards her." "Yes, Sair, I did, but when *I* have such thoughts, I can actually kill. And I would have, had not God—or my mother—I don't know how she did it, she can't cross water—stopped me."

I can actually kill.... Flautis sat silently, trying desperately to recall what little he had learned about josquins in clerical training. Josquins were a mystery among clergy. The fact they were a mystery among themselves didn't help matters. No one could articulate the relationship between inherent healing and the spirit of God, shalonn and Eucharist.

Flautis glanced back to his one class. Berea, leader of josquins, lectured them on the power and workings of healers. She left them all in a fog of confusion. In retrospect, it didn't seem that clarification was her aim. And while she spoke easily and authentically of her own love and devotion to God, the woman bore with her a distinct impression of sensuality. It was rumored Lady Berea had a special "ministry" among young men. The fact that she had spent her entire lecture partaking of a flask had done nothing to straighten his mental clutter.

And now, here sat another healer, one reputed to possess powers as none before. *Her thoughts could actually kill.* The woman squirmed under his silence. "I don't know what's wrong with me, Flautis. But I do know I almost killed someone last night. I confess this sin and beg your help." She was looking to him now. He could feel it, a desperate drive to rescue. But for the life of him, Flautis couldn't think of how to help her. How does anyone help someone who can think into existence life and death? He retreated to training.

"You have confessed your sin to God, Casica Elespoir," he declared. "Your sin is forgiven." There. That part he knew. The rest, God help him.

"Thank you, Sair," she breathed, relieved at the grace of acceptance. "But what of my hate...my rage? What can I do for this?" Flautis ached for the tender woman. She wept openly, broken by her desperate need. "Daughter," he comforted, "you've a good heart. I've heard your reputation and I see it now. But tis placed in a vise here in this country. What spurred your rage toward this baroness?"

"She tried to kill a little girl slave. And now this child kills herself through starvation, and I can't stop her. I can delay it. I can keep her alive for a time. But I can't stop her." Flautis watched as, even now, Casica's eyes hardened. "What kind of evil drives a child to end her life?" she demanded. "Slavery," he answered simply. The princess shook her head.

"That's what I thought once, Sair. But now, I don't know. I'm not enslaved, and yet I am. I would never have thought myself capable of murder and yet I almost did. Tis though," she reached for the image, "I live on a spider's web. I'm trapped. There is no way out. If I move, if I show signs of life, the spider will come. And I'll die. If I don't move, if I hide who I truly am, I might survive, but...," she squinted at the realization. "If I hide myself, am I not already dead?" Casica looked around tearfully. "I would sit in the balcony of this place, such a slave I am to my own fear and darkness." She stopped and looked down. "I'm so confused, Flautis." *So am I,* was his silent reply.

Flautis' mind was a diocese of turmoil. *"Do something, you idiot!"* his thoughts were demanding. *Say something! You're a priest, for God's sake! This woman is coming to you for help and you'd better deliver. Otherwise she may go around destroying God knows how many people!* A panicked drive to rescue spurred the young man. He had to fix this. Had to dive into this woman's chaos and order it. But how? His mind raced frantically. It was his job to have the answers, his job to fix....

Flautis' thoughts stopped in mid-frenzy. Only now did he notice it, the pallor of fatigue weighing the woman's expression. She was exhausted, the princess was. Like a spark, the revelation singed him. This woman did not need answers. She needed care. *Do I care for this woman?* he questioned. Do I care for her more than I do my need to have answers? Something Berea had said—something about josquins needing touch. Touch and sleep and food.

The man set his hand on the girl's woolen sleeve. She glanced up, surprised. "Princess Casica," he asked tenderly, "how long has it been since you've slept?" She looked away trying to remember. "Days." "How long since you've eaten, fully, a meal?" "Some time. My slave hungers," she explained, uncomfortable. "I feel guilty being full when she is not." "And have you heard at all from home?" Casica shook her head, despondent. "I send out letters...but no replies. They're as absent as Bastien." She looked up. Her gaze pierced the priest.

"You don't understand, Flautis. I've beaten my Clarece, at the king's command—but it doesn't matter. I've been threatened with my life. I've raised a sword against a woman. I miss my husband—who isn't even my husband, I saw a woman leaving for her death and didn't stop her, I can't sleep as I used to—," and thus she continued, spinning a litany of failure and worry. *No wonder she wants to kill something,* thought the priest, listening patiently. This woman had left a world of security and adoration and now lived in this desert of danger and contempt.

She stopped finally, exhausted by her outpouring. A tinge of sleepiness laced her body. "Princess...." She turned to face her confessor. "You are forgiven. Fully. God has cleansed you. Fully. It is said that when all familiar is stripped away, the journeyman stumbles. You stumble but you still journey. And well." The priest glanced at her boots. "What is familiar to you?"

Josquin considered the question. "My stones," she answered, bringing her hand to her throat. "My karosh. My horse. Cassican. Oaks. Someone else, but I rarely see him." The man nodded. "These are all external. What of inside? What's familiar?" These were harder to list. "My desire to heal. My love of worship. My enjoyment of music, painting. My love of food and rest," she added, shyly. "My anger...hope...that's been failing these past days. My concern for people. I love people." *Sure you do,* a voice accused.

You love them so much you almost killed one last night. "I do love people," she repeated, countering the voice.

"Yes, you do," Flautis rejoined. He watched the candles. Strangely, he didn't feel cold anymore. "You remind me of soldiers I've talked to. They stay on the front lines until they forget themselves. In their struggle to survive, they stop living." He turned his attention to his parishioner.

"You are at war Princess Casica. In our country, you lived in light and peace. Here, you dwell with darkness. This is a violent, treacherous land. Enemies...both of flesh and, I dare say, spirit... hate your presence here. You're in enemy territory." Flautis pointed to the candles. "You bring light to this night. I'm not surprised by what you feel and neither should you be. You seem to have forgotten who you are. For a moment. But you are not your enemy, Casica."

The woman blinked at this declaration. And at her name. It was one of her greatest fears, warring with herself. "You are greatly gifted," Flautis concluded. "We're always attacked in the areas of our gifting. The attack is proof you do good." He grinned as the woman smiled, encouraged.

"Here is your penance, Daughter," he announced. She listened carefully. "Go outside and sit in the sun until you feel sleepiness." That won't take long. "Then you go home and eat fully, alone. And then you sleep, sleep until rest rouses you. And you allow your slave and your Father to take care of what is going on around you. Do you understand your penance?"

The tired woman nodded. "Yes, Sair Flautis. I thank you." She frowned suddenly, convicted by the candles. "But I should tarry to pray, first." Flautis shook his head. "That wasn't on my list. Sun. Food. Sleep." He stood and took her hand. Again the warmth filled him.

The priest walked his parishioner princess to the door. She paused. "I'm grateful you're here, Flautis. Thank you for caring for me." "You're welcome, Princess," he bowed. "I, too, am grateful you're here. I wasn't allowed entry to the palace when you came. To see you now.... Well, your presence is a blessing to this place. I haven't buried a single slave. No fever this year." Casica smiled, knowingly. "Thank you, Sair. God's blessing upon you." "And upon you, great lady," he returned.

And then Flautis did something usually reserved for older priests. He embraced his parishioner. She sighed in his arms. A man's embrace. How deeply she needed it, Casica didn't know until this moment, resting in a uniquely masculine strength. She stepped back and bowed to his kneel. "I'll be back," she smiled.

Flautis watched her stroll along the path until she stopped to sit on a boulder, warmed by the morning sun. Josquin leaned back and smiled in the light. Even from this distance, he could see her shalonn, burning brightly in response to its owner. In a few minutes, she left for her chamber, finding it warmed by Clarece's attention to the brazier.

Casica ate directly from the stew pot. Ate until filled. She then wrote a note to Clarece telling her she was not be disturbed and fastened it, with Bastien's dagger, to the slave's side of the sliding door—which she closed. She entered her sitting area and there lit a large candle, placing it in her window as an oblation of faith, hoping against hope for Asla's early return. Then closing all other curtains, she sat on her bed and freed herself of boots, clothing and responsibility. Finally, invested in her nightgown, scented with the freshness of Clarece's washing, Josquin slipped into her cool sheets, drew the heavy comforter securely about her and closed her eyes.

Within the time it would take to offer a prayer of contrition, she slept. Penance never felt so good; felt, perhaps, as it always should.

XIII

Casica roused slowly, wakefulness coming upon her as had sleep, unawares. Her body lay quietly, enjoying the exquisite sense of warmth and coziness. If she'd dreamt, she didn't know it. Her room slept too, it seemed, still and silent except for the ticking of the clock and an occasional pop as her brazier stretched with the glowing coals. Not even the wind breathed. The woman relished the silence, relished the sense of well-being that stood in her like water in a stilled glass. Her body was fully rested and her mind, tranquil, with a peace she had not known in weeks.

After several minutes she opened, finally, her eyes. Shadows danced near her door as Asla's candle burned low. The healer breathed deeply, concentrating on registering the dim heat, playing with her shalonn. She smiled. She could feel it. She lay thus for half an hour, secure in the solitude and comfort of being closed in. The clock sounded eleven, then the half-hour. Twelve hours. She had slept half a day away. Penance, thoroughly, was satisfied.

When the quarter-hour struck, the princess moved, stretching contentedly in her warm bed. It was in the middle of a lavish yawn that she sensed her. Asla. Asla was coming home! The healer's heart leapt with joy. She watched as the door lever turned slowly. A figure, hooded all in blue, stepped soundlessly into her chamber like an apparition. It took the flickering candle and walked towards the brazier, glancing in the direction of the princess' bed.

"Welcome home, Asla!" Casica whispered happily in g'Helderleicht. The insulit stopped, seemingly confused, before stepping cautiously, towards the voice. The candle, she set on Casica's nightstand; her body, she set on the edge of the bed. The princess rose slowly. Something, clearly, was wrong.

"Asla?" she said, gently pulling the hood from the woman's face. The face dropped to hide in its owner's hands. A dark hand touched her, holding her shoulder comfortingly. The woman tensed at the connection; it was the first safe feeling she had known in days. "You shouldn't touch me, Casica," Asla whispered. "My body's been places your mind can't even go."

"Dear, Child," the kind woman offered, drawing the body close to her own. "*'Child,'*" something in the insulit thought. *This woman is the only person in the world who would call me that.* A familiar warmth began to penetrate the g'Helderleit but in a confusing manner, as though searching to locate the mistress of the body it filled. Asla was home in the palace but not yet home in herself.

"Two days," a distant voice offered. "No food. No drink. No sleep. Only men. Bastard. He subbed me. Rented me out to the others." Casica watched the thumb rub into the palm. "I earned him money faster than he planned; he let me go early. Frappin Edsner. Tis forbidden to sub an insulit. He'll pay for this."

The girl abandoned her palm to rub the comforter, then her sleeve, seeking desperately to find something, anything, to call her back to herself. She had almost forgotten her way to the palace, so broken away from herself was she. Had it not been for Casica's candle, she would still roam the palace grounds, searching for the chamber.

Casica held the trembling woman as she examined her for harm. There was much. Not severe enough to threaten physical life but enough to shatter the inner vessel. "Your cloak saved my life," Asla heard herself say. "I kept it near where they took me. I would touch it when I could. It was like having you there. It kept reminding me I existed someplace. I don't know where." She crossed her arms in front and rubbed them against themselves and her body. "I went away someplace," she whispered, confused. "But...I can't seem to remember where...." She bit her thumb. "I can't remember where...."

Josquin placed her hand upon the left side of the woman's head. Even before the physical connection, something in Asla grasped at the healing, closing the woman's eyes for her to rest in the sensation. For a long time, Casica ministered to the soulish breach that yawned in the insulit's mind. Slowly, very slowly, she could feel the gap lessen between Asla the held and Asla the felt. She was more in her body now, but her presence flickered like the candle on the stand. The girl turned to face Casica, finally. The gaze startled the healer; it looked frighteningly similar to that of Raina, empty and lost.

"How's Raina?" a hollow voice asked. "She's awake but not eating." The insulit nodded, understanding. "She's broken," Asla announced nonchalantly. "She'll die now. 'Twill be better for her." Asla looked into her mind. "Clarece says there's a Heaven for slaves. Raina's innocent. Not even God would keep her out."

Though Asla's words spoke as if encouraged for the girl, sorrow filled her tone. She had feared this would happen. On her way to her service, she had stopped by the cathedral and begged whatever god there was to spare the child. She had stood on her side of the gate, directing her plea into the open doors, weeping at the music that flowed from them. In desperation, she had approached a worshipper entering the holy place. She had opened her mouth to ask for their supplication on her little friend's behalf, to offer money for them to light a candle for her healing. But then she heard the howl of darkness. And cowered before it.

"To be dead is better," she continued softly. *For the souled, that is,* she thought. But for her...*If men are this evil, what will demons be like?* The insulit reached inside the cloak and produced from behind her, the large dagger. Casica watched cautiously as the girl stared at her arm. She pushed up a silken sleeve and began to scrape the blade against her wrist, absently, looking all the world as though sharpening it against her flesh. The healer winced at the sight and at the sights that joined it: the vicious bruise around the delicate wrist, the bloodied bite on the forearm.

"They teach us how to survive," Asla said to no one. "Teach us how to die, painlessly." In the light, tears crept silently down the expressionless face. "They don't teach us how to live painlessly. Don't teach us how to live a'tall."

Dear God, wondered Casica, *is this how insulit are broken?* Very slowly she reached for the knife. Asla offered no resistance. The princess took the weapon and set it out of reach on her nightstand. In its place, she offered her hand. Asla's closed around it.

"Come, my friend," Josquin invited softly, rising from her bed. She led the silent woman to a chair near the warm brazier. The heat bathed the golden face with comfort. Casica took the stew pot and ladled a goodly amount into an earthen bowl. She cupped her hands around the vessel until it steamed. Then carefully, she placed the bowl in the lap of the ravenous woman, praying as she did, that Asla would receive it.

The insulit looked at the food, debating. Survival was embedded deeply within her. She reached, finally, for the spoon and brought it deliberately to her mouth, and in response to the delicious taste, her body did, wonderfully, what her heart could not; it desired. Asla ate quickly now, barely noticing the glass of wine Casica placed beside her. The stew finished, she drained the cup, emptying it as Casica placed another bowl on her lap. This, too, she devoured, all in silence. The third bowl she ate much more slowly. She was returning from wherever she had gone. She could almost hear the clock.

The healer watched her friend intently. Asla looked weak enough to fall from the chair. She stopped eating now and bowed her head, still cradling the warm bowl in her lap. She stared into the stew vacantly, hesitating in her return to herself, fearful of what she might find.

A familiar touch drew her attention. The insulit watched, bewildered, as the princess kneeled before her and unlaced her ties. Casica removed the dirty boots and placed them aside, adding to them a pair of red woolen socks. She wrapped her hands around the small feet and began to massage them, filling the girl with warmth and kindness as she did. *Tis safe to come home,* she seemed to speak, somehow. *Tis safe to come home.*

The blonde woman sat, dumb, and wondered somewhere within her dazed mind, how a woman like Casica could touch a woman like her. She thought back to the cathedral, how she stood there outside the gate crying, aching to enter in, aching to join the voices that filled the air with music. But to enter was forbidden. She could never go to it.

It was here in this place of such helplessness, that the cathedral now came to her, gracing Asla with a pure and kind inclusion. It was as if Casica placed the Host into her mouth. Its sweetness overwhelmed her. Asla bowed her head and sobbed.

She never felt herself fall asleep. Never felt the healer lift her from the chair and place her in the warm bed. Never felt herself freed of belt and vest. Never felt the unique healings poured into her body. Never felt the heavy comforter tucked securely about her. Never felt the kiss upon her brow.

Asla of g'Helderlend felt none of this. Yet all the while, received more of God than had many a worshiper, ever, in the cathedral of stone.

XIV

Casica stood at the curtain, contemplating the scene in Raina's stall. Clarece slept, sitting straight as her chair, Soren's vast domain sprawled across her lap. His was the sleep of the contented, his belly being filled with royal morsels from Casica's unclaimed plate. The slave hadn't her owner's leave to eat the procured dinner, so she hadn't. Sir Tom, unfettered by such scrupulous restraints, had. The Cassican reached to touch her friend awake, but before she could, the chief slaveswoman opened her eyes, stirred by her mistra's presence. "Good evening...."

Clarece smiled at the welcome and even more at the fragrance of her owner's freshly bathed body. Her mistra positively beamed with a renewal of life. "Good morning, my lady," she returned, maintaining her stiff posture. "Confession becomes you. It looks much better than ever it has on me." Casica grinned, assuming her place opposite cat and woman. "Perhaps you should try confessing in Cassican. I've been fully graced. And how are you and Raina?" The slave looked sadly at the sleeping child. "She hasn't eaten or drunk anything, Mistra. She succumbs, I fear."

The healer placed a warm hand on Raina's head. She was dying. That was certain. She would do all she could to sustain life, but if God did not intervene, it would be not His will done, but Raina's. Casica examined her exhausted friend. "There's good news. Asla's home." "She *is*?" Clarece responded, brightening immediately. "How is she?"

"She sleeps in my bed," her mistra offered as explanation. Clarece bowed her head, relieved. She could rest now, knowing her sala was safe. "Now," Casica continued, "tis your turn. I'll free your feet and gather you some light." The slave offered not a single objection. Within minutes, she slept in her cot, oblivious as Soren to the waking pen.

"The big, black horse broke into the brook. The big splash of the big, black horse wet the dusty donkey. 'Go home, lowly donkey,' the big, black horse spat. 'Go back to your mud and sticks. Go back to your lowly way.' 'I will run with horses,' said the donkey. 'A donkey can run with horses. He can be a runner, too.' The big, black horse splashed the little donkey. 'You are not fairly fast to run with horses,' said he. 'You are made to bear big burdens. You are made to walk. You are not made to run.' 'I am made to run,' said the dripping donkey. 'I can run this race. I can run as a donkey runs.'"

Casica paused in her reading to examine the silent child before her. Raina continued to worsen throughout the day. Sighing, she lowered the book, humbled, once again, by the limitations of her power. A person's will was a formidable foe, even a little person's will. Raina's decision to die thwarted her gifting, and Casica found herself straining as she counteracted the child's refusal to feed her body. Normally, in such a circumstance Josquin would summon the powers of other healers and enlist them in the battle with her. But that was in Cassica where healers moved among each other's giftings as easily as thought; here, she was beyond the reach of her sisters.

Josquin caressed her shalonn. At least she could help them; her power was such that it flowed smoothly across the channel. Since coming to Byzanthia, she had on several occasions assisted healers at home.

Casica tucked Asla's cloak more closely around the little slave and sighed again. What she wouldn't do for any one of her peers' help. Help and companionship. In community was so much more strength found than could ever be known alone. It mattered not she excelled above all in power. Casica wilted in the absence of her sisters. They would be convening, soon, in Iveria. Iveria, heart of every josquin. Womb of every shalonn. Where to hold a score of pobble stones, one need only caress the dirt.

Casica remembered herself there, that first time, where as a child she walked in a meadow with her mother, anxious and excited. She would be inducted into the assembly of josquins this day. She had worn her shalonn several years, already, and had rendered many healings. But now, she would join The Circle.

Pelana laughed at her daughter's giddiness. "Here, M'Yat," she announced, kneeling on the cool, green grass. "You're surrounded by pobbles, you know." "Where, Maman?" Her daughter looked all about but saw none. "You mean you can't see them?" "No," the girl replied, concerned, looking more earnestly around herself. Perhaps it was a vision she could gain only after her initiation.

Pelana smiled at the puzzled expression. "Place your hand in the dirt. Feel it." Casica knelt beside her mother. She dug her fingers into the damp earth. That blessed scent of life filled her, as suddenly, for cubits all around, pobble stones rose to the surface. Those pobbles she could not see, she could feel. They were everywhere, a field of jewels, all of them reflecting the colors of her shalonn. Pelana joined her hand with the dirt. More stones rose and now all pulsated with light, alternating in shalonn color of mother and daughter. They laughed aloud at the symphony of color. From then on, this became their yearly ritual, their special game in the fields of Iveria.

Casica's eyes glistened. Who would play with her mother this year? Would she ever, again, stand on that sacred soil? The healer removed her necklace. She caressed it lovingly. In her hands, the stones radiated with the growing intensity of memory. Nowhere on earth was she so at home as Iveria, there among her family of healers, there among the presence of healing. The air itself breathed life into a josquin. How she longed to assemble with them this season, to spend the two nights in solitary cleansing. To kneel before the Council in blissful receivership of unction. To join with the others for days of corporate release upon their people, administering to their island health and life. Cleansing, blessing, release. The rhythm of a healer's world.

Casica shook herself. Time for this world. She took her shalonn and drew it about her neck. Instantly, the stones joined in their unbreakable union. She glanced around the pen. All was quiet. The afternoon's duties took everyone away. Even Clarece was gone, excusing herself after her short sleep to gather coal for an absent guildsman. How strange, determined the princess, that in the midst of Raina's life and death struggle, the mundane activities of daily living continued. She had observed this countless times in her homeland. Life stopped for nothing, for no one. Often, it seemed, the world, itself, *should* stop, so profound the impact of a broken body or ended life. But it didn't.

For many years Josquin resented this apparent disregard of life concerning the tragedies experienced in its realm. It seemed to prove the futility of existence in this world. Now, however, she interpreted things differently. It wasn't that human life and drama were unimportant. On the contrary; they were the essence of life. So essential to earth's existence was life that nothing, no one nor the absence of anything or anyone, could stop it. Life here or life in the afterworld: in either domain, Life ruled.

"Would you like me to keep reading, Raina?" Casica asked, hoping against hope the child would respond. She didn't. Though her eyes opened from sleep, the gaze that stared past the open curtain was as empty as the pen. "Alright. Then I'll continue...." The healer returned to the donkey who dared run with horses. The cat who dared run with mouses, well, she hadn't a clue where he had gone off. Soren had departed their company hours ago.

His Eminence was, at this moment, snoozing on the princess' bed. Asla was home, and where Asla was, Soren was sure to be—providing, of course, his kingly duties allowed him proximity to her person. It was a strange, peculiar affect of the insulit, all insulit, this mysterious allure of whiskered creatures. Rarely could Asla spend an extended time alone in the city at night (when animals roamed most freely), without attracting an entourage of pawed attendants. For herself, she found the attention most unwelcome. More than once while fleeing an assailant, the insulit had secured herself in a hideaway only to be found out by an admiring mew or bark.

Asla couldn't explain this attraction of creatures to her person. It certainly wasn't that she particularly liked animals. They were acceptable in their furry way, but a polite association was all she ever offered. Nothing more. Her life never had lent itself to developing affectionate bonds with anything living—except for plants. The g'Helderleit enjoyed a torrid affair with flora, one fostered in childhood by lonely play, and in this season of botanical sleep, Asla found herself pining for leafy companionship. But as for animals, theirs certainly was unrequited love. Even so, suitor Soren never balked at Asla's rebuttals. Happily he surrendered his kingly pride to bask a moment in the woman's presence and even now slept, shamelessly, at her feet.

In a few hours, his lady would waken to his regal self and, rousing as she would in an especially generous mood, scratch his scruffy form. It was good that Soren was a cat. If Asla must wake to an unwanted padded presence, one that mewed fared far better than one that barked. The insulit, all insulit, feared dogs with a vengeance, the reasons for which were kept to their own company.

Casica read to herself now, Raina having fallen asleep, heedless of the passing day. It was late afternoon; the clock had chimed four. The princess turned to the account of the rabbits' trick to spur the donkey's continued resolve when a familiar presence approached her post. Accompanying the presence were the aroma of Cassican stew and a kingly mew. Josquin looked up and smiled. Asla was standing outside the stall, within her sight but beyond Raina's. On her arm was draped Casica's cloak.

Asla placed the bowl of stew on the great table and motioned for the healer to come. His majesty flew by the princess as she rose and jumped directly upon the girl's cot. *So that's where you've been,* thought she. *Consorting with other women.* With a glance towards the sleeping child, she left the donkey's story to join another's.

"Good afternoon, God's Beauty," she whispered in g'Helderleicht, encircling the young woman in a warm, josquin embrace. She smiled at what she felt. The insulit was whole in body and mind, as much as she could be.

"Good afternoon," Asla wished. She withdrew and bowed, embarrassed. "I...I thank you for whatever you did and for letting me take your bed." She glanced over her shoulder towards the stairs. "I would change your sheets, but, scads, if I know where Clarece hides them." The princess shook her head. "I can never find them, either. I think the chief slaveswoman uses them to stake some clandestine game of chance." The insulit smiled, relieved at the woman's playful tone. "Uses them in some clandestine game of another sort, more likely."

Casica bowed her head, her face warming into a grin. Clearly Asla was on the mend. "And how is the little one?" Asla continued, indicating the stall with her head. Casica's playfulness dissolved. "Unwell. She refuses drink or food. I'm doing all I can, but she'll die if this continues."

Asla nodded with understanding and stood, uncomfortably, in thought. She had been thinking for some time now, basking in the light and coziness of Casica's room. As Soren and she shared a bowl of stew, she had ruminated many things, not the least of which was her role in Raina's life. It was a bizarre fact of insulit existence that the very people who secured their doomed fate trained the damned in the art of survival. Could not one doomed as she, Asla wondered, use her enemies' training to help one who yet had hope? She reached into her vest pocket. It was a small thing but she had learned, well, to use what was at hand.

"Wait here," she quieted instructed. "Give me some time alone with her." Casica nodded, intrigued, then as an afterthought offered, "She's deaf in her left ear." Armed with this information, the insulit nodded and taking the bowl into her hands, walked lightly towards the silent stall.

"Hello, Scamp!" she greeted happily, masking her shock. Raina bore a deathly pallor. The small slave opened her eyes to locate the familiar voice to her right. Asla moved her stool so that the girl could see her clearly and listen with her good ear. With a flourish, she added Casica's cloak upon her own and offered her most winsome smile. "Missed me?" she winked. The child said nothing but a light sparked in her eyes. It was Asla! Asla had come home. The beautiful woman now sat on the little slave's cot.

Asla studied the sunken face and took a deep breath. Gods knew, she had touched some of Earth's most repulsive issue. She could do this, and if it meant being burned, then so be it. She would burn, eventually, anyway. To the child's eyes there was no reluctance, no fearfulness. The insulit reached out her hand and tenderly traced Raina's cheek. "I missed *you*," she said softly.

At Asla's touch, the lonely child wept; her tears were cold to the g'Helderleit's fingers that kindly wiped them away. Asla reached for the stew. She set the bowl in her lap and ate several spoonfuls, letting the aroma tease her small friend. As she chewed her last bite, she returned the bowl to the stool and reached into her pocket.

"I brought something for you," Asla divulged intriguingly. "Tis a special treat." From her vest she produced some brown parchment. Something hid within. "Can you guess what this is?" The movement of Raina's head would have been imperceptible to another person, but the insulit saw it clearly. Slowly, mysteriously, she unwrapped the treasure. With her forefinger and thumb she took the gift and held it reverently before the child. "Do you know this?"

Raina examined it as closely as she could. She had never seen anything like the white, rounded substance. She looked to Asla. "Tis called 'peppered mint,'" Asla whispered. "Tis the most magical thing on earth. One taste and you'll never be the same."

Raina watched, captivated, as the insulit reached behind her waist and drew out her large dagger. She placed the candy on the stool and struck it, hard, with the knife's hilt. Instantly, the shattered offering rendered to the ladies its heavenly scent. Mint filled the stall. Raina had never seen nor smelled anything like it. Out the corner of her eye, Asla saw her lick her lips.

The insulit waited a breath longer then brought a sliver of the candy to her nose. She closed her eyes and smelled deeply, as she would if the mint were green, growing in the garden outside Casica's chamber. How she longed to rub that living leaf in her hands and drink of the crushed aroma. She took the sliver and, quite dramatically, placed it upon her tongue.

"Mmmm," she moaned. A grin pricked her face as she heard beside her the distinct sound of a little belly growling. She took another sliver and without even pausing to think of asking if it were desired, brought the candy to the girl's mouth. Instinctively, Raina's lips opened and received the mystery within. And for the first time in her impoverished life, the child tasted something sweet.

Raina smiled as she hadn't in days, savoring the sensation that dissolved upon her tongue. "Is it not magical?" her big friend asked, smiling. Raina swallowed as she watched Asla brush the candy pieces into her hand. One by one she fed the slivers to the child, then casually offered a spoon of stew. Raina received that too. Inside, the dancer pirouetted. Outside, she reached for the donkey book.

"Let's see how donkey is doing today," she announced, and for half the next hour read the story aloud, alternating pages with food. She stopped her serving and reading only after Raina refused more of either. But this time her rejection came not from her heart. It came from her body. Satisfied, the weakened frame dismissed Raina from wakefulness to concentrate more fully upon restoring her with nourishment.

Asla smiled. She tucked Casica's cloak about the sleeping child. A slight smile graced the lovely lips. Raina would live now. Sweetness had overwhelmed her. Her alliance with death was overcome. Again the insulit caressed the silent face, fearlessly this time. She would not burn, she now knew. She, the hollow, could touch the souled and not be burned. But she could blaze she realized, mystified.

Asla took her hand from Raina and placed it upon her chest, feeling herself intently. Something was aflame in her hallowed heart.

XV

Dolca, Countess of Halen, sipped happily. She enjoyed her visits with the Cassican. The princess of the foreign country truly did have a tongue to match her appetite, and with her tongue filled the afternoon with curiosity and humor. Today they had been discussing courtship procedures of their two countries. It appeared the only aspect similar to their respective rituals was that they both involved men and women.

"So you mean to tell me, men in your country do not...'partake' outside marriage?" Casica took another sip of tea, nodding into her cup. "Sin is alive and well in my country, Dolca. Though there's less now than before, what with my having left and come here. Infidelity and fornication certainly do exist, but such is an anomaly, a matter of shame. Of course," she grinned, "this might help explain why Cassicans tend to marry at relatively young ages."

"What a strange people you are in your small island kingdom," Dolca observed. Casica coughed on her sip. Clarece's shoulders shook in silent laughter where she stood, positioned behind the visiting royal. Casica glared in her slave's direction but not in view of Dolca. As much as she wished to defend her country's good measure, this was no time to start an argument: Raina stood in the balance.

"There is much about my country that's alien here," Casica said, instead. "I'm thankful the enjoyment of tea isn't one of them." "Indeed," her guest replied, "you do brew a very fine drink, Your Highness." Casica smiled in acknowledgment. Her palms were sweating. Her shalonn was burning. Scads, she'd better say something now before she lost all courage.

"Dolca, I have a confession to make." "Ah, your sin to which you allude. Well, I'm not accustomed to assuming a clerical role, but confess away," Dolca replied good-naturedly, placing her empty cup upon its saucer. The tall slave moved to refill it.

That was another strange thing, thought the countess, having a slave stand instead of kneel at attention. She observed Clarece with interest. More than once during her visits with Casica, she had noticed the slave and her lady make eye contact. She was quite certain that in private, Clarece and her owner lived face-to-face. The slave refilled her cup expertly, gracing her retreat from the guest with a humble bow. What would it be like, thought Dolca, to live with a slave as with a human? The princess summoned her back to the confessional.

"My inviting you here today is laced with an ulterior motive." She sipped from her cup encouragement. "Tis my understanding you may soon advertise for a slave." Dolca glanced over her shoulder. Clarece gazed slavishly at the floor. "That would be a correct understanding. But I was unaware, Princess, of your employment in the brokering business." "What I'm employed in might surprise you, Countess," Casica replied, rolling her eyes. "I know that it certainly surprises me at times. However, I have had in my—medicinal—care, a little girl, Raina."

"Oh," Dolca interrupted, raising her hand. "I've heard about Muriel's waif. I'm not interested. I don't want a slavechild. 'Never have." She turned back towards the woman behind her. "However, I'd be more than willing to take Clarece off your hands." Of course Casica wasn't selling her; Dolca knew this from previous discussions. Still, something in the playful royal wished to stir the water. Casica laughed. She would enjoy this.

"I'm afraid that's impossible, Countess. You see, we have a wager, Clarece and I, on who will tire of whom first. I'm betting she'll dismiss *me*.... However," she continued, playing Dolca's game, "out of curiosity, how much were you thinking?" Clarece glanced up, shocked. Dolca studied her cup for a moment. "I'd offer you 510 pounds."

"Five hundred ten?! Truly?" Casica gasped. "That much? Hmmm." The princess partook slowly of her refreshment. Her friend had suffered enough. "No," she declared decisively, "we're only now learning to tolerate one another. I think I'll keep her." "Well, if you change your mind...." "You'll be the first to know." The princess glanced at her charge. The realization she'd been played poured from Clarece's neck into her face. Her mistra got her good this time. Casica returned to the issue at hand.

"Well, as a royal courtesy, Dolca, would you please indulge my ramblings concerning the child?" "Of course, Your Highness." Casica set her playfulness aside with her cup. "Raina has suffered terribly," she began.

The princess' tone caught Dolca unaware as did her words. She had heard rumors concerning Muriel's attempt upon the slave's life. The thought of a royal the baroness' rank acting in such a manner turned the young woman's stomach. There was nothing she could do, of course. Muriel was well within her right to kill her own slave. But still, the baroness' behavior over the past year had grown increasingly irrational. Another rumor had her drinking herself mad.

The princess continued. "She was brutally wounded but recovers. The child's in desperate need of a new owner, however. It is thought, by some, that you and she would make a fine pair." "By 'some'?" repeated Dolca. "Yes." Dolca glanced over her shoulder. It was certain who the "some" was; she stood behind the countess praying for the miraculous. "And what of you, Princess?" Dolca asked plainly. "Why do you not assume her ownership?"

"Well," Casica replied, caressing the fleur d'lis on her cup, "tis thought by the same some that any interest I might show in the child would seal her fate."

Dolca nodded, understanding. Clarece was correct. "Well, as I've said, I've no need for a child. Tis not that I'm unmoved by her circumstance, but I'd rather an older slave. A young slave is nothing but trouble." "Such has been my observation about older slaves, too," the princess noted, dryly. (Clarece flinched.) "However, I've observed also that some slaves far exceed any trouble they may cause."

"True," Dolca capitulated. "Still, from what I hear, the girl hasn't *any* good qualities. And while I surely don't move in the circles of royalty as you, Princess, my rank does require certain trappings. Any slave I own must reflect well upon me. Is there anything about this girl that would do so?"

Josquin slumped, stumped. She hadn't a clue what an owner looked for in a slave. "I can't answer," she confessed. Dolca turned to Clarece. "Chief slaveswoman, what of you? What are this slave's assets?" The senior slave glanced towards her owner. "With your permission, Mistra?" "Of course."

"Raina is a young slave, tis true, but her youth may be her greatest asset, my lady. An older slave, such as myself, is set in her ways which may prove ill-fitted for a new owner. You may ask my mistra. My faults are legion, and I'm slow to learn her ways. Tis only through the long-suffering of her gracious, nay—divine nature, she did not dismiss me months ago. Raina, you may train as you wish for her slavery to be rendered. She is honest and bright and eager to please. And, before her injury, characterized by cheerfulness. She would make you good company and, in service, prove advantageous. She currently learns to read and write—abilities, I believe, you have not yet enjoyed in a slave."

Dolca sighed. These were good selling points but, clearly, Clarece was stretching. "And her liabilities? What are they?" Here, the senior slave spoke more cautiously. "Raina is young. Her age restricts her ability to serve you. There are tasks, ones requiring height and strength, she's not yet able to perform. Time, however, will remedy this situation. Also, she currently recovers from injury. Raina has limited hearing in one ear. However," she hastened to explain, for a physical weakness was intolerable, "the princess is working to cure this. The child has been raised poorly, thus far, and hasn't the social skills required by one of your rank. But she could learn from a teacher like yourself." The senior slave hesitated. This might be Raina's undoing, but it was true. "Lastly...Raina is broken, your ladyship. She hasn't the confidence a slave should."

Dolca snorted indelicately. She crossed her arms in thought. "So Muriel has broken her. A broken slave is as a broken cup," she observed, studying the one in her hand. "Neither is useful to anyone." Casica glanced down, fighting a wave of tears. God, how she had hoped for at least a chance for the child.

"If I may, my lady?" It was the chief slaveswoman. "Tis true; Raina is, at this time, unfit for a woman of your stature. However, it is in my belief, as equally true that she has within her person, the fabric of a fine slave. She needs only nurture and guidance to realize her potential. The nurture, your ladyship could most easily and naturally administer. As for guidance, should you choose to employ Raina as your charge, I willingly offer myself as her menta. By my mistra's leave, of course."

Dolca's eyebrow raised with renewed interest. "You're saying you would menta her?" "Yes, my lady. I would place Raina under my personal supervision and accountability." The royal leaned into her chair. "Well, that does sweeten the pot. If I can't have the shaker, I'd at least taste the salt."

Two women, one nervous and one praying, waited anxiously. Dolca was teetering. *Scads,* thought she. *What would it hurt to look?* "Well, bring the girl in. I'll have a look." Clarece glanced towards her owner. Casica nodded. The tall slave offered a half-kneel and retreated quickly to the pen below.

She found Raina sleeping as she spent much her time doing. Her body recovered quickly in the presence of rest and nourishment. She lay on her right side so Clarece touched her awake. "Raina?" The child turned, groggily. Her ear rang wildly. "Raina?" "Mistress...." The little slave sat up in her cot, concentrating on hearing her chief above the noise.

"There is someone in Casica's chamber wanting to meet you. The Countess Dolca. She's considering buying you." The child's eyes brimmed with fright. "A royal? I don't want a royal, mistress. I'm a stupid slave. She'll hurt me." Clarece placed a hand upon Raina's face. "No...no, she won't," she comforted. "Countess Dolca is a gentle woman. She won't hurt you. She only wants to look. I'll be there the whole time as will the princess. I promise, you'll be safe."

The child cowered in fear. Inspection. Only a few months ago, she had endured one. Now here was another. Panic burned in her stomach. "We must go now," Clarece prodded. Raina submitted. "As you wish, mistress," she whispered, rubbing her nose on her sleeve.

Clarece examined the sleeve. Raina possessed only one shirt, and it had suffered along with its owner these past weeks. "Come, let's get you a fresh blouse." Clarece waited as the child donned her worn, broken boots, then took her hand and led her to Asla's cot. The g'Helderleit had not a few blouses, and her size more closely matched the girl's. Clarece rummaged through the pile, choosing quickly a green one. Green for luck. Crispus knew, Raina needed all the luck possible. "Here," she offered, "let's array you." Raina smiled, encouraged. Green. And Asla's. The cloth felt cool but comforting.

Clarece reached for the arms with her maimed claws. "Roll the sleeves some," she instructed. *Curse, her useless hands.* She could not even brush the girl's hair. They hadn't time, anyway. It would take a good hour—and clothes they didn't have—to make Raina presentable for the master seamstress. The chief sighed. There were times when a body could only throw itself at the mercy of the heavenly court. This was one of those times.

She squatted before the little slave and coached, encouragingly. "Now. Remember, Raina. I'll be with you the whole time. Nothing bad will happen. You just do what Dolca says and be honest with any questions. Alright?" The girl nodded, worried. Her face was red with crying. Thank the gods slaves lived face down. Clarece smiled. "Let's go show the countess what a fine slave looks like."

Clarece materialized at Casica's doorway. She offered a greeting kneel to her mistra and continued a few steps into the room. Raina followed close behind her, but now, at her leader's instruction, moved to stand in front of the tall slave. She, too, offered a little half-kneel. The healer watched the movement closely; the child was unsteady.

"Countess," Casica began, kindly, "may I introduce, Raina. (She purposely omitted 'd'Muriel,' fearful of the girl's reaction to the name.) Raina, the Countess Dolca." The countess studied the girl, frowning. There wasn't much to her. She was the scrawniest slave she had ever seen, looking all the more gaunt for her adult collar and blouse. A patch of reddish hair grew pitifully over her head wound. Her threadbare pants were tight and short, exposing green socks that ended in a pathetic pair of boots. Every artistic nerve in the seamstress shrunk at the sight. The only remarkable aspect of the girl's plumage was the socks. Dolca had never seen such fine woolens.

"So child," she began the inspection. "I hear you're looking for a new owner." Raina remained silent. That was good. "So tell me about yourself. Who did you slave before your last owner?"

The little girl choked over her answer, remembering the old lady and her animals. Those were happy times. "I slaved the Lady Chantel of Byzanthia," her voice trembled. "I fed and walked her three cats and two dogs." "So you cared for animals. What of people? What can you do?" Casica watched, pained, as Raina fretted with her hands. Casually, Clarece wrapped her mittened arms around the girl's shoulders, drawing her comfortingly to herself. Raina relaxed at the touch.

"I...I can clean. And dust—what I can reach. And I scrub floors. I can make fire. I can wash and fold and iron. I like to iron. I...," she was floundering. What *could* she do? "I can serve meals." She glanced at the floor, desperately. That was all she could do. That and care for animals. "You can read," she heard a voice above remind her gently. "Yes," the girl nodded. "And I learn to read."

"Really?" the countess' voice asked. "And what are you reading?" The child smiled to herself, thinking of her beloved book. "I am reading the donkey story, mistress." Dolca smiled. She had read the donkey story, herself. "And what of the donkey. Does he win?" The girl shook her head, turning her face to the left. She hadn't understood.

"She didn't hear you," Casica whispered. Dolca frowned but repeated her question. "Does the donkey win?" The child shook her head again. "I don't know, Countess. I haven't got to the end of the book. I *hope* he wins." Dolca smiled, despite herself. It was certain this child would hope that.

"Well, it appears your accomplishments are many," she offered kindly. "Come here. Let me look at you." With a gentle nudge, Clarece sent the girl off. This was the second most difficult part of the inspection. The worst was yet to come.

Raina stepped to within two steps of the royal and kneeled humbly, trembling at the proximity of the strange woman. She was so far from Clarece now. Still, the princess was near.

"Walk to the cloak and back," Dolca ordered, thinking the girl seemed unsteady on her feet. Obediently, Raina stood and walked. She tottered once, imbalanced, but resumed the task, ending her trek at the woman's chair. Dolca raised an eyebrow at the healer. "That will pass," Casica mouthed, silently.

"Turn around. Show me your back." The child turned and raised her blouse. Beside the royal, the princess clinched her eyelids, fighting a streak of anger. Scars, bearing the telltale signs of fresh lashing, crisscrossed Raina's thin back. *Muriel did that,* thought Dolca, disgusted. For herself, she had never beaten a slave in her life.

"Alright. Your front." The slave turned to expose her chest. Every rib showed. The small belly moved in the quickened pace of fear. Again, there were stripes, red and ugly. These were very recently applied. The countess' practiced eyes scanned the flesh. Nursing would be unaffected.

"Alright." The blouse lowered. "Your legs and buttocks. Striped?" "Yes," came the weak answer. "Your arms?" The reddish head shook. "Let me see your hands." Raina held out her hands. They trembled, with fear, reckoned the potential buyer. "Your palms?" Obediently the child turned them up. Rod marks scarred the flesh but the hands were serviceable. "Open your mouth." Raina squeezed her eyes tightly before complying. Dolca looked carefully. The child had all her teeth. "Bite." Obedience. Good teeth. "Good." Raina dropped her head immediately, dreading what was to come. "Now. Your eyes...."

For a slave, any slave, to make eye contact with a free was terrifying. Raina could have as easily looked upon the face of God as to look this royal in the eye. She faltered, but finally, the instinct to obey overcame her inherent terror. The child lifted her face, and, squinting as though looking into the sun or coming into light from a dark place, met the royal gaze.

For an eternal moment, the damned and divine connected. Dolca saw her. Some slave had bred green into the child's blue eyes. The unique blending revealed deep, deep fear. Raina could bear no more and dropped her face, shamed. Dolca glanced over to Clarece. "Lice?" "No, my lady," came the quick answer.

The Princess of Cassica dropped her own face in shame. Shame for Raina. Shame for herself. For humanity. Never in life had she witnessed a more brutally humiliating exercise of devaluation. Her own public humiliation waned in comparison to what this little girl suffered now. To be inspected like a piece of meat, to have your entire future and worth summoned to this moment! The woman struggled with all her might for self-restraint. Everything in her raged against this violation of human sanctity. The injustice of it!

"Enough!" she wanted to scream. She wanted to break something, wanted to tear the metal from Raina's throat and spirit her to *her* world, a home where people weren't chattel and children weren't stripped and torn. Further infuriating was the fact that this inspection came at the hands of a kind, gentle woman. A just woman who saw nothing wrong with what she did. *Evil politely performed is still evil,* Casica fumed.

Another woman cringed in the moment but for entirely different reasons. From where she stood, Clarece sensed her owner's indignation. She panicked at the thought of what Casica might do. "Please, Mistra," she begged silently. "Say nothing. Do nothing. This is no time to react like we're human."

Dolca sat, oblivious to all except her assessment of the girl slave. It was quickly accomplished. "Raina," she instructed, finally, "go to Clarece." The child knelt, relieved, and quickly returned to the safety of her chief. Now would come Raina's nightmare, the final test in a slave inspection. "Raina," Dolca asked, "what are you worth?"

The question was an ancient one, carefully designed to pit a slave's assessment of themselves against a potential buyer's. The value a slave placed upon themselves spoke volumes about their confidence and spirit. And more than once, the answer to this question (and the manner in which it was delivered) determined the final outcome of an inspection.

The girl studied her feet, vanquished. Even to her young mind, the question did its work, exposing all her stupidity, all her deficiency. Tears dropped upon her worn boots. Clarece had said to answer all honestly. "Nothing," came the quiet assessment.

"Nothing?" rejoined the countess. She had never expected that. "How do you mean?" Thin shoulders shook with weeping. "My mistra says I'm a worthless slave," the girl managed. "Come now," prodded Dolca, "no slave whose mistra buys such fine socks can be worthless."

The socks. In all her life, Asla would never have imagined the pivotal role those green woolens would play in the girl's fate. The child shook her head. "My mistra didn't buy my socks. Asla did." Dolca blinked, incredulous. "The *insulit*? You mean the *insulit* bought you these socks?" What kind of slavechild would capture notice of the palace whore? "Yes," explained Raina. "Asla isn't a member of the guild. But she's my friend." A green sleeve passed under the runny nose.

The Countess of Helan rubbed her eyes, confused. This was the queerest inspection she had ever held. "Clarece," she pleaded. She needed some help here. "What of you? What is your assessment of this child's value?"

Leathered arms embraced Tarrant's child. Clarece gazed down upon the red head. She directed her voice to Raina's right ear. She wanted her to hear this. "Priceless," she answered. Dolca looked up. "Priceless?" she echoed, incredulous. "Yes," came the reply. "It is my opinion that Raina has the making of a chief slaveswoman in her time. I cannot put a price on such a woman."

Dolca slumped in her chair, defeated. She was outclassed. Outclassed and outmanned. Or womanned. "Raina," she ordered, relieved the session was over. "You are dismissed." The chief slave waited for her mistra. Casica was recovered enough to respond. "You're excused, Clarece. I'll ring if I need you." The chief slaveswoman bowed. The slaves knelt together then departed the chamber, the smaller leading the way.

Below, in the darkness, Raina stopped and bowed her head. She had failed. She had shown weakness and she had faltered. She had shamed not only herself. She had shamed her chief and her pen. "I'm sorry, mistress. I did so bad." Clarece dropped to her knees and pulled the child into a tight embrace. "No, you didn't, Raina. You did wonderfully. You were honest and brave. I am so proud of you, little one! I'm so proud to be your leader. 'So happy you're in my pen."

The child quieted some in the presence of such words. Clarece held her for a long time before looking into her face. Tarrant's eyes shone with what, she didn't know. "You are a fine slave, Raina. If Dolca doesn't buy you, tis because she's unworthy of you." She smiled genuinely. The child warmed with the attention. "Now. Tis time for you to rest."

Raina tugged at Asla's shirt. "You keep the blouse," Clarece winked. "I'm certain Asla would wish you to have it." Raina beamed with excitement. "Tis *green*," she observed. Clarece laughed. "Yes, it is." She lifted the girl and carried her lightly to her stall. Raina caressed a green sleeve with awe, causing the chief slave to wonder as she had before, *What does God have in store for you, daughter of Tarrant?*

The women, one very young, one feeling quite old, sat on Raina's cot. Clarece took the worn book into her mittens. "Let's read some of donkey before you sleep. I wonder if he wins."

"That is, without question, the most broken slave I've ever seen." The countess was fretting with her teacup. "Muriel has utterly ruined her. Raina might have made a fine slave, but now...," she turned to the healer.

Casica perched, her chin propped in her hand. Failure. Her grand attempt at redemption proved a dismal flop. "I've no use for a maimed, broken slave, Casica," Dolca was saying. "I'm sorry." The Princess of Cassica sighed. "No need to apologize, Dolca. I know exactly how you feel." Her guest gazed at her, askance. "What do you mean?"

Casica stopped mid sip. Her tea was cool. "I mean, I felt the same way when Bastien gave me Clarece." "When he gave you Clarece? But she's the chief slaveswoman!" Casica shrugged.

"So? What's that to me? I come from a country whose language doesn't even have a symbol for slavery, and this man I don't know is giving me a slave. I *hated* slavery." She snorted. No need for diplomacy now. There was nothing to lose. "I hate it even more now. But then, all I could think was, 'This man is giving me a houseslave that doesn't even have hands.' I hate to admit it, but that's what I thought. 'I've no need for a maimed slave in my life.'" Casica stroked her silver teaspoon. "That was months ago. Now, I can't imagine life without Clarece. Eventually I thought, 'Perhaps I can do her some good.' Well, you can guess who does whom good."

Josquin paused, thoughtfully spinning her cup on its saucer. "I agree, Dolca. A broken cup is no good to anyone. But Raina's not a cup. She's a little girl. And perhaps she is of no good to you—now. But God knows, you could be of great good to her." She looked into the seamstress' eyes. "Would you throw out a beautiful garment for a tear, or would you mend it?"

Dolca's gaze dropped. The image was a powerful one. Still.... "'Chief slaveswoman', indeed. I'm being threaded like a needle. Clarece no more thinks that girl chief material than do I." Casica frowned. "Clarece doesn't lie. She might skirt the truth at times or maybe adorn it. But she doesn't outright lie. If she says she sees a chief in Raina, she means it."

Dolca took a deep breath. This was ridiculous. She was a countess and had no business with a broken piece like that child. However, if nothing else, she *could* get her cheap. "Understand. I'm not saying anything by asking this. But if for some *fantastical* reason I purchased the girl, would you consent to Clarece's being her menta?" "Yes." The answer was immediate. "With no reimbursement required for her time?" Casica grinned. No matter how rich a royal, money was always in play. "None a'tall. I would consider Clarece's time part of the deal."

The countess' brow creased in thought. "What are you doing, Princess, trying to prick me with a broken pin?" She didn't wait for an answer. *I hope he wins,* she had said. "Still, there *is* something delightful about the child." Casica said nothing. Dolca's mere consideration was more than she could hope.

"*Green* socks?" She turned to the princess. "The palace *whore* gave her *green* socks?" Casica shrugged. "The child likes green." Dolca held her composure only a moment before bursting at the seams. Her hostess joined her laughter. It *was* all a little bizarre.

"Princess, can you warm my drink?" the Countess of Helan requested, still laughing. "Of course." Casica took her cup and topped it with cooled tea. She held it only a few seconds. China was so easy. The refreshment steamed.

Dolca gaped, amazed, as Josquin handed her the hot drink, looking all the while as if the fantastic were the most natural thing in the world.

XVI

Dolca gazed into the fireplace. In such a quiet evening, the afternoon seemed surreal, so peculiar it was. She studied the shirt in her lap. The mending it needed required only minutes, yet for hours it lay there, awaiting her attention. She lifted a soft kerchief to her eyes and nose; the embroidered piece was damp with sorrow. This whole evening, ever since dismissing her servant after supper, Dolca had wept. Wept as she did so often in this hour, the hour when nothing surrounded her but emptiness, nothing filled her but loneliness. The quiet ticking of the clock only compounded her aching. Minutes passing. Passing by the hundreds, the thousands, the tens of thousands. Her life ebbed away.

A contraction gripped her loins; she held her breath against the pain. Another month of bleeding, void and lifeless as the bloodied clots that passed from her body. She looked toward the tapestry on her forward wall, the one she called "The Fruit of Life." Vivid reds and precious blues shown even in the dim light. Trees heavy with fruit framed an idyllic scene of children playing with kittens and lambs and pups. Water flowed around its border and milles fleurs clouded the background. It was an early piece, amateurish in design and execution; still, the artist in Dolca treasured it. A first fruit it was, the first of many in her life.

She glanced down to her hands. A bronze thimble capped a finger. The shirt. Her clothing. The blankets. The taps. All the fruit of her hands. All the fruit of her fertile mind. Another painful contraction. Never the fruit of her womb. Never.

The woman bowed, uncertain what hurt her most: body or heart. She placed her hand low and to the left. Pressed hard. Harder. The pressure offered little relief. To hurt so much every month without benefit of life mocked her creativity. Bitterness, strangely comforting in its familiarity, rose in her throat. Why was she barren? Why? *Oh, God,* she cried, *Oh, God, will you never remember me?* Dolca knew this prayer. Had prayed it a million times and always to the same effect. It was hopeless. Hers was the power to conceive a hundred brilliant designs, knitted together and delivered wholly beautiful. But not once could she fashion a single breath of life.

She looked again at the rich, wool shirt. It was Nahalt's, the one she made for his last birthday. Tapestried roundels ornamented the sleeves, each bearing the likeness of his family crest. A fruit tree in the center. Water flowing around the border. Her husband was hard on clothing. He appreciated her handiwork, as much a man could, but how easily he spoiled her efforts.

This hole came from a jaunt into the woods. It was a simple tear, easily mended. She should do so tonight. Nahalt could return at any time. She never knew when. His visits became less frequent; whether by the king's demands on his skill or his reluctance to return to an empty home, she could not tell. Not that their chamber was truly empty. She lived in it and, like any woman, sufficed to fill it. Still, it was not the fullness he wanted.

No more was there compulsion for Sir Nahalt to visit the palace on a frequent basis to lay with his wife and increase his line. More than once, his colleagues advised him to divorce her. Barrenness was cause enough, even for the Church. He had every right to dismiss her but didn't. For Nahalt loved her; of this Dolca was certain. She wasn't like the wives she knew who dreaded their husband's presence. She had never felt a rod to her shoulders or a beating to her face. And though both she and Nahalt were passionate in their way—God knew, they had their share of misunderstanding—never in their lives had either spoken cruelly to the other.

No, Dolca didn't doubt his love. She came to him twenty years younger than he, the marriage arranged by her great uncle. They made a fitting pair, the knight and the countess. From the moment they met, she knew she pleased him, saw the pride and joy in his eyes. Those first few years were filled with his presence and laughter. She still anticipated his returns. Still ached at the thought of surrendering in his embrace. But something had changed between them, slowly like the fading of dye. With their physical pleasure was no longer mystery, no more wondering afterwards, "Is this the time our seed take root?"

Her thumb closed the tear. "Would you throw out a torn garment?" the princess had asked. A maimed slave. A maimed wife. Nahalt had not thrown *her* away. God may have, but her husband had not. Dolca repented of the thought about God. That might be another thing He held against her. She should attend confession the morrow.

The fire was dying. The countess stood and added more wood. The glow warmed her face. "I can make fire," the child had said. Dolca grinned. Those socks. Exquisite socks on a dreary appearance, like adding new cloth to an old garment. It would never hold. The old must give way to the new. Clothing. Cloth. *Forget the cloth, Dolca,* she chided herself. *What of the child?* She was the truest garment and so very young. And living.

The seamstress viewed the works of her hands. There was something glorious about her power to produce such beautiful things, to display them and share them and give them away. She was known throughout the realm for her skill. Known as greatly for that as for her barrenness. She loved to make things, to present beauty. It felt like worship to her. But still, they were only *things.* String and wool and dye as fleeting as the yellow on her tapestry.

It frustrated her, yellow. That dye couldn't hold its hue. And anything it permeated faded too. Even her beloved greens, made of yellow and blue would eventually yield to the blue in it. Passing things. But what of human life? True; it, too, faded. The body's fabric disintegrated so quickly; yet, nothing about humanity was temporal. God had ordained that life, woven into the warp of eternity, last forever.

Blue and green. The hue of Raina's eyes. That color would last as long as the light behind it lived. What would it be like, the woman wondered, to blend her life into another? What would it be like to weave herself into a child and see what unique and mysterious pattern would emerge? In this woman, accustomed as she was to mastery of threads and looms and color, there existed an ungodly absence of mystery. Such questions she now posed to herself provoked much. Mystery and hope lived fibre upon fibre. Hope had broken long ago. Perhaps that was why life held so little mystery for her.

Dolca returned slowly to her chair, careful of the cloth between her legs. Potential life flowed out of her now; but like the water on Nahalt's crest, it would cycle again....

She could not know it, but in this very moment life flowed more intimately than the seamstress could ever have imagined in that lush mind of hers. For within the woman's longing heart, God moved. The bobbin of time, He touched, and about the weft of need, strung compassion.

He had been remembering her all along. A little girl was being woven into her destiny.

XVII

Dolca despised her current circumstance. To mingle with the baroness in social situations was unpleasant enough. To sit in her chamber, acting the part of a welcome guest was incomprehensible. She should have postponed confession until after this foul-tasting enterprise. Her hypocrisy must reach Heaven. Her drink was untouched. It wasn't even afternoon, but already Muriel offered her guest wine. Dolca glanced around. The chamber was neat and clean but something about it stank.

She listened, absently, to whatever it was Muriel said, pondering instead her confession that morning. She had confessed to the priest all she could conjure. He had sent her to the altar to pray in penance, yet nothing he assigned comforted her. Just more empty words; that was how they registered to her broken spirit. After completing her recitations, she contemplated a warmer Word: the God who stood in stained glass and adorned the ceiling, the One who graced pillars of wood and shone in gold. The One woven in an ancient masterpiece of tapestry.

Naturally, the image portrayed in this medium most readily held her attention. In it God sat with children, blessing them. It was the only likeness of Him smiling. Had He not taught that to father the fatherless was to serve Him? The countess had a fallen but holy heart; she longed to serve the one she loved—and fought. Theirs was a vibrant romance.

Though this truth her religious mind never could have apprehended, Dolca's struggle with the Almighty was beautiful. She fought and clung to Him as only a lover could. She was desperate, like all women, desperate in a way no man could ever comprehend. Peering as she did through the lens of tradition, Dolca failed to see her desperation as mirroring the image of the One who created her. Such was true, also, of the priest who ordered her to repent of her hungry heart. Repentance of this kind proved inherently futile. One cannot repent away one's nature.

Dolca knelt at the altar, warmed by both the heavy cloth upon her body and the one hanging on the wall. *What would be the truest penance?* considered she. To rid herself of the battle of barrenness was impossible. That was clear. She exhausted herself in the vain effort. To give birth to a child was another matter she could not resolve. The impossible was beyond her. But within her reach, God now brought to her attention what He wouldn't to her womb: a child.

The woman meditated further upon the image of mothers presenting their children to God for blessing. In her imagination, the scene reversed: it was to her that God presented a child for blessing. The thought repulsed her. It wasn't what she wanted. How dare the Almighty offer a consolation prize....

God waited with His request. How would she respond? Would she grant Him the desire of His heart when He had, inexplicably, denied hers?

The Countess of Helan bowed her head to the floor and sobbed. She cried out freely, for the pealing of the cathedral's bells drowned all other sound. Had a slavish midwife seen her, she would have wondered if the woman at the altar travailed. Dolca had assumed a slave's position for delivery.

Throughout the joyous chime, she labored. And then, as the decrescendo of the final tone lingered, her heart gave birth. Dolca stood and dropped a gold coin into the receptor. A single candle she lit and over it, whispered her decision: "Yes." The word was as simple as the act profound. Surrender to the One she loved was complete. She turned from the burning lights, quieted in her resolve to embrace the life He offered.

"I have come to inquire about your slavegirl."

Muriel's eyebrows jumped in surprise. She knew there must have been a reason Dolca came; she never paid social visits. Still, the thought of the little waif concerning someone of her guest's rank surprised her. "You jest. That suckling? She's bound for the rubbish pit." Dolca winced. Her desire for Raina grew.

"That may be. She sustained a nasty fall...but even so, I'm interested in purchasing her. My own slave I send to my sister. I have need of a new one. I thought I might get a fair price on yours." Dolca grinned, knowingly. "The trash pit profits you nothing, Muriel. Why not sell her to me?"

Muriel poured more wine for herself. She hated the slave and nursed, like her drink, the scene of gutting the creature like the shoat she was. She sipped slowly. It was true. A trashed slave was of no profit and the baroness loved profit. The prospect of making money pleased her, almost as much as the prospect of stealing it from this countess. She despised the moral airs of this royal dog. Wouldn't it be a lark to sell her a carcass? Surely, the child would die in her care. That tattered rag hadn't two sound threads in her.

"The child is positively worthless, Dolca. She's an imbecilic brute. However, she's cost me a great deal of trouble, and I'll not let her go cheaply. How much are you offering?" Dolca drank, thoughtful. As a slave, Raina wasn't worth the silver around her neck. She would start generously low. "She's what? Four years?" "Five." "Five years old.... Alright. I'll give you a pound for every year."

"Five pounds?" Muriel objected. "You mean uncollared, I'm sure! There's nothing to her but as I've said, I've poured my best into that useless pig. I fattened her up, and while she may not be market quality, I expect to recoup my boarding expenses. She'll cost you fifteen if a farthing. And I keep the collar."

"Fifteen?!" It was Dolca's turn to act shocked. "You say, yourself, the child is worthless! I'll tell you what: I'll split the difference. I'll give you ten for the girl and buy the collar off you." Muriel smiled. Ten pounds. She'd only paid two for the slave. "You've a deal, Dolca. But don't come later saying I didn't warn you. The slave is worthless."

"Warning noted," the countess replied, relieved at the results. "Only I want this transacted today." "Happily," agreed the baroness. The women stood and shook hands. Raina's destiny was settled. "I'll get the East leader to mediate the transfer," continued Muriel. "We don't need the broker (*or his fee,* thought she)."

"Agreed," nodded Dolca. "Do so forthwith. I'll have your money waiting." She wished the papers in her hand quickly, before Muriel had a chance to change her mind. "I'll leave you to your business, Baroness," Dolca ended, acknowledging her hostess' bow. She quit the chamber; she would not linger in such a place.

Clarece lay outstretched upon the sofa, her boots placed neatly over its arm, her eyes riveted upon the ballad before her. "'The destiny of the soul is a flightless one, its course laid in steps—never in winded sail....'"

A knock interrupted her memory. Casica glanced up from her painting. Clarece jumped quickly from her post. "By your leave, Mistra," she asked. Her owner nodded, careful to shield her canvas from her charge. She needn't. She had told Clarece she painted a self-portrait and wished for it to remain unviewed until completion. Her wishes were shield enough.

The chief slaveswoman quickly covered the distance to Bastien's door. A servant met her at the entry. She bowed in deference to his superior rank as, without comment, he presented a sealed letter, addressed, surprisingly, to her. The slave accompanied the letter to her mistra, careful to kneel on the back side of the canvas.

Casica read the name, confused. "But it's for you, Clarece." "Yes, my lady. But all I receive must come through your hands. You must break the seal." "I see," the princess replied, cutting the wax with her boot dagger. Clarece received the letter, hopeful. She could think of only one reason for this. The contents jerked her to her feet.

"Yes!" she exclaimed in a most unslavish fashion. "What?!" Casica hadn't a clue what the letter might be. "Tis from the Baroness Muriel, Mistra. She requests my services as mediator in the transfer of ownership of the slave Raina! Tis the countess, my lady. She's buying Raina!"

"Madala!" Casica announced victoriously, referencing, instinctively, the greatest Cassican expression of satisfaction. The women embraced, laughing. "You did it, chief slaveswoman! You did it!" "I did nothing, my lady. Twas you with your god-like tongue that swayed the course of human plight." Casica glowed.

"Twas a teamed effort, Chief. Between the two of us, we make quite the royal flush."

Clarece perused the letter. "Bless her," she breathed, seriously. She looked into her owner's questioning face. "Dolca purchases Raina collared. The child won't be stripped. That means she won't have her collar removed and replaced." Clarece looked down, repulsed. "Collaring is a hellish experience, Mistra. Tis undoing." She thought for a moment before saying what she did next.

"When someday, you finally tire of me and sell me off, I ask you, in all earnestness, please: josquin me to sleep before you strip me. Tis unbearable. Dolca knows this. She wants Raina spared the ordeal. Already, she proves herself a worthy mistra."

Casica nodded. Indeed she did. "So what happens now?" Clarece surveyed the procedure in her mind. She had mediated many transfers. Usually, it was a despised role she played. Today it was wondrous.

"First, I pay a visit to the slave broker—by your leave, of course. From him I will ascertain the day's rate for Raina's collar. I present this assessment to Muriel who will then draw up a bill of sale. The bill I present to Dolca. She will give to me the money required. This I transfer to Muriel who will, in turn, hand Raina's papers over to me. I deliver the papers to Dolca and await her orders. She'll probably wish to meet with Raina this evening. I do have your permission to menta her, do I not, my lady?"

"Of course!" Her owner was beaming. It almost seemed that light shown through her skin. "God truly has shown mercy," Casica observed, reverently. "Indeed," the slave said softly. "I mean He has shown mercy by bringing *you* here, Princess." Clarece glanced shyly from the brown eyes that saw her so clearly. "You begin to replace Crispus as our slavish saint."

A dark hand embraced Clarece's mittened wrist. "If anyone supplants his heavenly throne," Josquin answered, "tis you, chief slaveswoman. Now to flight, good Hermes! Transact your saintly sale!"

Clarece grinned at the command. She kneeled happily before going below to change into her royal vest. A transfer of this nature merited a slavish livery. She would wait to tell Raina of her newly-found fate, she decided. Wait until the earthly pact was sealed in gold...the stuff of which heavenly streets were paved.

XVIII

The seamstress smiled with herself, pleased with the work's progress. The stag began to smile back at her. With just enough hatching, she might render the curved line believable. She turned from his mouth to stretch her eyes with distance. Sunlight poured into the window and lit her face. It served as an encouraging assistant, the sun. Without Solange, weaving went more slowly. But it was a good loss. Solange and child arrived safely, her sister had written, and were adjusting well to their new home. It was a good thing she had done, Dolca thought again. A good thing. She watched, now, her newest slave. While it mightn't yet be a good thing, buying Raina was a good thing in progress. Like the smile, it may require some sleight of hand.

For their part, Raina's hands labored feverishly, scrubbing the floor as though to strip the wood of varnish. All morning, on this, her first day alone with her mistra, she had plied herself diligently. Nervousness served as energy. Dolca lounged in her chair, smiling in memory. She saw that first night when Clarece brought Raina to meet her new owner.

The girl trembled under the gentle claws of her menta, fearful of this powerful woman, fearful of failing even in the introduction. She fretted with her small, dirty hands as, slavishly, she gazed to the floor. "Is there anything you wish to tell the countess, Raina?" her chief asked. The reddish head nodded. Humbly, the child went to her knees. "I thank you for buying me, Mistra. I will slave *good* for you. I will slave so hard."

Dolca shook her head. The child certainly endeavored to fulfill her promise. Under Clarece's watchful eye, she had dusted and polished, washed and swept, straightened and scoured. Clarece proved a kind and effective teacher and in her shadow, the child thrived. She felt perfectly secure with the great woman who patiently encouraged her.

But while Raina was a confident slave with Clarece near, she now slaved alone. Her menta had told her that, this day, she would slave the morning by herself. She had performed well, Clarece explained, and had proven herself worthy of this independence. The decision was a strategic one. Clarece hoped time alone with Dolca would facilitate bonding, for without bonding, Raina would never become unbroken. A broken slave was a vessel in pieces. Trust in an owner was required to accomplish the work of wholeness.

Dolca nibbled a barren bobbin thinking how this might prove a successful venture after all. She couldn't know what spun in the child's frightened mind. To Raina this morning loomed as a horrendous test in which failure would be the end of her. Every slave, no matter their age, lived keenly aware of the temporal nature of their existence—either as slaves of a particular owner or as living beings entirely, and no amount of assurance from Clarece could erase this awareness from Raina. The child had lived long enough to understand: Solange was this woman's slave and now she was gone. A big slave who had worked hard. If this mistra had sent a grown slave away, what might she do to her? The scrubbing increased frenetically. Worse things than transfer could happen.

Raina scanned the great chamber in her slave's line. For days she had searched for her owner's instruments of failure—a whip, a rod, a slate—but to her mounting fear, she found not one. There were vases, however, three of them placed about where they might easily be gained. Her bad ear rang from having bowed her head so long. Inside she trembled at the memory of pain.

"Raina." The child didn't hear. She had spoken towards the direction of the slave's injured ear, the royal realized. Dolca called louder. "Raina!" The girl looked up, startled. She glanced about to locate the direction of the voice. There. Her owner sat at the smaller wooden thing. Dolca twirled the empty bobbin in her fingers. She pointed toward the corner with her gaze.

"Fetch me that basket of thread." The slave already knelt so she touched her brow to the floor before rising. She ran to the basket and lifted. It was heavy, heavier than the countess could know. She wasn't accustomed to having such a small body perform her tasks. The weaver's attention returned to her loom, so she never witnessed the struggle waging between the little slave and her awkward burden. Raina battled valiantly, however, and had managed to gain half the ordered distance when it happened. The basket slipped from her hands.

Thread and bobbins dispersed with chaotic zeal, scurrying about the damp floor. Panicked, the girl moved to fix what she'd broken, for in her mind, that was what she saw. It was a vase she had dropped, and now its pieces lay all about, trumpeting her stupidity. She must hurry, hurry before the pieces came together and pounced. Raina glanced towards her owner. She was found out. Frantic, the child knelt to cover her mistake. In her slave's line she watched the royal rise from her place. There was no time—no time!

The little girl faltered in confusion. What should she do? She took a step towards a bobbin, then retreated. Another step forward, retreat. It was the confused dance of duty and fear, a ritual perfected in her months with Muriel.

Her mistra now approached. Defeated, Raina abandoned indecision. Slavishly, she backed two steps, collapsed to her knees and, in a practiced motion, stripped Asla's blouse from her body. Dolca winced at what she saw. Raina struck herself on the head, hard, crying, "Stupid slave! Stupid!" She cringed as her owner squatted before her.

"Where do you keep the whip, lady?" Raina wept. "I will fetch it." Dolca stared. She didn't even own a riding whip. "Raina," she asked, gently, "what's wrong?" Thin arms crossed tightly. She must not reach out, she must not try to cover her face. To do so was to fetch greater pain. The slave sealed her eyes against the scenes that flooded her, but what her mind tried to contain, her body summoned. It remembered everything. Her frame shook in terror. It was coming. Death was coming. The countess captured the situation in one horrified glance, but for the life of her, couldn't imagine what provoked this spasm. Instinctively she reached for the girl.

Raina saw and understood. She was going to be killed. Her mistra Muriel had often told her she could kill her with hands, alone, and now this mistra moved to do it. "Mercy, Mistra! Mercy!" Raina's eyes blinked at the sight of the woman. Death moved towards her.

There was movement, indeed, but it conveyed nothing of death. Dolca went to her knees and pulled the child into a protective embrace. Raina resisted and surrendered, together, careful even in her fear to hold her arms out, away from the free. For to touch was to die. The woman held her even tighter. "Peace, Raina!" Dolca spoke urgently into the right ear. "I won't hurt you! I'll never hurt you!" Her touch was kind and warm on the scarred back. But the child couldn't hear, couldn't feel, so terrified was she.

Dolca, a lifelong student of slavery, knew a slave's language. She spoke it now. Nearing her face to her slave's, she tenderly scented Raina's neck. "Shhh," she whispered. "Shhh. Peace, Little One." Her breath poured comfort upon Raina's throat. Dolca cradled the reddish head and continued scenting until she felt Raina quiet. Cries melted into silent sobs. "Please, don't rid me, Mistra," Raina whispered.

The royal's eyes closed to the plea. Something in her heart burst with pity. And in this place, Dolca's life was knit to the little girl. "Raina," she said, tenderly, "I will never harm you. I swear. Never." She placed a kiss upon the throat. And smiled. Two little arms wrapped cautiously around her. No one who would scent and kiss her would kill her, Raina knew. Her breath returned, deep and calm as silently, she brushed her mouth against her lady. Her mistra smelled of beauty, like Asla.

For a long time, they clung to one another, the free and enslaved. Dolca wept for reasons she could not know, but in her heart, she held the child fiercely. She would do all she could to see Raina live, to see her grow in confidence and joy. She would begin by filling her world with good and beautiful things.

Beautiful things. The tapestry of God receiving children flashed in Dolca's mind. Surely, the Father of all knew the way of scenting.

XIX

"Now hold still, Raina!" the countess mumbled around pins. The child strived to obey but the order proved near impossible. Never in life had she been measured for anything, and here was her owner, with needles in her mouth, using a knotted line to measure excited arms and legs. For herself, Dolca was having a grand time. She hadn't made clothing for children since her sister's brood last visited two years ago.

"I don't know why I'm bothering with hems at all, Raina," she observed. "You'll outgrow them by the morrow." The child liked that thought. She wanted to grow, to be able to pick up baskets and not drop them. "There!" Dolca declared, recording the stites in her mind. "We'll sew you brown trousers, though 'twill be a pity to hide those green socks." The girl glanced down, nervously. "What of your shirt? What color would you like?"

At the words, Raina cocked her head, trying desperately to understand what it was her mistra asked. She had heard the question but didn't know what it meant. *What would she like?* Her hands fretted with themselves. In her face brewed a storm of confusion. Choice was a stranger in her world. Dolca watched the struggle, as confused as the girl. Suddenly she understood: Raina didn't know what she liked.

"What about green?" she asked, kindly. "Would you like your blouse to be green?" Immediately the child brightened. "Green," Raina smiled, nodding. "I like green." Dolca smiled back. For an instant the slave's eyes met hers. They hid just as quickly. "Then green it is," her owner announced. "Let's go find some brown."

♞

The tin spoon tap danced on Dolca's door. Her own mistra's meal delivered, Clarece now conveyed the countess' tray. She anticipated her afternoon with Raina, anxious to teach her slavish tricks of washing. The chief hummed softly as trained eyes inspected the wood before her; it needed polishing.

The door opened. Dolca's slave offered a half kneel to the familiar boots. Clarece squatted and looked into the face. Her smile dissolved. Raina had been crying.

"Little One," she asked frightened, placing the meal beside her. "What happened?" The child wiped her nose on her sleeve. "I dropped a basket." Clarece blinked. "A basket?" Tears welled in the woman's eyes. She held Raina's face protectively in mittened claws. *God, had she terribly misjudged this owner?* she wondered, panicked. Tarrant's daughter, had she surrendered her to an abuser? The chief slave glanced about. "Did she hurt you?" she whispered. Raina shook her head and smiled shyly. "She kissed me."

Clarece sighed to the explanation. "She kissed you?" A nod. Raina's menta drew her into a warm embrace. "That's good. Tis a very good thing." She drew back and smiled. "Why don't you take your mistra's meal and then show me what happened." The child nodded, receiving the platter. She wished to give her mistra the greatest gifts of earth.

Two slaves, one quite small, one fairly tall, entered the dining chamber. Dolca glanced up from her work. "Glory! Tis the chief slaveswoman!" she proclaimed. "And how goes your day, today?" Clarece offered a half-kneel's worth of answer. "Well, great Countess," she bowed. "And yours?" Dolca watched as, diligently, Raina placed the silverware just as she'd been taught. "A good morning overall," she replied grinning, "A few snags but everything pulled through quite nicely." She motioned to the attending girl. "You've brought me a fine slave, Clarece."

Raina warmed at the compliment, pleased at the praise in her chief's presence. "Your meal is ready, Mistra," she announced, officially stepping from the table. Her mistra approached. "Raina." "Mistra?" "We need fresh greenery for the vase. Why don't you take the scissors from the hearth and go cut some from the garden." "Yes, Mistra." The child knelt obediently and rose to perform her task. Dolca waited until she had left her chamber before turning to the chief slave.

"Clarece, I have a matter to discuss with you." "If it's about the basket," the menta apologized, quickly, "Raina has already informed me and—." "What? No," Dolca interrupted. "Tis not that. That was my fault. The basket was too heavy. Clarece...." She stopped, struck suddenly with an idea. "Would you look at me?" At once, the blonde head complied. This royal was her mistra's friend; she was in no danger. Dolca smiled, though at what most, she wasn't certain: the ease with which this slave met her gaze or the exquisite hue of her eyes.

"You've the most striking eyes," she observed. "Thank you, Countess," the slave bowed. Silently, Dolca mused. It occurred to her that rarely in her life had she seen a collar and face in one look. She studied the scene carefully. Clarece warmed under her gaze, feeling somewhat inspected.

"Forgive me, Chief," the royal apologized, suddenly aware of her effect. "I didn't mean to stare. Tis just that, I wonder. What is it like to live with your mistra as a woman?" "My lady?" "What I mean is, well, what is it like to live face-to-face with your owner? Do you think that to grow like this would knit rebellion in a slave's heart?"

"'Rebellion'?" Clarece winced at the word; to even link it to a slave felt deadly. "Why, no, my lady," she answered carefully. "I wouldn't *think* so unless, well, it would depend on the slave. Any slave that responded so I would think already had that bent in their character." "So you would see no harm in my having Raina look at me—in private of course."

Clarece smiled broadly. So that's where this went. "No, Countess, I don't. On the contrary, I think the results may please you." "And what has been the result with you, slave Clarece?" The chief slaveswoman glanced away, uncomfortable. The countess asked probing questions. "Well," she ventured, "I believe the princess has, as her charge, better company. A slave makes for better companionship as a human than as a property."

Dolca grinned. She liked this slave. "I see." She took a few steps in thought then turned. "Well, tell me something more, great menta. Raina is terrified of life. What can I do to help her become more like you?" "*Me*, my lady?" "Yes: competent and assured." Clarece squirmed at the description. "Countess, Raina was broken by the baroness (she still didn't like to speak her name); it will take time for her to trust again, though it sounds like you've taken great strides already." Dolca nodded. "Still...there must be something concrete I can do for her. When you came to the palace, what helped you?"

The chief slave shook her head. "When I came to the palace," she repeated. She bowed her head in memory. It wasn't a time she liked to revisit. For a moment Clarece debated telling the truth. A slave's past was as their collar. They didn't like having others touch it. But she had shared with another royal some of her past and found it healing. Perhaps if she dared, again, another's healing might benefit. Her head remained bowed as she remembered.

"I arrived at the palace in a sack. It was all I had to wear. I'd never worn a pair of shoes in my life." Dolca listened intently. She'd never seen this side of the chief slave. "I was more animal than little girl. You see, my lady, a slave becomes what owns them. I was owned by livery slaves. They brutalized me and I became brutish." Her deep eyes moved from distant scenes to one more closely in vision. "As I remember, I spent much of the first months here snarling at people." She answered Dolca's disbelieving look. "Truly. The prince, himself, still bears on his arm a bite mark."

The countess shook her head slowly, unable to imagine the woman before her as that little girl. "What happened?" she asked. A smile answered her. "Kindness. The chief slaveswoman—she left before you arrived—she took me under her care. She won my trust, at first, with food and then my heart." Clarece glanced down into her memory. Besaida had redeemed the course of her life. "Her love reminded me what I was."

A thoughtful gaze met the royal's. "Raina is in a much better place than was I, Countess. Her last mistra was brutal, yes. But Raina has the memory of another mistra, a kind woman. And all the pen loves her. Her heart will remember quickly, I think, in the presence of your kind person."

Her heart will remember, Dolca thought. What all did this woman before her have to remember? Who dare would have brutalized a soul like her? *How could anyone burn a piece of metal about her throat?* someone had asked before. The owner glanced at the silver band on the slave's neck, and for the first time in her life, considered what pain its presence must cause. Her expression was contemplative as she turned again to the chief.

"What's Raina's present food allotment?" "The baroness allowed half a bowl." "Drink?" "Water." Dolca nodded. Casica had mentioned that food and rest were essential to Raina's recovery. "And what of her provisions? Tis clear she hasn't clothing. What else is she in need of?"

Clarece glanced away, embarrassed for the child. "Everything, Countess. Her former mistra provided her nothing." "Nothing?" *Curse, that Muriel.* "What would you suggest for her?" Clarece's mind spun in an orderly fashion.

"She borrows all she has now. Raina could use a bucket, a cup and towel, soap, a pillow." "She hasn't soap?" Dolca interrupted, incredulous. No royal would wish themselves an unclean houseslave. "None her own." "Go on." "A pillow would be welcome, as would undergarments." "She's no undergarments?" "No." The royal shook her head, angry. "Continue." "That would suffice, my lady." "Suffice?" "Yes."

The countess was considering. "What could I give the child to let her know she's precious to me, that I value her. What would you suggest?" Clarece smiled within. Already this woman turned like the seasons in her affection for Raina: "valued" was becoming "precious". "Well, my lady," she began, "Raina currently uses a broken currycomb some slaveman...found...for her hair. She appreciates pretty things. I think a brush and comb for her very own would serve as a daily reminder of her mistra's care for her. That and (why not ask?) a vest. No slave feels fully vested until...vested."

A vest. The seamstress liked that idea. A vest to match those exquisite green socks. She strummed through her mind. She knew no vendor who would carry such a brassy shade of green. "Where did the insulit get Raina's socks?" That was the last question Clarece expected. "I don't rightly know, my lady. Asla has many resources." "No doubt," mumbled the royal. "Tell her to see me." The slave bowed. That should be interesting. "As for the other, make it so, chief slaveswoman."

Dolca went for her purse. "Take what you need. And have the kitchen deliver me, daily, a mid-morning dash. A cup of soup with milk. That sort of thing. And increase Raina's supper allotment to a full bowl with milk as drink. Understand?" The slave nodded. She understood perfectly. The countess nodded also, pleased. "You do your part, Menta. I'll do mine. And with God's help, Raina will remember."

Within a minute the little girl gained the chamber. "Raina," her owner ordered, "I believe you and Clarece have some washing to do. Afterwards, I want you to rest in your stall until my supper." She took the greenery and scissors. "Ladies, I leave you to your work." The slaves knelt in unison. The younger preceded the older as together, they quit the dining chamber for Dolca's bedchamber.

"Now watch," Dolca heard the chief slave explain. "When you lift something, use your legs—not your back." She slapped her thigh. "You see, God knows our plight and in His mercy, gives us strong legs for lifting." She whispered in the girl's good ear. "And for kneeling a thousand times a day." She winked. The little slave grinned. God *was* merciful, she was learning. *And* He liked pretty clothing.

Memory often requires a present reality. As Raina's mind imagined God, the eternal Father began to look something like her mistra, a gentle Master with an eye for beauty. And the means to make beauty come alive.

XX

"What think you is the moon, my lady?" The women paused in their trek to view the subject at hand. Casica looked into the whitish half-disc and then closed her eyes, smiling. Sunlight warmed her cheek and blouse. Even Clarece walked uncloaked this afternoon. Both reveled in the warmth and light. After so many days below in the pen, to walk upon the earth—instead of living in it—felt like freedom even to one already free.

Casica opened her eyes and watched. Clarece was studying the distant object that filled her imagination. Today the blue, whitish areas of the one that ruled by night blended into the sky around it. Truly, it did look like someone had painted it on the firmament.

The slave took a deep breath, thinking to herself how she felt taller this day. It must be from spending so much time with Raina. Living around little ones could do that. Still, she glanced down at her sleeves; they appeared to come up higher on her mittens. She shook her head; this was ridiculous. A woman her age, whatever age that might be, did not continue growing. Maybe she was simply walking straighter. She looked to her lady.

"Well," voiced Casica, "I don't think tis what our poets say, that it's a round of cheese that time consumes and God restores, though the thought of its being food *is* somewhat romantic." "Indeed, Mistra. All food is romantic." "No," continued Casica, "I rather think it to be something like our earth, but without the benefit of life. You see the round areas? I wonder if they could be lakes, only frozen to give them the white appearance."

Clarece studied the frozen bodies of water. "So you think water covers the moon." "Well...not all of it. Only certain places. Of course, if they *are* lakes, they must be the size of the ocean. Anything that looks that big from this distance must be immeasurably huge." "And what of the lakes at night, Princess? Why are they dark?" "Shadows maybe?" "And its light?"

Casica frowned. That always perplexed her. "I don't know. If tis as the sun, it makes its own light. I don't know." She turned her gaze to Clarece. "What of you, learned scholar? What think you?"

"I used to think, in Kanasa, when I was small, that the moon was the eye of a monstrous whale. Not that I've actually seen a whale, but I saw a picture once in a book at my master's house." She grinned at the memory of the dark fish with its huge head and mouth and little bitty tail. "Anyway, the eye opens and closes to differing degrees depending on the fish's mood. And when the whale sleeps, no moon at all there is."

"That's the poet in you," Casica ventured. "Perhaps," Clarece nodded. "*If* I were a poet, but I am only a lowly slave, Mistra. And my slave eyes more often find themselves upon the ground. And that's given me another theory. You've seen rain drops fall upon dry dusty earth, yes? They form little craters, like pock marks on a man's face. At night, that is what the moon reminds me of. I wonder if what we see are craters." Casica snorted kindly to herself. She'd never thought such a thing, but her charge's observation was plausible. "I see your point, Clarece, but these are huge craters. What could form *them*?"

Clarece shook her head. Her scientific mind acquiesced to the poet within. "Something fearsome, my lady. Something like the tears of God...." Casica laughed at the phrase. "Too bad you're not a poet, Clarece! You'd make a brilliant one. And the light—what think you of that?"

Here Clarece turned and faced her mistra, carefully looking for witnesses to her eyes. There were none. The ladies were too far from the palace. "I'll tell you what I've told no one, my lady, for no one ever speaks with me about such things. But I think it is the sun that lights the moon." "What?!" "Yes, my lady. The Book says that God made the sun to rule by day and the moon by night. They are both rulers, but the one by day is greater than the ruler of the night. The moon is the subject king, and like all subjects must glean his glory from the master. This would explain why the moon shines in both day *and* night. The sun never goes out, though we do not always see it. This could also explain why the moon is full and then gains his horns and goes out completely."

"How would it explain that?" "Well," the teacher continued, "the greater king always assumes the position of honor. The center. I think what we see is a shadow upon the moon." She took her mitten and slid it across the other. "You see the shadow? My mitten doesn't change shape, but appears to. The moon does not change at all. Something is moving across it and blocking the light of the sun." Casica was captivated. "But what could be so big as to block out the sun?" Clarece smiled mischievously. "Us. Earth. Tis the earth's curve that we see upon the moon. It gives the horns."

Casica frowned in disbelief. What Clarece said felt somewhat heretical. "But Earth is *flat*, Clarece. It has no curve. Or do you say...*are you saying the earth is round?*" The tutor grinned. "If I do, I'm not the only one. For centuries others have written as much. And why not, my lady?" She glanced to the sky. "The sun is round. The moon is round. Why not Earth?" "Because the Book mentions four *corners* of the earth. Something must be flat to have corners."

Clarece shook her head in disagreement. "Not necessarily. A box has corners but it's not flat." "Tis not round, either." "No, but a sphere is. And the ancient ones, the true keepers of measurement, explain that a sphere can have four corners in its design." "A sphere?" "Yes, my lady. A sphere is a—." "I know what a sphere is!" Josquin interrupted, flabbergasted or frightened, she wasn't sure which more. "So you're saying the earth and the sun and the moon, and let's just say all the stars in the sky, are orbs. Balls, floating in the heavens?" "Yes, my lady. More than just an orb. Geometrically...." And here the teacher began a recitation on geometry of such galactic proportion, her owner's head spun. Left her feeling, in fact, quite dizzy. It wasn't until Clarece ended her lesson that Casica understood why; why she felt dizzy, that is. Clarece's explanation literally took her breath away.

"...so that's how a ball can have four corners, my lady." The teacher beamed with excitement. "'It is He who sits above the circle of the earth'. You see, the Mighty One fills us with questions but gives enough clues to answer them. He's teases us, I think.

He's a good teacher. He enjoys the chase, to watch His students gain on His heels." Clarece stopped and glanced at the ground. "At least concerning little things, like the moon and earth. But the greater things, they are as a king's bedchamber. Those secrets He keeps to Himself." She only now stopped to glance shyly to her lady. "You do not think me mad, do you?"

Of the two women, it was Casica who bore the expression of madness. "No. Never," she decided, finally. "I feel rather bedazzled. If the earth is round, as you say, then you have managed to undermine everything I ever thought I understood. Tis like you've snatched the ground from under my feet. I feel...." She paused. (Was that a headache she felt?) "I think, chief teacher, my mind cannot gain your heels. You are too fast for me. As the heavens are to the earth, your thoughts are to mine." Clarece blushed at the reference. "I will think later on these things and hope for you to have an audience worthy of this discussion someday. But that's all the thinking I'll do now. Show me this palace of yours."

Clarece regained their pace, glowing with the release of thought, lost in the satisfaction of tutorial expression. Her student felt lost too, but in an entirely different manner. Casica glanced up at the moon then turned to face the sun. She looked at it directly, like a josquin could. Walking, she watched the ground pass under her feet, feeling strangely imbalanced. Never again would the woman from Cassica look at her world in the same way. Her charge was speaking again. They were approaching the ancient structure....

Clarece's glow grew. "This is it, Mistra. Byzanthia's oldest palace. Tis hundreds of years old, no one knows exactly." Casica studied the building, relieved. Wood. Stone. Solidity. This was something she could wrap her mind around. Clarece was pointing with her mittens.

"You can see, it is not a large building, and it contains little of stone and even less of precious stone. Tis made of trees taken from here," she motioned around. "This explains why there are no trees in this area. The foundational structure was made quickly, by necessity. Early Byzanthian kings hadn't the luxury of long-term planning. Too many enemies. But the second floor is built more ornately, lavishly. The wings, only two, were added by later sovereigns."

Casica listened carefully. She could see what her teacher taught. The building did indeed look like a work in progress. It was not large by any means and stood by itself, apart from the present castle and its buildings. The building closest to it was the soldiers' barracks. "Is it unlocked?" she asked.

"Always. Anything of value that once here was has long ago been moved to the palace. Tis nothing more than a storehouse for dust and discarded furniture. But it holds a surprise. Come!" The women wound up the steep hill and ascended forty-one steps. Clarece knew them all by heart. She opened the heavy oak door with the familiarity of one who owned it. She waited for her lady to enter and for their eyes to adjust to the darkened light.

There's nothing to this place, thought Casica. Plain paneling lined the walls. An occasional stone pillar supported the ceiling. A lonely, musty odor filled the air leaving her with the impression of a tree stripped of bark. She looked at her friend. Evidently, Clarece saw the building with different eyes. An unusual sense of ease settled upon the slave.

"It looks like nothing to you, I'm sure," she said. "But to me, this is my most holy place." Her eyes brimmed with emotion. "When I first came to the palace, years ago, I lived in constant fear. Fear of Prince Bastien; fear of the other slaves. This city. I came from country places—a kitchen, a barn. To move into the palace.... Scads. I thought I would go mad so busy and vast was this new world. Everything and everyone confused me. The only thing that was the same was the language, and even that was spoken with a different accent." She smirked at the floor. "The slaves and servants made fun of my bumpkin tongue. I thought the changes would suffocate me.

"Then one day, I snuck out the palace and thought to escape. I didn't care if I were gutted. I just wanted to find somewhere I could think. And that's when I discovered this place. It was dark and quiet and empty. God, it was so empty...." She took a deep breath. "Here, I could hide. Here, I could think and remember myself. I would run away to it any chance I had. It was my healing place."

Clarece turned to her mistra. She was smiling with the story. "I've seen crabs now. This was like my shell, I think. I haven't been here in years. Life is so busy now." She looked down, embarrassed. “But I wanted to show you, Princess. For if I had a picture locket, it would be this.” “Tis beautiful, Clarece,” Casica observed, reverently. The building had become so in the moment, transformed from an abandoned relic into a cathedral.

“I know every stite of this place,” Clarece continued. “Though it’s not big, tis confusing. The halls run like a maze. I won’t bore you with it all. But wait till you see this. Come!” Their steps echoed softly in the vacant building that was not completely so. Here and there sat a chair or empty crate. A pile of bricks mushroomed by a door. A table stood silently. All about were recesses and corners.

Casica imagined Clarece as a girl; surely her inquisitive mind would have led her down every passageway. The darkness and quiet would ease her busy thoughts. The solid walls would surround the frightened child with security. ’Twas a good hiding place. A secret garden made of wood.

They had walked long enough, now, in maze fashion so that the princess hadn’t a clue where she was. She did have the sense of being somewhat underground, though not once had they descended a single step. The air was cooler, however, of that she was certain. Clarece made a sharp turn to the left and there, Casica saw it. The delightful secret of the secret place. Here along this hall ran a series of stained glass panels. Sunlight shone through the ancient glass and graced the hall with colored light. Casica laughed delightedly.

“This is beautiful!” “Is it not?” Clarece agreed smiling. “I cannot tell you how I felt the first time I saw this. I’d never seen colored glass in my life and here these were: not only color but each telling a story. I used to make up my own stories to accompany the scenes, but after I learned to read, books told me what I saw. Most these mosaics portray the histories of kingly residents in this place. They’re like parchment made of glass.”

She led them to the first panel. It showed an angry looking man relieving a dark figure of a dark head. Casica winced at the sight. Even in the ancient glass, she recognized the resemblance to herself.

“This is King V’liet,” her guide was explaining. “He’s one of the earliest kings recorded in written word. A mighty warrior. He conquered many peoples.” “That’s a Cassican he conquers there,” her owner observed quietly. “I didn’t connect it till you came. But yes. He killed many of your people." Casica studied the haunting scene. "I don't like that king," she decided. "There's too much pleasure in his expression."

And then it happened. Berea's containment of her memory loosened, and into her consciousness seeped mental images that, until now, had been only a blur....

What would take hours to speak, the princess saw in an instant. Saw herself that unspeakable day she arrived in Byzanthia. She was kneeling before the crowd. They were screaming at her, mocking her with words that were indistinguishable to her ringing ears. She couldn't understand anything but the intent; overwhelmed, instead, by the shame of her nakedness. Her blouse, which only hours before Maman had buttoned and caressed, hung from her body, tattered. It was no longer the pure white it was in Cassica; it was crimson, crimson like the color of her royal seal, dyed red with her royal life. The shell buttons were stripped, revealing her bare chest and shalonn. It glowed intensely in its struggle to contain the breach in her veins and arteries....

Blood was everywhere. On her breasts, on her hands, oozing from the fabric of her shirt. The lining was heavy with it. Her flesh, hot with it. The mob in the city square was frenzied, bludgeoning her with hate and cursing. She tried so hard to see it, the sea of faces that pounded her with its vengeful surf. But she couldn't. All about her grew dim.

Except for the pain. That was a crystal shard. It seared through her sharp as a knife as the caller seized her left arm and yanked. The shoulder, all but severed from her body by the flogging, popped. She felt herself scream and wished with all her might for the power to put herself down. She rose, instead, in obedience to some invisible tyrant. She gained her feet and walked submissively with the guards who flanked her.

A carpet of gold swished around her feet and for a single absurd moment, the princess thought she walked the bride's aisle, with rose petals gracing the floor of the cathedral. But these were leaves, not petals that carpeted the blood-stained scaffold with scent. She paused and breathed deeply. For a moment, every single leaf came into focus. "Tis beautiful," she smiled. Like coins scattered before her they were, coins whose currency of autumn fragrance God spent lavishly upon the doomed. A drop of red fell upon her foot and her legs gave. She collapsed helplessly upon the scent. Something spirited her up and away. And then she saw him.

It was her groom, hooded all in black with two holes revealing deep blue eyes. The voices faded. All she heard now was air, as deep slow draws filled her punctured lungs. The hooded man took her and kneeled her before the large trunk of a tree. Notches, she remembered seeing something like notches, scarred its length. Dark stains splattered everywhere. He took her right arm and stretched it full upon the trunk. She offered no resistance as he secured her wrist. She only watched him, watched the hooded man slowly move as in thick, dense air. He grasped her left arm which hung limp at her side. She cried out in agony as he tried to extend it.

The executioner knew his work. Quickly, expertly he placed his foot on the shoulder and jerked. A popping sound took her breath and with it, the pain. He fastened this arm to the trunk. Her breath quickened as much as her body could manage. She needed air. Precious air. Terror invigorated her.

Then in the midst of all this confused state, she heard his voice. It came out of the haze clearly, like the leaves a few minutes before. "Peace, child," he said. Their eyes met. He pushed her shoulders back, and the kindness with which he bid her head rest against the tree, she now remembered. It was the second kind touch she knew since the prince surrendered her to the ghastly day. "Rest. All will soon end." Something of the deep voice lulled her and everything, every muscle, every fear settled. She relaxed. "Good girl," the words droned.

Drums sounded. They pulsated into her body as they pounded on the platform. Her own heart pounded with them, drowning out all the noise, all her breath. The executioner lifted a huge, glistening ax.

Time stopped. And into that endless moment poured all her life. Her mother was everywhere as was the seashore. Her father and Berea and the feeling of a horse beneath her. Images and music. Laughter and weeping and healing and light.... Her shalonn lit her face as the man circled the ax once, slowly in his right hand. On the next pass, he joined to it his left. The blade captured a ray of sun as it rose and pierced her sight with the brilliance.

The light flooded her and suddenly...she smiled, overcome with a peace she never knew existed. It rushed upon her, advancing the falling blade....

"Princess?" Casica turned quickly, jolted from the horrifying scene. In its place stood Clarece, looking concerned and confused. "Princess?" she repeated. "Are you alright?"

Only now did Casica realize she wept. Her hand went into a vest pocket, producing a royal blue kerchief. She wiped her nose and nodded. "Yes, Clarece. I'm sorry. I was...I'm alright." "We can leave if you'd like." "No." The healer closed both her eyes and the door of her recollection. "This is good for me. As you say, this is a healing place." With a deep breath, she regained herself. The light and color around her dispelled the darkness.

She looked again at V'liet. "This is one Cassican head you missed," she informed him in her tongue. Clarece understood and smiled, despite her concern. "If tis any consolation, my lady, he lost his own eventually. A son, jealous of the crown that rested upon it, took it from him. Of course, his he didn't keep his for long before an even more jealous brother laid claim." "Those were dangerous times." "Indeed. One never knew when the world would crumble about one's feet.... If you like, we'll continue," the guide invited. "Kinder faces line our way." And to the princess' delight, they did.

First there was showed King Ruttlund, a priestly king who in his pane, showered his subjects with holy water, the hyssop bright green in the light. Next was the scholar king, Elkhart. In his mosaic, he sat at a desk, a quill directed towards the viewer. Books made for a kaleidoscope of background. The women continued for three panes more then stopped.

Here was a pane to set the others apart: in it shone a likeness of Byzanthia. A gold star marked the royal city in which they stood. The sea surrounded one side and in it was set a tiny, green piece. Cassica.

"Look, my lady. Tis your island kingdom. It pales in comparison to ours, but in size alone—not in color." Casica shook her head, playfully, at her grinning companion. It was a beautiful pane, but what held her attention was the sun, masterfully rendered with bright colorful pieces. It crested the entire scene like a crown. It almost *could* be the center of the universe.... "Look, learned teacher," she observed. "Tis your ruler of the day. The morning light crowns your suzerain." "Yes," Clarece nodded. "This is my favorite of these panels. It fairly explodes with brilliance."

In the time it would take to repeat Clarece's statement, the observation transpired. As the women watched, the sun, and all it embraced burst into a thousand razored fragments. Both royal and slave spun in self-protection. As she did so, Casica reeled at the force. Something outside lifted the solid structure and dropped it stites to the earth. She fell to the granite floor.

"My God, Clarece!" she cried. The slave stood; balance was inherent to her class. "Does the earth shake in Byzanthia?!" Her owner yelled though she didn't know why. All was deathly, ominously silent. "No, my lady," Clarece answered, quietly. Her mind raced. "This is not of nature." "Then what is it?" asked Casica.

Clarece didn't respond. They were spinning, her thoughts, and the differing understandings of the women showed clearly in their differing postures. Casica stood and looked toward what might be the end of the wide hallway in which they stood. Clarece's gaze was fixed upon the ceiling. In her memory she sorted out the structure above, the heavier, newer section of the building. *Where are we—where?! Where?!* she reasoned frantically. Her mind showed her what she wanted. *Scads!* They stood under the throne room—the marble and granite-floored throne room. *Dear God!*

Casica turned casually to her companion "Do you think we should—?" She never completed her question.

There was no time to escape. Clarece exchanged thought for action and with the same intensity of the former seized her owner by the waist and ran her towards, or rather into, the center wall. The princess cried out as her body Clarece flung down. She fell hard upon the floor and gasped as her charge added her own weight upon her and lay stunned, both by the events and the shocking exhibition of Clarece's physical strength. All surprise gave way to anger.

"What the devil do you think—?!" Casica stopped. Somewhere, something shifted. The solid floor buckled beneath her. "*Crispus,*" she heard her friend breathe. A terrorizing realization welled within her. Instantly, Casica strove to insert herself into the seam where wall and floor met. She could smell leather and couldn't understand why until the mittens touched her face. Clarece wrapped her arms protectively around Casica's head as she positioned her body upon her. Something above them wretched. Plaster and wood, mortar and dust fell with a sudden belch. The slavish shield did its work. None of the ceiling touched the terrified royal. For a quarter minute, the women lay perfectly still. Casica stirred to move. "Hold, Princess," the familiar voice ordered.

Somewhere far away and deep within the bowels of the ancient place was expelled a single, agonized moan. Years ago, Casica stood near a frozen lake, smiling at the eerie voice of expanding ice. She heard it now and almost wretched with fear. The building swayed at the source of the moan. A contraction swept across the skeleton of the structure, transforming the palace into a ship. It convulsed in an invisible storm as every timber popped in succession—far away at first but advancing quickly, a wave hurtling towards the women.

"Crispus! Save us!" Clarece cried as with all her strength, she shoved her mistra and self into the wall. Her heart pounded into Casica's back. And it happened. The tidal wave crashed upon the vessel. Its supporting beams and pillars buckled, and the palace began to sink upon itself.

Casica never heard the scream that fled her. It was swept up in the surge and carried away as all around rained the ancient palace of Byzanthia, swallowing the women with the deafening deluge of destruction. Casica felt her shield give as something heavy grazed her friend. After an eternity, it stopped.

All was silent except for the panting of the women. For how long, neither knew, but they lay as they were, frozen by the fear that any movement of theirs may waken the deadly course. Casica felt Clarece's breath against her face. It was slowing as was her heartbeat. Finally, carefully, the slave moved. Casica turned from the wall to face her. Dust filled the hall. It shrouded Clarece with an eerie sheen.

"Are you alright?" Josquin asked. Clarece glanced overhead. "I'm not sure. Are you?" "I think so...." Unsteadily, the slave rose and helped her mistra up. Behind her was what she had felt. It was a granite block about a cubit square. Casica looked upon it with horror.

"Crispus must have heard you," she mumbled. "Twas the first time," the slave replied, wincing at the thought of what might have happened. "And I salute you, Crispus. Twas a good time to be the first." She concentrated now on their plight. "Clarece," she heard her owner say, "if we survive this, I propose a moratorium on tours of all types." "Agreed, Mistra. Indefinitely."

They stood silently. It was darker now with the windows gone. Something moaned above them. Casica voiced the obvious. "We need to flee this place." *But how?* thought Clarece, frantically. While the ceiling had not fallen completely, it seemed to droop above them. The way in was blocked by debris. The outer wall where they had been standing had collapsed upon itself sealing them in. The only way available meant to go further into the building. That was the last move her instincts wished. But whatever they did, they must do quickly.

"Come!" She took Casica's arm into her mitten and jogged lightly. Neither woman commented on the growing frequency of creaking and popping noises scattered above and around them. They stopped at a pile of rubble. "Go ahead," Clarece instructed her owner. Casica easily cleared the pile and waited anxiously for her friend. She joined her quickly.

They continued their way more slowly now, clearing away what they could and scrambling over what they couldn't. Their movements were silent but desperate, like running a race against some unseen opponent. The building would not hold long. Finally they neared what Clarece hoped would still stand. A supporting wall. It too was graced with panels of glass. She spun and glanced all around. There. A single rough brick. She picked it up and took it with her. "We're almost there," she told her frightened companion. They made a sharp right and froze.

Light, colored light, glistened in the narrow hall. For some reason it seemed as though the day should be cloudy.... Clarece glanced up. The stained-glass panels were high here, placed to where they could catch the sun's rays. "Mistra," she asked, motioning to the window, "can you throw this through that?" Casica grabbed the brick. "I can today." She drew back her arm and aimed.

"Stop!" her friend cried suddenly. "What?!" "Not this pane! I like this pane." "*What?!*" Casica exclaimed, incredulous. "Clarece, the building falls!" "I know Mistra, but—not this one!"

Casica looked up despite herself. The mosaic was round and filled with colored flowers. She still stared at it disbelievingly as her charge pulled her along. "Here!" Clarece pointed. Her voice was angry. "King Tustinlck! He was an evil king. 'Killed many slaves...." "Are you certain?!" Casica asked sarcastically. "Are you sure there isn't some other sovereign you'd prefer disintegrated?" Clarece considered the question, all sarcasm lost in the moment. "I'm certain. Destroy *him*!"

Casica cursed under her breath. "Stand behind me." She lifted the heavy brick that some slave long ago had fashioned and hurled it with the might of her shalonn. She threw like a man, the princess did, and her aim was deadly. King Tustinlck shattered and fell at their feet. Clarece snorted and kicked at the pieces. A forehead and two eyes looked up at her. She ground them under her heel. "A slave laughs last after all," she muttered. Casica shook her head. *Only God knew the mind....* "You go, my lady. I'll help you out and then find another way."

"No," came the reply. "I'll not leave you. You've risked your life enough for me." Josquin judged the height. Seven cubits, maybe more. Still, her shalonn burned, she could do it. "You go first," the princess ordered, turning to her friend. "I can scale it." The slave objected. "No, my lady. Tis too high." "I'm Josquin, Clarece. I can do it." She was removing her vest. "Here. When you get to the opening, cover the shards so you don't cut yourself. I'll lift you up."

Clarece wanted to argue but the sound of something falling somewhere spurred her to faith. Healers could do all sorts of things. Her mistra wouldn't lie—she hoped. Casica stood by the wall and held out her hands. The slave stepped into them and, amazed, felt herself lifted to the healer's full stretch. Quickly, she cleared the larger pieces of glass with her elbow then placed the vest over the rest. It's astounding how mightily terror empowers the human body. Maimed hands and all, Clarece pulled herself through the window and disappeared from sight.

Casica stepped back to the far side of the hall. Another sickening sound of the building crumbling spurred her frantic thoughts. *You can do this, Cass,* she encouraged herself. She took two deep breaths and ran, springing with all her might.

In its eagerness to save, the shalonn almost killed its host, tossing her up with a dazzling zeal. Only with great difficulty did the princess avoid crushing her head against the ceiling. "*Kai!*" she yelled as she prevented the impact with one hand and grasped for the window ledge with the other. She threw her left arm over the vest-covered glass. *Poetry in motion,* K'net used to say, teasing about her clumsiness.

The poetry dangled on the frame for a moment before gathering her strength in a more controlled manner. She lifted herself easily and fell through the opening. Casica expected to hit hard but didn't. The ground was only several cubits away. This part of the palace was built into a hill. No wonder Clarece chose it as their escape. The slave helped her owner gain her feet. She stood and looked in the direction of Clarece's gaze. Smoke filled the air.

"Dear God," Casica breathed. She could feel it. Pain and death were everywhere. It was the soldiers' barracks they saw, a huge portion of it blown away.

"Powder," Clarece determined, somber.

XXI

Activity had begun to organize around the flaming building. The women ran to join it. Frantic soldiers rushed all about dragging and carrying wounded comrades from the burning rubble as men lay on the ground, screaming in pain. Casica stopped short.

"Come, my lady!" her charge urged. "They need you! Come!" Josquin resisted. She was breathing hard. Her shalonn blazed like the building but in a confusing way. "Princess!" Clarece begged. "I can't," Casica declared quietly. "There are too many. I can't help them." Clarece stood helplessly, the voices of dying men blocked by her own desperate thoughts.

She couldn't know what her owner fought. Casica was gifted above any healer, it was true. But the healings she faced had always involved individuals—not groups of people. A healer felt pain. And now, with the suffering of dozens of people assailing her, the young woman was overwhelmed, like trying to focus on many conversations at once. Josquin stood paralyzed in her power as she struggled, desperately, with the urge to run. The moment exposed her greatest weakness: to flee in the face of confusion.

"Lady," Clarece now stood directly in front of her owner. She held her as best she could with her claws. The healer looked beyond her. "M'Yat!"

The name did what nothing else could. With a jolt, Casica returned to herself. "My mistra," her slave implored, "you don't have to help them all." She was leading the panicked girl to the nearest man. He lay on the ground, burned and unconscious. “Here,” Clarece invited, soothingly. “This man. Only this man.” Casica gazed at her. Clarece recognized the uncertainty that filled those brown eyes. “Here, my lady. Help this man. I’m here. You’re not alone.”

Josquin blinked. *You’re not alone.* Here was the cure for her weakness. Casica Elespoir could do anything if she weren’t alone. Haltingly, she placed her hands upon the man’s heart and brow. He awoke to her touch and stared, unfocused at the dark woman. Casica felt his emotions; he was afraid of her. “What is your name?” she asked, examining him all the while. “First Stage, Calitar.” “Calitar. I’m Casica.” The man tried to nod but couldn’t. “’First Stage.’ Is that like being a Private?” “Yes.” “Well, we’ll see about getting you to the next stage, yes?” “Yes.”

Casica smiled. She could have asked him anything, and he would have said ‘yes’. The burns on his abdomen were deep. His head was injured. But he now felt no pain. Josquin reached into her boot for Bastien’s dagger and with it, carefully cut away the cloth from Calitar’s torso. *God, you’re so young,* she observed. He wasn’t even old enough for hair on his chest. He might be younger than Asla.

She sighed, relieved at the burn site. It was contained to a single area. She placed her hands around it and concentrated. A particular type of healing flowed from her into the scorched and bleeding region. Calitar closed his eyes. As she put him to sleep, she felt herself wakening. She felt solid inside, at home in her gifting. This was all she could do for now. He would not die. The healer looked up from the soldier. Men, all of them young, lay around her, crying out in pain. She must act quickly. She closed her eyes and concentrated; if she could only take the katala and filter it, find the ones most grievously hurt.... *There.* She looked to her left and moved quickly to a man who looked to be Clarece’s age. He moaned in agony. With his hand, he covered the wound in his groin. He looked up at the dark woman and gasped.

“I’m Casica. Who are you?” The man’s eyes widened. He didn’t answer, from pain, she thought. “I know this man,” the voice beside her said. “He’s a lieutenant. Batis is his name.” “Batis. You know Clarece?” “Yes,” he managed. Josquin asked him more questions, trying to calm him with her touch. It came slowly, for

Batis resisted her help. "I need to see, yes?" She placed her hand on his and in that instant caught her breath. Immediately she put him to sleep.

"Mistra?" Clarece could see the change in her owner's face. "I know him," Casica turned. Her eyes were hard. "It was he who flogged me...." Clarece gaped. She didn't doubt her mistra's knowledge but wondered at the information. Cruelty was not the guard's reputation. "Are you sure, my lady?" "Yes. This man tried to kill me." Casica's voice was filled with contempt. No wonder he feared her so. For a long moment, she debated leaving him to die. Memories were already beginning to stir in her. She used her anger well. With it she cast fear aside.

"What will you do?" It was her charge that was fearful now; she'd seen what Casica did when she was angry. The shalonn burned incessantly, demanding attention. "I'll help him, of course," she replied, her face bearing a mixed expression, "but I'll deal with the other later." Clarece could only wonder what she meant. Royal fury was a fearsome thing.

Casica lifted the bloody hand from the wound. "Scads," she breathed. It wasn't just the wound Batis covered; it was the sliver of plank that had been blown into his body. It nestled into the artery. This was going to be a bloody mess. "Clarece, take your vest." Quickly the slave unfastened her garment, retrieving her tin spoon from the pocket. "I'm going to pull this out and when I do, it's going to burst. I'll cover the wound with my hand; you cover my hand with your vest. Alright?" Her charge nodded, ready.

The princess took a deep breath. She must do this perfectly. She grasped the wet wood and yanked straight up. In the instant it took for her to cover the opening, Batis' heart beat, christening her and Clarece with red. She pressed hard and filled the torn vessel with healing. Clarece's presence helped greatly. Josquin closed her eyes and willed powerfully, feeling the artery heal with an ease she'd never experienced. An ironic realization made her laugh despite herself. Clarece was panting with adrenaline.

"What, my lady?" "This brute.... I've never been this good with bleedings," she explained. "I survived his flogging. That's why I can do this now. His evil has saved his life." She held the healing for five precious minutes. The bleeding stopped. She looked down at the guard and memorized his face. "You meant it for evil;

God meant it for good, *your* good today." She'd done all necessary for now. The women left him sound asleep.

For a half-hour the healer and her assistant went from man to man treating those with the most life-threatening injuries. Josquin's healing flowed like water, efficient and powerful. Many of the men were wounded by the collapse of their living quarters. These injuries, involving organs and bleeding and breaks she treated quickly. The burn victims were a different matter. Healing burns took time but what she could not minister in healing, she could minister to pain.

They kneeled now beside a corporal whose arm was deeply gashed. Casica tore off Clarece's left sleeve, her own having left her six wounds ago. "We're running out of clothes, my lady." "Agreed. Can you get some cloths?" "Yes. I'll be back as quick I can." She didn't wait for her owner's permission to leave; an emergency like this trumped slavish etiquette. Casica listened as she ran swiftly towards the palace.

She paused from her treatment of the gash to study the scene around her. Interestingly, her efforts at saving life and limb waned in comparison to efforts at saving the building. Dozens of men in fresh and soiled uniforms—some wearing only their undergarments, swarmed around the blazing structure. No one seemed to fear additional explosions. All were consumed with finding comrades and fighting the fire. A water brigade formed, thirty men long, as they desperately drained the barracks' well. The healer glanced from the black plume of smoke towards the ocean. It hid from her view, just beyond a high hill. How ironic, to be near so much help and yet unable to tap its resources.

She couldn't know that at this moment others, people keenly interested in her well-being, looked upon the same smoke. At the watchtower of the Cassican capital, men argued among themselves what the smoke might be. Was it war? Was the Byzanthian city on fire? K'eran couldn't determine as he watched through his glass. His daughter was there, though, somewhere near that smoke. It was certain she was helping, if not harmed. He turned to his commander at arms and ordered him send a delegation to the Byzanthian consul. The people of Cassica were prepared to assist their Byzanthian neighbors. It was the first offer of its kind in the countries' recorded histories.

Casica continued on her trek. It did occur to her to wonder where the palace physicians were. They would be of great help with the lesser injuries. As if in answer to her thoughts, she saw them come, unmistakable in their long, black robes. She never understood that, the donning of black by a healer. Black was the color or mourning. It seemed to portend a patient's death.

As for the healers in her land, they were indistinguishable in a crowd. They looked like every other woman, except for the glowing stones about their necks, and the fact they tended to be somewhat taller than the general female population. Berea said that for an ailing man, a pretty face was good a medicine as any shalonn and advised her pupils to look their best for the trade. (Not that she herself put any special effort into personal appearance. She needn't. Even at a hundred years, the chief healer caused many a masculine head to turn.)

The healer went to her next patient. This boy did not appear to be more than sixteen. He didn't stir at her touch. Tenderly, Casica closed his eyes and in the midst of all the commotion, spoke a short Cassican prayer over his body. "S'Aduou leit ta dachna, e coma pol tale kana shew." *May God usher you safely home and comfort those you love.* She released him and continued. The next man needed nothing more than a quick touch to his ribs and something she did not have. "Water," he coughed. "Please. Water." "Yes, soldier," she answered, comfortingly. "I'll see what I can do." All these men needed water, but all the water there was went to the building.

Something startled her shalonn. She looked to her right. A man lay still and quiet. She ran to him and fell to her knees at his side. He looked up at her, confused and shocked. His eyes turned to his wrist. It appeared to be a simple fracture but it was not. A splinter of bone about the size of a needle stuck out of his flesh. Nothing hurt, really; it seemed harmless enough; yet the quiet man was slowing bleeding to death.

"Tis nothing, lady," he breathed. "I'm alright...the others... help them." "What's your name?" Josquin asked, taking the wrist into her hands. This was difficult and for a moment, she faltered. The bone was threaded though the man's vein like a needle. She must unravel it before anything could be done. She must do this quickly. Her hands were slippery with blood.

"I'm Sagina. And you are the Princess Casica. We have not met, my lady, but we all know your slave. I serve with Poul." A bizarre thought came to him. "Tell me, Your Highness, we all wonder... where the devil does your slave lay that sneaky cur?" "In her mind," Casica laughed nervously. Here this man was, dying, and what he wanted to know is where his sergeant takes his woman. Military men. They were a breed among themselves.

Sagina chuckled weakly. "That's most certain, but where in the flesh?" "In the flesh?" She shifted her healing. "That place where men usually take their woman, I would assume." Sagina laughed till it hurt. He was getting very sleepy. "Please...I beg you...." "Alright, Sir Guard, but only if you lay very still for a minute." She had unthreaded the needle. Quickly, she set the bones and poured healing into the wrist. He was going to live, this man. Compliments of Batis. "You didn't hear this from me," she divulged, "but Clarece rendevouses with her man at the—."

"*Casica!*" She never felt his approach. Didn't even know the voice except in memory. The princess looked up from the sleeping man to the one that studied her with deep concern. The blue in his eyes stole her breath.

"Bastien...."

XXII

For a long moment they gazed at each other, oblivious to the noise and activity about them. It was he who broke the silence. "Are you alright?" She nodded, speechless. She couldn't believe what she saw. After so much time, here he was, the man who lived only in her imagination. But he was not imagined now. Bastien squatted across from her, his face streaked with the black of smoke. His shirt clung to him with sweat. Her voice returned from wherever it was. "When did you get here?" she managed.

It was his turn to pause. She was safe, thank God. Her flesh and clothes were covered with the blood of his men. Her face ran with toil, and her brown eyes pooled with an energy he didn't recognize. The necklace at her throat shone in brilliant color—like stained glass. He could only wonder where her sleeves were. She was positively beautiful.

"I returned this afternoon. I went to the chamber, but you weren't there." Bastien glanced around. "Where's your slave?" He wasn't concerned about Clarece's well-being, only irritated that she wasn't where she belonged. "She's gone for cloth." He nodded, approving. "Is there anything else you need?" Casica looked at the field of wounded men. "Water. These men all need water." "Alright. I'll get some." He spun and ran quickly from her.

Casica returned, bedazzled, to Sagina. She felt his heart and head. He was very weak from loss of blood but stable. She could leave him safely for now. The moans and cries were less frequent now, due partly to her presence, partly not, but for some reason, she felt bolstered as though Bastien brought with him an encouraging air. She continued to the man nearest her.

This soldier lay unconscious, blessedly so. His hands were burned severely as though he had reached into a fire. She felt him. Only his hands were injured, but that was enough. He stirred at her touch. "Still," she ordered him, smiling. "I'm going to help you." She asked no questions; the man struggled even to breathe so frightened was he.

"My hands...." "I know. You're in luck. I'm handy with them. I've been working with a pair for months now." Gently she placed one of his hands between her palms and did what she wished someone could have done for Clarece. She spread the fingers out to match her own and filled the destroyed flesh with healing. During the treatment, her flesh never touched his—only her energy did.

The young soldier moaned with relief. He was betrothed. His marriage was a mere month away. This day was to have been his last at the post before the wedding. *Will you give me your hand in marriage?* he had asked her. Now he would have nothing with which to receive Breanal. His tears weren't lost on the healer. She took his other hand and applied the same type healing. He breathed more easily now.

"What's your name, soldier?" "Dan." She smiled. "Tis my brother's name.... And your wife's?" The man swallowed. To weep before a woman was shameful. "Breanal. We're betrothed. We marry in four weeks." Casica nodded. No wonder he wept. "Congratulations," she offered encouragingly. "Breanal is a blessed woman."

"She'll not be blessed with a handless man." Casica wiped the sweat and tears from his face. Her touch filled him with peace. "Don't fear. You won't be handless, I promise. You'll be playing love sonnets on the lute for her in a month." He smiled wanly. "I don't play the lute." "Then you should learn. The surest way to a woman's heart is kindness and romance." She held the hand carefully in her own. "I'm going to put you to sleep for now, Dan. Dream of Breanal."

This time she saw him. Bastien came quickly to her, a bucket of water in tow. He glanced at the sleeping soldier; it was Dan. Wordlessly he dipped the gourd ladle into the bucket and brought water to her lips. She covered his hand with hers, startling him with the sensation. A cool warmth and something he couldn't identify filled him.

Casica sighed at the wetness but what truly refreshed her was Bastien's touch. She emptied the vessel quickly. He offered her two more ladles. Satisfied, she looked into his face. "Thank you, Bastien." Her eyes shone with gratitude. He smiled.

"I'll leave this bucket with you. I have men giving water to the wounded. I told them to listen for you in case you need something. Is there anything else I can do?" She shook her head. The prince glanced around. His blue eyes were pained. "Thank you, Casica. These men are my friends." Without awaiting her response, he stood and ran towards the fire. She was still watching him when she sensed her.

"Mistra," Clarece called dropping beside her. Her arms were filled with clean, rolled cloth. Around her shoulder hung the satchel. "Forgive my taking so long. I brought your bag and found some slaves to tear the cloth into strips. I thought that's what you'd want." "Exactly what I want," Casica replied, studying her friend. The slave breathed heavily with running and the burden. She wiped sweat from her eyes with a mitten. "Here, Clarece."

Casica took the ladle and offered her water. It was received enthusiastically. The healer took the dipper and poured water along the back of her friend's neck—a trick she'd learned from her mother. Clarece bowed her head at the sensation. "Your lord has returned," she observed. "Have you seen him?" "Yes. He was just here." The smile that met Casica was filled with meaning. It was only then Clarece noticed the injuries of Dan. She winced in horror.

"My God," she breathed, "...his hands. Can you help him?" Casica studied her companion's worried face. Her eyes were moist with empathetic fear. "Yes. We can help him. Give me your cloth." The princess tore thin strips of fabric. Expertly, she wrapped each blackened finger, then joined all with a thick layer of covering. "Is that all?" Clarece asked; he *must* require more care. "All for now," she was answered. "I'll treat them more thoroughly later."

"Will he...he won't be like me, will he?" "As you are now, no. As you could be, yes." There was glint in her mistra's eyes, like she held some secret. The slave compared Dan's white shrouds with her leather mittens. "You're certain he'll be alright?" Her owner placed a warm hand on her claw. "I promise," she comforted. Clarece considered the dark hand. Casica's fingers moved so deftly, like a weaver's. What would it be like, she wondered, to have fingers?

The women moved quickly now, for most of the injuries were easily treated. As they went, the healer noticed how excellent an assistant was Clarece, speaking comfortingly to the men—many of whom knew her—encouraging them and assuring them of her mistra's abilities. And while she couldn't tie knots or tear cloth, she could give water and wipe faces. There was about her a mothering presence to which the injured responded readily. As she set a broken arm, Casica smiled into her friend's sweaty face.

"Has anyone ever told you, you're a motherly figure?" Clarece laughed. "I've been told I've a *matronly* figure, Mistra." "That's not what I meant." Something in the man's arm popped audibly. Fortunately, he was in no condition to feel it. "I refer to your maternal way. Would you want children, Clarece?"

Clarece pushed back a damp strand of hair from her face. The question took her by surprise though strangely, not for its being asked in such a setting. Josquin moved among the injured easily, bearing with her a tranquility that felt somewhat like afternoon tea. No, it was the matter, itself, that surprised Clarece; for while children were a subject breached often in her heart, she rarely had discussed it with anyone. It wasn't the kind of thing slave-women talked about. Her eyes grew soft with thought.

"If I could keep them, Mistra...and love them, and know them as a free woman, yes. I would have many children—a handful at least, more if God grant it." She smiled shyly. "And if my husband grant it." Casica adjusted her healing. "You remind me of a man I know," she said. "His name means 'a quiver filled.'" "And how many arrows has he?" Casica shook her head. "None. He's unmarried." "Has he not found the one he loves?" Clarece inquired, handing her mistra a roll of cloth to wrap the healed fracture. Her owner sighed deeply.

"I think he's found her," Josquin answered, meeting the blue eyes of her friend. "Only, there are complications." "Dowry?" The healer frowned. "Something like that." The slave nodded, understanding. "Sometimes I forget that being free doesn't solve all life's troubles. I will pray for them." She lay her mitten on the man's chest. "Tis a bitter lot, to be denied your love's desire." What she wiped from her eyes was not sweat. She glanced at her bucket. It offered an escape from her stirred emotions. "We're running low on water, Mistra. I'll fetch more."

The princess stood with her to survey the scene, noticing the fire felt not as much oppressive as it did warm. She turned her face toward the ocean. A damp air moved in, a harbinger of cold weather. "We need these men moved, Clarece," she observed. "Tis a bitter night that comes. Is there an infirmary nearby?" "Very," her charge answered, motioning to the burning building. "There's another. The west barracks." Casica nodded. "Good. When you get water, ask someone about transporting them. These men need food and warmth." "Yes, my lady."

The slave kneeled before turning to run to the well. Others waited ahead of her. As she stood, she noticed a group of men striving to remove burned debris. Even now, after so long, they struggled to find life in the ruins. A hand exchanged her empty bucket for a filled one. She took it and jogged towards that group. A lifetime of slavery taught her many skills, not the least of which was how to run without forfeiting her bucket's contents. Clarece stopped at each man and offered them water. They'd had none, they said, and gratefully paused their work to drink.

A large man lifted a blackened beam and, turning, dropped it near her feet. She smiled broadly at his ponytail. "Excuse me, Sergeant." Poul looked up. *"Clarece."* "My lord." She kneeled and offered him the dipper. Poul gulped his drink then knelt in front of her. She glanced for witnesses before looking into his eyes. They were red with smoke.

"How are you, Poul?" "Better now," he coughed. She gave him more. He drank and bowed his head, exhausted and discouraged. "We're finding bodies, Clarece. Only bodies. God. This is worse than battle." A stream of cool water flowed along his neck; he surrendered to the sensation, allowing himself to rest under the exquisite bath. Just being in her presence strengthened him. He looked up.

For once, their eyes truly embraced. In that sapphire blue, he saw her all: the bloodied and ripped blouse clinging to her body;

the scarred, thin arms; the brilliant silver band about her grimy throat; the sandy eyebrows and lashes; the lovely face streaked with sweat; the full lips parted slightly for breath. She was glorious. Instinctively, he reached out his hand. She didn't move. His flesh was a mere breath from her face. She closed her eyes, anticipating his touch....

"Slave!" Clarece jerked as though struck. She dropped her head guiltily and turned towards the voice; it was another slave to whom the man yelled. She bowed her face to hide the tears. Almost. Almost they had touched.

"My lord," she said, resuming herself. "My mistra says the wounded men must be moved to warmth and food. The west infirmary is nearest, but I think the physicians would make this decision. Would you inquire, Sir?"

K'net sighed deeply. God...they were so close. "Yes, Clarece. Tell the princess I'll see to it." The slave bowed her head to the ground. "With you permission...." "Yes." He watched her stand, take two steps back, and turn as a slave does. *"Clarece!!"* he called, *"I love you!"* The water bearer did not look back. It was only in his mind he spoke.

Someone had only now been found and lay, screaming, on the ground. A commander rushed to his side. He'd spent the entire afternoon searching for this soldier, waiting for news of his whereabouts; for the smoke-streaked, broken man was more than a lieutenant: he was his son. "Physicians!" he yelled. Three physicians and their assistants ran to his voice. The commander dropped to his knees and clasped the hand locked into his own. His child's agonized cries tore his heart.

Casica looked up, startled. "Come, Clarece!" They ran to a crowd of black-robed men gathered around the soldier and his father. For her height, she could see them—the crushed shins of the lieutenant. A beam had fallen upon him and all this time he lay, numbed by the weight. It was with the lifting of the pressure, she knew, that the agony came upon him.

"Father!" he cried, gripping the commander's royal vestments. The physicians moved quickly, silently; they cut the leggings and boots from the injured and consulted among themselves. "They'll have to come off," the leader said, calmly. He nodded to his assistant. A large, rough saw was produced. "No! Not my legs! Not my legs!" the lieutenant screamed. "Can't you help him?!" the commander demanded. "No, my lord," the physician answered coolly. "There is nothing to be done except take them off."

Casica's heart pounded as loudly as her shalonn burned. They would kill him. To cut off both legs was almost certain death from bleeding if not infection. Her ears rang with a desperate anger. "You'll kill him!" she yelled. The gowned men turned to her voice. She broke into their circle.

"Who in Hades are you?" the commander spat, knowing full well who she was. She was the Cassican, the prisoner from the hated land. "I'm a healer. I can help your son." "She's a demon! Take her away!" ordered the physician. At once three men seized the woman and moved to drag her off. "Please!" she begged. "I can help him!" The physician thrust his hand towards the ocean. "I said, *away* with her!"

"Stop."

The voice came from above. Sitting on his mount was Ars, King of Byzanthia. "Let her go," he ordered quietly. Instantly, she was released. Casica looked at him only a moment. "Clarece, my bag." The slave knelt beside her owner as, quickly, Casica placed her hands on the man's brow and heart. All pain left him and flowed into her. He quieted. She smiled encouragingly. "Don't fear. I won't hurt you." He blinked twice and fell asleep. "She's killed him!" someone observed.

"No, she hasn't," the father answered, quietly. He could feel his heart. His son rested free of pain. Clarece had already opened the bag and held for her mistra what she knew she wanted. It was a knife, strange in its blade; in place of iron was an edge made of stone. Few of the men recognized the obsidian. Sharper than any metal, it would never rust. Again, Clarece did what her owner thought. She placed several drops of the cleansing ointment into her water bucket. As she waited, Casica quickly examined the man's body.

"What is his name?" she asked the father. "My own: Macartus." Casica smiled. Macartus: Son of Might. "So you are a mighty man," she whispered in Cassican. "Hold onto your might. This won't come easy." The water was ready. She washed her filthy hands and dried them on Clarece's offered towel.

Josquin took the blade and dipped it into the water. She placed her hand on the leg nearest her and concentrated. The blood all but stopped; she must hurry or lose the limb after all. Deftly, she slit the leg from ankle to knee, crossed over the bone then continued the incision on the other side. She cut under and carefully lay the strip of flesh back. Clarece held it in cloth. She'd never seen such a thing. Bone and sinew lay open.

Casica closed her eyes and prayed. Taking a deep breath, she took the broken bone in her hands. She could heal bone like nobody's business, she had once said. Now she proved it. Purposely, Casica blocked the view of the audience, however; otherwise they might burn her, yet, for a demon. In her mind, she visualized what Clarece saw with her eyes; bone knit together at her silent command. The slave glanced from the sight to her owner's shalonn. It glowed with a red intensity. She lost track of time, but at some point the princess winked at her.

"'You alright?" Josquin whispered. Clarece nodded. "Good," Josquin continued. "Now I'm going to seal the cut, but I don't them to see me do it. I need you to follow after my hand and cover his leg with cloth, understand?" "Yes."

Her owner beamed. She was positively enjoying herself. She took the flesh and replaced it, and, with her assistant doing as instructed, sealed her work. She concentrated and blood returned to Macartus' limb. "Wrap it, Clarece." The slave obeyed as the healer moved to the other leg, holding the knife by the handle in her mouth.

By the time the women finished with the Macartus' legs, it was growing dark. The dying fire offered a necessary light. Around them men moved, stretchers in hand as the wounded were transported to the west barracks.

All the physicians had dispersed—all except one. The leader. Jealousy strangled his heart. The king stood beside him, his hand on the commander's shoulder. Macartus the elder was his personal friend and advisor. Casica finished her work and smiled. Pleased with the effort. Pleased with the result.

"Your son lives his name, Commander," she said. "We need get him to a warm place. He'll sleep the night. His recovery will be slow. But he'll keep his legs." The father's eyes shone. He kissed his child's brow and cradled his head against him.

Casica looked up at the king. Beside her, Clarece kneeled at attention, not upon the ground as required in the presence of her sovereign. After such a day, something within her refused to prostrate itself.

The posture was not lost on Ars. In perfect Cassican, he addressed the princess. "You did well, royal guilt." Casica blinked, shocked. "I wasn't alone, Your Majesty." Ars considered the silent form. "She did well, also." He turned to the father. "Macartus," he instructed in Byzanthian. "Go with your son." Stretcher bearers conveyed the wounded man. Wordlessly, the king returned to his mount.

Clarece glanced cautiously towards her owner. "I didn't know the king spoke Cassican." Casica shook her head. "Neither did I. He's like a slave, that one: filled with surprises." The women stood quietly, each lost in her own thoughts.

Behind them, the fire blazed on. In front, the unseen ocean grew black with night. Casica turned to the fallen palace. It seemed an eternity ago they were there. "Your holy place is destroyed, Clarece. I'm sorry."

The slave was considering the structure, too. Slowly she shook her head. "Don't be," she answered; something about her voice was different. "Twas a child's hiding place." Clarece surveyed the field of wounded and departed men. "Here," she motioned with her gaze. "They are the holy place…." She faced her owner, and the eyes that met her mistra's shone with something new. A satisfied smile graced her lips.

Casica nodded. She knew the feeling well. "Let's go to the infirmary and check on our patients, shall we?" she asked. Silently, they began walking to the west. The moon burned in his setting glory and shadowed them along their way.

Clarece stumbled down her stairs. She couldn't remember ever feeling so exquisitely exhausted. Something in her thrilled at the sight of the men snug in their beds. Four had died, but many more would have joined their number had it not been for her owner. As for Casica, she wasn't the least tired. The work of the day utterly invigorated her. She beamed as she shared with Clarece her meal of roast, commenting on the improvement of the men and on her friend's fine assistance.

"If we were in Cassica, Clarece, I would knight you. I'd still be cringing if it weren't for your presence." Her smoky face teared with gratitude. "I thank you." Clarece ducked at the expression in those brown eyes. The healer was seeing something she couldn't. "You would show purple," Casica said softly.

Show purple. What can she possibly mean? the slave wondered. But she didn't ask. She was too tired. Tired and too confused to want to know. What she asked instead was, "Do you know where your husband is?"

Casica choked on her bread. Her husband. *Good, God, I'm married!* Bastien was back! She'd forgotten. She looked behind her through the doorway into his chamber and stared. After so much time, there would be an occupant in that room. Only a wall would separate them. A wave of panic welled within.

"No. I suppose he's still at the fire." Her charge remained silent, conspicuous in itself, as she continued eating. "Say something, Clarece." The slave swallowed. "I'll light his brazier and draw your bath, my lady." "That's not what I meant and you know it. What do you think will happen to me now?" Her friend took a deep breath. In her mind she glanced at what would happen to her mistra, but it would not be now. It would take time to come to that place.

"Deeply maddening and satisfying things, I would think, Princess. But not tonight. You and he have had a long day. You have much time to know one another. Rest and see what tomorrow brings." She motioned to the doorway. "The door slides and locks on your side. He designed it so. He waits for you to open it." Her words only stirred more within the dark woman. How was she to open such a door? How could a man and woman from enemy lands ever become one?

The princess stood, looking nervously toward the chamber. "Would you like something stronger to drink?" she asked. God knew *she* did.

"Mistra...." Assurance was what the girl needed, not drink. Clarece rose and pulled her owner into a kind embrace; Casica smelled of smoke and of herself. Tenderly, the bound bestowed a knighthood of her own: she scented her lady and kissed the warm neck. It was a slave's gesture, but to the troubled royal felt like coronation itself. She melted at the touch. Clarece held her mistra and offered a quiet benediction. "Tis been an honor to serve with you, this day, my lady. Truly, you are God's gift to this country. May its son be His gift to you."

So now the bath was drawn; the fire was lit. She made her way to her cot. Excited voices filled the pen. The chief slaveswoman didn't announce herself. She didn't feel like facing anyone more; she simply wanted sleep. Clarece ducked into her stall. And blinked. There, on what she thought was her cot, sprawled a rich, royal purple comforter.

Scads! I'm in the wrong pen! she thought, confused. She paused. It *was* her stall: that was her pile of books—and Asla's schedule. A red comforter draped her stallmate's cot. The woman still stood, dumbfounded, when a voice found her ear. "We'll sleep like queens, Clarece!" Penelope exclaimed. "How on earth did you ever manage this?"

Clarece faced her, speechless. It wasn't the explosion everyone was talking about; it was the covers. "I didn't do this," she said, dumbly. "Of course you did! Who else?" Clarece shook her head. "Truly. I've tried for years, but this isn't me."

"Well, whatever you say. Thank you! You definitely get our votes next selection!" Penelope hugged her quickly and ran back to the happy women. Lacking mental energy to solve this puzzle, Clarece surrendered it for the morrow. She didn't even bother with her boots before slipping under the heavy cover. Already, its down warmed her.

She barely stirred as hours later, Asla worked at unlacing her boots. "Taken up smoking I see," the g'Helderleit quipped. "I can't wait to hear who you 'comforted' for these."

The chief slave coughed. "I'll tell all tomorrow," she mumbled. "It *is* tomorrow," a voice may have said, she wasn't sure. Slumber pulled her down quickly, dragging in its wake the puzzle's solution. *Purple.* A smile blanketed her sleeping face....

XXIII

That's the last time I'll rush to welcome his royal highass home. Clarece winced where she knelt in her master's room, smarting from another blow. His words cut into her like leather, tearing at her character and spirit. *Kai,* she thought now, *'twas worse than a flogging!* With a flogging, she might anticipate the end, either through the torturer's fatigue or her unconsciousness. But this—would he never cease?

"And what's *this* I hear?" he yelled. "A soldier says he saw you and the princess come from the old palace. Have you *seen* that place? *Tell* me you didn't have her there! Blast you, Clarece! I entrusted her to your keeping, and you put her in harm's way all about. What the *devil* were you thinking? Or can you think?" He prowled near her. "I swear, you're becoming as lame of mind as you are of body. Is it time to sell you off?" She trembled at the statement. "What have you to say for yourself?"

Silence. She had nothing to say for herself. He wasn't truly asking, but she had much to say *to* herself. So much for donning her best vest and allowing herself joy that her mistra's husband was safely returned. So much for showing herself to him at all. She was *Casica's* property and cursed if she would allow herself placed in such an idiotic, humiliating position. "...and so that's the way you reward my trust in you, slave. You turn idiot when I need you the...."

"Good afternoon, prince." He stopped. He'd never heard her approach, had no idea how long she'd stood there in the doorway. Clearly she had heard him. To haven't was impossible. Even from the slave's stairway she had ascended after visiting the injured. She had hoped to find Clarece, below, to care for her hands. It was most certain they ached from her toil the day before.

"Princess Casica," Bastien answered coolly. "I didn't hear you come." "Obviously," replied she as coolly. Her gaze met his bluntly. It wasn't unkind. She wasn't a fool; she knew his attack upon the slave was misdirected. Still, his anger at her friend riled her.

"Clarece," she asked softly, "would you excuse us, please?" The slave bowed her head to the floor and moved to rise. "Stay." His tone sounded all the world like ordering a dog. The chief caught herself mid-rise and slowly lowered. Inside she shook her head. *Pony,* she thought. *That's just what I need: to be the object of contention their first day together.*

The dark eyes hardened, and for a moment, the princess thought to challenge the prince to his face. She stood her ground, instead, and when she spoke, her voice was warm wax. "Yes, Clarece. Stay. In your stall. I have need of you. But for now, leave us, please." Bastien's eyes pierced Josquin as the slave rose and quickly withdrew. Casica slid the chamber door closed behind her.

"You breed rebellion in her!" Bastien said ominously. "I?" Casica replied, anger rising in her tone. "*I* breed rebellion? By treating her as human? Tis slavery you mean. Slavery breeds its own rebellion. How *dare* you treat her that way!"

"How *dare* I?" he demanded. "Do you forget to whom you speak?" "If I do tis because of your former absence and your present behavior. But as best I recollect, I address a prince with no more standing than I!"

No more standing. Well, he did continue to stand and stared at the woman as though he'd never in his life seen her. He had half-forgotten her height but never her countenance. Her eyes burned at him with that pool of energy he could not name. Beneath her vestless blouse, a ring of light blazed, responding to its owner's passion.

For herself, she stood wondering why she'd bothered dressing up for him at all. Not even she had believed her when she told herself she wore this clothing for the injured. She had wanted to please him, to welcome him to his home, and to herself. *And for what?* she considered now. She'd been a fool to hope for mutual affection between them. Not five minutes together were they before the hideous issue of slavery raised itself between them. She glanced past him to the bed. What a fool she'd been, indeed. All these months of hoping. Ridiculous. She studied him now. He wore, still, what he had the day before. His face reflected fatigue that reached deeper than the body, and his eyes brimmed with defeat.

"What are you thinking, healer?" he asked suspiciously. He would not be thought foolish by this woman. "I'm thinking I don't need to be a healer to see you're in great need of rest and sustenance, my prince. And you don't need me to bother you further." She bowed graciously. "Forgive my intrusion. I'll leave you to yourself. Good day." With that she turned to leave. Her hand was sliding the door when he shot at her.

"Going for tea with your slave?" Slowly, she faced him. Her voice was kind. "Yes," she nodded, smiling. "We share tea at two—though I'd hoped to have *you* as my guest this day. I wished to hear of your time in Valdera." "Why?" he asked, softly. "You never replied to any of my letters." The dark head cocked in surprise. "Letters? I've received no letters." Bastien studied her even as she did him. For a moment he thought she might be lying but clearly she wasn't. "I wrote to you every week. You never heard?" She shook her head. "No," she said simply.

The young man glanced down at his muddy feet. His anger towards Clarece, his anger towards the foreigner dissolved. So she hadn't been ignoring him, rebuffing him, after all. His vision shifted quickly to her view. What must she have thought, not hearing from him all this time. "Again, my prince," she was saying quietly. "Perhaps, another time I'll the pleasure of your company." She bowed. "God's blessings upon you." With that, she left and secured the door between them.

Bastien scanned his empty room. His deep sigh filled it. Blast. Another false start. Like two draft horses that couldn't jump together they were, this woman and he. "What an incredible teamster you make, great prince!" he announced to himself. The engineer within scolded as it often did. He would never get this right.

"How is your mistra, slave?" he asked between bites. Clarece knelt invisibly as possible. Despite the princess' reassurances at tea, she felt certain she wasn't yet out of anger's way. She paused before selecting an appropriate answer.

"Gone, master." Bastien choked on his chicken. "*Gone?* Good, God! Where?" "To the injured, my lord. She's gone to treat them." The royal head dropped in relief. Inwardly, the slave smiled. 'Served him right to panic and choke. For his part, Bastien never suspected he'd been played; to have done so would have required suspecting the speaker reasoned. But as he chewed his meat and drank his wine, something in the man began to wonder. So the princess has tea with this slave. What did one do at tea except talk? Talk about what? What could Clarece possibly have to discuss?

"Will she return after?" Again a pause. He desired an answer. "Doubtful, my lord. She expressed her intention to visit with Countess Dolca after her ministration. I would not anticipate her return before midnight." Bastien nodded, approving. At least the Cassican mixed some royal blood into her social cup. He returned to his meal. His former property provided large portions, much more than she ever brought to her mistra, though at times, Clarece considered she should serve Casica as a man. Josquins possessed a mighty appetite. And it had been her increasing observation that while her owner seemed to lose weight, she, herself, gained.

He was finished except for his wine. Bastien leaned into his chair and studied the silent form. Clarece looked very much like the table by which she knelt. Knees firmly planted; body straight in attention; gaze riveted slavishly to the floor. He caressed his cup thoughtfully. Bathed and full, he was feeling much more himself. "What are you thinking, Clarece?" A pause. "Nothing, my lord." Bastien snorted to himself. Just as he'd suspected. "Except that I wonder...." He turned more fully to her.

"The ancient mathematician, Collaudius, asserts the earth possesses much weight, weight such as cannot be fathomed. Yet he speculates additionally, that nothing of mass upon Earth is without impact. That if one were to jump and, thereby, deprive the earth of his mass, he would subtract, to some minuscule extent certainly, but subtract, nonetheless, from the earth's load. I wonder if the same is true, equally, concerning points of force.

"I observe here my knees. Clearly my weight, let's say nine stone, is distributed unequally upon the support of this floor. My knees create the most prominent site of force. If I redistribute this force by leaning back, then theoretically, the floor is affected by the change of force. Is the same true for Earth? Are its foundations affected in anyway by the concentrations of forces derived by weight? What if all cities and all peoples could, somehow, be fixed upon a single point on its surface; would the earth's structure shift? Would it tilt—if only theoretically? And if it did, would e'Manite's principals of counter-force alleviate...."

Bastien forgot his wine. He sat, dumb, as the human/slave table continued to set its own course. He was familiar with much of what she said but never, *ever* had he arranged these ideas on such a grand scale. Quickly, he was drawn into her speculation, mesmerized by its possibilities. And for a space of time, forgot entirely that this teacher wore a collar about her neck and kneeled before him as property. Even more than the content of her lecture was the slave's delivery fascinating.

"...of course, all is moot if Puklackin's premise of universal mass proves valid. But that's all I'm thinking, Master. That and that I need fold your wash before it wrinkles." Clarece shifted, uncomfortable. After months with Casica, her knees were out of practice. She bowed. "Forgive me, Master. I speak as the mute. You are one trained in these matters. What think you?"

Bastien blinked. What thought he? Blast, if he knew what thought he. He was gone just a few months, and his whole frappin world had changed. "I think you're right," is what he said. "You should fold my wash before it wrinkles."

The slave bowed to the floor. She rose, and in her slave's line, skillfully removed all his course. She retreated two steps before turning on her heel as a slave does. Bastien eyed her retreating form. He rubbed his forehead, befuddled. He felt a headache coming on.

XXIV

It was raining. Cold drops pelted the hood of Dolca's cloak. Casica didn't have a black cover in this land; graciously, the countess provided one of her own. Dolca stood somewhere in the rear of the crowd, escorted by a former squire of her husband's. Beside the princess stood Bastien, cloaked also in black.

In honor of the friends who would rest this awful day in wet earth, his head remained uncovered. Rain dripped down his blonde hair, causing it to curl playfully; but nothing was playful about this procession. He watched, thankful for the water running down his face; it helped mask the water running from his eyes.

As a prince, Bastien sponsored many things concerning military personnel: the guards' dance, the soldiers' tournaments, the summer games. This day he helped sponsor the funeral. As a minor prince, he stood farthest at the right of his father, Bastil filling the place of honor at the king's side. Ars stood, stalwart and somber. Four of his soldiers killed in an explosion that defied explanation. Already, there was speculation of sabotage. The rain turned heavy.

In the distance was heard the dull drone of percussion. Drums, played by a black- uniformed corps of military men filled the air. They were coming, the dead, ascending the hill to rest, finally, in the land of their service. Beside the princess, Bastien coughed. The rain chilled him but not as greatly as the horror. Death in battle was to be expected; death in barracks was not.

A black-gloved hand emerged from Dolca's garment. Silently Casica took his own. Immediately warmth filled him. Startled, Bastien glanced at the woman. After the fight they'd had only yesterday, he wondered at her attention. Even her presence at his side surprised him. The hood hid her face, but her kindness revealed her intention. Reconciliation must come in such a time as this. Life was too short for prideful battle.

He returned her grasp and clung gratefully to her. It wasn't the warmth only that encouraged him. It was she. He glanced up. Cresting the hill came the funeral procession. Four coffins, advancing side-by-side made for a ghastly review. The bearers of them wore black—even the sashes about their waists. Behind the caskets drooped a parliament of flags, all black and weary.

Black on black on black, thought Casica. What a bleak and hopeless commendation of life was this. She gazed at the gaping hole before her and cringed. May God spare her a watery death.

A watery grave awaited the approaching soldier. His mother wept openly; his father stood, numb. These were young men. Too young. Draped over the coffins was the Byzanthian flag. Its deep green relieved the black setting. The procession stopped. Men with solemn and grave expressions waited patiently on their comrades as the clergy arrived to bid them well. "Good, God," mouthed the princess. Even the clergy dressed in deathly black.

Her mind returned to the first funeral she could remember: Anasis'. Then it had rained, too. Then she and her family and mourners beyond number dressed in black, too. Then the casket bore a flag, too. It was the royal standard of her family: a fleur d'lis adorned all in burgundy and gold. A ring of white encircled the flower, signifying the dead belonged to the order of healers. It was assumed Anasis would have been a josquin, coming from the womb of one. No one would ever know for certain; life had left her before her eyes could testify with the telltale blue at night.

But in the midst of all the black and bleak and rain that day shone the clergy. As was her people's custom, the holy men dressed in the purity of white and hope of green. For God never wore black. Even darkness was as light for Him. And in the holy garb of their priests was embodied a necessary reminder; death was the ultimate release of life. This little babe who never once had drawn an earthly breath lived, at that moment, more fully than did any of the attendants at her funeral.

Her sister, dead. Casica blinked aside her tears and clung more tightly to her companion.

The priests' sermon was memorably forgettable. Their droning held less meaning than had the drums'. Finally all that could be was said. Reverently, four coffins lowered in unison. The flags remained on them, signifying the remaining presence of Byzanthia with the men. Casket bearers retreated in orderly fashion and in their place marched the bearers of black mourning flags. In turn, each bearer stripped from the shafts their black banner. The naked shaft revealed itself as a spear.

The Princess of Cassica had never witnessed such a ritual and watched, somewhat unnerved, as the stripped flags were cast into the open graves. The symbolism was unmistakable to the former ambassador: their comrades and family would, forever, mourn the fallen and sent their sorrow into eternity with them. The naked spears signified each bearer's pledge to assume the fallen's place in battle. And reprisal. Warriors. Casica had known many; they were a fearsome class.

Now advanced the families. Silently, they cast mud upon loved ones. Greenery was offered and, unlike Cassican funerals in which family representatives remained to witness the completed burial in dirt, all waited as professional gravesmen shoveled mud unto the deceased.

Boom! Casica jumped. How on earth could a drum sound so loud? In the distance, what must have been several massive instruments exploded in unison, like four cracks of thunder. Their reports echoed in the cold air and seemed to thicken the already suffocating experience. *Where is hope in the midst of this observance?* Josquin wondered, shivering. What possible light could family and friends, the living, take with them from this place? *This land excels in death....* The princess shivered again, but this time her spirit riled against the darkness. The best response to death was life, she knew; slowly her head bowed as in prayer.

Thick cloth concealed what happened beneath her cloak. The woman closed her eyes and smiled, willing something powerful inside her. In response, the shalonn glowed with an irresistible intensity and at that moment every witness, every mourner, every bored and distracted participant, each experienced the same sensation but in his or her unique perception. Each warmed inexplicably as every man and woman received a renewed application of health towards their bodies. Not a few mourners interpreted the sensation as a message of peace from their beloved. In her desire to bless, the healer extended her work to the palace and palace grounds. This evening, she would flood the region with this ministry. Byzanthia was in desperate need of Life.

Bastien glanced down. Holding her hand as he did, he could sense the source of what he and others felt but didn't know what to make of it. He only knew that the woman did something good. The closer drums deflected his thoughts. The flag guard spun and marched toward the palace. Family followed next, then dignitaries, Ars and his sons leading them. Casica accompanied the fifth prince, holding still his hand. The congregation of mourners ascended the hill wordlessly.

At some point, Bastien paused his trek and turned to the hooded figure. "Princess," he whispered, allowing others to pass them. "Would you walk with me?" She released his hand and removed the deep hood. The rain lessened to a zanzan. Her eyes were the color of earth. His were the color of fatigue. "Of course," she mouthed. He took her arm in his and led them north, away from the palace, away from the crowd. Here was a garden he loved, lined with trees and trellises and a childhood dream; it was there they went.

As he walked, Bastien gathered his thoughts. He always spoke better in motion; men are side-by-side communicators, not so much face-to-face as women. Finally, alone and beyond the view of others, he spoke. "Josquin."

Casica blinked, first at the sound of that name in his voice and second, at its Cassican pronunciation. Bastien said it correctly: Josèn. *How could he possibly know that?* she wondered, gazing at him.

God, her eyes are so dark, thought he, so rich with something. He didn't know what. They made him almost to forget his message. He cleared his throat. "I thank you for attending the funeral. After all that's happened and what I've said. Well, you didn't have to come. No one...." "Expected me to?" she asked, finishing his sentence. The Byzanthian nodded.

"Tis just...you're Cassican. No one expects a Cassican to stand in the rain and watch Byzanthian soldiers buried. I thank you. Your presence, tis meant much to me." She nodded. "And," he continued, embarrassed at the truth, "I know you won't be told this officially, but we are all, the guard, my father, everyone... we're all grateful for your assistance that day. Many more men would have died without you." He grinned, despite himself. "If you were Byzanthian, you'd be knighted. Woman or no. As it is, my gratitude must serve as citation enough." The woman bowed, graciously.

"Citation received, Your Highness. You and your compatriots are royally welcome." She watched their surroundings. They headed towards a garden of sorts, more an arboretum perhaps, in the north lawn. She was unfamiliar with this place. "What of the explosion?" she asked. "What is thought to have happened?"

Here the man paused in reply. It was the question of the day. "We don't know for certain. It could have been accidental, no one knows. We're new with powder. But there's much suspicion. Byzanthia has more than a few enemies. Cassicans...." He glanced quickly at her expression. "You're not under suspicion." "Thank, God," she nodded, genuinely relieved. "But there are others: the Selians have cells of resistance as do the Kaints. And then there's always the slaves." "Slaves?" "Yes. Renegade slaves. They're always up to something. But tis impossible to prove, and we've so many slaves with access to the palace grounds. Interrogating them all is impractical."

The princess cringed. Interrogation meant only one thing. Surely Clarece and her people were safe from such response. "What of traitors in the ranks? Is that not possible?" The prince nodded. "Tis possible but highly unlikely. Probably, we'll never know what happened until something else does. We haven't had insurrection in years. I tell you: the crown never is secure." Casica nodded, knowingly. No ruling family, no matter how powerful, could rest secure on a throne.

Josquin paused. "May I ask a probing question?" Bastien blinked. "Well, of course." The woman weighed her words carefully. "What was powder doing in the barracks? I mean...the Church has made it clear: no military development. Only industrial...." Byzanthia's prince frowned. "Ah. I see where you're going. We abide by the agreement, Princess. Here, tis soldiers who transport powder to the mines. That's all this was." Josquin squinted. It all seemed rather improbable. She brushed her doubts aside. Now was not the time for this conversation. She nodded and continued her walk with him.

They had reached the garden. Under the canopy of trees, the two could walk protected from the rain—except for periodic drippings from above. Bastien stopped and looked at her. *How unlike other women,* he considered, noticing her damp, black mane. It didn't seem to bother her, getting wet. Her breath steamed the air. "What are you thinking?" she asked. Now *that* was like other women, always asking a man's thoughts. He made something up.

"I'm thinking how much I like this place. I've missed it. I used to play here for hours when I was a boy. I've measured time by these trees." She smiled, gazing at his living rulers. That wasn't what he truly was thinking, she knew.

"Would you like to see something?" he asked, suddenly. She nodded; something was afoot in him. "Come!" He led her quickly to an oak that looked to be hundreds of years. Curling up the tree's trunk was a complex stairway, a spiral staircase made of stone. Its steps disappeared into a curtain of green.

The creator was grinning. "My first professional architectural endeavor. Commissioned by His Royal Majesty, Ars, King of Byzanthia. 'Paid me a pound to build it.... What do you think?"

"What do I think?" replied the princess laughing. "I'm amazed, Sir Architect! How old were you?" "Eleven years." "Eleven?! When I was eleven, I was delivering babies and setting bones but never, *ever* could I design, much less build something as this!" Her admiration was genuine, he could tell. Bastien beamed with pride. "Want to try it?" "It still holds?" Casica asked suspiciously. She didn't feel like setting her own bones today. Bastien had already taken her arm.

"Only one test to ascertain its structural integrity...." As he led the way, he tossed over his shoulder, "A builder always falls first with his work." *That's not very comforting,* thought his companion, dryly. But she wasn't afraid. Clearly young Bastien knew his work. She marveled at how closely fit were the treads and how cleverly laid was the staircase wall. Bastien explained his design, describing how it was made to accommodate growth of the trunk up to a hundred years.

They ascended cautiously up the mossy and slick stone and found themselves, finally, on a firm fortified platform. The boy Bastien had rounded it with merlons and crenels. And the walls of his fort were made of stone—like a true tower. He must have engineered the weight carefully. Their roof comprised of the ancient foliage. Rain patted the outer leaves.

"I spent hours in this place," Bastien shared, thoughtfully caressing a crenel. "I dreamed of making my own castle someday. But in the meantime, I ruled from this one." The princess leaned on the wall beside him. "What a magical playground this must have been." He nodded. "Only God knows how much of my life I've spent here. I would camp out in the summer. Live on it for days. Even when I was older, I would come here to think."

"And what would you think, Prince Bastien?" She turned and faced him fully. He grinned to himself. *Just like a woman....* "Well, I would think about the mistakes I made in the construction. And I would think about life—hunting, war...God. The future. After Mother died, I thought of her." His eyes grew distant. "I fell once. Broke my arm...."

"You seem to have a knack for bone breaking," Casica offered playfully. "What?" "I hear that's how you and Clarece first met...." Bastien smiled unbelievingly. "She *remembers* that? She *told* you that?"

The slave's owner nodded. "Clarece remembers everything, I think, and tells a great story." The man rolled his eyes. "I can imagine she does. I hope she hasn't reflected too dim a view of me." Casica shook her head. "On the contrary. Clarece has made a fine mirror for you. She esteems you highly and speaks gratefully of being under your care." *Really?* his eyes asked. She smiled a reply.

"Well," he observed finally, "tis good to hear I do some things right." His words trailed into another thought. This one he needed to speak. He looked away from her. His sigh was audible. When he returned his attention, Bastien's eyes had welled with tears.

"Princess Casica," he began, "I have never properly acknowledged your inhuman treatment coming to my land." He choked on the words but not from pride. It was the memory of her broken and bleeding form that tightened his throat. Even now, after so many months, he couldn't believe what had happened to her, what his people did to this woman. He thought back quickly to the sensation at the funeral. Surely she meant his land nothing but good.

He gazed into the dark face. Tears crept down her cheeks. "I'm so very sorry, Casica. I had planned differently. But none of that matters. What matters is you. You were harmed in a most unjust, evil manner. On behalf of my people, I beg your forgiveness." He swallowed hard. "And in my own name, I beg your forgiveness. It was my place to protect you and I failed. My failure is inexcusable and irredeemable."

He glanced at a wet leaf. It seemed fresh in its hue. When he looked back at her, her gaze had not shifted. "I can't make right how you've been wronged," the man continued. "God knows, I've tried to find a way, but I can't. All I can do is ask. Will you forgive me? Can you give me another chance? I want us to begin anew, to start over. Do you think that's possible or...." His voice faded. It was shameful to weep before a woman.

Silently, the Cassican removed her glove. A dark hand spanned the silence. He took it into his own. Warmth flowed into him. The prince of Byzanthia would never know what it cost for her to speak these words. "Yes, I do. I forgive you," she said, decisively. "I forgive you and your people."

The statement was so very simple, yet it released between them, these ancient enemies, something that a thousand words could not convey. Creating, as it were, to span the channel formed so long ago by catastrophe, a bridge. Certainly, much more must transpire if ever the two peoples could unite; but forgiveness will not be denied. The offering of it releases from Heaven healings that flow so ecstatically, time alone can align earth in the path of its accomplished work. The Prince of Byzanthia bowed his head. It was as if she were a priest and had blessed him. "Thank you," he said, grateful. He looked again into her face.

A puddle had formed as they spoke, pooling in a waxy, curled leaf. It filled beyond containment and, as fate would have it, chose this moment to spill itself upon a clutch of leaves that in turn, showered their pools upon the couple, christening them with an icy baptism. They laughed in surprise and looked up together at the source. Still laughing they captured each other's eyes. Bastien shook his wet hair playfully upon the woman. He bowed officially.

"I am Bastien of Byzanthia, Prince, albeit the most lowly of princes, of Byzanthia. It is my pleasure to welcome you, Princess." She bowed in turn. "Thank you, great prince. I am Casica Elespoir, Princess, albeit the most displaced of princesses, of Cassica. Thank you for your splashing welcome." His grasp tightened and then released.

He glanced at the cold sky. "Shall we retire to more comfortable accommodations, Princess Casica?" So Bastien said, but in truth he thought how being in her presence was comfort enough. The princess nodded. "Would you join me for tea?" The man grinned; his answer was immediate. "Yes, my lady. I'd be honored to sit at your table." "The table you made...," she ventured. "Do you like it?" he asked, pleased she knew he had made it. "Indeed! Your handiwork precedes your person. What I'd like to know is how you placed windows into a stone wall?"

Finally! thought Bastien, something in which he could move confidently. "Well, twas a challenge," he began. "First I had to determine the structural supports from the foundation...."

They descended the mossy steps and, arm in arm, made their way to the palace. As she listened to his explanation outwardly, within Casica visualized priests adorned in white. *Amazing,* thought she, clearing a puddle in the path. Only God could author newness on a day such as this.

But the day had not finished with its surprises. For on Josquin's table awaited a much-anticipated arrival: a parcel of letters, tied with a satin cord, sealed with the crimson crest of Pelana, Queen of Cassica.

XXV

Sumer is icumen in. She knew it by the warming temperature in the pen and by the empty stalls at night. And from the fact she must first supply coal to Jasmine's mastra before procuring some for her own mistra. A pulled back muscle: first casualty of warming evenings. Everyone was affected, it seemed. Asla, with her, "It's to where an insulit can't even walk the passages with all you slaves rootin' round like so many gena in heat. Tripped over three couples two nights ago. Enough to make me blush...." And Raina with her heightened interest in the curious activity.

Just a week ago she and the little slave were taking bucket baths in the women's area. It was a beautifully bright day, warm enough to where bathing outdoors wasn't such a penance. The child was admiring her new bucket and soap as they washed and listened intently to her menta's explanation concerning the manufacture of the slippery substance. All at once, Raina interrupted.

"When will I get my woman's hair?" The chief slave blinked. For a moment, she hadn't a clue what it was the child asked; she glanced down at herself and understood. "Your woman's hair?" "Yes. When will I get mine?" Clarece soaped her foot thoughtfully. "Well, when you become a woman." The answer didn't satisfy.

"And when will that be, Menta?" The woman considered with her mind. "Well, let's see. You're what, five?" "Almost six...." "Six. Well...I would venture within five or six years." The child beamed. Time meant nothing to her, but certainly her first five years passed so quickly; the next should also. She would be a big slave then, able to do what the other slaves did at night, whatever it was that took them away from their stalls.

Clarece shared this story with her stallmate. They hadn't seen each other in some time and had much to relate. The story had Asla smiling as she massaged her senior's unmittened hands. Though Clarece no longer experienced pain, the two continued their ritual. To feel another's flesh was as pleasant to the maimed woman as observing the changes in her friend's hands was to the g'Helderleit. Clarece's hands and forearms were thickening (for lack of a better word), and tonight the little white growths in what would have been finger tips revealed their identity more fully. Asla shook her head.

"I tell you, Rece, that child frightens me. I fear she turns insulit. Notice how she's gone to cuffing her socks over her boots like me?" Clarece chuckled. "Who *hasn't* noticed? You're her hero, Asla. She wants to be like you."

"*That's* what I'm talking about," the blonde countered. "Tis not natural for a child to want to be a me. And I tell you something else, if she starts sporting an earring, I'm going straight to that Dolca woman: I can *not* handle the competition!" Clarece burst into laughter. Her friend was on a roll.

"And I tell you, tis worse," continued Asla. "Just the other day, we were reading that donkey story? Well out of the blue, it starts telling about this foal falling out of its mother's rear. You tell me, Rece. Who writes these books? Sailors? Who puts something like that in a child's story?" "The mare's giving birth, Asla. It's natural..."

"Natural for you! You grew up in a barn. But for Raina, she's spent her life in civilized settings—lap pets and sewing machines and such. What's she know about that? So she turns to me and says she thought babies came from belly buttons but is that where they come from, their mother's arses? And if they do, how do they get there in the first place? Now what kind of child asks questions like that?"

The chief slaveswoman wept with mirth. "A normal five-year-old," she managed, "and what on earth did you tell her?" "What'd I tell her? I told her what any decent insulit would tell her. I said that 'god' put babies in women and that they come out the same place he put them in, and if she had any further questions, she should refer them to her esteemed menta whose knowledge and experience in such matters *far* exceeds mine...."

Clarece still laughed with herself in memory as she performed her duties. The walk upstairs to her owner's chamber taxed her, laden as she was with a pail of coal. Warming days or not, the nights still required heat. It was gratefully the slave knelt before the brazier. She drew a sooty mitten across her brow. Coal was messy business. Her camisole was smudged with it. She must change before her mistra returned this evening. Clarece paused to catch her breath, rubbing her wrists together against the strain placed on them, considering as she did, those little white growths.

Her arms tingled with a familiar sensation. The startled woman glanced around the room for its source. She found it. There was her mistra, sitting on the floor by the windows in her camisole and bare feet, grinning mischievously. Between her expression and simply gathered hair, Casica looked positively girlish. And for a moment, Clarece concluded that in her own home, this must be more truly her owner's carriage.

"And what song is it you hum, chief slaveswoman?" Clarece hadn't realized she was humming. "A forgettable one, Mistra," she replied, rising to kneel beside her lady. "I thought your ladyship was out to the city with her prince this day."

"She was," Casica explained, placing the painter's knife in her mouth like a pipe. "But then so overcome by inspiration was she, she begged leave for an evening lavee´. Tis a perfect day to paint."

The slave glanced at what was painted. Casica had covered it with a cup. It must be small. "Tis a bright day, Mistra. You must be warm sitting in the sun. I can feel your heat from here." She voiced a question she'd often wondered. "How is it you get so warm and yet never sweat?"

The healer smiled. "I know I feel warm, but I don't feel warm. My shalonn keeps me at a pleasant temperature, like my cloak. I rarely truly sweat. If I do, it's because I'm experiencing extreme physical or emotional stress." "Even in summer?" the slave asked, amazed. Josquin nodded. "Yes. The stones cool in summer, warm in winter. If you ever need to cool yourself, chief woman, don the cloak."

Clarece considered her own weak, sweaty body. "It must be a joy to be josquin," she voiced aloud. "Tis," her owner answered, smiling. "Not that I've anything to compare it to, but I love being a healer." She offered a sideward glance. "You might try it someday." Clarece snorted in a kindly fashion. "I might," she teased, "if it weren't for the burning eyes. They're positively unnatural."

Of course, she argued within herself, this whole reality of healers and necklaces of glowing stone was unnatural. She studied the pobbles around her owner's throat. They looked heavy. "I would think being josquin is also burdensome." Again her mistra nodded. Her mind traveled many scenes, settling, finally, upon one that seemed so much more distant than it was. She was thirteen, standing before her parents' throne, surrounded by officials and dignitaries. The ancient vestments hung heavily upon her. She was sweating....

Her eyes softened as she gazed into the memory. "I remember when I was invested," she began. "It was such an incredible day, Clarece, the conclusion of a series of incredible days. The fasting... the vigil in the cathedral...the cleansing.... I was standing before my parents—fully vested. I had answered the throne's questions to everyone's satisfaction and been adorned with the mantles of my people. Baba stood to place the diadem upon me. Tis a simple gold band," she described with her hand, "ringed with the stones of Cassica. It isn't the true crown," she explained, "that's only for those coronated, but the diadem is its precursor. I'd never even touched it. I'd no right until that moment." Casica's eyes teared into a smile.

"I remember how startled I was at its weight. Baba grinned at my expression." She touched her cheeks. "I still see his dimples...." She closed her eyes, now, lost in the scene. "And then Maman, she stands and she looks into me. She's sad in her pride, and I understand why. She knows where this day will take me...so very far from one another." Casica wiped a tear. She then laughed lightly as her eyes opened to see more clearly her mother's.

"But suddenly Maman, she smiles and presents an alabaster vial. She breaks its neck and the room fills with frankincense. That's the fragrance of healers. Our eyes never part.... Maman anoints my crowned head, and I feel it, I feel the oil flow through my hair, feel it running down my cheeks. I'm drenched with its scent. And something in me rejoices." Clarece watched her lady intently. Casica breathed deeply. She could smell it. She looked to her friend.

"It was in that moment that something was released in me. You see, up until then, I'd been seeing myself as a victim. Doomed. Cursed by destiny to play this role I do. But in that moment," she smiled, "I didn't feel doomed: I felt chosen. God had chosen me for such a time as this and was providing healing in advance for whatever might happen."

Josquin focused on the cup. "I think my mother could sense what I was feeling. She whispers to me, 'The crown is sweet as it is heavy, M'Yat. You cannot bear the weight without drinking its sweetness. Remember.' And then she held my head in her hands and kissed me and the whole assembly cheers." She looked up and raised her hands.

"And then the bells of the cathedral peel to tell all that a successor has risen to the throne. And I get to run outside, finally, and present myself to the delight of all my people and spend the rest of the day celebrating. In all my life, I will never forget that day. I mustn't ever forget it." She swallowed and turned back to her companion. Clarece was lost in the scene. "That's something of what being a josquin is like," her owner was saying. "Sweet in its heaviness."

For a time the women were silent. One in memory, one in imagination. *What would it be like,* wondered the slave, *to be anointed with destiny? To know, truly know, one lived for such a time as one lived?* "And what is most burdensome?" Clarece asked finally. Casica's brows rose at the question.

"In Byzanthia? The isolation, the noise...." "Noise?" The dark head bobbed. Another healer would know exactly what she meant but to a non-healer...she struggled to explain. "Need—physical, spiritual, emotional feels to a healer like noise. We call it 'katala'; like holding a conversation near a brook. Tis distracting...disorienting. In Cassica, tis not so severe. There are other healers and with our combined presence, it lessens the effect." "And how many healers are there?" asked the slave. This was fascinating.

"I can't tell you," was the reply. Clarece glanced away, somewhat shamed. That information must be forbidden to a Byzanthian. It wasn't. "I mean I don't know," the josquin continued. "There are 216 of us shalonned but we know there are more healers who've not yet been identified." She grinned playfully. "Despite its minuscule geographical girth, Cassica's populace is quite scattered. We concentrate on identifying healers through family lines. We tend to branch from common blood."

The student nodded. Two hundred sixteen. She knew the effect of having a single healer in her midst. What would it be like to live in a place with scores? "And in your absence of fellow healers," she inquired, "how do you lessen katala here?" Casica snorted softly. "Not very well, I'm afraid. Wine is one way, my use of which I need to curtail considerably. Healing helps: the less need, the less noise. Prayer, meditation—that's the best thing... music, painting. They help refocus my attention."

Clarece studied her mistra's paints. "I could never be a painter," she mused. "I could never be a you." "And what would you like to be, Clarece?"

The slave fretted uncomfortably with her left mitten. It bore a fresh tear. She weighed answering the question before looking shyly at her mistra. Only two other people knew this.... "A harpist." Casica blinked. "A harpist?" A nod. "Yes. I've always admired the one in the library. Sometimes, at night? I dream I'm playing. I actually hear the music. And I've never even heard a harp." She blushed at her confession and tried to drape it in humor. "Asla says the harp represents something else I'd rather be playing."

Casica laughed. That sounded like an Aslatic interpretation. "*Asla...*," she said to herself and with the name, removed the cup. Clarece gasped. There, set in a leaf of a portrait locket was her sala's image. She stared in wonder. It was as if her mistra had captured Asla, somehow, and placed her in the ring.

"Mistra," Clarece breathed. "I'd no idea." She looked up at the smiling artist. "It was you. *You* painted the faces in your locket." Casica nodded. The slave frowned. "But I thought you were working on a self-portrait?" Her owner shrugged. "A lie to throw you off my scent. I've done only one true self-portrait, and it hangs safely from view at home. No," she lifted the leaf and studied it. "I thought Asla would like this. You see, your portrait will go in the next leaf. She can carry your friendship as she goes about her day alone." She smiled delightedly. "Look at the clasp. Bastien found one with a hawk attached." And he had. A silver bird graced the silver chain with flight. "I hope she likes it."

"You *hope*?" Clarece echoed. "Princess. You don't know what this will mean for her! Asla...she'll be overcome." She looked down again at the face. How could anyone capture such beauty? Even the eyes were perfect. A twinge of yearning rose in her heart. How she wished to have her friend's portrait. How she would enjoy such a gift, she wanted to say. But to want so much was unfitting, so she remained silent and, instead, shook her head, bowing. "I am amazed. You are indeed a gifted painter, Mistra, and thoughtful as you are gifted."

The healer took a deep breath. "Thank you, Clarece." She looked tentatively at her companion. "And tell me: when will you allow me assist you on your journey of thirty-one strings?"

Clarece's mood shifted visibly. She had known that, one day, her mistra would breach this topic and now it had come. She squinted, circling herself with resolve. "I've given this matter much thought, Mistra," she answered softly. She looked into the brown eyes. They were moist with the anticipated answer. "I have decided against pursuing the healing of my hands."

Casica released a sharp sigh, stunned. How could she possibly say that? How could anyone who dreamt of playing harp say that? "May I ask why?" she replied, careful to hide her attitude. "I know tis not a matter of trust or lack of desire. What keeps you from wholeness, Clarece?" The slave glanced back to Asla's portrait.

"God," she said simply. Casica frowned. She must have misunderstood. "God?" "Yes." "Whatever do you mean?"

The slave dropped her gaze into her hands. They seemed happy with themselves. From her hands she went to her boots. They were new, fashioned at her mistra's instruction with hooks in place of eyelets so that their wearer might lace and unlace them with greater ease. She glanced to the table where she enjoyed teas and silverware, to the sofa where she napped and read and held long conversations with a royal. She glanced now to the royal, herself, an owner who loved her as friend. She'd been given much. Too much. Tis the lifted head that's lost.

"God has given me so much, Mistra," she explained, "so much more than any slave should even imagine." She smiled at her leather. "I have no pain. Ever. I can feel. And Asla has noticed something she thinks are fingernails?" The healer nodded, sadly pleased. She had poured much of herself into the formation of so delicate a creation. She'd never made nails and now they had come...and for no purpose.

"He has given me so much," Clarece was saying, "that to ask more, to ask for healing...." She paused. "Tis unwise to ask for more than what one is allotted. God, He is the Mighty King. To want more might be to insult Him, to provoke His wrath." Something in her cringed. She knew much of wrath. She looked nervously to her claws. "He might erase all He's granted. Tis more pleasing to Him to be content and remain silent in wants." She looked again at the locket. "Tis better not to desire. Desire is dangerous." Such was her conclusion.

Clarece waited, hoping against experience her owner would leave her alone with the decision. Of course, she didn't. "I see," Casica said finally. "You fear that to want complete wholeness may be to appear demanding of God. And as a consequence, you would lose all you've gained?" The slave nodded. Perhaps she would be let off the hook after all. Casica brought her hand to her lips as was her custom.

"I think I understand your view, Clarece," (here it came) "but I must say, from the perspective of one who is the daughter of a king, I disagree. I've seen my father insulted, and as you say tis a fearsome thing. But I don't think I've ever witnessed him so much insulted as he was hurt in a matter concerning his adopted son." Clarece stared. What on earth was her mistra talking about? "Your father has an adopted *son*?"

"Yes," Casica replied, spinning the painter's blade in her fingers. "Seven, in fact. He and mother have twelve adopted children in all." Clarece was incredulous. "I don't understand."

The blade resumed its pipe imitation. "In Cassica, adoption is an ancient tradition. We believe tis unfitting for anyone to be without family. So people, rich and poor, take into their care orphans." "You mean orphaned children." Casica shook her head. "Not necessarily. Often they're adults who've lost parents." She took Clarece for a visit to her homeland. "You see, we have two kinds of adoption. The most common is the type of my parents' where the adoptive parents assume financial and social responsibility for nurturance of the adopted child." She nibbled thoughtfully on the brush.

"This man, my parents adopted years ago. Baba knew his father and was delighted to take the son into his care. A few days after the adoption ceremony, Baba called Elien to his throne room and asked, 'Elien. You're now my son. What may I give you this day?' I was playing jacks on the floor so I saw everything. Elien, he bows his head and says, 'Nothing, great king. You've given me more than I can ask with your care.'

"Baba kept pressing him. He knew Elien needed employment and had determined to give him part of an estate. But Elien continued to avoid father's request. At first I thought it seemed humble, Elien's response. But eventually, I saw its effect on Baba. Father wasn't feeling honored by his son's refusal; he was hurt. Here he loved this man so much he adopted him, and now that he offered him generosity, Elien refused. He wasn't acting like a son; he wasn't even acting like a beloved subject before a kind king. He was acting like a man too frightened or too proud to receive what his sovereign wished. It hurt Baba, greatly. Elien was his child, and yet, he wouldn't acknowledge his need to the one who could provide for it. Who knew it. Who reveled in anticipation of meeting it."

She looked at her friend. "The Book says God knows our desires before we ask and rejoices in giving good things to His children. You acknowledge His good gifts to you and in doing so, you give Him glory. Why would He wish to stop?" "He stops to make us more pleasing to Him," Clarece countered. "Lack develops character." Casica caressed her shalonn.

"So I've been taught, but I don't think it. Some people believe that it's godly to rid the heart of longing. I disagree. Twould be like wishing the eye free of vision. *God* made us to desire. Even *He* desires...deeply. A life void of desire isn't godly; tis sickly." This last she said to herself, an image of Bastien prompting her. She turned to her friend, hesitant to press but convicted to speak truth.

"Clarece, you want more in life for a reason. It is God who's awakening your heart and when you desire, *that* pleases Him. Tis not demanding. To come to a king with hope and longing honors him; it acknowledges that he's good and generous and powerful." She nodded to herself. "Tis a great compliment to a sovereign, the asking and expecting of great things. We only ask great things of ones we deem great."

The slave looked, again, to the portrait and then to her hands. She didn't know what to say. Truly. The thought of approaching a sovereign with any request, much less a great one, was utterly foreign to her. She'd spent her life avoiding Ars, her sovereign, and look at what had happened at that encounter. She must ponder this matter and said as much. "I will think on what you've said, Mistra," she ventured. It was time to turn the topic. "But may I know, what is the other type of adoption?" Casica laughed lightly. *Elusive as water in fingers of sand....*

The healer stretched her legs and wiggled her long, dark toes. "The other adoption is extremely rare. I can't render the word for it in Byzanthian except 'adoption,' but it is much more profound. In this adoption, the 'parents' approach the orphan and offer *themselves* as the inheritance. Tis not a matter of only supporting the individual; it involves that person's becoming one with the parents as though they were literally born into the family." She studied Clarece. The teacher was absorbing this information.

"Tis a fascinating process. The parents offer themselves and if the person agrees, they respond with a simple statement of acceptance. And that's all they do. Nothing more. The parents do everything else. A covenant is prepared and in it all responsibility, all the work of adoption is assumed, solely, by the adoptive parents. A report is made of any outstanding debts against the adopted party. These debts must be cleared or paid fully by the parents before the adoption is finalized. It's an incredible contract. Completely one-sided: the adoptive child doesn't even sign it, only the adopting parents do." Clarece shook her head in amazement. Who would have conceived such a concept? Her mistra was continuing.

"Now the adoption ceremony is something to behold. Tis glorious. I've only witnessed one. The morning of, the future parents and child meet at the cathedral. The cathedral has a special bath room designated for this ceremony. There the adoptive child is bathed by either a member or representative of the adoptive family. The bathing signifies a washing away of the child's former life and cleansing of any outstanding debt. After the bath, the child is attired in clothing of the family and presented to the congregation. Prayers are offered on behalf of the new family, the way you would pray at a christening. A public charge is given to the parents and their covenant sealed." Casica paused, remembering the upcoming scene. Her eyes glistened with its beauty.

"And then...," she smiled, "then a beautiful thing is done. The *parents* christen their son or daughter. Tis a symbol of rebirth into their lives. From that point on, there's no distinction between the adoptive child and one born of flesh. No one ever refers to them as adopted. They are called 'son' and 'daughter' because that's who they are. The day ends with a great party where the new child receives gifts—birthday gifts—and everyone eats and dances the night away. We do alot of dancing and eating in Cassica."

The princess sat, lost in happy thoughts. Beside her, the chief slaveswoman sat, perplexed, wondering within herself who in their right mind would *ever* enter into such a one-sided covenant. Such "parents" must be mad with love for the desired child. A warm voice interrupted her thoughts.

"So...Clarece, you deny my offer to help." She sounded content with her friend's decision. "May I assume it's acceptable with you if I continue praying for your healing?" The slave glanced up. "Why would you pray for healing, Mistra? Tis you who heal." The brown head disagreed. "No, tis not. I don't heal." She motioned to the curtains. The sun was not so intense. "It's like in the morning. You draw back the shade, but the sun lights the room. I only pull back the curtain, Clarece. Tis God who's been healing you."

The slave looked down, embarrassed. She knew of no one who truly prayed for her. Asla would, but she couldn't. "You pray for me?" she asked, shyly. "Yes." Clarece fretted with her mittens. "What...what do you pray for?" The healer's voice filled with tenderness. "Well, I pray for your healing. For your safety. Your freedom...." The blue eyes teared. Freedom. "You pray for the impossible," Clarece whispered. "Why pray for anything else?" Casica replied. "And...and I pray for your adoption. For you to accept God's offer to draw you into His family."

Something within the slave burst. She was slave and every slave was an orphan. How often had she, as every slave, longed to be fathered and mothered. To be familied. "How does one do that?" Clarece wept. "Only receive," Casica answered tenderly. "Only respond to God, 'yes,' and rest in His having done all the work, paid all your debt."

Cleansing. Adoption. Receiving. Rest. Massive, alien concepts to Clarece's slavish heart. She struggled to contain them, but could not. And how could she? *They* are the containers. Clarece rested her mouth against the comforting familiarity of leather and gazed upon the portrait in silver. Here she was wanting a portrait locket, yet fearful of asking for hands to open it. What a mess she was.... She looked deep into herself. Could God truly know the desires of her heart? Could He want someone as soulishly maimed as she for His daughter? It was too much, too much to resolve now.

A movement distracted her. Casica reached to her right. "For you," she said, presenting something covered with a blue scarf. "I thought you'd prefer yours framed." The maimed woman left her confusion and shyly wiped her nose on a mitten. Somewhat suspicious, she received the gift. She uncovered it with a gasp.

In all the world, there is nothing so beautiful as people who love. Before her was captured a moment of such beauty. There, framed in burled cherry, was herself and Asla. The two of them glanced at each other with expressions immediately recognized, smiling at one another with some joy freshly shared. It was last night she was seeing.

The slave wept openly. Never in her life could she have hoped for such a treasure. Yet here it was, a desire taken straight from her heart. She looked from the face she knew so well to the one she knew not at all. Could her countenance, truly, be that pleasant? She wondered. The eyes with their blue intensity; a noble brow; the mouth, tentatively revealing its owner's thoughts, and the silver about her throat, looking more a necklace than a sign of bondage.

She could bear no more. The woman closed her eyes against the loveliness, her own, and embraced the gift to her heart.

XXVI

Their laughter filled the narrow stairway. "Now be careful!" he instructed, holding tightly her hand. It was warm to his touch. "'Be careful?' How can I be careful with my eyes closed?" "Well, you just have to carefully trust me. I can't see where we're going, and if I can't, neither can you...."

Josquin laughed again, relishing the queer sensation of ascending a circular path in total darkness. The corridor was damp and cool with stone; even with her lack of vision, she could sense the proximity of the walls to their persons. Occasionally, she'd pass an arrow loop, she knew, from the drafts of cool air escaping the openings in the tower. Her boot slipped on a chipped step; he caught her.

"Careful, Cassican!" he teased. "Tis a long roll down." "Yes. Well, one of us will fare better than the other, Byzanthian, should I fall and take you with me!" He grinned. What he enjoyed more, the play or the excuse to touch her for so long, he wasn't certain. He surprised himself with a thud. "Blast! I always do that," Bastien muttered. He reached up, felt for the trap door and strained against the rusty hinges. They gave. "Mission accomplished!" he announced.

He reached down from the tower and pulled her up. Blue eyes burned into the night. They were smiling. "Well, what do you think, Princess?" he asked, careful to close the door behind them. Casica made her way to the crenelated wall. She leaned into one of the crenels and breathed of the night air. "It's lovely, Bastien." And it was. Below them bobbed lights of the palace grounds, torches of guards moving along their watch. Beyond these were the lights of the night market and the city itself. An endless fleet of light sailed the night sky and reflected in the castle moat. Casica glanced from sky to water and smiled; it wasn't difficult to imagine herself suspended in the universe.

His warmth moved beside her. "I love this view," he said softly. "So many times, I come here to refresh my mind. There's nothing like seeing things from above to right a low perspective." She nodded in agreement. He could just see her silhouette against the darkness. Strange, how her eyes glowed without casting light.

"Walk down a ways," the man invited. He counted the merlons and stopped at three. Here, he reached to his left. "Feel this." Casica lay her hand where he led. The left side of the opening had been carved into a smooth curve. "It makes a pleasant chair," Bastien invited, "if you're not afraid."

"Afraid of what?" she asked, jumping too easily onto the wall. She stood and raised her hands to the sky. Someday, Josquin thought, she would fly; but until then...she spun and dropped into the curve. "Aren't you afraid of falling?" Bastien asked. Casica shook her head. "No." "Because you're a healer? The fall wouldn't kill you?" The young woman looked down. She estimated the height. "The fall? No. The *landing* on the other hand...." "Oh...," he groaned, "that hurt." "Sorry. I couldn't resist. But seriously, if I landed on my feet. I'd likely survive. I just might wish I hadn't."

Bastien hopped to the ledge beside her. "How did this resting place come to be?" she asked. "Some bored boy spent a summer chiseling it out. The guards learned quickly enough to stay clear below." Her laugher met him. "I can imagine a bored lad doing that. He must have been tenacious, though. This would make a daunting task." Bastien felt the rough stone. "It was. But it was something to do, and he enjoyed the results." She grinned. "So do I. I thank him."

Bastien looked fully at her face. Somehow it didn't feel like staring. She was blinking at the breeze. It made for a playful effect on her eyes. "What are you looking at?" she asked, knowing very well what it was he looked at. "Your eyes...they're fascinating." Casica shook her head. "Well, then you must be the only person in this land who feels that way. Mostly people fear them. Clarece is, only now, not telling me how 'positively unnatural' they are."

"Well," Bastien thought aloud, "I guess they don't bother me since I was expecting them. I guess that's the difference." His companion blinked, again, but in surprise. "How's that?"

Bastien scraped his heel against stone. The image of his informer warmed him with a sad smile. "My mother told me about your eyes. She was telling me about your mother's eyes and said that yours would be the same...."

"Wait," Casica interrupted. "My *mother's* eyes? You make it sound as though they've met." It was his turn for surprise. "They *have.* You mean you didn't know?" Blue orbs narrowed. "What are you saying, Bastien?" the princess asked suspiciously.

Bastien was somewhat suspicious, himself. Surely this wasn't news for her. "When Mother heard of Pelana's betrothal to King K'eran, she requested a meeting with her," he explained. "They met in Cassica someplace, completely beyond the knowledge of my father, of course—at least that's what she told me. She made me swear secrecy."

The dark woman brushed aside a strand of loose hair. She scanned her memory, frantically, but knew the result. Her mother had never mentioned anything of this to her. She felt suddenly alone. "I didn't know any of this," she voiced, bringing her fingers to her mouth. "Why on earth would our mothers have met?" Bastien sensed her anxiety and rushed to comfort it.

"For a good reason. Mother said she wanted to congratulate Pelana, but mostly they talked about The Edict." He paused, choosing his words carefully. "She told me they made a pact; that if by some fate you and I came to be, well, they agreed to ready us as best they could to help us make...," he glanced away, "the most of it. I've assumed you knew."

Casica's fingers migrated to her shalonn. She did know. She did know her mother had spent her life encouraging her daughter about The Edict and the prince it would join her to. She did know that Maman spoke highly of the boy Bastien and of his family. She did know Pelana hoped for God's goodness to intervene in something man intended for evil. But she didn't know this. Didn't know of her mother's action. She must have been very young, Josquin reasoned, and something in her wondered if her father knew. Something greater wondered what *other* secrets had been withheld from her. When she spoke, her voice was tinged with hurt.

"I can't believe your mother would tell you this, Bastien. And not mine." "Well," he speculated gently, "it *was* a secret meeting. And my mother didn't tell me of it until." He paused. "Until secrets no longer mattered."

Until secrets no longer mattered.... Casica's indignation quieted. At least her mother still lived to honor vows. "What courage Clarece must have had," she observed finally. "And what a great love for you—even before your birth...to have been acting on your behalf." Bastien nodded to the compliment. His mother was the brightest sun in his memory.

"She *was* courageous. I wish you could have met her. She and my father—people say they loved each other once...but I guess...I don't know. Something happened." His mind traveled many scenes. "They lived a distant life. But for me...she was always there." He took a deep breath. "Mother made me feel I could do anything. She always told me she never doubted I could 'make the leap.'"

Casica smiled at the reference to the knighthood ceremony when a newly-knighted man would leap, fully armored, to his high horse. "She said I could leap anything life would ever bring me," Bastien continued. He sniffed away a tear. Strangely, he didn't feel embarrassed. "Mother had great hopes for me."

Silently, the princess leaned towards him. "Then she left you a great legacy, Bastien," she offered softly. "Hope is its own courage. It beckons us into the future." Clarece's son considered the words. *I wonder if you have hope about us,* he asked in silence. He had failed so miserably at their meeting; had fallen so disgracefully, and his failure had almost killed her. Even now it eluded the prince, how his plans had been thwarted. And he wondered, also, if she ever would trust him again.

A warm energy surged through him. He glanced down, startled, at the source. Her hand lay gently on his arm. He looked from it to her eyes. They seemed to burn away his doubt.

XXVII

She expelled a long, satisfied breath, pleased with what she beheld. The colored stones were coming together finally, appearing on the board as they did in her thoughts. Something of the game's geometrical workings fit snugly the pieces of her mind. Like puzzles. She'd always excelled at them, as she did chess, though only one person in the kingdom knew that, the one who challenged her on a monthly basis; their kingdoms fell with mutual frequency.

She placed another stone and scooped up five. Her opponent snorted but not unkindly. It wasn't her play he studied most this day; it was she. The delicate fleta'i streamed into a delta of silk rivaling even her silver collar for brilliance. He wanted to touch her, wanted to wade into that river and explore the region beneath. But he could not. He was of the Order and kept its rigors in a most austere manner. With her he could test his resolve fully. Look all you wish; but never, never touch the Forbidden One. It was a strange contest he held with himself.

Asla stretched, relaxing into her chair. She sighed. It would take many moments for him to move. They would play, for another two hours, this peculiar game of his. She glanced past the man towards his open window and breathed again of pleasure. The fresh air mingled with his incenses and lulled her into a sleepless dream.

The night was still as death and strangely chilled. She watched warily about her as she washed, her dagger to the left of her right foot, alert. She hated this part of the city, feared to pause in it at all, but loathed more the completed service. Moonlight filled the bucket and flooded the alley. A fence, one she could scale easily, served as an escape in front. For the moment, this was the safest place to wash.

She reached under her blue cape and took from her insulit's bag a piece of bark. She bit of it and chewed then, cautiously, cupped her hands to the water. She drank and gargled deeply, trying best she could to cleanse herself of his presence. She spit him out and repeated the ritual. Next from her bag she took her mouth stick and brushed her teeth all about. The cathedral sounded two. Two hours before the lieutenant.

She jumped, startled. Only a rat. How easily she blended into his realm, she thought, smiling wanly. Two hours. Time enough to drink and forget at The Stone.

Casica paced her chamber, restless. The shalonn burned fiercely though she hadn't a clue why. It could be release. She hadn't released in so very long. But it seemed something more, something she couldn't quite arrest. She sought the ones she knew. Bastien was absent from his chamber. It was Hultsday and on this night, the fifth prince shared the late watch with his guard. Her heart went below. Clarece slept in her cot. Asla was absent. Raina slept, also, but several other slavewomen were missing.

Her shalonn swept the palace. People scattered everywhere; she passed over certain of them, blushing, and went directly to Ars' chamber. The king was present but awake. He rarely slept, she was learning; she brought upon him a particular movement of will. Soon, his wakefulness dissolved. He would be of clearer mind for the council meeting tomorrow. Meeting. For some reason, a lord's queer invitation brushed her attention.

But they were all here, all well. No sickness stalked the walls of Byzanthia but still.... Casica shook her head. Something was amiss. Something festered in the palace that had nothing to do with disease of the body. The woman kneeled in her place of prayer by the chamber table. If the light shone under the sliding door, Bastien was not in his room to see it. She bowed and breathed, willing her shalonn to do what already it wished.

In time, it burned with a pure white light that seeped into her being and radiated from her flesh. The small chamber exploded with a brilliance that disappeared in its race through the palace. It met resistance and conquered. The unsettling force fled but only for the time. It would regroup. It was brewing. It was summer and all was restless....

"Asla—my goddess! Is it tonight you will kiss me?!" Asla grinned from her seat on the bar. The inn's owner was making frequent withdrawals from his liquid treasury again. Barn positively gushed with exaggerated lover's zeal. He propped his face in his hands and gazed hopelessly.

"Not this night, good Barn," she laughed, running her hand through his oily hair. "But I swear to you, some night, before I...."

"Don't speak it!" he objected. "Tis I who will die with want of your divine lips. Here. At least caress them upon my cup." She obliged heartily. Ironic, how he saved his best drink for the nightly crew. "To Barn!" she toasted. "Patron saint of night laborers!" Cheers rose happily to hers. She smiled at her sister whores. Their day was almost spent.

Helderlesce was smiling as she wend her way to the cathedral. It was a good sleep she'd had last night, the kind enjoyed by her sort. Hearth and heart were content; children and husband healthy and filled. The tune she hummed joined in chorus with the tower bells, their peals greeting morning and parishioner with the knowledge that, yes, it is good to go into the house of the Lord. She had much for which to thank Him. Her hand went tenderly to her belly. And more to come! Her smile only broadened at the sight of a figure ahead.

She hadn't seen her in weeks, but there she was, standing at her usual spot outside the fence, a cat brushing her legs and, as always, the deep hood hiding the unknown face. She must be returned from her trip.

"Morning to you!" Helderlesce wished. "And upon you!" the woman returned, bowing graciously. "And how was your journey?" "Well," the hood nodded, "though tis good to be home. And your family?" "We are blessed," the mother replied. "Very much, indeed. Tolase is completely recovered—as you said she would be. That very night after we spoke? She improved. And the babe is still in my womb. I begin to believe you," she ended softly, "that this one will stay." "He will," the hidden voice encouraged. "You'll see. A good power is at work."

The chimes sounded. The hood glanced towards them. "So...," Helderlesce hastened, for the caped one was restless. "For whom do I light a candle this day? The usual?" "Yes. And if you would, light another for a woman, Dolca, in repayment of a great kindness done."

Helderlesce studied the hand that now offered the candle price. It bore neither rings nor jewelry but was uniquely adorned in flesh of bronze. As always, the caped one was generous. Her family would have meat tonight. She bowed to the gift. "I will do as you wish, but tell me, great lady, when will you give me your name to present to God?"

The hood shook, somber. "As I've said...." "You're joined to an infidel: 'to speak your name would be to erase the others'," her companion quoted. "I do not believe it. And I pray for you anyway, name or no." The hood laughed. "You are kind, Helderlesce. Don't forget to mention yourself. Goodness to your family and to you!"

The mother nodded. The woman would not linger, she knew. Helderlesce watched as the secret worshiper rounded the wall, blue cloak dancing, two dogs racing to join her.

Dolca glanced from her work, uncertain of what she'd heard. It came again. A knock, light and tentative. She rose from her sewing and met the door. "Asla!" The insulit bowed, shyly. The parcel under her arm explained her presence. "I bring your cloth, Countess." "I see. Please, come in." The blonde hesitated but entered. "I thank you for getting this so quickly," Dolca was saying. She led the woman to her table and took the offered package. "I could never have matched the color...."

"The vendor says he's an unlimited supply, should you need more. And offered a good price," Asla explained, placing a handful of change on the table. "He's anxious for your business, I think." Dolca glanced at the money. *More likely he's anxious for yours,* she thought wryly. But she was pleased; the cloth the insulit chose was perfect in shade and texture. "'Twill make for fine vests, Asla. You've a good eye."

With her observation, Dolca became excruciatingly aware of the whore, and from a side-glance, studied her. Not only was the woman's eye good, but so were her mouth and throat, her face, her body. Asla stood not closely but closely enough for Dolca to smell her fragrance. Sage. In a flash Dolca saw Nahalt. He was the king's man. The insulit serviced them all. The woman cringed at her imaginations.

Dolca clothed her panic with activity and lifted the cloth from the table. To her surprise, another bolt hid beneath. *What's this?* she thought. The whore was smiling to herself. "This is from me," she was saying. "I thought it might fashion a livery vest." Asla unfolded the piece. A small golden horse was woven into it. She caressed the creature. "The weaver said he placed it so that it would prance between Raina's shoulders.... Did he do so correctly?"

Dolca found herself. "Yes...yes, quite." She handled the green velvet. It was exquisite. "But this is a costly fabric, Asla. Let me reimburse you." An unruly strand of hair, disobedient from the day it grew, fell to the insulit's face. She brushed it back with a smile and, in that instant, looked the child she was. "No," Asla objected softly. "Investment is a slave's greatest day. This is my gift."

She glanced into Dolca's eyes with her reply and, at once, saw it. That familiar look of suspicion. She felt it from so many women, women who stared through her back as she passed, cursing her for all they imagined she did. She's wondering, Asla knew, the countess. Wondering if the woman who stood near her knew her husband as she. The girl looked away, shamed.

"Well, at least let me dash you for your service." Dolca bit her lip. "Errand." The blonde's smile had long dissolved. "No," Asla said softly. "Keep it. You might use it to dash Raina someday. It will make her feel a big slave." She stepped back and scanned the room. "Where is the scamp, anyway?" Dolca lowered the cloth. "Come."

She led Asla to her sewing hearth. On a pallet, lay the child nestled in a colorful quilt. Beside her were neatly placed an empty bowl and cup. She slept soundly. "I see why she grows so quickly," Asla whispered. "All the pen marvels at her transformation." "Well," Dolca smiled, "everyone should be allowed transformation."

The women returned to the table, awkward and silent. "I should go," Asla offered, *and should never have come*. "Good day, Countess." "Thank you, Asla," Dolca answered, chiding herself. She watched the insulit turn to make a graceful retreat then looked, fully again, at the exquisite cloth. Her vision blurred with moisture.

Asla took several steps and stopped. She spun silently. "Dolca." The royal looked up, surprised. Their eyes met. "Three of the king's men have never had me. Your husband? Is one of them." The insulit paused only a moment. She turned and removed herself from the room.

Nahalt's wife dropped her head and wept.

XXVIII

Asla lay perfectly still. It didn't matter that her neck ached or that her nose itched. She lay perfectly still. For to move might stir him and to stir him meant continued suffering. She lay on her right as she stared into darkness, keenly aware of his grasp on her hair. She hated this man, detested him but not nearly with the vengeance he did her. And not only her. Asla blinked slowly. Every man hated whores to some degree as they hated themselves to another. But this man ruled his own hell and treasured dragging her through it. He hated beauty and sought in every way to stain it. She was the most beautiful of women and therefore the most tortured.

The insulit knew his kind. His kind lived with a perverse code of honor. A righteous perversity that allowed no overt violence but chose instead as its weapon, humiliation. Degradation executed his judgments concerning the nature of woman. To a man like him, woman was a dangerous, weaker enemy that threatened to consume. But she was nothing, and it was his duty to convince her of that. Or more truly, to convince himself. He gloried in drowning her in his depravity, and all the while, wore white gloves for the task.... The insulit serviced all manner of men. Three would she have erased from her life forever. He was the first on this list.

She dared not sleep, for in slumber she might move and waken him; so she lay perfectly still and thought. She thought about the next chess move she should make with Baron Parcelat. She thought about her visit with Dolca and wondered what the countess did at this time. She thought about Clarece and silently scolded her friend for not reaching for handedness. Her mind wandered finally to the strange interlude with Casica two nights before. She had sought and found the princess in the library, playing soft melodies in the darkness. It was summer and all were restless.

Casica hadn't heard the woman enter through the windows but she felt her presence soon enough. Blue eyes turned expectantly. "Asla," she greeted, surprised. "What on earth are you doing here?" She considered the height of the chamber. "*How* on earth did you get here?" "I come in through the windows...." Casica glanced towards them. "Aren't they locked?" The insulit shrugged. "What of locks?" Casica persisted. "But there are no trees nearby...how do you gain this level?" "I climb the walls," Asla offered, settling on the bench beside the Cassican. The healer shook her head. "I would say something about the dangers of falling, but you don't seem the falling type."

The insulit dodged the dark woman. "On the contrary, Casica. I'm the final word in fallen-ness." She looked towards a distant memory. "When I was young and being trained, I fell once from a cliff at the ocean. Seventy cubits up. I was scared skinless but after my initial terror, I found the whole experience quite exhilarating. Fortunately, I sliced the water clean." She brushed the keys soundlessly. "They say the dark one fell from heaven. The landing must have stung but, oh! what a thrill....“ She was smiling to herself, and Casica wondered for the thousandth time what sort of spirits lodged themselves in Asla's past. The g'Helderleit startled her with a question.

"And why on earth are you awake this hour of night, Your Highness?" Casica brushed the keys herself. "I couldn't sleep...." "Because of your chambermate?" the blonde teased. "Only in dreams," Casica bantered. "No. There's something brewing in the palace, something seething. I can't place my shalonn on it." Asla studied the glowing stones. "Tis summer, Casica. Lot's going on in the palace. Best stay clear of the slave passages whatever you do. There are sights enough to make my fleta'i curl."

The healer frowned, somewhat afraid to ask. "All right," she capitulated, "I'll bite. What exactly *is* a fleta'i?" Asla laughed her answer. "Tis hair g'Helderleit women grow on our chest when we reach our time. 'Want to see?" A hand objected quickly. "Thank you—no."

The insulit grinned. Even in the darkness she knew the princess blushed. This was fun. "We've another," she continued. "It grows in the small of our back but that's only after we give birth." Curiosity won out. "What do women who don't have children grow?" Josquin inquired. Asla shrugged. "Bitter, mostly...."

The princess shook her head. She was about to comment when suddenly, her friend ran her fingers over the keyboard. She played a short arpeggio and ended in a pleasing chord. "Since when did you play?" Casica asked incredulous. "Since forever," Asla replied. "Insulit are a multi-faceted instrument. Entertainment is our forte." The princess laughed, delighted. "Will you never cease to amaze, mighty g'Helderleit?"

"Most certainly, Casica," came the whispered reply. Asla caressed the ivory. "I won't live out this year." Casica gaped. "What do you mean, Asla?" The insulit glanced around herself and shrugged. "Edsner begins to hate me," she explained. "Every handler hates his insulit eventually." Her eyes glanced towards her companion's.

"At first, they are the master. They control our life but then... then it is we who rule. One day they look around and see that all they have comes through what once they mastered, and at that moment they realize they've become the slave. They can't live without us, and they despise us for it. Edsner walks this path." Casica looked worriedly at the young woman. "What makes you think this?" The whore looked away. "He begins to torment me. The other day, he took the pipes to me." "What pipes?"

Again Asla glanced around. "Insulit, we are an unruly order. Our creators make different ways to control us, like using a whistle to control a dog. Mine used pipes. Just metal pipes that are struck together. Tis my leash." She thumbed her palm. "I'm obedient to Edsner—mostly. He only used them to hurt me." Her voice trailed away. She didn't want to show her fear; she didn't have to. Josquin could feel it. "Edsner, he's...he's too royal to kill me himself. It's only a matter of time before he gives me a bad lay or calls a henta or something."

A familiar warmth spread comfortingly to her arm and did, instantly, what it was Asla had sought out the healer to do for her. The ache in her shoulder ceased. "What's a henta?" The girl's voice was all but inaudible. "A hunter. They're used to cull insulit," she breathed. "They're our nightmare. They hunt the souless and send us away."

The touch increased in warmth as did the necklace of light grow in intensity. *Dear God,* Casica was thinking, *this can't be true. Is there* nothing *I can do?* She couldn't know that listening was, in itself, an act of divinity.

Asla turned to her and confided. "I used to have a soul, Casica," she wept. "I can remember it. When I was small? I used to lay in the sand of g'Helderlend and look up into the sky." She smiled. "Light would fill me. I would be filled with light and the darkness...it couldn't contain me. Sometimes, when I dance? I feel the light, but I daren't look upon it or it'll come, the darkness will come and snuff me out." She intoned to herself. "But I remember. I remember what it's like having a soul. Until they came and took it away...."

A surge of rage crashed upon the healer. It washed over her and beyond. *Truth,* she reminded herself. She must live truth. She must reveal it. Her shalonn burned in agreement. "Asla...." The girl's haunted eyes met hers. "They never took your soul. No one can take your soul. Tis in God's keeping." "They did," Asla objected, "...he did."

All pretense collapsed. Asla sobbed. It was hopeless. All was hopeless. She wanted so much to live. She hadn't truly, before the healer had come. Desire for life was stripped away with the soul; but in the person of Casica was Asla exposed again to light, as on the shores of g'Helderlend. Like the child then, she craved the very thing forbidden insulit: life. But it would never be. Too far had she strayed from the ocean; a lake of fire was all that remained for her. "I am so lonely, Casica," Asla confessed. She lowered her head and groaned. Another's groan joined her. Josquin's soul was torn. *Please,* she prayed silently, *let me do this for her.*

"Asla...." The woman looked up, shamed for sharing her deformed heart. "Here," Casica whispered, "I *can* do something." She reached out her right hand and lay it gently to the g'Helderleit's chest. Asla closed her eyes to the familiar sensation. Suddenly, something changed.

Asla's eyes jerked open. She looked into the burning blue of Casica's gaze. But Casica wasn't seeing her. It was something else the healer saw. Something so glorious it would blind her. So she closed her eyes as she summoned it. Summoned it as one does always the holy: fearfully. The room began to lighten, illumined, but not by the stones that glowed with joy.

Asla gasped, fearful. Then fear surrendered to something else. Someone else. She looked away inside and then to Casica. The healer's eyes glowed. She was smiling.

"You feel it, Asla?" she asked. "You feel it? That's not me...it's you. Tis your spirit." Asla looked down to find the light's source. A person's spirit is larger than its vessel. For this instant, a veil was opened and through it, Asla could see what the healer sensed always. Asla breathed as though to inhale the light; something within her brimmed to explode. The healer could not contain it. She released and the room burst into darkness.

But like a note, the sensation lingered.

For a long time there was silence. Asla turned, stunned, to her companion. Her expression asked all. "You see, Asla," Casica whispered, "you *do* have a soul. It's not missing." "Then why," Asla breathed, "why...."

"Are you so empty? Tis *you* that's missing, Asla. God is always present but you aren't. You live beside yourself. And you must," Casica quickly added, "for now. Tis the only way you can survive this madness you live. But the day is coming when it'll be safe to return." Casica's smile saddened. "The journey will be rather rough, I think. But you *will* come home, Asla. Life will quiet around you and you'll hear yourself. God's working on your behalf to make this so. And when you do return, He'll be waiting...."

A tear now crept across her nose. The pillow was wet with the memory. The young woman awakened as from a dream. Sun. The sun had come in her absence and now lit her face.

He was waiting.

So now her hell was almost ended. All that remained for was for her to tie his boots, but it was a struggle. His free foot pushed at her face in a frustrating game. He loved it. He could sense her frustration and hoped she'd strike, but she wouldn't. She knew this game and how to win it. Her shirt hung open so he could gaze upon her. He would enjoy every minute of his money. The man smirked. And the best was yet to come. That is if his guest were the punctual sort. He leaned back into his chair.

There was a knock at the door. Asla heard and understood. It wasn't uncommon, his inviting a spectator to enjoy this sport. His servant was speaking. The guest approached. Asla gritted her teeth against his latest kick. The steps behind her stilled. In mock surprise, the man jumped to his feet.

"Princess Casica...." With a jolt, Asla spun and in one horrified glance saw the healer see her. "Kneel whore!" the man ordered, but he needn't. Already, Asla had collapsed with her head to the floor, frantically buttoning her blouse. Blood flooded her face. For Casica to know what she was, was one thing. To witness it, another.

"Forgive me, Your Highness," he was saying, kneeling. "I'd meant to have this removed by now. A man's oversight...." He waited, anticipating. Surely the Cassican wench was mortified. Outraged and shamed. Surely he had outdone himself by outdoing them both. He expected reaction. He was terribly disappointed.

Certainly, Casica realized she'd been lured into a trap. And as incensed as she was at her and her friend's humiliation, she wished to retaliate with more than words. But she realized also who this man was. For while she never gave names, Asla had begun telling stories. Some games Casica could play as well as anyone. So when she spoke, her voice betrayed nothing but bored distraction.

"Rise please, sir!" the princess announced, "And a good morning to you." She examined a glass decanter at his drink table. "May I?" The man gaped as Casica poured herself a drink. She deposited herself in the chair opposite him. He still stared when another voice spoke beside him. "Are you done with me?" He glanced down. "What?" "Are you done with me?" Asla repeated, cringing. Her service grasped desperately for the upper hand.

"Of course, whore," he sneered. He reached into his vest and produced a coin. "You've the mind of a rabbit, insulit, but you're the best lay in the kingdom—let no one say otherwise." He held the coin to her. Asla hesitated. She would see it; the pure woman would see her receive her whore's due. The hand trembled as she offered her palm. He dropped the coin, disdaining to touch her now that her rent had expired.

Asla stood to escape Casica's sight. A tender voice paused her flight. "He's an ass, Asla," she spoke in g'Helderleicht. "An ass."

The alpine eyes remained riveted to the floor. "Will you be at tea?" Asla bit her lip. "No. I've a service to attend," she lied. Casica nodded. "Then I'll miss you," she said kindly. "Tomorrow, perhaps?" "Perhaps." Casica set her free.

Outside the insulit leaned against the cool wall. Her mind raced as quickly as her heart. The coin was sweaty in her palm. She looked at the bronze and with a silenced scream, cast it brutally down the hall. It bounced with a metallic echo. The woman ran into the nearest slave passage and in its darkness fell to her knees and sobbed.

The man didn't understand. The Cassican spoke with the insulit. And in her own tongue. What could she have said? And now, here she was thanking his servant in a most ladylike manner for the bread and raisins he offered. His mind was spinning. He would not be beaten. Not here, not by this foreigner in his own chamber. He would force her into shame. Resuming his best face, he repeated the coarse observation.

"Our palace whore is the best lay in the land." Casica studied her drink contentedly. "You'll have no argument from me," she agreed.

He blinked. She turned and smiled pleasantly, hoping her response would end the subject. She couldn't know what it stirred in her host. As it is said, to the pure, all things are pure; but the wicked flee when no one pursues.

The man blinked again. "You mean...you know Asla?" Casica sipped her drink, surprised. Surely *everyone* knew that her houseslave and Asla were friends—or so she'd assumed. "Of course," she replied, innocently, "I've often the pleasure of her company...."

His mind raced. What kind of woman would associate with an insulit? Only a dark woman would do such a thing, and this woman was darker than most, ringed with an unrighteous light. His heart pounded in a panicked race. The insulit knew many secrets about him. Which of them had she deposited into the Cassican's dark keep? And what might she do with the knowledge she now held over him? His stomach turned with a vision of the dark alien dragging his body through a vat of filth.

The healer frowned at his expression, utterly confused. She brushed away her concern. This man was not worth her time.

"So," she asked, casually, "Prince Bastien tells me you've some questions concerning wild game in Cassica. What is it you wish to know?"

He barely heard above his mental din. All he could think was never, *ever* would he entertain this woman or the insulit again.

Somewhere the One who waited, smiled.

XXIX

"Rece, I've services to attend. Can we get on with this?" Clarece was pacing her stall nervously. Kai, what does one say to a queen? What kind of queen writes a slave anyway? She thought of the queen's daughter. If Pelana were anything like Casica, or vice versa, it made perfect sense. Still....

"Scads, As. What on earth do I say? I mean, this is a *queen*. A real queen. I need something short and direct. You can't go around wasting a queen's time with mindless drivel." She scraped her mitten on the table. Her hands had been itching for days. "I need to sound intelligent. Competent. Otherwise, it would be like a courtier who's all thumbs."

The blonde rolled her eyes. Tempting as it was to touch that last statement, she thought better of it. "Clarece, just be yourself," she replied instead. "You *are* intelligent. You talk circles around the *princess* of Cassica all the time. The queen can't be much different."

"You think not?!" Clarece objected. "Well, let me tell you, g'Helderleit, you know what 'Pelana' means? It means 'Mighty Tower,' that's what it means. How does one go about entering a 'mighty tower'?" Asla frowned sarcastically. "The same way one enters a piss chamber: with a first step. Just *begin*. Your scribe awaits...." The chief slaveswoman nodded. She would begin:

"Greetings Your Royal Majesty, Pelana, Queen of Cassica...." Asla's feather flew. *Beloved Mother of Casica*. "I wish to express my deepest gratitude at your concessional attendance of correspondence to a slave of such insignificant circumstance...."

Receiving your letter has brought me much joy. "It has been my great honor to serve in the capacity of domestic slavery for your esteemed daughter." *Living with your daughter is such a pleasure.* "Your daughter, Princess of Cassica, has provided me a cornucopia *('corn of Copia?')* of knowledge upon the table of learning. Both her instructional and experiential presentation of your distinguished nation have served to increase my hunger—no, make that 'appetite'—to dine further upon the understanding of your culture." *Casica and I have many conversations about your country. Her words and the manner in which she treats me and my friends makes me wish I could visit your island.*

"I anticipate the privilege of slaving—I mean, serving your gracious daughter for the remainder of years I have been allotted." *I look forward to a life-long friendship with your daughter and hope I can be as great a gift to her as she is to me.* "I humbly submit this reply through the hands of my friend and stallmate, Asla, of whom you inquired. Blessings upon you and your people. Respectfully, Clarece d'Casica." *I am Asla, Clarece's friend. Thank you for giving your daughter to us. Rece's and my life and many others' lives are so much better because Casica is here. In g'Helderlend, we say that digging a hole in one place provides dirt to fill another. I know that Casica's absence must leave a big hole in your home because she fills so many here.... Blessings on you and your people. With warmest affection, Clarece d'Casica.*

Asla presented the letter to her friend. A glance read all. Clarece's frown surrendered to a smile. "You've missed your calling, insulit," she observed wryly. "The way you translate, you should have been a magician." "I *am* a magician," Asla mumbled, corking her ink well. "If you saw me perform tonight, you'd know that." She looked at her senior friend, curious. "I thought I'd eaten everything. Where on earth *is* 'Copia'?"

What a perfect ending to the day! Nahalt was coming home. Dolca reread the letter as Raina prepared her bedchamber. She brushed her fingers over the familiar handwriting. Nahalt always wrote her himself. As usual, his letter was direct but its contents warmed her with anticipation. There was something to anticipate in the coming weeks. The countess surprised herself with the tune she hummed with her reading. It was a slavish song, one Raina sang often as she cleaned. Dolca smiled. Surely Nahalt would enjoy the newest member of their family.

"Your bed is ready, Mistra," a soft voice announced. Dolca studied the child approvingly. Already the sleeves of her blouse crept beyond her wrists. "Thank you, Raina. And guess what: I've news! Your master is coming home the end of the month."

The girl's response wasn't what she'd expected. Raina frowned worriedly. "My master is your husband?" she asked cautiously. "Yes," Dolca replied, rising from her seat. Raina fretted with her vest. "He is a man?" The countess squatted before the nervous slave. "Yes, he's a man," she laughed softly. "What's wrong, Little One?" The greenish eyes glanced anxiously about the room. "You would like I should ask Asla come slave him?"

It was Dolca's turn to look confused. "No. Why would I do that?" Raina clutched a button. The memory frightened her. "I'm not old enough to slave a man," she divulged. "The baroness, she wanted me to slave her nephew, but Asla said I wasn't old enough so she took my place. I wasn't supposed to tell anyone. That was only a little while ago. I'm not much bigger yet."

Dolca's eyes dropped in understanding. Her ears rang with rage. She must confess away, again, her hate for Muriel. "So Asla slaved the man," she repeated. "You never saw him?" The child shook her head. "I slept in Asla's cot. She let me use her red cloak. It smells pretty...."

Dolca sighed. That's another sin she must confess, her judgment of the insulit. The woman brought a hand comfortingly to Raina's face. "Asla is a good friend. She was right. You weren't old enough to slave for that man. But my husband is a different man. And you're just right for him. He says in his letter, he looks forward to meeting you." She grinned. "You'll like him; he laughs all the time."

The small slave relaxed but worry clung to her. She glanced at a basket. "You would like I should spool more bobbins for you?" Her owner glanced from the basket to the child. "No. You've worked hard all day. Tis time for you to rest.... Raina?" she asked quietly, "Is something wrong? Is there something happening in your pen that makes you not want to go there tonight?"

The little girl cringed, caught. Her fingers kneaded one another. "No, ma—I mean, Mistra," she blushed. "There's nothing wrong. I...I just miss you." She looked at her mistress with tearing eyes. "I miss our home." Dolca smiled gently. She drew her girl into her arms. "I miss you, too, Raina," she whispered. "I love you...."

The power of her confession impacted the woman more than it did the child, for Raina knew she was loved. "I love you, too, Mistra." Dolca drew her back. She felt strangely free. "I tell you what: why don't you sleep here tonight? I don't have a red cloak, but you can share my big bed."

Instantly, Raina brightened. "I've never slept in a bed," she said, excited. "Well," explained Dolca, "it can hold all my sister's five children. I'm certain 'twill hold us. Come." The two ladies made their way to the warming bedchamber. Raina undressed while Dolca selected a soft, red nightshirt. She bundled the child into its warmth and placed her in bed. The two nestled together under heavy covers. Dolca brought Raina's head against her and silently caressed the reddish hair. "You're so warm, Mistra." Dolca kissed her brow. "Raina, you can call me 'Ma'—when we're alone. I mean...if you *want* to call me mother, you can."

The little slave clutched her owner's hand, comforted. They lay silently for a few minutes before a voice whispered, "I love you, Mother." Dolca sighed. "I love you too, Little Queen. Good night...." Dolca felt the small body quiet and within moments, the breath beside her drew deep and steady.

The countess relaxed. The crackling brazier. The ticking clock. All seemed content and at peace. She thought back to evenings in the past. Evenings before Raina's arrival when she would mourn the night away. Somewhere in the midst of all this change something had happened. With the subtlety of dye, bitterness had faded, and in its absence revealed a new color: Hope. She studied the sleeping face. Some slavewoman had carried this little life, for months had felt the knitted body dance in her womb. A nameless, faceless woman that, perhaps, even this moment slept somewhere in the city. A woman just...like her. The countess' mind traveled months back in time. She was sitting at tea with the strange woman from the alien land. "I am no physician," Casica had said.

Beside her, Raina hiccupped. Dolca smiled at the movement and drew the covers more tightly about her. Children. In her imagination, she viewed the tapestry of parents presenting their children to the happy God. What was she, she now wondered, if not a child? "He is not angry," Casica had said. He is not angry.

Dolca brushed some reddish hair behind Raina's injured ear. Nahalt was coming home. Hope beckoned. Her heart pounded with resolve. Tomorrow, she would visit the Healer of Cassica.

Clarece returned from her hands' time with her healer. She glanced around the closet to Raina's stall. Still, she had not returned. Asla was buttoning her red cape. God, she hated to go to the city. She should leave early and fortify herself with drink.

"Have you seen Raina?" her friend asked. The insulit glanced about the stall. "No." Clarece fretted with her mittens. "I'm sure she's alright," she told herself, "but…." She was wavering. She should go to Dolca's to make certain.

"Oh, she's likely asleep in Dolca's bed," her stallmate was saying. Clarece frowned. "Highly improbable." Asla stamped her boot. "I tell you what: I'll swing by Dolca's on my way out. If she's there, you won't hear from me. If not, I'll come get you." Clarece nodded. It would save her from having to disturb a royal so late at night. "Are you sure you have time?" Asla adjusted her collar. "Positive. You go to sleep, chief slaveswoman. I'll see you at supper tomorrow."

The senior slave embraced her friend, praying silently that she would, indeed, see her the morrow. "Blessings upon you," she offered. "I reek of blessing," the insulit quipped. "Sleep well."

Dolca watched the milk. It should be warm soon. A soft knock came to her door. "Who on earth would be coming at this hour?" she asked herself, removing the kettle. She opened her door tentatively. The last person she could have imagined stood there.

"Good evening, Countess," the insulit bowed. "I'm sorry to disturb you this hour, but we're concerned about the scamp. Is Raina here?" "Yes, Asla. She's staying the night with me." Memory of her previous treatment of the young woman convicted her. Why wait till tomorrow for repentance? "Asla," she invited, "I'm about to have night milk. Would you join me?"

The insulit blinked. Why would a royal be inviting her to refreshment? She had no desire to visit with the company of suspicion, but still.... "Please," the countess urged. The word swung the balance. Asla entered the darkened chamber, a tinge of fear pricking her. Instinctively she scanned the room: *this could be a trap,* her mind said; she despised herself for the thought. Here was the only safe place she would know this night, and yet she entered it as danger. What a mess she was.

"May I take your cloak?" her hostess was asking. The young woman handed Dolca her cover. The seamstress studied it admiringly. The buttons were true bronze—not gilded, and into them was etched an ivy design. The lining was of rich velvet. But the true surprise awaited.

"The cloth has seagulls woven into it!" Dolca exclaimed quietly. Asla smiled at the observation. "They're osprey, actually. The birds of my land." Dolca shook her head. "This is an exquisite garment, Asla. You've elegant taste." "I do treasure my cloak," Asla replied. "'Twas the last thing I bought on my way off g'Helderlend." Her voice quieted. "I knew I wouldn't see my home again. I wanted to have something of it." The countess understood. She poured milk for her guest and added to it cinnamon.

"You use cinnamon," Asla observed, removing her large dagger from her belt. She placed it on a stand to keep the countess' chair from being torn. "In my country, we commonly add nutmeg." "You must miss your people," Dolca offered. "You share this aloneness with Casica, yes?"

"Yes," Asla nodded, sipping her milk casually. "Except that it seems Casica makes those around her more like her people. I would not wish for others to become like me."

Something of the honesty took Dolca off guard. It was the reputation of the whore to be arrogant and insolent. The insulit knelt to no one—not even the king. But clearly, Asla's opinion of herself was not as rumored. Asla smiled in memory of Clarece and the queen's letter. "I tell Clarece she's turning Cassican." Dolca smiled at scenes of her own. "She certainly learns the language," the king's royal observed, "but I'm certain the chief slaveswoman's loyalties rest with her own country."

Her guest turned to her quizzically. "Why?" Asla asked. "Why would any slave's loyalty rest with this land?" Dolca frowned, confused. "Because tis the land of their birth—the womb of all they have," she answered defensively.

"Such as what?" countered the slave. A raw anger brimmed Asla's heart. "You love this land because you're royal: you've title, wealth, freedom—a future. Your husband fights for it for many the same reasons. But how would you feel as slave? How would you feel if because of this land—and for nothing you've done other than being born—you have metal burned around your neck? You are ravished and flogged and stripped and sold like an animal. The children you bear and the man you love are taken from you. Your very freedom—your humanity are stolen forever." Her eyes hardened. "Byzanthia doesn't give to slaves, Dolca: it steals, it kills, it destroys...."

"How can you say that?" the countess parried. "In all my life, I've never heard a slave complain about their state. Clarece, for example. You could not find a more loyal subject of the king."

Asla smirked into her cup. If only the countess lived in her pen a single day. Her reply softened. "There *are* some slaves who are content to live in bondage," she conceded, "but in common, most slaves aren't. Loyalty to a country, patriotism—these don't exist. Slaves are loyal to owners—not thrones. Clarece wouldn't give her life for Byzanthia. But she would give it for Casica, a foreigner, because her owner inspires loyalty through her love. But for many slaves, this isn't so. They've no reason for loyalty to anything."

The countess' tea was cooling. Something in her chilled as well. "You make it sound as though owning a slave could jeopardize one's life, Asla," she voiced cautiously. The slave shrugged. "I wouldn't own one. And I think if many owners knew what slaves truly felt, neither would they."

Dolca considered the sleeping slave in her bed and her decision to see the healer. She fingered her saucer nervously. Asla watched the gesture and knew what was thought. "But you've no cause to worry, Countess," she offered softly. The freewoman looked up. "You love your slave like a daughter, as does Raina love you as a mother. Your connection will engender what would come naturally in such a relationship. It'll look awkward because of the collar, but Raina's joined to you by the heart. And that's the strongest bond." She grinned. "Small as she is, if a 'big slave' would say aught against you, they'd answer to her. She's devoted to you." The slave thought of her own handler. "You are worthy of devotion," she concluded.

Dolca studied the woman silently; her perception of life teetered as it did so often when conversing with Casica. There was so little she truly knew of the world outside Byzanthia. Increasingly, the royal began to question if a nation, any nation, were meant to be center of anything at all. Did not God say He was center and that people were second only to Him? He didn't seem impressed with nations as a whole. She looked at her guest, newly curious. "Asla, what is your island like?"

The g'Helderleit brightened at the question. "Tis eight islands, really. We were formed by fire and lay as in a ring. I'm from the main island, g'Helderlend. Tis verdant. Life everywhere." She remembered into her cup. "We have orchards and vineyards, crops. Our population is small, but the people are as lush as the land."

"And your people—are they all as...striking...as you?" Asla nodded. "I'm quite common, except I'm tall for my age, though I know you won't believe it." Dolca didn't. "You jest! Are your men much taller than the women?" "No. Only as much as you see here." Dolca laughed kindly. "Well, why then are you called 'The Mighty'?"

Asla snorted. "You Byzanthians! Always occupied with size—especially your men. You don't understand that size has little to do with power—or pleasure." Her hostess blushed. "We're called 'The Mighty' because unlike Byzanthians, no one's ever conquered us. Your country tried several hundred years ago. What few were left of you made certain no more ever tried. And the Kaints? When they swept through the sphere? They didn't attempt invading our land so terrified of us were they." She caressed her cup. "We're not as 'civilized' in our way of war as you. Our gods are not so polite."

"And what of the saying about your lives?" Dolca inquired. "Is that true?" The blonde grinned. "So it's said. We g'Helderleits have three lives: one to lose, one to give and one to find. Tis so because our gods love us so much. That and because they know our appetite for enjoyment."

Dolca smiled; not only the gods knew that. "So you have many gods to serve...." "As much as we wish, yes. Your god didn't arrive on our island until a couple hundred years ago." Dolca straightened with pride. "I hope His addition has enhanced your country's fibre (*cleansed you of your barbarism,* is what she wanted to say)." For a time, the girl was silent. *It was your god's men who created insulit,* she wanted to voice. "He's not yet popularly received," she answered instead. "Well, may His popularity increase," Dolca wished. Her guest bowed humbly; it was unfit to insult another's god.

Asla was finishing her milk. The clock ticked comfortingly. The room smelled clean and fresh with flora. Texture and color spiced it more. It was a good place Raina's god had sent her, the slave considered. A good place. "Thank you for having me in your home, Countess," she said. "I haven't had night milk in ages. Have you ever tried adding chocolate?" "Chocolate?" her hostess asked, surprised. "Yes. A friend introduced me to it. If you melt a piece of chocolate in milk, it's mortal nectar." Dolca considered the concoction. "If I ever can find chocolate, I'll try it," she decided.

Asla glanced about and thumbed her palm nervously. She'd been in a lady's presence too long. It was time for her to leave; time to make her way in darkness. She met her hostess' eyes tentatively. "I should leave."

The troubled expression wasn't lost on the countess. "Well, I thank you for visiting, Asla," she smiled. "Your presence honors me." The girl thumbed harder. "I rather doubt that," Asla offered quietly. "When I come, I bring a whore into your home. I'm certain your luncheon guests won't approve."

Dolca studied the saddened face and wondered what it must be like to live outside the circle of feminine acceptance. "On the contrary," she replied. "I rather think your presence will only enhance my table." Ethereal eyes glanced up. "The truth is, Asla," Dolca continued, "you're something of an enigma. Tis true, women generally...distrust your presence among their men. But on the other hand, they can't help but wonder what makes you so...desired by so many. You are not an infrequent topic of conversation at my table. And the talk is not so derisive as you might imagine."

The insulit smiled wryly. "Then you must entertain some rather bored guests, Dolca, if a woman like me holds their interest. They should talk to their husbands instead of each other. The lack of enjoyment most married couples have in each other rather surprises me." She scratched around her collar. "I would think no greater adventure would there be than to love one person. 'Twould be like...holding a mirror before a mirror: the reflection never ends." She looked at her hostess. "Your husband returns soon, I gather." Dolca blinked. How could she possibly gather that? "I hope your reunion is fruitful."

The royal stared incredulously. Was the insulit reading her heart? she wondered. Asla was reaching for her knife. It was time to leave. The countess rose with her. Something within made her risk invitation.

"Asla," she asked, "are you often to the city on Weldsday?" "Yes," Asla replied, cautious, "every Weldsday night." "Then would you consider visiting with me before you depart? I retire late...and your company, tis a pleasure." The blonde was debating. A woman like her had no business with a lady. But what was Casica if not a lady? "Next time, I'll have nutmeg," Dolca enticed. Her guest grinned playfully. "Well, in that case...but if you decide differently...." "I won't." Asla received the offered cloak. "Then until next week," she bowed.

Dolca closed her door, thoughtful. It seemed her vision of life had deepened. She accompanied a lamp to her bedchamber and glanced at the child. Raina hadn't stirred, so soundly she slept in the warmth and security of her mistra's bed. She smiled at the peaceful face, somewhat relieved, and then caught an image beside her. It beckoned.

Dolca approached her wall mirror and stared. The woman in it looked intrigued. She reached for her hand glass. It took time to align them correctly. And then it happened. Dolca gazed in wonder. Her eyes now saw what her heart had so recently experienced.

A mirror before a mirror. The reflection never ends....

XXX

Bastien swept the hand mirror side-to-side. It seemed a child's game, this illusion. Still it held him spellbound, an endless tunnel of reflection. "Tis like a curved tunnel, as something you might see in the afterlife," he mumbled. "Fascinating...." He turned to his hostess. "Nahalt showed you this?"

Dolca hesitated. "The insulit, actually." Bastien blinked. "Asla? You know Asla?" Dolca took the offered mirror. "I begin to. She was here last night visiting. I've never truly spoken with her before," she shared into her likeness, "but she's not as she appears. She's quite provocative."

Hundreds of men won't argue with you there, the prince answered silently. Still, the thought of the palace whore visiting with the countess of Nahalt, it perplexed him. All the palace was going queer, it seemed, and he needed look no further than his chambermate for the reason. Everywhere Casica went, strangeness followed. What'd be next? The insulit turning priestess?

"Well, I thank you for humoring me," the woman was saying. "It seems childish, I know. But I find the effect so wondrous, I needed to show someone, and when I saw you in the hallway, I couldn't resist." Bastien bowed his smile. "It is I who thank you, Countess. Rarely have I the pleasure of your company, and frankly, tis the most fascinating thing I've seen in some time." "So you haven't been seeing the Princess of Cassica, I take it?"

The man grinned. "Well, not as thoroughly as I've seen this." Dolca tossed a look only a married woman could properly execute. "Perhaps you should do something about that, great prince."

Bastien coughed. "Well, I will...I mean, I will see her, forthwith, and deliver your message." What she said afterwards, he couldn't remember, so loudly his ears rang with embarrassment. Scads! Did the whole palace speculate on his and Casica's intimacy?

He wondered this still as he stepped into his chamber. His bed Clarece had already prepared in anticipation of the coming night: covers drawn, pillows set, fresh water as well as fresh candles on his nightstand. The brazier glowed, covered. A small fire crackled to his left. He went to it, propped his foot on the hearth and leaned into the heat. It bathed him comfortingly, eliciting a sigh and thoughts of Casica. Her touch was heat; her voice, light; her person, a hearth inviting rest and comfort.

He took the poker. How easily she stirred him, he considered, stoking the flame. Was it time for him to stir her, to spark into their relationship the ember he truly desired? He glanced toward her door. It was slightly ajar. She might be there now, reading or writing as she oft was accustomed. He walked silently to the opening and peeked. And shook his head. *Unbelievable.*

There they were. On the cushioned chair, slept the palace whore curled up like the sleeping Soren against her. A plate of crumbs sat with an emptied teapot on the serving table. Across from Asla, snored her friend, his former property, sprawled full length on the princess' sofa. A book lay on her chest.

Bastien snorted. All those months he'd spent fashioning that sofa, (and with it not a few fantasies of what he and his coming guest might do upon it) and for what? His slave to enjoy. He looked to the table he'd made. There she was, wife of Byzanthia's prince, dozing in the hard chair, feet propped on his cherry finish. A wine goblet balanced on her knee. He took in the scene wholly. God help them if the eyes that watched had been his father's. The palace whore, a slave and a Cassican tribute lounging about Byzanthia's furnishings like so many queens in a—. He jerked to his right. Someone was watching.

Brown eyes smiled mischievously. His blue ones rolled in response. She repressed her laughter and rose to meet him. "I swear, Casica," he offered in his chamber, "if Father ever sees that—heads will roll! And mine among them! Care you nothing of owner etiquette? Your behavior's become a plague. I just saw Dolca. Even she's infected. Consorting with Asla, no less. She wishes see you, by the way, at your convenience—that's if you're holding court with underling royals anymore."

"Tis not as bad as all that," Casica defended, accompanying him to the fireplace, "and besides, we rarely have Asla's company these days. She's never home." She sat beside him on the hearth and turned to the flame. It flared. "Edsner's killing her."

Bastien blinked. "How do you mean?" Her face turned somber. "Her 'services.' They are more and more brutish. Less selective. The diseases she gets...." She looked uncomfortably into his gaze. "I wasn't allowed to treat such illness in Cassica. No maiden healer is. I'm learning here as I go." Her voice lowered to a whisper. "Asla would not live the next two seasons if I weren't here. Why does he do this, Bastien? Why does Edsner destroy his greatest source of income?"

Bastien clawed a finger into the hearth. How Casica's forays into the slavish world rattled his. With her, no longer could he deny the injustices and horrors of his palace's silent population. With her, all excuse for oblivion was stripped. He'd known Edsner since childhood. The man was not evil; an evil man would not have been his friend. Yet what kind of man would treat even his horse as Edsner did this young woman? *Blast!* he cursed inwardly. *That was the problem!* Before Casica, the insulit of g'Helderlend wasn't woman at all. Now, however....

"I don't know," he answered. "I...I sometimes think Edsner's lost his mind. He doesn't know what it is he does anymore. For him to rent her to these men means he associates with them. The Edsner I knew would never have allowed their kind in his shadow."

She took a deep breath. "Bastien, I've been thinking—." "I know what you've been thinking," he interrupted. "You're wondering if I can't buy Asla off him. If we can't save her in that way." "Yes!" "We can't, Casica. He won't sell. He's been offered three times her worth." "But if *you* approached him..." Bastien smirked. "No. Tis not a matter of money with him. It's one of power. You see, with Asla, Edsner has something no one else has and everyone wants. Now if Father approached him, or Bastil, he would acquiesce. But me? Never. She makes him something he's not, otherwise."

The dark eyes that stared into the fire glistened with sorrow. Clearly, this discussion was done. There were limits to her power in this land. If her husband were helpless to save, how much more was she. "I can keep body and soul together for a very long time," she said quietly. "But should some man decide his pleasure is to slit her throat or drown her in the ocean," she shook her head, "I can't remedy that." She smiled sadly at him. "But for you to even regard her lot, Bastien, I thank you. You and Edsner began life with much in common, no doubt. You've chosen a nobler path than he." He wanted to kiss her. "I should see Dolca. God's peace, my prince."

Casica rose but hesitated in her step. "I'm happy tis your eyes and not your father's that see me." He listened as she closed the door behind her and imagined he heard a step or two of her boots in the hall.

Bastien waited until he was certain they wouldn't meet before leaving his room. He followed Josquin's path down the hall but passed Dolca's door for another. Edsner was within and genuinely surprised.

"The devil, you say! To what do I owe this honor?! Come in!" Bastien settled into the offered chair. He surveyed the room as Edsner poured them drinks and thought how little of the rich furnishings existed five years earlier. The heavy desk and table, velvet, silks and silver, all lavishly placed. How the Hollow filled Edsner's world.... He lifted the crystal goblet to his lips; even the quality of Edsner's wine had improved. "Well," the lord asked, gesturing to his chamber, "what think you?"

Bastien sipped contentedly. "I think your lands are garnering a tremendously fruitful yield." Edsner grinned knowingly. "Tis the soil. 'Most verdant you've ever tilled, or in your case, never tilled. Or course, you've your own estate." He leaned forward intimately. "Tell, me, Bastien, are her stones as magical as we all think?"

Bastien winced. *Blast! The whole palace* did *speculate!* He faked a slight grin. "I guess it all depends on what you think...." His host laughed lightly. "God, to be in your place for a night! Too bad you can't rent her, eh? To women and insulit!" Bastien joined the toast half-heartedly. He thrust himself into his mission.

"Edsner, I've come to ask you something." "About what?" "Asla." The lord stopped mid-sip. "So, she's *not* as good as we think after all, eh? Not surprised, Bastien. Cassicans, they're a cold lot." Something like anger rose in the young man. "I don't mean that, Eds. I'm wanting to buy Asla."

Edsner leaned back into his chair. It was tangible, the way he felt their relationship suddenly tilt. All the gold was on his side of the scales now. And while he'd reveled often in this balance shift with other men, never had he imagined this pleasure with his childhood mate. The whore of g'Helderlend leveled every playing field. Prince or peasant, all found their way to his throne, all wished possession of his golden scepter. He paused before answering as he did in every similar occasion. Let them wonder. Let them hope. He mused with his wine then offered finally, "No.... I have a hunting bitch for bid, but this one's not for sale."

The prince expelled a knowing sigh. "Of course," he acknowledged, admiring his goblet. "How powerful it must feel to have something everyone wants, eh, Edsner? But the wealth she yields is passing. Surely you want something more." Bastien glanced from the room to memory. His gaze fixed upon his former friend.

"You know, I remember when we were children, how us boys would spend summers at your family estate. I remember how you would pretend ordering everyone about. How you dreamed of the day all that land would become yours. 'Lord of the Harvest,' you'd make us address you. How you loved surveying the fields.... Well, we're not children anymore, Edsner. I and your fellows, we've gone on in life. We've become men. Become the true lords of the estates entrusted us. But what of you? All that good land in the north and do you till it? Do you tend it? No. You till the body of a woman. You harvest a whore while your true fields lay fallow. What honor is there in that?"

"Honor?" Edsner spat. "Who speaks to me of honor? I see the way you look at her. You've wanted that wench since the day she arrived. You're no different from the others. You've just more self-control. For now. You have a distraction. But mark my words, Bastien: the day will come when you'll take her. And as for 'tilling', I'm a business man. I make more with her flesh than I ever could with land and with much more ease. She's an investment, a wise investment. You only wish you'd thought of her first."

Bastien's look told all. "No," he replied simply, "I only wish you to think of me last. The day will come when she no longer can yield. Her use will be up, and you'll be wanting money—much of it. When that day comes, I want her sold to me. I'll give whatever you ask, no matter her condition."

Edsner stared at the prince, puzzled. He'd known this man all his life; never had he heard Bastien speak this way about anything, especially a piece of slave flesh. What on earth was changed in his old friend? "Why this interest in Asla?" he voiced. "Why care about her at all? She's slave. You say, yourself, she's nothing to you."

Bastien nodded. "True. But she's much to my wife. Tis my wife that keeps your property intact, Edsner. Tis my wife that heals her wounds and illness. That makes Asla my business. 'Happy wife, happy life,' yes? You should spend your resources seeking one for yourself. Till some ground that'll bear a legacy of life. But," he shrugged, "that's my opinion. As you say, you're well within your rights to do whatever you wish to your slave. But when the day comes to sell—and it will—you come to me. I ask your word on it."

For a moment, a blink in time, Edsner Lord of Gottanae felt sanity's tap on his soul, like a man wakened from a daydream. For a moment, he was that little boy again. The fields sprawled before him and beckoned him take that step into the better, truer self he now remembered. He need only relinquish the illusion that defined his life. He teetered, ever so slightly, in the balance of choice. Then fell.

With a thoughtless brush of his heart, the man swept aside holy desire for one feigned. In an act as ancient as time, he exchanged truth for the lie of something which, while seemingly required nothing of him, would devour his very soul.

So he nestled, Edsner did, as into a downy bed, more comfortably into his own grave. But the effect of the moment would have its work. "I give you my oath," he declared. "When I at last sell her, it will be only to you. I swear it."

As Bastien passed Dolca's door a few minutes later, he could not know that behind it another contest for life was waged. The stones about Casica's neck flared upon Dolca's sleeping face. Josquin focused, as she healed, upon the striking tapestry of red and blue, its fruit-laden tree and flowing river depicting Nahalt's family crest. The scene reminded her of an ancient song: *We feast on the abundance of your house and drink from the river of your delight. For with you is the fountain of life; in your light, we see light....*

Light. She infused it into Dolca's body. Life surged irresistibly into the soil of a barren womb. "'Fountain of Life'," Casica prayed, willing it to be. Joy flooded her. The Lord of the Harvest was coming....

XXXI

Ars sat at the field, nursing his wine. He looked at nothing but saw much. It was a quiet evening; rain splashed against his darkened windows. Silence filled his darkened chamber, pierced only by his breath and laughing fire. It lit the board with a kindly light, joining the rays of the little table lamp that flickered in their presence, shadowing the few surviving warriors with themselves.

The move was his, but he waited, mired as much in an unseen field of battle as he was this miniature one. His opponent sat, sipping his scotch as she studied his face. There wasn't much he could do now in this game, she knew. His quest for the little pawn was ending. He would take it this night and there was nothing she could do to prevent it. There was nothing she wanted to do. The pawn represented what, she couldn't know, but whatever it was possessed him; he must exorcise himself.

He could take her. He had taken her once and now he would take her again. That cursed, worthless vassal that plagued him night and day; she, he would take from the game of life. She had haunted him long enough, waking him with sweats and horrid dreams, prowling about his house and thoughts. She would die; he would take her from this board and dash her to pieces. Except that she didn't merit the attention. Insignificant piece of onyx. How dare such a pitiful specimen pester him at all? How dare, indeed. But it was that time of year when she haunted him most. That time when the world became black with regret. He would take her from life; take her in the presence of one whose very name meant Life.

"Say good-bye to your pawn, wench. Tis cluttered my battlefield long enough." With a flourish, he moved his warder and toppled the broadfoot. He studied it now in his hand, debating whether to throw it into the fire or crush it under a blade.

The woman refilled her glass. She took a long sip. The anger and sorrow in her opponent permeated the small space between them. "Do you feel better, Father?" she asked quietly. Ars cleared his throat loudly, leaned back into his chair and gulped his wine. "Much," he replied, returning to the present reality, "I always feel better after vanquishing my enemies." "And what of this broadfoot? What made him your enemy?"

Ars smirked. As though one needed reasons to have enemies. "He irked me, wench. His presence was a thorn in my side. It is my practice to pluck such splinters from my flesh." "I see," Casica replied, nodding. "Have you many such flesh dwellers, Ars?" "Why do you ask? Would you like a peek?" he answered, suggestively. "I can see enough from here, thank you," she replied, unfazed. "And what exactly is in your field of vision, royal gilt?"

Casica lowered her drink. "I see you have more than any man would wish. They haunt you, these dwellers, I think." "You think?" "Yes." "That'll be the day, when a Cassican thinks. Especially a woman. Your sex is good for one thing, and it's not for thinking."

Casica did not parry. Strangely she would have a few weeks before, before Bastien arrived; but with his presence, something of her drive to defend lessened. She walked completely from that jousting field to another. "I know the crown attract enemies, Ars. Tis its nature. But what of friends? No crown can bear its own weight without them; yet, I never hear you speak of any."

Ars rolled the small piece in his palms; it felt strangely warm to his touch. "Friends," his mumbled. "Would you believe my friends fare not much better than my enemies, Healer?" She shook her head. "Well, they don't. You should keep that in mind. There's room enough for only one king on the board. I have killed friends who thought otherwise, whether their existence posed a threat to me or not."

Casica studied the king of Byzanthia and his pawn. He held it now, trying to crush the fine stone with sheer force of will.

He couldn't. He was waiting; she could feel it. Wondering if she would dare ask.

There are times when to question is to wittingly open a door to sights one wishes never to see. Josquin could pass this one by and leave the man in his lonely place. But she was a healer and ignoring wounds was not within her. It wasn't challenge that prompted her response but need. "So what friends have you taken from the board of life, Father?"

"The best." Ars gazed upon faces and scenes more clear to him than his own reality. They would send him to hell, these faces would. One should know who it is that sends one to hell. He stared into his companion. She was lovely and alluring, and he hated it. Hated how her presence enticed him to speak. Something in the fabric of her race, no doubt. Something in the necklace about her throat. He walked into her invitation. To confess to one's enemy was easier somehow. He slid back the grate, desiring a witness to his sin.

"They were childhood companions," he began, his eyes drifting away. "The two of them. Grew with me and mine in this place. He became my most trusted knight; she became his wife. When my queen moved into my bed, she took her as her chambermaid, both for her fine company and for our friendship. They became fast friends as you women often do. The Countess Silva and her Sir Almed dined at my table. We would visit, the four of us, here in this room, and talk and laugh the night away." He smiled. Those were happy times.

"Silva swaddled my sons and bathed my wife. She never had children of her own, barren as she was. Still Almed kept her. She pleased him. She pleased everyone who knew her...." The smile faded. "Almed I lost in the Sarciany wars. Silva mourned with my wife as her kerchief then asked to be returned to her people in Calmahn. I sent her away with my blessing. Often my wife would visit her." He grinned to himself. Women. What a mystery. "I used to tell my wife she was half a heart without her Silva....

"Several years later, Silva sent a request by my own wife's hand borne. She had bought a slaveman, a tutor, to learn the children of her village. Having no children of her own, I suspect, she lost herself in the care of others'. Well, this slave, this lowly piece of nothing, this slave stole her heart. She begged for me to release him that they might marry." Even now, after so long, the disgust of such a thing rose in the king's face like vomit.

"Can you believe that, wench? Can you believe a woman of noble blood would ever humble herself to such a thing—to wish her body joined to a brute? My wife begged on her behalf. She had met him and found him honorable, she said, brilliant and noble in his way." Ars snorted. "'Honorable.' 'Noble.' Words fit for her dead husband accorded to this not-human. I rejected Silva's request and chastised her for even considering such a thing. Twice more she appealed to me. The final time in person."

He looked toward a particular place in the room. "She knelt on this floor where she and her good husband had stood. Like a slave she knelt and begged me release her to marry this man. She loved him, she said. *Loved* him. I told her she was mad. To love a slave would be as loving an ox or boar. Such perversity would I never permit...." He fretted with the pawn.

"Silva left me and continued to pay her taxes and remember all our birthdays. Of the matter, I thought nothing more. Nothing, until one day, word came that my wife's former chambermaid had given birth. It was the slave's issue. Being more brute than man, his seed overpowered her natural state. My wife begged mercy.

"I tell you, Cassican," he offered viciously, "I'll be cursed if I give mercy to one who deserves it not. I sent my guard to Calmahn to hunt down that vermin slave. I needn't bothered. He was waiting for them, Macartus told me. Waiting. Didn't even attempt to run. Can you believe that?" His face bore the same expression of confusion as it did then. "Mindless, stupid slave. I had him gelded and gutted and his carcass hung on the gate of her home. It rotted there, filled the village with the stench of his defiance. Warning every slave of their fate if they dared rise above their place." He looked away for a long moment. "And I found her, too. She hadn't run, either. She waited for them in the chapel, in the presence of my village priest. I intended to drown the spawn but the Church stood in my way.

"You see, Silva was more cunning than I, as is the way of your sex. She'd had the issue sealed by God. The Church had christened it." His eyes glared. "That wouldn't have stopped me. God himself couldn't have stopped me so great was my wrath. But Silva was wise." A slight smile crossed his lips. Outsmarted by a woman, he was. “She covered that bastard with something greater than God. She had sealed it with the name of her best friend. *Clarece*. I couldn’t drown my wife....”

He looked now at Casica’s face and smiled at the effect: it was whitened with shock. “Silva was royal, and I would not spill my own blood. So I stripped her and paraded her in her village like the whore she was. Macartus said none would look upon her nakedness. Then I took her and banished her to the mines of Pulca. I knew she wouldn’t live the winter. And she didn’t. Her issue, I collared and sent north to Sladishen. I told my wife I had killed the mother and drowned the ‘son’. I knew what she would try if she had any hope. I had no desire to fight that battle. Clarece never forgave me. From that day on, she withheld from me the only thing I’ve ever needed.... Her heart.”

His eyes teared in the firelight. “Later, I wanted to beg her forgiveness. I wanted to make things right, somehow. But I am king and I bow to no one, not even my need.” His eyes turned hard. There was a greater King, one he could never usurp.

“But God, God found me out. He brought my sin upon my head and into my very home. Years later, I’m walking in my house, and there is this little slave in the hall. God made me to stop and look at her. I tell her, ‘Show your face.’ And there they were: eyes like God poured the sea into them and contained it with a ring of night. Silva had come to haunt me in that freakish beauty bearing my wife’s name. God had bested me....

“But He wasn’t done. No. Not Him. He took my Clarece and filled her with fever. And you think I repented? No.” He looked at the princess and smirked. “Queen Pelana, your *mother* sent an envoy, begging permission to cross the channel and heal my wife. My *enemy* begs help me. I sent a note attached to his corpse telling her I would rather my wife dead than to be indebted to a Cassican healer.”

The man looked at what only he could see. “I defied God. And for recompense, He required the love of my life. Seven years, this day....” His gaze shifted to the woman before him. She barely breathed and sorrow filled her face. “Don’t dare weep for me, Cassican. I will not be pitied. You see what I do to those I love. Imagine what I do to those I hate. The life of your pawn is as dung to me. Like the life of her lover. Your cousin.”

Her blood ran cold. K'net. *Dear God,* he knew about K'net. On impulse, she almost fell before him and begged mercy but somewhere wisdom ruled. Casica's training served her well now. She was a poker player and at this moment presented her best game face. Nothing of the din within her showed without.

"K'net is my altage," she answered plainly. "My guardian. Nothing more. If you thought differently, you would have killed him long ago." He smirked. She was a cool one, this girl. "I know he's your altage. And I know he's served me well in battle. And I know his men love him. But I swear to you, Gilt, if you move against me, I'll do what even a healer can't undo. I'll send his bones to you in a bag."

The princess leaned into the playing field. "And what is it you fear of me, Ars? That I'll kill you? Kill your son? Your people? You need no leverage to contain me. You know the power of love—or once did. Ask your physicians if you haven't noticed yourself. I offer nothing but help to your people. If you would send me the body of my envoy, I'll do nothing to stop you." With her face, she motioned to the pawn in his hand.

"And as for Clarece, why do you tell me this if not from conscience? I know that with great power is potential for great harm. My own father is not immune. The harm you have caused cannot be undone. But the harm that continues, you *can* quell, Ars. You can repent and free the one that lives."

"Don't dare speak it, Cassican," he warned. "You've heard what I do. I will not repent. God, Himself, judged the wickedness of her issue. Gave her claws like a beast. From the womb He marked her. I will *never* give her freedom."

"If you did, you would give her nothing," Casica rejoined passionately. "Twould be a thief's offering, returning only what you've stolen." It was her eyes that hardened now. Indignation filled her but discretion softened her response.

"God did not mark Clarece, Father. You did. *You* gave her claws through an owner that boiled her body like meat." She looked at him unflinchingly. "You speak of kingly honor...you dishonor yourself. Slavery is determined by the womb—not the seed. A free womb never bears a slave. And your own laws plainly state that a free man or woman cannot be made slave." Her mind reasoned quickly.

"All about Clarece proves her free state. God ordained it; she came into the world of a free woman. Your civil law attests to her freedom; there are no original papers for her; there couldn't be. She was born free. Your Church attests to it. A slavechild cannot be christened, yet your priests sealed her. The Church. The law. God—all recognize Clarece's free state." Her tone softened. "You have stolen it from her. Her freedom, her name, her history. But not her future. That God has preserved. He safe-keeps it for your ransom. Release her, Father. Release yourself."

"I do not release anyone, Cassican," Ars answered darkly. "I fear no one, not even God. I spared not even my own wife. Don't you ever forget that." "I won't, Ars. Nor will I believe you are the souless fiend you make yourself. If you were, you would bear this sin easily. But you cannot. Tis proof you bear still the image of God."

"I bear the crown, daughter of a defeated race. That is what I bear. And I will crush *anyone* who dares come against me."

"As whom?" Casica ended quietly. There was much more she wanted to say; her mind riled with righteous indignation, but to shed light upon a darkened mind was futile for a human. Another must enlighten...it was not her place. The queen capitulated and turned her focus to the chessboard. "I assume by your telling me all this, you mean for Clarece to know. Or do you wish me remain silent?"

"I fear no knowledge, Cassican. Tell anyone you desire. But I warn you: if that slave dare raises her head in this knowledge; if you use it to pose her against me, I swear, I'll take her from the board of life." Casica didn't flinch.

"She doesn't need my interpretation, Ars. Clarece knows the playing field better than I. But she won't rebel. Your slave is loyal to the law. Even in her dealings with your sergeant. They do love, yes. But they aren't lovers. She honors you too much."

Ars studied the fallen pawn. Why couldn't he destroy it? "Nevertheless, Princess. Remember your pawn." "I will remember," she said, evenly. "As I remember this: pride topples the crown more often than ever an assassin's dagger. May God save you."

With this Josquin reached for her bishop. He'd been waiting patiently for weeks. Now with the pawn dismissed, he could exercise his calling. Ars watched as the bishop glided into his realm. She set him like a rock.

"Mated."

XXXII

Casica locked the library door. Only then did she allow herself release. Leaning against the judicial section, she wept, sliding down the volumes to collapse on the floor. It couldn't be. What Ars told her couldn't be true. Her hands, her enslavement, her tortures, her abuse. None of this was Clarece's lot. None of it. She was the daughter of a countess, and even a bastardized daughter of a woman like Silva the Church would have taken, or a distant vassal, a villager, someone.

Casica slammed her fist into her hand and stood. *Nepa!* She prowled the room enraged, all sense of justice violated. "Why?!" she kept demanding in her tongue. "Why did you abandon her to such a hellish fate? She was innocent!" No answer came. She knew none would.

She surrendered finally to the familiar hammerschord. There was Clarece's key, the one key she played in "E'lanesce": "A Sunset Walk." Such a simple little tune, a child's song. Yet it stood as one of Clarece's favorite Cassican compositions. She enjoyed its different renditions based upon her mistra's mood at the time of performance.

The beginning of the piece required a single low note that Clarece had made her own. Waiting on the bench beside her owner for the proper measure and beat, she would press the key, smiling, pleased with her role in creating music. Casica stroked the ebony key. Her fingers took a life of their own and performed the piece. Tears scored its delivery. Sorrow and rage; of the two, sorrow always ran deeper.

As the final note lingered in the dark room, she quieted, breathing deeply the smell of old books. Books! Casica glanced about. There was a section...Clarece had shown her...a section of lineage. There. Shelved low and at the end. Casica stood and walked purposely to it. She scanned the volumes intently. *Clarece looks to be about twenty. Let's say Silva was thirty? at her birth.* She reached for the appropriate years and gathered three books.

At the table she lit a candle, not of necessity but for its comfort. She reached also for a glass and poured two fingers of scotch. Light was good company but spirit was better....

Silva's village was Calmahn. Both Cassicans and Byzanthians identified their royals with the towns from which they ruled—not family. She would start there. The chronicles were thorough but disorderly. She must scan each entry. *Scads.* Clarece was what was needed here, she thought. Oh, well. She was armed with drink and determination. If Silva, Countess of Calmahn, existed in these accounts, she would find her.

Hours later, she still read, her latest scotch propped against her forehead. Beside her Soren, having entered from somewhere, lounged on the table bathing his scruffy form. Slowly, the glass lowered. "Silva," Casica breathed. There she was. One volume back: The Countess Silva, born in Calmahn of the Countess Nashura and Count Conon...born of Duke...the list continued. Silva's family spread like a tree among the earth of Byzanthia. Hers was an ancient line, the titles blood borne, not granted. No wonder Ars said he wouldn't spill his own blood; the roots of her people grafted into his own.

The princess read frantically now, oblivious to the sound of lapping. No reference to anyone following Silva. No siblings. The two of them died of fever (everyone, it seemed, died of fever or horse falls). *No children. Calmahn.* Surely a history of the village would produce something. Another search she made, this one more easily accomplished. Geographical information was readily organized.

She found Calmahn and learned much, the most striking fact being the abrupt end to its history. The village was disbanded by decree of King Ars. *Disbanded?* frowned the princess. According to the documentation, Calmahn was a prosperous duchy. Why would a sovereign disband a profitable region? The act was senseless, like amputating a healthy limb. It was irrational; it was impetuous; it was Ars. He determined to wipe from existence everything of this chapter.

Josquin slumped in her chair. Absently, she petted the cat. What appeared to be drool ran from Soren's mouth as he lay cochfadala—flat on his back, legs sprawled. He snored profusely. She turned from her books to the window. In a few hours, day would dawn. She stood and opened the door.

"Gilian!" The guard jerked up, surprised. He jogged to the royal and bowed. "You know the Cassican intern, Flautis?" "Yes, Your Highness." "Get him." The guard couldn't imagine what was needed with a priest at this hour but he didn't hesitate. Anything to get him from this graveyard watch. She returned to her chair and quickly took note of pages and volumes, all referencing Silva. Books were replaced by the time Flautis burst into the room.

"Princess!" he panted, kneeling. "Is anything wrong?" (Dear God, he hoped she hadn't killed anyone!) She took his hand. That blessed sensation filled him. "Nothing wrong," she answered in their tongue. "I need information. 'Calmahn.' Have you heard of it?" "Of course, my lady. The relic of Saint Solgostis derives from there." "Its christening records, where are they?" Flautis frowned. That was an obvious question. "In the village abbey, my lady." "But what if the town were disbanded? Where, then, are its records stored?"

"Disbanded?" That was not-so-obvious a question. "They would transfer to the monastery of the region. The Grimillion Monastery...." "And do you know the way to this monastery?" "Yes," Flautis smiled. Finally, he was proving useful to his sovereign. "I know it. Tis half a day from here. It's headed by...."

"Here," she interrupted, handing him a paper and quill. "Draw me a map." The priest swallowed his reply. "Of course, Your Highness, but..." he inquired, tracing the way from the palace, "my lady is not going there this time of night, is she?" Casica grinned, roguishly. "She is...."

She stepped quickly through Bastien's room, noticing as she walked the distinct scent of its owner. Her heart ached for him.

Hunting. The grandest substitute for war. Next time, she would join the men. She found what she wanted and quickly jotted a note for Clarece: "Gone today. Everything's well. Eat all. Will return this night." As an afterthought, she added. "Don't fret."

Leaving the note on her dining table, Casica slipped out her door and into the night. Her eyes burned excitedly in the darkness. A trip. She hadn't been on a trip since coming to Byzanthia. She ducked her head as guards passed not wishing them startled by her eyes. A livery met her at the stable. She allowed no conversation, simply asserted her rank and waited, impatiently, as he saddled Rigel. From the wall she took a crossbow and secured it to her steed. She prepared to mount when the livery stopped her.

"My lady," he bowed. "Are you certain you wish no escort?" Poul had made it clear the foreign royal was to be attended well; if he learnt he'd let her go alone, there'd be hell to pay. "No escort necessary, livery." As he prepared to mount, he stopped her. "Are you certain, Highness? Tis imprudent for a woman to ride alone." "I'm fine, livery. Thank you."

He stopped her once more. This time her expression squashed all further questioning. The man offered, instead, his jacket. She took it. He felt better. "Thank you, livery. I'll see it back to you." With this, Josquin hopped easily into the leather. Rigel nodded at her weight. She tapped her heels, and the two companions dashed into the fading night.

Casica passed through the portcullis and reined. Before her plied the business of slavery, as collared men, women and children brought their owners' wares to market before dawn. Their lamps made for a sea of stars, their voices stirred as surf. Laughter and yelling filled the dark places. She rode silently through the sea, careful to shield her eyes as she glanced about. The slaves worked as a great machine setting up booths and filling carts.

Life in the city stirred but beyond it, a half-hour to the north, the forest slept. Casica followed the map easily; years of josquinning and circuit riding had developed in her a confident sense of direction. The air was damp and cold from the earlier rain. She loved it. Alone with the woods as she had been so often in her homeland. A light or two shone in breaks in the clouds. An occasional movement in the brush or call of a whippoorwill or owl beckoned her attention; otherwise she rode in thought.

The envoy was killed: she would have been nine or so, old enough to remember events in the castle but of the death of an envoy she wasn't aware. She wondered if the man were a spy or port authority. Certainly her parents had never mentioned anything to her. She thought about their meeting, Pelana and Clarece; how did it feel to Maman, to be helpless to save the woman who had initiated their contact? She considered, also, Ars' private hell: a legion of guilt plagued him. Would he ever be free? Would he ever surrender to his Sovereign and receive absolution?

She ducked under a bough but not quickly enough. The leaves christened her with rain. The woman laughed at the cold sensation. Crispus! How invigorating this was! In her joy, she broke out in song. It was a traveler's song, a piece about the journey of earth upon an eternal path. The lyrics and melody she enjoyed as much as the pleasure of her voice. Rigel liked it too, finding the familiar music comforting in this unfamiliar place. They rounded a bend and ascended. Upon their faces poured the morning light. "Whoa...."

Light crested the horizon, spilling like a wave through the treetops. Deep orange quickly turned yellow. The cloud bank began its retreat. It should be a fair day. "Yip!" Rigel broke into a gallop. Mud flew from his hooves and steam, his nostrils. He was a runner, like his lady, and restraining him proved difficult. "When we come to a clearing, I promise," she told him. She reached into the livery's pocket and found a strip of jerky. She chewed contentedly, humming along with Rigel's gait. They splashed through a shallow brook and left the thick trees for a meadow. She loosed her hold and kicked. "Ya!"

Yes! Rigel charged as he always did, increasing speed in a muscular crescendo. He flew into the meadow; his mistress lowered her head to his neck. God, could he fly! She closed her eyes and melted into the cadence, the pounding heartbeat of flight. He reached his apex now and flowed like water.

Casica dropped the reins and sat upright, arms spread out, head back, eyes closed. On him she could fly. Someday she would for real, but until then she reveled in this equestrian ecstasy. Cold wind whipped her ears and face as she surrendered to an exquisite trust. Her laughter filled the meadow. With time her wings tired and slowed of their own volition. She reclaimed control and patted Rigel's sweaty neck. Between her legs his sides heaved like a bellows. "Rigel, I love you!" she declared, as she had countless times before. The white mane nodded in agreement. He loved him too....

They walked now at a healthy pace. A fork in the path approached them. She paused to let her mount rest. Flautis' map directed them to the right. For a long time they followed this route, the sun bathing them with warmth and comfort. Cassica or Byzanthia, the same light fell on both, she thought. Her people worked and lived beneath the same rays, another reminder she was not alone. How much she struggled with a sense of isolation, only God knew. But it was often.

Perhaps if she were blonde and fair, Josquin's foreign-ness would be experienced differently; she might blend in at times. But as it was, seldom did she lose her keen awareness of being dark in a white world. Sometimes when she imagined being with Bastien, she saw him dark, too. Surely their offspring would be more dark than not; what would life be like for them? Who in this land would possibly marry them, children of a mixed race? As she wondered this, she wondered if Bastien ever wondered it. She felt it doubtful, though she couldn't know. He had a way of surprising her. Bastien.... Her thoughts wandered to other sights now; she smiled at the vistas.

A shrill cry arrested her. Two hawks sailed the sky together. It was impossible to see hawks without thinking of Asla. Casica offered a prayer on her friend's behalf. The prayer was well-timed; for there, not a mile before her, sprouting like a chimney in the open, stood the parapet of the monastery. She kicked her heels.

Monasteries were only slightly less fortified than castles. A high stone wall separated the world from the holy. As the world breached the open gate, a black-cloaked figure approached her. He shed his cowl and stared. Never in life had he seen anything like it: a woman clearly, (an oddity in itself) but a dark woman, with hair darker still. "Welcome, daughter," he wished. "I am Brother Petter." She slipped from the saddle. The monk looked up. *Dear saints in Heaven!* thought he. What fate brought this dark female giant to his brethren?

"Thank you, Petter," the giant smiled. At least her teeth were white.... "I am Casica. I come from Byzanthia." "Not at birth, I would venture." "No, very recently was I delivered, quite grown." Petter struck his head in realization.

"Of course!" he exclaimed. "You're the Cassican tribute. We've heard of you." Tribute. That was one way to view it, she thought. "Yes," is what she said. "I've come to pay such to your great place." Petter bowed humbly. "You grace us with your presence. Tis payment enough. Come. You will meet our abbot."

She bowed to the man and to the doorway. It was low on her. "You will wait here," Petter instructed. As she stood, the healer viewed her surroundings with misgiving. She wasn't fearful; just unsettled. Why would God's followers live in such gloom? If there were any windows in the structure, she hadn't seen them. Instinctively she buttoned the livery's coat around her neck, feeling it prudent her shalonn stayed hidden here. She stood contemplatively as a man, followed by three others approached her.

The abbot stopped and in a most un-abbot manner studied her person. She was tall and dark and damp and girded in a man's coat. She was a healer, and he had heard rumors of healers. What would a spirit like hers want in a holy place as his? The princess felt naked under his stare. She decided to cover herself with word. "Abbot. I am Casica, wife of Bastien of King Ars." *Wife,* thought he. Perhaps she was not so unnatural as she appeared.

"Your Highness," he bowed. "I am Ruftus. I welcome you," he offered guardedly. "And to what do we owe such an honor?" "I come for information, Father. I wonder if I might see the church records for the town of Calmahn." "Calmahn?" he asked quizzically. "That town no longer exists. It was ruined by plague." *Yes, a plague,* she thought. A king's mind plagued by guilt.

"So I hear, Abbot Ruftus. I hear, also, that its records were transferred to the keeping of yourself. I have interest in its population. I wish only review it and I'll be on my way." "And may I ask the reason for your interest, Princess?" "A woman's curiosity, Abbot, and for that, reasons are known only to God." A chuckle came from a man in back.

"Indeed, Princess. For a woman's mind, the Maker formed a chasm of curiosity." Ruftus considered only a moment. Calmahn was veiled in mystery, like this woman. Probably its mystery drew her. If knowledge would send her away, then let it be. "Brother Mott." The chuckler stepped forward. "Accompany our guest to the chronicles and assist her search." "Yes, Father," the man replied somberly, motioning for the woman to follow. She nodded as she passed the others.

Beyond their sight, Brother Mott presented his face. It beamed with a manly pleasure. "You can breathe more easily now, Highness," he grinned. "We go to a kinder place. Novitiates await you. The abbot is a good man. Only suspicious." She smiled but without reply. The less said here the better, she determined.

Mott led her to a circular stairway. They descended not a few paces before coming into a lit chamber. She stopped at the sight and grinned. If only Clarece were here. Book, hundreds, crept up the walls like layers of an endless cake. Tall ladders and men on them lined the volumes. Her gaze was fixed above so Casica failed to witness her entrance. Male faces, a dozen at least, lifted from scroll and parchment to stare at the dark form. Every mouth smiled. A woman. Confession must cover their thoughts, but God knew how long it had been.

"Welcome to my world," Mott offered. "My brothers and I honor your presence." She smiled winsomely at the admirers and wondered for a moment if this might not feel something like being Asla. "I thank you for your welcome," she bowed. *Byzanthian clergy: pity them,* she thought, (considering their vow of chastity) and as alms offered a holy flirt. "It is my pleasure to enter your sanctum. Your order's gain is *my* world's loss."

Grins swept the room. Her host invited her to a table. Immediately its chairs emptied as young novices happily offered their seats. She sat alone. "What years of Calmahn do you wish view?" "The last christenings recorded." Mott disappeared, leaving her to examine the surroundings.

The smell of books fragranced the air as did the smell of lamps and the scratching of quill. Toward her left in a corner hung a score or so of saintly portraits; paper and pen scattered her table. Casica took a quill and began to sketch. The search took quite some time, and during the interval she completed her work, blotting it and turning it over carefully to dry.

"My lady," Mott greeted, presenting his success. "The final volume." "Thank you." "Is there more I may do for you?" "Not at this time." The monk bowed and excused himself. She opened the heavy work at its end. Depending on when Ars disbanded the village, Clarece might be toward the back. Names were recorded under yearly headings. She began her search. At some point, a cup of wine and a plate of bread attended her. She nodded gratefully to its bearer.

She had consumed half her wine and a third her bread when Casica found her. *"Aduou,"* she breathed, staring in wonder as though she'd stepped through a portal of time. There, written in the distinct script of clerical strokes, was her friend's genesis: *Clarece Aerasa, beloved daughter, born live to Silva, Countess of Calmahn, this day, Apela 21. Baptised into the family of God for the pleasure and purpose of the Almighty Father....* Tenderly, dark fingers caressed the writing; it warmed at the touch. Aerasa. A second name Silva had given her daughter. An anomaly in the culture.

Casica's eyes closed as she imagined the desperate mother. For months she had kept her secret but now all would be known. Surely she anticipated Ars' reaction. He called her wise. Such a woman would prepare for the worst. Were she to die, she would have nothing to leave her daughter. No inheritance. No provision. Nothing but a name. She bequeathed one rich with meaning and added to it a second to embellish her child's verbal dowry. Added perhaps, as a message to her friend, a memorial to her lover....

Aerasa, Casica whispered. *"Undying love...."* The lovers died but their love lived on. Lived under the very gaze of the one who erased them from life. Clarece's friend wept quietly in that silent place of knowledge. The novices took notice but none spoke. None moved. She wiped her eyes on a silk kerchief and then taking her quill, wrote the entry verbatim. She finished her wine and bread thoughtfully. Communion between the past and present ended. Closing the book Casica stood, and as an offering, placed the sketch upon the volume. She glanced at Mott. He came to her. "I'll see myself out. For your order," she whispered, offering him a heavy gold coin. He bowed to the gift. She turned and ascended the stone way.

The men waited until she disappeared from sight, then as one, congregated around the table. Mott took the parchment and turned it up. The sight evoked a collective sigh. Before them was drawn a paragon of divine loveliness. Surely she must be an icon, they reckoned among themselves (no superior consultation was deemed necessary) and having decided as much, framed the image. They would gaze upon her often for inspiration as joined with her company of fellow saints was displayed the Beauty of God....

XXXIII

She stepped lightly up the stone stairway, scraping her feet for the sheer pleasure of the sound. What an amazing day it had been, one of beauty and revelation. Her face still warmed with the sun who long ago had transferred her to the keeping of his softer friend. An even lesser light welcomed her now. Clarece had placed a candle in her window. Though the hour was late and sleep missed for two days, no fatigue weighed the young woman. Her journey invigorated her as did the knowledge she carried in her mind and vest.

Josquin played with the idea of waking Clarece but decided against it. The chief slave needed rest; morning would rouse her soon enough. At her door Casica stopped and gazed a final time into the night. Stars blazed everywhere. "Mun gode, Aduou," she wished her maker and turned to her chamber.

She opened the door. Warmth greeted her. She stepped into the cozy room and smiled. A lamp and a glass of wine graced her table as did the aroma of supper warming on her brazier. Her mouth watered. Softly she retrieved her meal and sat to eat. Her note rested in its place. Casica glanced at it and stopped. Two words were added to the bottom, written with what one would have thought was a child's hand, so uncertain and labored was the print.

"Welcome home," the chief slave had penned. Casica teared. She was born to write, the poet was, but her body failed her. Failed her for a king's ungodly judgment. Casica took the paper and studied it. It was the only example of Clarece's writing she had. She folded it and placed it in her vest.

The princess enjoyed the meal with hunger as her companion until the last bite; it was then she sensed her and turned in time to see Clarece offer a greeting kneel. Her vest was gone for the evening but her boots remained; she'd been waiting. Casica smiled at the image. Nothing about Clarece had changed; yet adorned as she was with newfound understanding, nothing about her would ever be the same.

"Welcome, Mistra," the slave bowed, approaching. "I wished to establish your safe return." Her owner stood and enveloped her warmly. "Safely returned, my friend." Clarece scented her and sighed. "Mmmm," she moaned, "old books. Where have you been?" Casica chuckled. "You can smell that?" "Indeed. Tis the most evocative scent on earth," Clarece observed, joining her owner at the table. Casica poured her a glass of wine. "To life," she toasted in her tongue. "To life."

Casica took a deep draft before speaking. "And how did you spend your day?" "Like a royal," was the shy answer. "I ate your breakfast. I ate your lunch. I drank your wine. I read and slept on your sofa. Tis wisdom slaves have so little free time. I'd positively mold." She took a pleasurable sip. "It was a delightful day. But very quiet...." Very lonely. "I missed you." Casica nodded. "And I you." "Impossible. Not while gathering a bookish scent." The dark eyes studied her wine. "Especially while gathering such a scent," she answered softly. The expression on her face worried her companion. "Princess? Is everything well? Your note said it was. But is it?"

Casica gazed into the eyes of a royal. She took a deep breath. There was no need to wait. If it were she, she'd want to know without delay. "I spent the day at Grimillion Monastery. Do you know it?" The slave shook her head. "Well, tis a half-day's ride from here." Clarece leaned forward with interest. Her owner wove a great mystery, she felt. Casica rested her elbows on the table, offering a silent prayer as she began.

"Ars told me a story last night, Clarece. I want to share it with you. Years ago, Ars had two friends who grew up with him. Their names were Almed, who became his First Knight and Silva, Countess of Calmahn. Do you know Calmahn?" "No." "Well, Almed and Silva wed—they had no children—it was thought she was barren.... When Ars married, Silva stayed in the palace and served as his wife's chambermaid. She and the queen became confidantes. They were, the four of them, dear friends."

Clarece was smiling. "I'd never imagine the king's having such a circle." "Tis hard to believe," Casica agreed, "but it's clear he loved them." She caressed the smooth table. "Almed died in the Sarciany wars. Silva eventually asked to return to her village. Ars' wife visited her there regularly." Casica paused here, wanting to reach for her wine. She didn't but continued with the story instead.

"Ars said that several years later, Silva sent word by the queen asking him to free a slave, a tutor she'd bought to teach the village children. She loved this man, she said, and wished to marry him. Three times she made the request. Even the queen spoke on her behalf; she'd met the slave and thought highly of his honor and brilliance."*What a foolish woman,* thought Clarece. The king would never agree to such a request. "Of course, Ars refused," her owner confirmed.

Again the storyteller paused. Her eyes teared when they returned to Clarece's. For some reason, the slave found her heart beating wildly. "And then what happened?" she asked. Casica bit her lip. "Some time later, Silva gave birth to the slave's child. A daughter." She looked tenderly into her friend's face. "She named her for her closest friend...."

All this time, Clarece had sat with her chin in her claws imagining with a witness' detachment the scenes her owner weaved. Now, she slowly drew back. Detachment gave way to disbelief: she wasn't an observer. She was a thread. The realization immersed her. Casica answered her speechless question.

"It was you, Clarece," she spoke softly. "You are the Countess Silva's baby." For a quarter minute, Clarece held her owner's gaze. The statement settled upon her like a billowing sheet, drifting down of its own weight. It covered her as with a dream. She must be dreaming. The blonde head shook.

"No. This can't be. You're mistaken, my lady. The king, he was misinformed. I am slave." "Tis true, Clarece," Casica countered gently. "It's in the library. Countess Silva is real, her line an ancient one. Ars knows of what he speaks." The blonde head continued to object.

"No...how could he possibly know it's me? I've no original papers. He'd never even met me until that day—." "In the hall?

That's how he knows you. Your eyes, he said. It was your eyes that frightened him, Clarece—not your hands. You've your mother's eyes. 'Like God poured the sea into them and contained it with a ring of night'...that's how Ars describes them."

"My *mother*?" Clarece stared at her owner, utterly confused. Her confusion gave way to sorrow. It flowed down her face. "But if this is true, then...then where are they?" she whispered. "Where are my mother and father?" Casica glanced down. "They...died." Clarece frowned, suspicious. "How?" *How?* Casica wondered. How to tell her friend her parents' terrible fate. She could not bear to disclose the grisly story. Clarece saw the struggle.

"Please, Mistra," she begged, "please. Hold nothing from me. Tell me all." Casica glanced from her friend to the table. She nodded, finally, and spoke what she knew, oblivious to her desire to defend the sovereign. "Ars was insane with wrath, Clarece. You must understand that. He sent a guard to find your father. He was waiting for them. He hadn't tried to escape. Ars ordered him... he had him castrated and disemboweled. And his body hung on Silva's gate...as a warning." The slave's eyes hardened. "And my mother?" she asked, swallowing her fear of the knowledge. "What did he do to her?"

It was Casica who teared now. "She was waiting, too, in the village chapel. Ars...he wanted to drown her baby, but she was wise, he said. Silva had had you christened. He says he would have killed you anyway except that she covered you also with his wife's name. The Church and his own conscience stood in his way. So instead, he sent you to Sladishen as a slave and your mother to the mines of Pulca. She died shortly thereafter...."

Clarece leaned back in her chair, bewildered and silenced, her mind lost in revelation. He had not run. She had not run. Surely they knew death awaited them, yet neither had abandoned the one they loved. Gutted...it was her worst nightmare; it was every slave's worst nightmare. Yet he had faced it bravely, faced it like a human. Like a man. For a long time, she sat. Her surroundings seemed strangely distant. Something inside her kept saying none of this was real.

She turned finally, to her right. Her owner waited silently. Clarece breathed deeply and with her breath inhaled the scent of books. "You say you found proof?" she asked. Casica nodded, retrieving from her vest the papers. "I wrote references for you," she explained, unfolding the list. At the sound of parchment, something in Clarece woke. She reached for the list.

"You can find these in the library. I looked for information on Calmahn. Ars had the village disbanded. I learned its church records were transferred to Grimillion. That's where I've been." She unfolded the second parchment with a tender smile. "You *do* exist, Clarece. You are christened." Silva's daughter received the offered record and slowly read it. A slight smile crossed her lips.

"My original papers." A piece of her life had been returned to her. She *was* real. She had a beginning and held it now in her hands. Lovingly, mittened fingertips caressed the words. Her owner had a beautiful hand. "Aerasa...." She grinned in her tears and turned shyly to her mistra. "I've a second name. I know no one with two names." She studied the year of her birth.

"I'm older than I thought," she announced, issuing a soft laugh. She tossed the princess a wan smile. "My resale value has dropped considerably." Casica offered a labored smile of her own, wondering what Clarece truly felt. Surely, under that relaxed veneer was the knowledge of unjust enslavement. She awaited her friend's response. When it came, it wasn't as she expected.

Clarece leaned back her head and took a deep breath. And smiled. "They loved each other," she told herself, told the world. She opened her eyes to tell her companion. "My mother, my father—they *loved* one another." A mittened claw went to her heart. "I am born of *love*, my lady. Undying love." The hand moved to her collar. "*Freely* given." She brought a mitten to wipe her nose before continuing. Her owner knew as did she.

"I know I am wronged," she acknowledged, looking away to something in her mind. "But even so, I am among the most blessed of women. Tis not every woman, not even free, who can say their parents loved."

A hundred questions hung between them, the one born free, the other living free. None was asked. The chief slaveswoman looked again at the list. The library. Information. They beckoned with comforting familiarity. "Mistra?" she asked now. "May I your leave to visit the library?" The princess nodded. Clarece started to rise, then remembered herself. "May I have these?" she asked in reference to the parchments. "Of course."

Casica watched, as her charge stood and offered a parting kneel. Wordlessly, she left the chamber for Bastien's room. Casica heard the door close behind her. She cradled her head and prayed.

XXXIV

A warm ray insinuated itself between the curtains. It found her face and fretted her eyes. Clarece turned away but even then, the light teased her sleep. She snuggled more deeply under the heavy tapestry. The room was cool. Her body registered the chill, registered the weight of her cover and the scent of books. The one she smelled most lay open across her chest on top the fabric's regal horse, covering his flowered trappings.

Very slowly awareness crept along her warming face, waking her in a kindly fashion. She opened her eyes to a blinding light. Disorientation melted quickly into recollection. She blinked into the morning sun which was less morning than she wished. *Pony.*

Clarece knew without a clock: she'd missed not breakfast only but lunch too. *So what,* she thought. She didn't care. Like the heavy tapestry securing her from cold, the knowledge she'd gleaned during the night sheathed her with a comfort and sense of well-being she never knew she lacked until now. She'd read all there was concerning her family: her grandparents, their grandparents, all the way back to the spring of blood from which she and the kings of Byzanthia flowed.

Kingly blood or not, if she were caught like this, she'd be flogged and stocked. But instead of panic, she felt present, yawning happily as she stretched full on the sofa. So what if she were flogged and stocked. She was Clarece Aerasa. She had a name. She had a history. She didn't care. However, she realized suddenly, someone else would. Casica! Casica would come check on her, late as it was.

She disentangled herself from tapestry and carefully replaced all she'd handled in the night. She tucked her shirt into her trousers, arranged herself as properly as possible, and stepped quickly from the room, striking a single key on the hammerschord as she passed. Thank God she lived face down, she thought, passing puzzled guards along her way; otherwise, she'd lose all composure. She'd advanced two minutes towards her pen when her slave's line detected a colorful figure ahead. It was the Princess of Cassica, coming to find her wayward slave.

Clarece dropped to her knees and awaited acceptance. It came as it always did, with a tender caress on her head, filling her body with a healing warmth.

"Good morning, Mistra," she mumbled embarrassed. "A thousand pardons for your meals." Her lady laughed kindly. "Come. I was on my way to the library. Would you care to join me?" Her slave bowed with her half-kneel, pausing for her mistra to gain a step ahead before following her. In the privacy of the library, the women faced each other. "Again, my lady, I ask your forgiveness for neglecting you." Casica dismissed the comment with a flick of her hand. "Forgiven. So how are you, Clarece?" The slave moved to the sitting table.

"I'm not quite certain, Princess," she said, presenting a seat to her owner. They sat. "I've read all in this library concerning the family and history of Calmahn. Calmahn's existed hundreds of years. The king's disbanding it was senseless. But I think I understand why he did it. He wished to end my family's memory." She looked at her companion. "Do you know I trace back to his line? The king and I are distant relatives. No wonder he hates me."

Clarece fiddled with a fastener on her mitten. Tears filled her eyes. She'd thought she would have run dry after the night she had spent. Outside, the cathedral peeled the half hour. She met Casica's gaze.

"I read once of someone who said they were a bell and didn't know it until they were lifted and struck. I feel like that. I feel like I did that day I learned to read. Except this time, *I'm* the text." Casica nodded at the image. A puzzle piece failing into place is what she imagined.

The slave dropped a clawed hand to the table, her face scowling. "But I'm confused, Mistra. For years the king has known me.

His son buys my food, and yet he's waited. All these years. Why tell you? Why now? It makes no sense." The princess twirled a quill in her fingers.

"I don't know. I do know the night he told me marked the seventh year of his wife's death. Her death haunts him, as does your mother's. Ars is tormented by his deeds." "As he should be," Clarece muttered under her breath. She stood and walked to the windows. She drew a curtain aside. Casica studied her in the light, Ars' words rising to her memory. "'If she raises her head in this knowledge....'"

The princess contemplated the impact of knowledge. She was cognizant of the unfolding of Clarece's personality. She had purposefully done all she could to facilitate and nurture the process. She remembered her prayer of a thousand years ago, to offer tastes of freedom in the midst of slavery. In Clarece was found not so much tastes, as the banquet itself. Love, joy, hope—powerful emotions these were, but conspicuous in its absence was anger. When a sleeping limb, numbed, comes to life, it hurts. It riles.

The form at the window seemed settled enough. But inside this collared woman was garrisoned a battalion of injustices. Would the knowledge of her birth create a warlord? The healer couldn't know. But of one thing she was certain; Clarece seethed like a volcano. Casica had never thought otherwise. Her friend was passionate and brilliant—and bound. Chains could not hold so powerful a soul forever, anymore than they had constrained a slave's passion from being poured into a personal friend of the crown. His release brought forth life. Her soulish release was inevitable. What fruit would it bear?

A mitten brushed a spider's web from the windowsill. "My mother and I have more in common than our eyes," Clarece observed, still facing outward. "Hers was a forbidden love. I wonder if it was worth it? I wonder if she had all to do again, if she would?" She turned to her owner. "You're a healer. Is the taste of life worth one's death?"

A silent gaze answered her. The slave's hand went to the band about her throat. "Sergeant Poul. I love him, Mistra. Surely you must know that." She watched as Casica ducked her head, uncomfortable. The reaction puzzled her. "I mean you must hear the rumors, that he and I are lovers." She turned from the Cassican's embarrassment.

"Well, the reality is, we've never touched—much less been together. Tis forbidden. Everything of humanity is forbidden a slave." She grimaced at the truth. "I've bent rules beyond number but never, never have I trespassed the boundaries of my collar. My father did. I wonder...I wonder while they yanked life from his body what he thought. To live as he truly was, to embrace his heart's desire, was it worth everything? Was it dignity that gave him courage to defy the king...or rebellion?" She turned again to the princess. "Tell me, Princess, what do *you* believe? Is living, truly living worth every kind of death?"

Casica expelled a long, deep breath. *Oh, Clarece.... To explore such things as a freewoman would take you only God knows where, but to embrace them with a chain about your throat....* "The Book says that life, truest life, requires death of the most deadly sort: death to self. But as to what you ask...." She shook her head. "All I know is that it's the essence of woman to bleed for life, even when we're not bearing it. Even though there's no potential, we bleed in preparation of giving it. But our shedding of blood is not the *loss* of life, tis the giving of it."

"As opposed to the gaining of it," Clarece rejoined, nodding. "I don't know," she concluded, finally. "I don't know what to do with my life." She leaned against the sill and asked a most unexpected question. "How long do you expect to live, Mistra?" Casica blinked. "I don't know. Barring personal calamity—sixty, seventy years, perhaps."

"You mean one-hundred-sixty or seventy years, I assume." The healer nodded. Clarece laughed, shaking her head.

"*Crispus*.... Well, we more mortal than you can hope for a third of that though, I begin to suspect that living in your presence, I may hope to live longer than typical. Still, I have a short wick. My life is a meaningless riddle. Perhaps, it is preferable to go out with a flash, like a falling star." Casica cocked her head at the statement. The scene from a night in her life came to her. Still, something of her friend's tone, she found disturbing.

"Clarece, I have a question. For years, you lived in the presence of Queen Clarece. How is it she never knew you?" Clarece hid her smirk. Her owner would never grasp this. "Furniture, my lady. I was in the proximity of Prince Bastien's mother countless times. I remember scrubbing around her feet. But the prince has only recently referred to me by name. I've always been 'slave' or 'girl' to him. The queen never 'saw' me. She was a kind royal. But a queen, nonetheless, and a queen does not look upon a slavegirl."

"And for that she missed the one thing she most truly wanted," Casica replied. "To redeem the memory of her friend. Ars lied to her concerning your death. He implied he knew that he'd have a battle on his hands if she thought you lived." Clarece stared at the information. "You mean, she would have tried to find me?" "Yes," nodded Casica. "She loved your mother, Clarece. Ars said that his wife was 'half a heart' without her. When Silva died, a part of Clarece died with her."

The thought pierced a hardening place in the slave's heart. "A *queen* would have bothered herself with a bastardized slave?" Casica stood to join her friend. "Yes, and while *she* couldn't find you, God did. And He brought you under her roof. You aren't meaningless, Clarece Aerasa. You've been spared for a purpose—a high purpose. I don't have the answers to your questions, but I do know tis no accident you live. I pray you, bring all this matter to the One who finds you."

Silva's daughter turned her gaze from the royal. She viewed instead the world beyond her, a world which always would lie outside her slavish grasp. With a destroyed hand, she caressed the bondage she wore about her throat. Why should she bring anything to the one who put it there? "I don't know," she said, finally. "I simply don't know."

The statement stirred dread in the healer's heart. It felt all the world like a dangling bobbin on one of Dolca's tapestries. Clarece was a work in progress. Her indecision hung ominously, like a thread that could unravel all.

XXXV

The dark woman walked quickly, desiring escape for a most riveting reason. She wanted to think, to go away with herself and savor a change of life. She wanted to pray and, perhaps most of all, wished release. She would send healing to her own country in celebration for the happiness she was beginning to know in this one. After so long of living in dread, joy was returning. And she knew why. It was Byzanthia's son who freed her to laugh.

The course of her heart took Casica on what she had come to call the gazebo path. She paused to glance at the sky; it had the queerest look to it. Clouds hung high, too high for a summer season, she reasoned. She couldn't remember seeing anything like it in her island home. *Oh, well,* she thought, continuing, even the weather was changing, like her spirit.

She peered down the path and smiled. A blonde head was bobbing towards her. Asla glanced up, also, but too late. She'd be seen; there was no avoiding the princess this time. For days she had skirted Casica's company, surrendering even the safe passage of her chamber for the southwest door. She couldn't shake her shame, try as she might. Their unexpected meeting at the baron's was too befouling; any sense of normalcy the insulit enjoyed with the Cassican princess had drowned in a flood of darkness.

Even now, Asla winced in memory. For Casica, a pure and innocent woman, to have witnessed her whoredom in flesh.... Nothing, none of Clarece's reasoning and pleading would ever set it right. And yet here she was running right into the person she least wished to see. "Blast," she cursed herself, "if I were still hunted, I'd find myself ripped in a day." Casica was smiling. There was nothing to do now except bear the stain of sight.

"Mighty g'Helderleit!" the princess hailed in her tongue. "For too long I've not seen you! Clarece and I grow fat from your share of cake and tea!" The insulit paused only to bow in greeting and then moved to continue. "Hold, please, Asla," Casica asked, no teasing in her voice now. The young woman obeyed. She turned to look awkwardly at her friend. "I wish to speak with you about the other morning," Casica began. Asla thumbed her palm viciously.

"Casica, I was only doing what—." The princess raised a hand. "As I was saying, I was shocked and appalled at what I witnessed. The sight of your accepting a mere pound dash from that man.... I only *spoke* with him for an hour and, God knows, deserved at least a crown for my labor. Tis none my business, Asla. But I do think you should reconsider your dashing rates." She grinned.

In the company of such gracious humor, Asla relaxed somewhat. "I've missed your eyes," Casica offered kindly. "I've been busy," the blonde lied. "So I see," observed her companion. "Busy running this day. How far have you gone?" Asla calculated silently. "Several skene. A short jaunt before the weather changes." "So what do you make of this?" asked Casica pointing her face to the sky. Asla's joined her. "I think if I were on the hunt, I'd be looking for a cave or hollow to hole up in this night. 'Twill turn bitter."

Casica started to ask what Asla meant by hunting when it came. More and more did they come in Byzanthia, glances that shone with great frequency at home. There was a reason so much gold shown in her shalonn and the giftings the stones facilitated increased with life. In this moment, time stopped, and in the measure it would take for the healer to blink she entered a scene: it was Asla. The g'Helderleit was speaking somewhere strangely familiar to the princess. Casica glanced at the surroundings. Huge trees hung low, forming some sort of canopy. Their shadows brushed markers made of stone and wood. It was a cemetery she saw. Her friend stood in a graveyard.

"...so I've been wearing the brace as you suggested. My ankle sustains more," Casica heard, waking into Asla's conversation. She forced a smile, shaken from what she'd seen. She could not know all the vision meant, but one impression was clear; Asla lived no longer in this land. She dwelled in another, her life poured into a garden of death. The young woman was catching her breath.

"So you ride?" Casica glanced towards the west. "Yes. Before the weather sets in." "Then you should leave now," Asla advised, "as should I. I've services soon." The princess studied her expression. "Will we see you for tea, tomorrow?"

Her friend smiled wanly. "Yes," she decided. "I've...I've missed you." She looked uncomfortably away. Surely the healer would not embrace her as was her custom. She could share tea, from kindness, but she would never touch her again, not after what she had seen.

Casica answered the thought immediately. "Tis so good to see you again," she said. She took the woman into a warm embrace. Healing flowed into the harmed body. The sight of tombstones haunted Casica. "God's blessings upon you, Asla," she prayed.

The slave almost wept at the blessing. She let go, instead, wordlessly resuming her way to the palace. As she walked, she could feel it. *She's standing there,* she said to herself. *She's standing there waiting for the reply.* Something burned in her heart. *Well,* she argued, *when horses dance! I'm not saying it. I'm a frappin insulit and insulit have no business....* "Rigel dances, you know!" Bronze feet skidded to a stop. The Mighty took a deep breath.

To Asla, all the world's a dance floor. She spun upon it now in a most graceful fashion to face the healer. Casica stood in the path, arms crossed challengingly. The blonde stared a moment at the whimsical expression meeting her. And smiled despite herself.

"And upon you!" she yelled with a flourish. There. She had said it. Casica caught the words and clutched them to her chest. She raised her hands to heaven. And for a moment, the insulit could have sworn she saw light burst from the dark woman. She blinked. She couldn't have. And yet.... She smiled and spun again, and with a heart lighter than she had known in weeks, sprinted towards the dawn of her day.

Casica dismounted lightly. She paused at the saddle, relishing the scent of sea. Her eyes gazed directly into the sun. The strange weather hovered above, hesitating its ascent. Rigel's flanks glistened with sweat. His head bobbed hopefully. Surely his mistress would free him of saddle. "I know what you're thinking," she told him. The young woman tossed over his stirrup and reached for the cinch. Wind, sweat and leather mingled into a queer brew. Berea's containment loosened.

She stood, troubled, in a dark, empty place. Her bare feet were cool on the cobbles. The silence rang uncomfortably after the noisy entry into the city. Their quiet ride through the woods had ended abruptly. Bastien held her protectively as they rode through the market, shielding her with defiant glances and muttered threats. The whole city, it seemed, had come to gawk at the Cassican sacrifice. Eggs, stones and dirt were kept in hand, fearful of striking Byzanthia's prince. They would wait, the mob would, wait for her presentation in the square. Their hate assailed, unchecked, in curses and screams of protest. Few if any in the crowd guessed the man's intent. All assumed a royal execution this day.

Casica's heart pounded wildly. He felt her quickened breaths and held her more tightly. "It's all talk, Princess," he said under the violence. "You're safe. No harm will come. We've only a short ride to the hall. You'll pass through the guard unmolested. I've paid your ransom, but I can't be with you. I'll be in the antechamber. But don't worry; I'll be there in time to cover you."

Numbly, Casica nodded. She knew the script as well as he. She would be surrendered to the king's guard as the prisoner of war she represented. If not for Bastien's ransom, they would have absolute right of her body; that had been her greatest fear, more than death. The guard would present her to the people who could do as they wished. But only from a distance. From the people, she would be escorted to the executioner. If Bastien abstained, she would lose her life; if he covered her with his mantle, he would gain a wife.

Rumors swept through the crowd like wind through a meadow. She couldn't know how little speculation pertained to her; it was the necklace the crowd wanted. The alien string of light reputed to possess incalculable power and value. No one could gain it while she possessed life.

He rode through the crowd quickly possible. They ducked through a narrow portcullis, its thick masonry mercifully shielding her from the noise. Xerxes' hoofs echoed loudly. "There, that wasn't so bad," he observed more to himself than to her. He slowed to a walk. "We're here," Bastien announced quietly. "I'm to leave you at the door. They'll come and escort us to our places on stage." His breath was warm on her neck. "Soon, this will all be over, Princess." He was going to say more but the clang of a sliding gate stopped him. They were coming for him. He dismounted and helped the young woman to the ground. A voiceless person took his mount's reigns. "I'll see you soon," he encouraged. "Don't fear." She nodded, knowing not if he saw her. Mount and men were leaving. So she stood.

Josquin fretted with her bounds, fretted with her feet. The wait was suffocating. "Come and get me," she mumbled through her hood. "I'm here. You've waited five hundred years. Why wait longer?" She strained at every sound. Water dripped somewhere. It could be the walls, she determined. It might be very dark. The place smelled of urine, the result, doubtless, of frequent guarding. What she did not yet realize was while they didn't come, they watched.

Eyes, all of them differing shades of blue, peered through arrow loops lining the narrow tunnel. They smirked silently at one another, the guards, relishing the girl's increasing fear. For hundreds of years they'd awaited this hour; they wouldn't rush a moment of it. The healer concentrated on the pulsing presence of her shalonn. With time her mind quieted and in its silence, she could feel them, feel their eyes upon her. She straightened determinedly. *You may look all you wish,* she thought. *You cannot touch. I will not cower before your game.* They grew tired of it. A large man bearing chevrons on his sleeves removed his tankard from the keg on which it balanced. Drink had flowed freely this day....

Casica jumped. A rusty lever sounded to her right. Warmer air crept into the darkness. "Welcome, Princess of Cassica!" a voice bellowed. "We've been waiting." A powerful hand grasped her arm. She felt, suddenly, very small. "Come," the voice sneered. "You've many friends who wish to meet you." He took her forcefully and pushed her into a room. She stumbled but maintained her feet.

The chamber smelled of mead and men. The woman took several blind steps backward, away from the wall of flesh she sensed. She backed directly into a body and spun away. For a minute, she stood perfectly still, panting through her gag. The wall laughed as it encircled her. It was closing in. And in the midst of her growing terror, a memory flashed.

She was fox hunting. Hounds had cornered the terrified creature, and she rode upon them just as they moved to kill. The fox lunged and snarled in futile desperation. Something in the girl winced. It would be torn to bits. She recoiled at the thought and called the pack off. It was the last dog hunt she accompanied, sickened by the sport.

This time, however, it was she who was prey. And there was no one to intervene.

She could smell them, the pack. They panted more than she. Frantically, she looked around the darkness. "'No harm will come,'" he had said. The promise fell from her like armor.

Something from her left rushed. He locked his arms about her chest. She flailed against the force as another man ripped from her head the hood. A foreign hand grabbed her shalonn and yanked brutally. Casica gnawed her gag. But it wasn't the external attack she fought; it was her shalonn. To attack a josquin was suicide. The stones would not surrender to any force apart from their owner and even now riled dangerously in defense. She must contain her power or she could kill them all. The men cheered in ignorance.

"Take her! Take her!" someone yelled. She was lifted then flung viciously to the floor. The granite met her. She gasped at the breath that fled but before she could gather it, the man was upon her. His arm pinned her throat as, laughing, he fumbled with her karosh. She strained frantically to rein her shalonn. The guard's comrades jeered him. "Need some help?!" The man rose slightly to object. "Tis this cursed foreign buckle!" he answered, turning. "I can't—."

He never finished. Her foot had traced the inside of his thigh and found what she wanted. Her heel struck him with all the might of her shalonn. He couldn't even scream with the agony, collapsing, instead, into an unconscious heap.

All attention turned to the fallen soldier. In the confusion, Casica struggled to stand. The leather bonds snapped from her wrists as she reached desperately for her blindfold. A flash of light downed her. She lay dazed upon the floor.

The lieutenant tossed the shattered spear from him. "You want to play?" he demanded. Casica didn't hear him. The blow that would have killed a non-healer left her teetering on the brim of unconsciousness. She felt herself lifted and half-dragged by her necklace. Her captor wrapped something heavy, like chain, around her wrists. She struggled against the metal when suddenly a force stretched her arms up and out. It pulled until she hung fully extended. Her lungs strained against the weight of her body.

A sweaty hand gripped her face. "Come now, Princess. You're not afraid, are you?" he asked, forcing something against her nose. The scent of leather met her. "Even Cassican blood spills here," he breathed. Casica hung helplessly. The blow to her skull, the act of breathing, they were all she could manage. "*Nalada*," she begged through her gag. "*Aduou, nalada....*" The pack howled.

She heard the whip crack at her left ear. Felt its wind on her face. The howls crescendoed. Twice more he taunted her. And then it came. Like fire, the leather sliced into her back. She felt the extended flesh rend as cloth. A scream passed her gag as another, then another, bolt seared her. She heard nothing apart from her body's cries of confusion as artery and vein split with flesh and sinew. All her shalonn's energies surged in a fierce containment.

Had he known her deepest secrets, the lieutenant could have not chosen a more deadly torture. He did not know her secrets, but he knew his work. The whip flew expertly, focused exclusively upon her back. With blind loathing he shredded her, targeting finally her left shoulder. He smiled at the game. He could sever it, the shoulder, and would, had someone not arrested his endeavor. "You've killed her!" a voice screamed. The man blinked.

The white blindness of rage faded and in its place was revealed his target. The woman hung limp at the chains. Blood such as he'd never seen, soaked her body. The whip dropped with a thud. It echoed in the silent chamber. All the soldiers gaped, horrified. They'd not been given permission to kill....

A captain raced to free the body of chains. It fell heavily. He turned her over. Beads of sweat popped from his face. If she died, here, in their custody.... He struck her repeatedly. No response. His mind raced. They needed her only conscious, only alive enough to present to the people. If she died there, no harm would come.

"Water!" he ordered. He took the offered bucket and emptied it slowly upon the dark face, upon her nose and into the gagged mouth. Drowning would waken the dead. The face moved. A slight moan escaped the gag. He continued pouring until she jerked away. "Hurry!" he demanded. "Get her out of here before she dies!" These words Casica heard. She felt herself lifted and dragged away.

Her face lay against Rigel's saddle. Its familiar scent woke her from the memory. The leather was wet with tears. The horse nosed her, worried, as his owner stood strangely still. The woman clung to the saddle. Batis. Batis did that to her. Her shalonn burned in harmony with her anger. She clung more tightly as something sinister and heavy pressed against her mind.

"Tis a lie," it said. "Your happiness, your hope—all lies. You're alone. You're abandoned. You're already dead. To believe anything else is to be a fool. Bitterness...despair, they are the only rational response. Tis your right to hate." The voice was familiar, as familiar as was its battle for her mind. Her hand caressed the smooth leather. And she remembered.

She was fourteen and rode drunkenly home. Usually, Berea required her competitors to wait until their sixteenth birthday to face her but this healer wouldn't wait. She couldn't wait, she had argued, and issued her challenge. For hours they'd met on the battleground of whiskey, a poor choice of weapon by the novice, giving as it did, the ancient healer home-field advantage. The girl couldn't remember mounting her horse and knew even less how she managed the ride. But she wasn't so drunk as to not recognize the blue orbs watching by the hitching post.

"My maternal majesty!" Casica announced, flailing her arms wildly. "Your sacrificial subject submits to your royal *ness*." She bowed. The eyes watched as Josquin oozed from the saddle to land with a most un-regal thud. Pelana squatted next to her daughter, shaking her head slowly. Casica squinted at the stars. "I drank that frappin witch under the table!" she declared. "Of course," her mother nodded. "That's what we all say." The stars were looking dazzlingly clear now. "How on earth did they get *there*?" Casica whispered. "I think...I think I'll just sleep here tonight."

Pelana sighed. She took Casica and lifted her gently to her feet. "Thank you, Rigel," she said. "Now go home." The white horse nodded and began walking toward his stable. His mistress stumbled in her mother's arms. Her legs gave completely. Pelana carried the girl up the garden stairs to her room.

In a few minutes, Casica lay quietly in her sleeping gown. Pelana sat beside her on the bed, her hand caressing her child's forehead. Her mind ached with turmoil. For months now, Casica fought her every step. Angry words had passed, followed by intimacy and then repeated anger. The queen felt more a tilting dummy than mother, absorbing blow after blow of Casica's awkward emotional thrusts. Tonight, she knew, was another act of rebellion. She braced herself for a verbal assault; she received, instead, something entirely unexpected. Her daughter began to sob.

"Please, Maman. Don't send me away," Casica wept. "Don't abandon me to death." Pelana winced. Her own eyes glistened with sorrow. "M'Yat...," she began. "I know I'm wicked," Casica continued. "I know I'm not what Anasis would've been, but please, Maman, please...love me. Love *me*." Pelana broke.

"Casica, my Casica," she breathed. "I do love you—you're my heart." "Then spare me. Save me," her daughter begged. "I can hide. You can say I'm dead. It won't be a lie. I was born into The Edict. I was born dead. Please...save me." Pelana moaned in agony. Her child pleaded with eyes as brown as her own. They closed finally in a throbbing sleep.

For a long time, Pelana held her daughter's face. There was no healing for drunkenness; if there were, she would administer it. Casica would feel wretched the morrow. She pulled the comforter close to her child's throat and kissed her. The shalonns burned at her proximity. She turned and blew out the candle.

It was with another sort of drunkenness the queen of Cassica stumbled down the hall. The guard watched anxiously. His sovereign wept. She bypassed her chamber for another. The family chapel stood one floor above. By day, the small chamber would bathe in sunlight channeled through a large central window. Now it was dark but for the single lamp on the simple altar.

Pelana removed her shoes and royal vest. She approached the light. She looked beyond the darkness into the night. Stars hung. The woman dropped to her knees as she had countless times, helpless in this matter. This night she could not pray, could not speak at all. She lifted her head and wailed.

K'eran ate awkwardly. Usually this time with his wife was filled with quiet conversation, a precious touch of communion before the busyness of the day separated them. But this morning his mate was silent. She ate none at all, merely nursed the cooling tea in her cup. It warmed with her changing emotion. Helios stood, worried. The chamber door opened.

All eyes studied the young princess, startling in her appearance. Black lines smudged her dark eyes, black as the trousers and sweater she wore. Helios thought how the daughter's face reflected her mother's haunted expression. "I need speak with you," she declared calmly. The servant bowed and made his way from the room. Casica clinched her eyes against the pounding door as it slipped quietly shut. A wave of nausea rose threateningly. She spoke where she stood.

"I'm leaving," she said simply. K'eran blinked. These past months between his wife's and daughter's struggle, he'd been raked raw. "Where are you going?" he asked, restrained as possible. She gazed blankly at him.

"To Hell, Father. But before I depart for our neighbors to the east, I wish see more my own land." She winced against a new throbbing assault. "I've never been to the Highlands. I hear the healers there live in isolation. Twill behoove me, I think, to learn their ways. I'm packed. I leave immediately. I've sent letters to my tutors and the canter. I'll complete my coursework when I return. I've sent word to DeLeah. Mother, if you'll inform the council to remove me from the circuit and tell K'ardan. I've looked for him. Of course, he's nowhere to be found." K'eran bit his response. This was no time for battle. "When will you return?"

The dark eyes teared. "I don't know, Baba. But I swear, I'll be back in plenty of time to pay our debt to Byzanthia." The king looked to his wife. She remained silent; after all the skirmishes she'd had with her daughter these days, to enter this fray would only exacerbate matters. This decision to leave certainly didn't smack of rebellion; it seemed a reasoned resolve. Casica looked to herself. What if they forbade her? She would defy them. For too long, her life had been directed by others.

The father fought his urge to fight. The Highlands lay weeks away. A woman alone.... He studied his child, sad. So much like her mother she was. So much like herself. From her stance, it was clear she desired no embrace. “We’ll miss you,” he said finally. His daughter bowed. She never looked at her mother, simply turned and exited the room.

Wordlessly, Pelana stood. She went to the side door and stepped onto the balcony. Her husband’s arms encircled her. They looked below. Casica had left the rich cloak Pelana made for her birthday, choosing instead a simple black one. She’d packed lightly. Two travel rolls. A crossbow. Her healer’s bag hung to the side.

She hopped none too easily to her saddle. Rigel reared as she spun him. With a kick, she ran them away.

XXXVI

Pelana surveyed the field of battle. Evidence of fierce combat remained: several bottles of whiskey, bread crumbs, a small division of glass. The ancient healer washed a cup for her guest. Berea looked fresh as always she did. "So, she's left you." Pelana nodded to the flowing libation. "And you fear you'll never see her again." The queen nodded more slowly. Berea waited. She knew where this conversation traveled, had met it countless times in the troubled mother. Large tears fell to the smooth table.

"What kind of parents are we?" Pelana asked finally. "If K'eran and I had half a soul between us, we'd fight for her. We'd stand against Ars and that cursed Edict. But instead...." Her voice faltered.

"Listen, Lana," Berea countered, "we've all been through this a thousand times. Cassica isn't ready for war. In ten years or so, maybe. But any move now 'twould be suicide. And besides," she added, determinedly, "we can't know what God has planned. It might not be M'Yat's death He requires at all. It may be life He gives. It might be, through her presence, the need for war is erased." Pelana's eyes turned hard.

"Highly doubtful," she replied bitterly. "I haven't forgotten my envoy, nor Clarece. Any man who would kill his own mate...." She shook her head. "What would he do upon the flesh of an enemy?" Berea sighed. "We can't know that Ars will kill her," she repeated. Her words pricked the mother's truest wound.

"I don't need Ars' help to kill my daughter," Pelana offered distantly. "I'm doing it all by myself." She averted her face. "She begged me last night to not send her away. Begged me." She closed her eyes against the words. "She begged me to love her. My own flesh *begging* me to love her." Cold tears fell shamelessly before her mentor: "What kind of mother have I been that my child begs me love her?" Her friend remained silent. The other tormentor would come quickly. Unconsciously, Pelana's hand went to her womb.

"I kill one babe by failing her at birth; now I kill another by succeeding," she whispered, moaning. "Anasis." Berea desired to comfort but nothing she knew, no touch, no passing of time, no understanding nor debating with God—nothing could erase this deep ache of guilt. The child had lived; for the fullness of time had grown joyfully in the womb, only to arrive, gone. Sobs wracked the broken mother as they had years before, fresh as they flowed that unspeakable day.

Berea said nothing, merely held Pelana's hand. There was nothing to speak to this sorrow. No poultice. In the truest wounds of need, was there so little a healer could do. Pelana quieted; the wave had passed for now. For months, perhaps.

"How is your freedom with Casica, Lana?" The mother met her confessor's eyes. "Not well. I try, Rea. God knows how I've tried since the beginning." She looked for confirmation. Berea nodded it. "You've fought, well, this battle."

The queen sighed with exasperation. "But I don't *win* it. What use is the fight if you never win? The closer the date comes, the greater I desire retreat. I mean, to try to love her, to enjoy her as though she'll be with me forever when I know she won't. I can't bear the pain." She pounded the table. "I can't *bear* losing another child. Not another. How many will God take from me? All? K'ardan?"

Berea smiled despite herself. "Not likely. He'd have to find him first. And that one? Even the Almighty has trouble keeping track of him." Pelana smiled wanly. 'Twas true: her son was a whirlwind of activity. Berea held Pelana's gaze. "But you're living that old lie," she continued. "The truth is, you *can* bear losing another child. And refusing to enjoy her and enjoy yourself with her, Pelana, won't work. Distancing yourself from M'Yat will in no way protect you from the pain you're going to suffer in the future." Berea fiddled with a cork. "If you'd known Anasis would be taken from you at the moment of birth, would you have chosen to end carrying her?" Pelana shook her head, insulted. "Never. I would have loved and nourished her as long as I could."

"Tis the same here," the ancient healer explained. "In two years or so, you're going to lose Casica. She *will* be handed over to our enemies in compliance to an edict some men formed centuries ago. These people may or may not kill her," she said plainly. "You cannot know. Only God knows. But she is foremost *His* child. He created her for such a time as this. Tis her life, Pelana. Not yours to prevent this. It is *your* life to love and nourish her for as long as you can." Berea's voice softened. She realized she spoke of flames as one who had never touched fire.

"Casica's not the only one written into destiny," she continued gently. "Only God can free you to give yourself to her. He gives you permission to live and even *enjoy* every moment with your child. You don't need to apologize to the future for living fully in the present."

Pelana considered the words. They rang of truth. "But what if she doesn't let me?" "What? Let you love her?" A nod. Berea laughed kindly. "Pelana, no one can prevent you from loving them. What they *do* with it is another matter. But they've no power to limit your love. Look at the great Father. How many people receive His love?" Pelana scanned the table. "That might be," she agreed, "but she won't even let me sense her; she's cut herself off from me." The ancient healer took a long drink.

"Well, she hasn't me. She's fine. Of course, when she reaches the Highlands, no one will be able to feel her. Unless she chooses to send her stones, which I think highly unlikely in the present circumstance." Pelana snorted. "She's raging at me." Berea shrugged. "She's raging at everything. M'Yat needs to break away. Consider it: from the day she was born, people who've never met her have determined her course. She's felt powerless all her life. She needs to assert her will, needs this time away—to live her own life and gather whatever treasures God has waiting for her." She looked evenly at the queen mother. "She'll come back to you, Lana. The course you must determine is your own; how will you respond when she *does* return?"

The Queen of Cassica walked soundlessly into her daughter's empty room. Its stillness stirred uncomfortably, like Rigel when Casica was quiet for too long. The rich, blue cloak she'd so loving fashioned draped a chair. Pelana caressed it before hanging it in its place. Her daughter was in the fabric. Already the servants had attended their princess' chamber. Fresh flowers sat in a vase on her writing table. An unfinished portrait, Casica's own, waited, covered, on an easel.

Pelana lifted the cloth and for a long time, considered the work. For weeks her daughter had struggled with this painting; still, all she'd accomplished was the initial outline. What would it reveal, the mother wondered, when completed? She strummed the collection of brushes thoughtfully. God had placed a brush in her own hand. What strokes would she contribute to her daughter's emerging self?

Evening was falling. She turned from the fading light to Casica's bed. The gesture would be futile; M'Yat wouldn't return for weeks. Perhaps months. But Pelana listened to her heart; it was what she wanted to do, what she would do if no chains of propriety or self-protection bound her. God offered her freedom. And somewhat embarrassed, she acted upon it. Lovingly, the mother turned back the covers and fluffed her child's pillow. She took scent and sprinkled rose upon the sheets. Casica loved the fragrance.

She glanced about the room. What else could she offer? She saw it and smiled. The candle was large and having lit it, Pelana placed the token reverently in the window nearest the garden door, the entrance Casica would most certainly use when she returned. The healer encircled the flame with her hands and blessed it and the one for whom it burned. The light shone with increased brilliance. It looked like hope.

She now stepped back to smile at her offerings approvingly. Only God knew what the servants would think, but something of the foolishness of her actions felt holy. It didn't matter what others thought. What mattered was fully honoring her heart. She would present this oblation every evening until God's child of her love was delivered.

XXXVII

Casica dragged Rigel's saddle free. She grabbed blanket and halter and bid him run. He delighted in joining his new friends in the corral. For weeks now, she'd used this barn and stayed at the home that owned it. Healings. So many healings and so many fascinating people. The Highlands lived their name. She gazed upon the horizon and from her perspective saw nothing but peaks. Plumes of snow rose like smoke. She smiled at the effect and thought to herself, again, how easily she could live in this place.

"So how was your circuit this day?" Benzaka asked. "Long," she grinned, "and beautiful. I'm pleased to announce the Walsta family has a lovely pair of girls to complement their fourteen boys." "And Ma Walsta? How is she?" "Quite well, I'd say," replied the healer, amazed. "She was fixing them all dinner when I left." The young man grinned. "That's the Walstas. They take the command to multiply seriously. 'More Walstas than rabbits! And talking about dinner, the village's come out to our house for a feast. I hope you've light left in your stones. You'll need it before the night's out."

He took the saddle and blanket and accompanied her to the stable. They talked of his day as they went and he considered, again, what a pleasure it was, her company. A Lowlander here, in his village; a woman who knew the works he'd read, who knew the South and the royal city. A visitor who'd brought with her more than healing. She brought wonder and mystery and curiosity. Rarely did anyone express interest in his life, but just the other night they'd sat on her pallet at the hearth and spoke hours of the world. And the week before, they'd danced the Hoovelaust. 'Twas a pity, his father said, her being betrothed. Even worse, her betrothed to a man she'd never even met, much less loved. Still, the betrothal had one good gain; it ushered her here in a final trip before marriage determined her life.

"Ho! Tis the Lowlander!" a voice hailed merrily. Casica smiled broad as the greeting. Warmth that far exceeded the fireplace welcomed her as a covey of children ran to her arms, laughing. She blessed them with health and spoke to each. She knew all in the room. It was as Benzaka had said: the whole village had gathered to send her away. For tomorrow she'd continue her quest to meet Anna, the ancient healer who lived near the peaks. The meal was delicious, spiced with as much conversation, laughter and argument as it was thyme and pepper. Casica added her unique spices to the offering, enjoying again the fellowship of countrymen who looked so much like her except for their paler complexion. The conversation wandered to politics.

"And what think you of the throne?" she inquired, her standard question at every place she had dined on her journey. A large, bearded man snorted. "I'd think more of it if they ever troubled themselves with us. You never see a representative of—what's his name? Kerton? Tis enough to make a vassal forget whose allegiance he holds." The table murmured with agreement. "If there were war, now, he'd find us soon enough...but in peace, he forgets us here." "All the Lowlands forget us here," a man observed. He pointed towards Benzaka. "If our student was a Lowlander, would not the university take him?" The table grumbled. Casica looked about, confused. "What do you mean? What has that to do with anything?"

"Everything," the man explained. "It was what—two, three years ago?" "Three," Benzaka replied softly. "Three years ago, he sends an asking to attend the royal school. The trader took it. And last year, this trader comes and says the school, Benzaka can't go. He hasn't any 'sponsor.'"

"But your village...you could sponsor him," Casica argued. Benzaka frowned. "It doesn't work that way. Your sponsor must be affiliated with the university. 'An alumnus or patron.' There's no one in the Highlands can be that." Casica shook her head, dumbfounded. "I was unaware. I thought we, it, practiced open admissions." The young man saddened. "Not open enough...."

"Tis the way of the Lowlands," his mother, Osa, added. "And not just the schools and royals, but the clergy and the healers, too." The table agreed. "I mean, look at them. We've a handful of healers in our lands. Tis true we are few in number, but still, to be circuited once a year, twice if we're lucky." She indicated the visitor. "You're a healer. But even so, it took a bad marriage to drag you up." The guests laughed. "Why can't your kind send more to help us?" Casica was denied an answer. "You'd think we're Byzanthian the way the Lowlands avoid us," a wrinkled woman rejoined. Murmurs turned to anger. "And what think you of Byzanthia?" Casica asked cautiously.

The wrinkled woman's husband spit a chicken bone into his plate. "Dogs!" he grunted. The table nodded. "Tis high time we fight for our freedom. But the king hasn't stomach for it." Casica reddened. "Perhaps he doesn't think it's time," she defended. "The head knows things the feet don't...."

"That may be," the man conceded, "but when a man chooses to sacrifice his daughter, he's no man a'tall." Her host responded. "You're wrong, Vojtek. The king's no coward. He's no choice but to obey. Tis our country he does for." "You mean he loves his country more than his daughter?" Casica asked, uncertain. Benzak shook his head.

"No, no, child. No man loves a country more than his blood. But he's not just a man. Take me.... Some man in another village tells me, 'Benzak, give me your daughter to do with as I please.' I tell him, 'Come. I'll speed you on your way to hell.' I can do this, for the fight is between me and him. The king, this isn't true. Tis not his own blood he risks. He defies Byzanthia? They cross the channel, kill us all. And this girl, God help her, she's not most truly his anyway. She's the Princess of Cassica. She belongs to us. God made it so. She belongs to us more than she does father or mother. Even herself." Benzak took a long draw on his pipe. "I do not envy him," he concluded softly.

"Nor I her mother," his wife added. "To have carried her, to give her suck, only to lose her. And to know it from the day she bleeds in giving her life." Feminine voices concurred. "Tis cruel. I hear she's lost one child already. Now to lose another...." Osa shook her head. "Queen or no, I don't know how a woman can bear that. God give her strength." The table bowed to the prayer. "And to the girl," another woman added. The guests grew somber. "Indeed," Benzaka offered. "May God spare her life—as we pray." Casica looked to her companion. "You pray for her?" she asked, surprised. "Yes," he nodded. "Every service, we do. She is our own."

The Princess of Cassica closed her eyes. Silently, tears coursed her cheeks, but they fell not of self-pity. They flowed from gratitude and repentance. Many at the table saw her tears through the dim candle light. Her friend watched awkwardly. "What are you thinking, Elespoir?"

Casica glanced up, embarrassed. She wiped her nose on her sweater sleeve. "I'm thinking.... I'm thinking the Princess of Cassica is privileged to belong to people such as you. I only hope she represents you worthily in Byzanthia, whether she live long there or no...."

The fire murmured quietly as did the couple. It was the last night they would sit at her pallet and visit. "I'll be missing you, Elespoir," Benzaka told her. Casica sighed sadly. "And I you. I've come to love your family and village." She gazed into the fire. "This has been such a good trip, Ben. I wish I could stay." "As do I," he acknowledged quietly. "You've brought something fresh, something exciting, to our sleepy ways. You make me think about setting out, myself." The young woman smiled. "When you *do* attend university, what will you study?" He grinned sheepishly.

"You mean in my dreams if I went...." He tugged at her blanket. "I would take my teacher's course. I'd come back here and teach the village and not just the children. The men and women... we may be sleepy, but there are students here in this place." He glanced at his mind. "We could use the chapel...invite other villagers. Books would be a problem. They always are. So expensive. But perhaps if I spent an extra year working in the royal city, I could earn enough to start a small library. Who knows," he smiled, "with time, we might have a sister university here in the mountains. That's what I'd do if I had two wishes to rub together."

As he spoke, his companion smiled with him, for him. "Tis an unselfish ambition, Benzaka. Your village will be blessed greatly." The young man grunted. "Have you always been a dream catcher, Elespoir?"

Casica stared at his words. Dream catcher. Hope was the stuff of a catcher's web. For so long, she had felt trapped in darkness; how freeing it was to be a catcher again. In this journey, she'd begun even to dream for herself. "In the past, I have been," she answered finally. "But these recent months, I've forgotten how, or maybe tis felt easier to live in despair. I don't know. But I see things sometimes. I see you as a mighty man among your people."

Benzaka glowed. The fire was dying and in its fading light, her eyes began to shade into blue. She reached for her boots and removed a prized object. "I've a friend, my cousin. He's a mighty man," she said. "He made this for me. I want you to have it…to remind you." Casica offered the boot knife. Benzaka received it reverently. It was exquisite. "This is too much," he said, studying the blade admiringly. "I've nothing to give you." Her expression puzzled him. "You've given me more than you'll ever know, Benzaka."

For a time they gazed at one another, memorizing the other's countenance. He knew what he desired was utterly impermissible. "If things were different," he whispered. She nodded. If they were different, indeed. His eyes teared. "I hope that man, your betrothed, he loves you. I will pray for it." The smile she offered now filled with affection. "Thank you," she said, "God's blessings upon you." "And upon you."

The flame was dying. Their shadows danced lazily in the falling light. She would be leaving in a few hours. She would never see this man again. Casica leaned forward. She drew his face to her own and offered his cheek a tender kiss. His sprouting beard tickled. Benzaka sighed as healing and something else flowed into him. For a long time they rested in their warm embrace. For both, their worlds would never be the same.

She departed a few hours before sunlight, pausing to drop a heavy gold coin in Osa's egg money jar. She then stopped at the village chapel to pray…and to complete one final task.

The villagers gathered later in the morning for service. Their chapel seemed strangely empty without the Lowlander worshipping with them. It was time to read the Word for the day. Benzaka took his place at the simple altar and opened the Book to its ribbon. A letter welcomed his confused frown. It was sealed, and though he'd never seen it, he recognized immediately the mark. A fleur d'lis pressed into crimson wax. *Dear God,* he thought, glancing from the parchment to the puzzled congregation. "We've a letter," he explained. He broke the seal reverently.

"Dearest Friends," it began. "My Lowland tongue fails with words to express my gratitude for having shared your fellowship. I came a stranger; I leave a friend. I thank you. And I beg forgiveness for neglect. You will see more of your Southern brethren: in royals, clergy and healers. On this, you have my word. And you, Benzaka, have a sponsor. Present yourself to my parents; they will know of you. You'll be welcome at the university, and after meeting you, I'm certain it will desire more of the Highlands' children. As my family's gift, a library of your selection will accompany you home to enrich your people with knowledge as they have me with hope. God's blessings upon you all. I ask your continued prayers. With deepest gratitude, Casica Elespoir, daughter of His Majesty King K'eran and Queen Pelana of Cassica."

The worshippers sat in a stunned hush; a queen had lived among them and they hadn't known it. But for the reader, his mind spun with an unforgettable image. A rough hand went to his blushing cheek.

XXXVIII

The old woman propped on her cane. For days she'd felt her coming and this evening would bring her. A cloaked figure materialized in the foggy mist. "Bless my eyes!" announced Anna. "If it isn't the Princess of Cassica." "Whoa," Casica ordered Rigel softly. "How is it you know me?" she asked, hopping from the damp saddle. The old woman limped happily to her guest. "I've met your mother. One can't see you without seeing her. That...and you cause quite a stir!" She embraced the tired girl. Rich power flowed from her. "Blessings on you, Child," she wished. "You are welcome here."

"...and how is that old crone, Berea? Does she still walk the earth?" Casica ate hungrily. "Yes," she answered over her stew. "Walks as though she owns it." Anna laughed kindly as she poured her guest more drink. "So. God's still not ready for her. Sanctification takes longer for some of us than others."

Casica couldn't know how much her sanctification would be nourished by her hostess, but over the coming weeks, she would learn. During her stay, Josquin never left the home of the ancient healer. She did no healing, only basked in the love and nurture of one who had walked the earth one-hundred-sixty years. So different was Anna's way with her than Berea's. The old woman listened attentively to the girl's story of her life and journey. Often she wept with Casica. More often smiled. Encouragement filled her home like air and breathing constantly of it as Casica did, the princess healed in places no one else had eyes to see.

Strangely, Anna never asked the motive of her journey. Never questioned the hours-long solitary walks; never confronted her impassioned arguments; never rebuked her wordless tears. Never placed any demands upon her at all. Rather, she served; always listening and answering when asked and ending each day by tucking her precious guest into a pobbled-warmed bed and a kiss to her brow. Casica would wake as she slept; nestled in the soulish knowledge of being cherished. In such an environment, she flourished. Comfort turned to courage as Anna's stories rooted her wandering spirit in the rich soil of history.

Clearly, Casica wasn't alone. Like a pobble in the chain of a shalonn, her color joined her sisters' and mothers'.

She lay thoughtfully in bed one evening as Anna spoke of Hadas, the young healer who lived alone even farther up the mountains. Her mother had been killed in the Lettings. "I'd hoped to meet her," the princess shared. "She's my age. It sounds as though she lives the way I'll be living in a few years."

Anna's dark eyes twinkled. She gathered the quilt closer to the girl's throat. "She's not so isolated as that. There *are* dark people around her...but yes, she's young to be living as she does. But...her mother greens the earth where she dwells. I doubt she'll ever leave." Casica considered herself for a moment. If she were Hadas, living alone in a rugged place, what would encourage her? What would help remind her of a kindred heart? She smiled with inspiration. How wonderfully easy it was to part with so beloved a possession. She reached to her bedside.

"Here," she said, placing her healer's bag in Anna's lap. "Would you see Hadas receives this? It might remind her she's not alone." The old healer studied the beautiful leather satchel with its exquisitely hand-tooled embellishment. Hadas knew nothing of finery. Such a treasure would enrich her impoverished world. Tears moistened the ancient eyes. "Thank you, M'Yat," she said softly. "I never leave my house nowadays, but I know the josquin who checks on Hadas each year. I'll see she receives your gift."

And so the time passed and with it, the season stirred to change. Summer surrendered to autumn. Casica strolled beneath a canopy of gold. She paused and breathed deeply of the cool, crisp evening and thought again how, truly, mountain air captured the scent of heaven—like the ocean, only richer. She gazed past the quaking leaves towards heaven. Wispy clouds sailed the sapphire sky.

"No wonder Your children live here," she prayed. "They brush against the dome of your house." She turned her gaze to a nearby peak. Snow capped it. Winter was coming. If she didn't leave soon, the snows would hold her until spring, and while a few months earlier such a prospect would have appealed to her, now it did not. She'd found what she had sought. It was time to take it home. So with the same compulsion that drove her into the Highlands, she determined to leave it.

It was with that strange mix of grief and excitement, Casica shared a final meal with Anna. The old josquin readied her guest well, filling her with meat, eggs and buttered bread. She placed a round of cured ham in Rigel's saddle bag. "Now don't you tarry too much, hear?" she was saying. "The snows come suddenly. And remember to take the west path; twill be easier on your mount." The girl nodded over her tea cup. She sopped the remaining gravy with bread. "And when you crest the range," Anna continued, "you let someone know you're coming, yes?"

Casica smiled broadly. "I will. I promise." Anna sat back and sighed. Tears filled her eyes. "I'll miss you, Casica Elespoir. What a gift, God's allowing me this time with you." The girl bowed, tearing. "The gift's been mine, Anna. To live with you," she glanced about the little cottage. "Tis like living in a shalonn. You are light." The woman nodded quietly. "You should know, Princess. That same gift dwells in you."

Casica frowned, embarrassed. "I know you know what I say," Anna confirmed softly. "Where your shalonn is taking you, that release, don't shun it. Tis God's gift to you and to us." Pelana's child fingered her necklace. Rarely did she ever speak of this burgeoning energy in her. "It frightens me," she confided.

"Don't let it," Anna countered plainly. "Tis not the light that unnerves you; tis the darkness. The evil one would have you neglect it. 'Have the world deprived of that blessing. Don't let him." She grinned mischievously. "Crush him under your feet...." The words fortified Casica with resolve. She nodded decisively.

"And now, a gift for you," Anna announced. She disappeared from the room and when she returned, held a most precious companion. Casica gasped. In her hands, Anna bore a rich, dark josquin's bag. Its design was foreign to her eyes, fashioned in another century. Anna caressed the leather lovingly.

"It was an anniversary gift from my husband. No one knows the hide. Some of the implements are older than me, others new as you. Friends over the years have filled it with their tastes. Now...his leather stays fresh with touch so don't neglect him." Casica shook her head, speechless. "A healer's bag," Anna declared, presenting the satchel to her successor, "for the Healer of Cassica." Josquin clutched the bag to her chest. It felt of Anna. "But your daughters...," she suggested. Anna stopped her. "No. I've been saving this for you. May it remind *you*, you are not alone...."

Casica hopped to Rigel's saddle. "Thank you for everything," she managed, weeping. "And to you, Child," Anna replied. "We won't meet here again but in Heaven. Look for me." The girl hesitated before asking. It was a terrifying question, and her heart trembled at its voicing.

"Do you...Anna, do you think I'll live?" The wizened eyes squinted. "You mean...survive the transfer?" The woman smiled broadly. "I'm certain of it." The girl swallowed, relieved. "But as for *living*," Anna continued, "that's entirely up to you, Casica. To *live* is a choice granted by God and nothing...no edict, no king's word, nothing can take that freedom from you. The battle is never for your body: tis always for your mind. Remember." Casica nodded. She would remember.

She pulled Rigel's saddle and blanket from him. The white horse kicked happily. *Freedom!* his tail swished as he pranced about the meadow. She lowered the leather and remembered still. Remembered leading the horse up the range, walking slowly on the steep path. As she crested the summit she stopped, her heart pounding in the thin air. God, her country was magnificent! Behind her stood the continuous peaks of the Highlands. Below her lay *her* world. Home. Days away. The woman blinked. Little pieces of crystal were falling upon her. She squinted into the white sky and smiled at the sensation of ice on her face. The white beckoned her above.

She dropped to her knees. "I am Casica!" she yelled, her voice echoing through the mountains. "I am Life's and He fills me with glory!" She raised her hands to the surging energy. And yielded. Light consumed her stones and poured from her body. She directed the energy, and for the first time, sent it across the ocean, across the channel to break upon the shores of the eastern land. And she thought of him, and prayed it would bless the fifth prince of Byzanthia, the one called Bastien.

She caused quite a stir. All about in the Lowlands, her sisters wondered at the force. A particular healer winced, startled, in the midst of a boring council meeting. Pelana closed her eyes in joy. Her daughter was coming home!

She came at night, secretly, having restrained her stones the past days to mute her return. Casica hopped to the familiar soil of her garden and held Rigel's saddle, sensing his eagerness. "We're home!" she whispered. "You'll be in your stall in just a little while." She looked up to her room and noticed the candle in her window. "Look at that!" she breathed then jerked quickly to her left. A door exploded open.

"Casica!" her mother yelled. "Casica!" The girl laughed in amazed delight. It was her mother. Her mother was running. She must have been watching for her. Before Casica knew what more to think, Pelana had her in an exuberant embrace. "I love you, I love you!" she kept saying, unabashedly covering her child with kisses. The girl melted at the unbridled display and clung to her mother, weeping. "Maman," she began to say, "I'm sorry—."

"Shhh," Pelana breathed. "No.... Let me feel you, let me know you are home." She clasped her tightly. "Oh, M'Yat, dear God, how I love you. How, always, will I love you." Love.... *How I love you Maman,* Casica thought, and conveyed her words with a most intimate gesture, one she hadn't offered in so very long. She reached for her mother's shalonn and held it. Both necklaces burned with joy....

And so they rested in one another, the mother and daughter. There was so much to share. So much to hear. So much fellowship to enjoy. But there was no rush. They had time. Not many years, perhaps, nor many months. But countless moments by God granted. For both had determined to live, despising the fears of the future for the joys set in the present.

And what will I choose now? thought Casica. She ascended the hill to the oceanic horizon. It lay before her, her home, and her future. The battle raged. Would she dwell on scenes of torture, cursing and death? Or would she choose to hope? "I have given you a choice," a voice spoke within. She smiled into the light of the strangely clouding day. She stood on a precipice, like the summit of a mountain. She fell to her knees.

"I choose life!" she declared with outstretched hands. Light surged from her being to join that of the heavens above....

XXXIX

So soundly she slept, she didn't register the first knock. It came again, something hard on chilled wood. Drowsily, Casica turned to the sound. It couldn't be Asla; the candle was gone; that meant she'd already gone to her stall. The knock came again, this time followed by a voice.

"Casica!" he called softly. *What on earth?* She sat on her bed for a time trying to clear her mind. The intensity of her release earlier had left her delightfully drained. She caressed the stones that still burned to her touch. The voice grew insistent. "Casica!"

"I thought I'd been freed from the night circuit," she mumbled, but she wasn't angry. Bastien never disturbed her at night. And why was he at the garden door instead of in his room? Something must be afoot.

She opened the door only a whisper, but it was enough to take her breath. "Tis freezing out there!" she exclaimed to her night caller, "Come in!"

"No!" he countered, grinning, "You come out!" "I'm not going out there. I like it here." "Oh, come on!" he laughed. "Where's that Cassican spirit?! Tis a magical night out—one in a thousand. Put on trousers and your cloak. You won't regret it." He was smiling so broadly even if she hadn't her healer eyes, she could have seen it. "I swear," she replied, "if you're not a little boy...." "Well, if you feel *that* way," he offered suggestively, "I could always come *in* and play." The woman groaned her defeat. "I'll be right out."

She slipped on trousers and boots and gathered her cloak about her. It warmed in anticipation. As she stepped onto the landing, all drowsiness shattered. “Crispus, it’s freezing!” she exclaimed. “What kind of Byzanthian magic is this?” He laughed at her expression.

“You don’t have weather like this in Cassica?” “Never! It must have something to do with our being an island.” “A pygmy island at that. Most likely, you do have such weather but it misses your land, so little of it there is. Probably, it falls into the ocean or comes here to grander quarters.” She rolled her eyes but then gazed in wonder. There was a reason for the eerie cold. Snow. A fine layer of white blanketed the ground and flora. Even as she watched, it fell silently through the air. Snow in the dead of summer. What a fantastical sight. “Amazing...,” she breathed.

He sensed her pleasure and grew in excitement with it. “Come, Your Highness. Your kingdom awaits.” They walked, laughing, down the stone way, careful in their steps. In her sight Casica noticed the smaller prints leading to her door. The g’Helderleit’s premonition of the strange weather had proven right. Bastien led her to his horse but it wasn’t Xerxes this time. It was his high horse. The white steed bobbed his head at their approach. No saddle. No blanket.

“Hello,” Casica greeted kindly. His nose caressed her warm hand. “And who are you?” “I am Gelderdesch,” her companion voiced horsily. “I am the great steed of the mighty Prince Bastien, Champion of Jousts and Defender of Maidens.” “Well, Sir Gelderdesch,” Casica answered huskily, glancing beneath the steed, “there’s certainly nothing maidenly about *you*.” Bastien whinnied passionately. “‘Women for the women,’” he quipped. “Then what am I doing here?” she asked, tossing a grin he barely could see. But her eyes, those he could see. He blinked at their intensity. What he wouldn’t have given to read them.

He answered thought with action and with a practiced leap, gained his mount. The hand he offered trembled slightly. “Shall we?” She took his arm and jumped easily behind him. *Too easily,* thought the soldier, puzzled. He moved to voice his confusion when suddenly warmth and something else embraced and filled him. All questioning ceased at her touch. This was no time for speech, he thought, tapping his heels into the horse’s side. Gelderdesch started with a lurch and she laughed in his ear.

Silently, the shadowy pair made their way on the garden path before diverting to the meadow beyond. It was beautiful to him, the sense of power beneath him, the silence, the sting of ice, her body. She brought her face near his. Her breath caressed him and once he felt her nuzzle his hair. Her arms tightened about his waist, drawing her body snugly against his. Even through their cloaks he could feel her softness. She felt him feeling and in response, the flowing warmth intensified like her shalonn.

The most peculiar thought came to him. How often had he ridden this steed, had reveled in the surging power of Gelderdesch thundering towards an opponent. How often had he boasted in strength and masculinity as armor met armor and force, force—shattering spear and body. How often had he gloried in victory, in the sweat and muscle and yet, nothing he'd known on this war horse—no combat or contest made him feel as manly as did her presence, vanquishing him with a tender femininity.

"What are you thinking, Bastien?" she asked quietly. "Nothing," he lied, clearing his thoughts with his throat. She smiled into his neck. "Are you catching cold, great prince?" "What?!" he asked, startled. "No...I'm—I'm wondering what *you're* thinking."

"I'm considering the damage this beautiful night may cause your people's fields." *Is that what you're thinking?* he wondered. "Little harm, if any," he assured calmly. "Tis only the air that's cold. The ground is summer warm and will melt the snow quickly. If this were later, though, it might be bad." He cocked his head toward her. "Are you always so agronomically minded, Princess?"

"I love the earth," she answered. "Most Cassicans do. We're people of the land." "Pity your island has so little of it," he teased under his breath. She snorted something in Cassican. "What was that, my lady?" "Nothing, my lord...." He grinned as he urged Gelderdesch on. The horse trotted with them up a hill and into the forest. Prickly boughs showered them with snow, the swishing mingling with their laughter as they cut through limb and glade to prance eventually into an open field.

The trio stopped. Before them the grayish light of an earlier moment melted into a present blue. Cloud had given way to star and the ruler of the night assumed his summer glory. The bright moonlight lit their world to where Bastien could see as clearly as she.

Casica watched as he looked. His breath steamed the air like Gelderdesch's. The horse was looking too, and seemed to turn his head with his master's. She smiled at the effect. *Surely these two comrades had partnered on many a mission,* she thought. She closed her eyes, sensing the bellowing sides of Gelderdesch. His warmth permeated her inner thighs. The mount had seen enough and moved to continue on. "Whoa...," Bastien ordered softly. He was in no rush.

Slowly his hand found her own. His caress was awkwardly tender. Josquin rested her face against his back and sighed. How wonderful to have chosen life. Had she allowed bitterness to bind her heart this day, she would have missed the joy of this moment.

"Shall we walk?" he invited. He helped her as she slid lightly to the ground. He joined her more heavily and took her arm into his. For a long time, they walked thus, their long shadows gliding silently as they, each lost in the magical beauty. Occasionally, their eyes would find one another and smile, soft as the night.

What would it be like? wondered the young man. *How would we celebrate such beauty if we were man and wife this night, joined in flesh as we are in Edict? What would it be like to discover the source of warmth that flowed so naturally from her body into mine?* Such questions he had considered countless times working on the dam of Valdera. They followed him home, keeping watch with him as he lay in his bed nights, knowing she slept not twenty cubits distant. Questions that demanded answers. Answers that required a course. A course he'd determined to set this night.

He could not know that as he thought, so did she. Her shalonn and heart burned at his proximity. The romance of the magical evening did its part to inflame them. *He must kiss me tonight,* she was thinking. *No man could walk with a woman—any woman—on such a night and not savor her lips. I'm his lawful wife. I'm willing. Surely he must sense that...surely—.*"

Her thoughts arrested themselves. It was a queer thing, being a healer. At any given moment, any given musing might abandon itself to physical knowledge. Even romance fell victim to a startled shalonn.

"Whatever on earth happened to you?" she asked, stopping. "What?!" She was pushing up his sleeve. "Your arm. You've the most awful bite mark on your arm. See?" He looked, confused, at the scar. "Oh, that." "That's a *human* bite. Who did this?" "Well...," he began suggestively, "there was this former lady—companion you might say...." She glared at him. "Your *slave*," Bastien laughed. "Clarece, did this to me." "*Clarece?*" "Yes, Clarece. Years ago when we were children." Casica shook her head, incredulous. The wound was deep. "Why on earth for?" Bastien smirked at the memory. "I got in the way of her cornball." "Corn ball?"

"Uh, huh. You see, she couldn't have been at the palace more than a few weeks. Looking back, I'm sure she was scared to death. Anyway, she was scrubbing my floor when all a sudden this cornbread ball falls out of her vest. I don't know where she got it, but it rolled across the floor and I reached to snatch it. To tease her, you know. Well, claws or not, she grabs my arm and bites the cush out of me. I mean blood...." The memory of the crouching, snarling girl seemed impossible, set against the chief slave now. He kept this image to himself. Casica was squinting in astonishment. "What'd you do?"

"I did what any future defender of the throne would do: I ran crying to my mother." "What did Queen Clarece do?" Casica laughed. Bastien offered a hurt look. "You're a healer; you shouldn't be laughing." "I'm sorry," the josquin repented. "And what did your mother do?" she inquired tenderly.

"Well, she washed and wrapped the wound. 'Told me it served me right, messing with a slave's food like that. I learned my lesson. You take my advice, Princess: never come between your slave and her cornball. She'll take your hand off."

Casica shook her head at the image of Clarece attacking a prince. She rubbed the scar kindly. "I'm sorry for your pain," she told it in Cassican. He watched her gentle hand; even in moonlight, her flesh was so dark against his. She felt his gaze and smiled shyly at him. "If you ever want it removed, let me know. I can't erase my own scars, but I could take yours easily enough." His eyes were tender. "Thank you, but this isn't a painful memory...."

He covered the dark hand and silently reached for the other. "Casica...." She turned quickly to her name. He paused to consult the moon before speaking. His palms were moist. "Casica," he repeated, gazing fully into the burning blue, "I've a question to ask you." *Yes!* she exclaimed inside. *Yes, you may kiss me!* "If I had the freedom to properly do so, I would ask your father's permission.

I haven't that opportunity. So I ask yours." He glanced down at his feet.

"Seeing your family are unavailable for inquiry, I ask you: Princess Casica Elespoir, it is my desire to court you. May I the honor of pursuing your hand in marriage?"

Blue orbs blinked. *It is my desire to court you.* It wasn't a kiss. It wasn't a proposal. It was a proposal to pursue a proposal. It caught her entirely off guard. *What he disappoints in imagined delight,* she determined, *he certainly delivers in surprising reality.* He was waiting, awkward. She came to herself. He saw her smile. Courtship. Surely the framers of The Edict hadn't imagined that. "Yes," she answered, bowing her head. "On behalf of my parents and people, I happily welcome your pursuit."

His face beamed. "Well, in that case," (*Now he will kiss me!*) "may I have this dance?"

Pony. No kiss. The young woman wrapped her emotions in laughter. "With pleasure." Bastien took her in his arms. And there, in that miraculously magical ballroom, spun her into a rapturous waltz, danced to a hushed orchestra of white.

XL

Casica's eyes glowed still from the night. What dreams she had had, beckoning her irresistibly to memory. It was the night of the magic snow that bid her to wakefulness this morning. Though weeks past, it clung to her like a sweet fragrance scenting everything about the couple's flowering relationship. She breathed the roses on her nightstand and glanced outside. The rain had ended but still dripped from the eaves of the house and limbs of her garden trees. On occasion, a drop would snag sunlight on its way. *Shining like a pobble,* she thought, caressing the glistening stones about her neck.

She considered the colors, mostly varying shades of red and blue and gold and much, much white. A married woman gained another color, that of her husband. The girl closed her eyes to watch what it would take for that to happen to her. She stopped. She should surrender that fantasy. Bastien and she only now began to know one another. He said he wished to court her. They may be months from his bed, his body, his....

"Good morning, Mistra," Clarece wished, offering her half-kneel. "Good morning!" Casica greeted. The light in her eyes wasn't lost on the chief slaveswoman. It was progressing well, Clarece thought, happy. Surely it wouldn't be long before she washed linens for one bed only....

"And how was your breakfast?" she asked noticing Casica's uncovered plate. "Actually, tis yours this morning, Clarece. I'm not hungry. I'm going to blades *to see Bastien,*" but this last part she didn't voice. Clarece smiled. Poul might be in blades. "Would you wish me go instead, my lady? Is it a message you wished delivered?"

Casica grinned playfully. "A message of sorts, but this time, I'll deliver it myself." "Oh," the slave answered, nodding. "I understand. Will I see you for tea?" Casica considered the brightening day. "I don't believe. I want to spend some time walking. I need to think." "Of course, Mistra."

How uncharacteristic of Casica, considered Clarece, to not eat. To skip tea. To go off by herself. Still a woman in love does many uncharacteristic things, she decided. She watched as her owner uncharacteristically left the room without a parting wish, neglecting even to gather her cape.

The slave toiled diligently in her solitude, sweeping under her mistra's bed with her sinsia. The small hand broom was altered with a strap to secure it to her mittened claw. She worked barefoot, a great pleasure this time of year and an even greater pleasure with her new boots which she could remove and shod at will. Her vest hung on a chair and her voice filled the chamber as she sang an ancient cleaning song any houseslave in the kingdom could join. So engrossed was she in her labor, she didn't hear the door of Bastien's room.

Bastien approached the princess' chamber, anxious for her presence. Even in her absence, she had cost him his match with Poul this morning, filling his mind as she did to the detriment of concentration. His friend reveled in the clumsy sparring and added many words to further his royal humiliation. "I think the great Prince of Byzanthia was smitten ere he stepped into this arena!" Poul struck. Bastien grinned good-naturedly. "Well, if I had the choice, there is another arena in which I'd like to perform!"

"Careful, Prince," his opponent warned, striking a particularly powerful blow. "In that arena, no man comes out as he went in!" Bastien laughed. Such a grand thing was sparring, and his good friend was the best of trainers. Afterwards, the two men drank together on the balance beam. Bastien thought still of the princess, and her image provoked a question.

"Poul," he asked, studying the hilt of his blunted blade. "The slave Clarece. Do you love her or do you only take her?" The sergeant's mind drifted to a different place. He caught the eye of his friend. "I'm in love with her," he said quietly. "So you don't just gain your pleasure," Bastien pried. Poul kicked at his blade.

"Oh, I gain much pleasure. The pleasure of her eyes, her mind, her glorious heart. But truth be told, Bastien, between you and me, we've never touched, much less been together." "What?!" His friend must be lying. "You jest! Everyone knows about you and your slave." "I tell the truth," Poul replied calmly. The prince shook his head. "If you're serious, why not?" Poul studied the royal crest of his blade. "That's why," he said, displaying the insignia of Bastien's father. "Tis a crime against your father to do so." Bastien shook his head again.

"No one cares about a guard having some slave." "I do. Tis my duty to honor his law, and a higher law still." "Your religious convictions," the prince observed. All knew of the sergeant's devotion to God. "Yes, and my convictions concerning Clarece."

"Clarece," he continued, "she isn't just any woman. Take that collar from her and she would outshine any courtier. She's the morning light," he smiled. "And she is my love. I would not treat her as anything less."

"Then why this façade? Why do you continue this ruse?" "I continue nothing," countered Poul. "I've never told anyone I take her. That's something fertile imaginations of men with too little battle devised." Bastien frowned. "Well, you've certainly done nothing to dispel the rumors."

"No, I haven't," the guard confessed. "I encourage them, in fact. They serve a strategic purpose." His face sobered. "A slave-woman like Clarece, she's vulnerable to harm. Tis my hope that the knowledge of my having her may shield her." Bastien nodded, reminded again why he liked this man so much.

"What will you do though?" he asked. "Tis not like she'll ever be free." Poul lowered his gaze. "I pray for a miracle," he voiced softly and *hope for Casica,* he thought. It had been his observation that wherever his cousin went, the miraculous often followed.

The other man didn't know what to say. Clarece had existed so invisibly for so long in his life; the thought of any man seeing her, wanting her as a woman was alien to his thinking. Still, another door had been opened, or rather the same opened more widely. Perhaps he needed to adjust his own vision....

"Slave!" a voice bellowed from the other chamber. The slave struck her head trying to extricate herself from the far side of the sofa. She'd been wrangling a maverick olive, evidence of the g'Helderleit's presence. She looked in time to see her master standing at the doorway; his eyes scanned the room for not her, she knew. She knelt humbly. "My lord."

Bastien turned to the kneeling form. "Where's your mistra?" From her low perspective, Clarece watched muddy water puddle her freshly cleaned floor. "She said she went to visit the blades room and then planned to walk, master." "Blades?" Bastien repeated. Could it be she'd gone looking for him? "Tis well," he voiced and then suddenly noticed the woman. "Stand, Clarece."

Her head touched the floor before complying. She stood. He considered her. Clarece was taller than many a female slave; her body filled her unvested blouse. Her mittened claws hung quietly at her sides. An unbred waist crowned the trousers that hugged very slightly her thighs, hinting at the slavish muscle beneath. He glanced at the bare shins and feet. Deep scars lined her flesh. An ugly ridge circled her right ankle. He'd never noticed that. Never noticed anything, really. "Look at me."

She met his gaze easily. The eyes that saw him shined exquisitely in her face, a face that was not, in any way, unpleasant to view. He noticed the full mouth and from there followed the course of her throat, stopping at the silver band. "Take that collar from her," Poul had said. Indeed. A patch of red formed on her neck, making its lazy way to her cheeks as she blushed from his attention. Bastien smiled within. She even responded as a woman.

"Would you go find Casica and bring her—no—ask her to come see me?" '*Would*' she? Did Prince Bastien just *ask* her? What was happening in her former owner? "Of course, Master," she replied. "I'll go at once." He turned and left the room. It was with no small amount of rumination the chief slavewoman shod herself with her boots. She laced them more easily now with practice. She stood and took her owner's cloak. It stirred at her touch. She might be able to catch the Cassican before she took her walk.

Casica laughed almost as profusely as she sweat. K'net was merciless. She'd missed Bastien but to her delight found the master swordsman. He glanced up from oiling his blade when she walked in. The door of the room closed softly. His cousin had hoped to startle him but while she hadn't, her presence surprised him, nonetheless. It was only the second time the two had been alone.

"Tis the Princess Casica," K'net announced in Cassican, bowing low. "And to what do I owe this esteemed honor?"' "God's good favor," she replied, grinning. "I came to find Bastien." "That Byzanthian? Why waste your time on him? He's useless nowadays. Seems to have lost his mind with his heart. However...," K'net offered, reaching for another sword, "your mission isn't completely failed. I hear you beat the queen's guard, Princess of Cassica."

"Twas a fluke, truly," Casica replied, slowly removing her vest. She watched him carefully. "But a blessed one. I owe whatever skill I showed to my teacher at home." "Well, let's see what you've learned in your teacher's absence." The sergeant tossed the sword to her. She caught it easily. Cautiously, the two opponents circled one another, twirling the blades in their grasps as they did. For once, she attacked first.

It was no competition truly. K'net outfought every opponent and the healer was no exception. It would have challenged him more had she drawn from her shalonn's power, but even then his skill would triumph over her greater strength. Her master blocked a thrust and smiled, pleased. She'd improved since last they sparred; she was more aggressive.

Poul steered the battle closer to the swords having decided, impishly, to sweeten their match with a spicy turn. His right foot found a blade on the floor and with his boot, he now tossed it to the startled woman. *Kai!* she thought, catching it on the fly; she *hated* when he did this: two-handed play taxed her coordination as nothing else. K'net laughed at her consternation. "That's no fair!" she exclaimed. "Battle never is, my lady!" He took a second sword for himself and attacked.

For a full fourth-hour the game made for an iron ballet as, fiercely, the two Cassicans fought. And while neither wore armor, they fought as though invincible; Josquin would mend whatever happened.... K'net considered his strategy. She could outlast him, he knew, so he needed to disarm her. Skillfully, he maneuvered her to the side wall against the leather dummy and feigned double blades to her right. She went for the ploy: with her one blade she moved to block, with the other to strike. The striking blade he captured with his own as with a loud clang, it fell.

Frantically, Casica tried to recover but too late. Twin swords crossed her throat. She caught his gaze and smiled, panting. Josquin or no, if this were for real, she would die. As it was, the man who held the swords did so flat-bladed, disdaining even the thought of touching her vulnerable neck. Her shalonn glowed intensely at his nearness. "I surrender," the vanquished conceded, dropping her remaining weapon. Her cousin's laughter wasn't for her. *That's what Bastien's praying to hear,* he thought.

His arms lowered as he backed from the cousin who was queen. She smiled now, soft with the closeness of her dear brother. How she missed him. "Are you alright?" she inquired kindly. He winked. "Just a few nicks...." She shook her head. It truly was him. "K'net," she whispered.

She took his face into her hands. Her touched filled the man with Cassica. He closed his eyes at the sensation and sighed. God, he was so homesick.... Tears crept from the corners of his eyes and with her thumbs she wiped them away. It had been so long since she'd ministered to him. There were nicks and bruises and injured muscles and a deep, deep longing for home. She closed her own eyes now as silently she poured healing and comfort into him. He quieted in the familiar embrace.

As she ministered, Casica thought of another woman who loved this man, a precious friend who still did not know whom she loved. "You must tell her," she whispered. "I'm under oath," he objected. Casica rested her forehead against his. "I release you. She's my friend. I disdain this sense of deception. She *must* know. Tell her." The Cassican captain nodded, relieved; for years he'd longed to tell her. Now, he could. Casica ended her healing. As a final blessing, she offered his brow an affectionate kiss.

Neither noticed the silent form that stood, numb, at the door. The cloaked figure gaped. The man she loved rested in the hands of the woman she trusted. Clarece blinked. *No! No!* her mind screamed. She turned from the door and flung herself against the stone wall, trying desperately to buttress her thoughts. Her ears burned hot and her breath came quickly as she brought destroyed claws to her face.

The familiar scent of leather eluded her. Reality eluded her. For in that instant, the past recoiled: Poul at Casica's bed whispering her pet name; Poul knowing exactly where Berea may be found; Casica twirling the blade in her hand; Casica blushing at her confession of love that day in the library. The notes. *Dear God!* All those notes.... The woman slid to the floor.

In her mind, the scenes fell together like some exquisite china plate slipping from her grasp. It exploded with comprehension. She must scream. She must run. Clarece spun on her heel and fled, finding eventually her dark and lonely stall. There she surrendered to her knees to wail in slavish silence, as shards of a thousand injustices thrust into her hardening heart.

XLI

Rece, for someone so smart, you sure can be frappin stupid! Casica wouldn't lay a man who's not her husband! She doesn't even lay the man who *is* her husband!" "I'm telling you she is," Clarece countered. "I saw them!"

The women held their quiet duel in the privacy of Casica's quarters. It easily could turn explosive; the insulit was tired, for one thing, worn raw with endless services. For another, the two hadn't seen each other in days. Asla hadn't been aware of the trouble between her friend and her owner. Only the night before had she come into its knowledge when she slipped into the Cassican's prayers.

The distraught woman had inquired of Asla about her stallmate's anger, something she now did herself. And the information she learned only served to irritate her more. The insulit had little time between services this morning and had hoped to spend it in a comforting bath; instead, she must spend it confronting an irrational belief of someone in whom she wasn't used to experiencing such irrationality. Scads, her little world was turning queer....

"You say you saw them," Asla now repeated prowling about the sitting area. "And what exactly did you see? Did you see them lying together? No." Clarece parried the statement, her voice laced with uncharacteristic resentment. "I saw her holding his face in her hands, Asla. I saw her kiss him," she glared. "And that's not all. He knows her Cassican pet name. Only those most *intimate* know it. *Intimate* she said." "'Intimate means alot of things, Rece," Asla blocked. "*We're* intimate and it doesn't mean *that*."

"But the fight, Asla—the fight. She twirls her blade just like he, and when I shared with her, (*God, she couldn't believe she had let her tread this holy ground!)* when I told her I loved him, she couldn't look me in the eye. She positively blushed. With all this, what would *you* think?"

What did she think? *I think your jealousy is making you insane* is what she thought. The insulit fretted with her dagger. Jealousy was something she'd never witnessed in her friend; she wielded it clumsily, like a poorly-balanced sword. Clarece's heart wasn't formed for such dark passion; she must disarm her before her sala severed something she couldn't restore. Asla's voice calmed to a breeze.

"I think, I might think what you think. Except for what you *know*. This is *Casica*, Rece. Your friend. She wouldn't lay Poul anymore than I." Clarece dropped her face. "I know what I *saw*." "But you don't know what it *means*. Look, Rece.... Just because you know everything doesn't mean you're right about everything. And why all this wrath at Casica? Where's Poul in your equation?"

Clarece glanced up, defending. "Casica is royal. Poul hasn't a choice." "Hasn't a choice?!" The insulit rolled her eyes. "Poul's a *man*, Rece. Men always have a choice. They're always on top... unless being under suits them better," she added, fading. *What a mess,* she thought. "Look, Rece, there's only one way to know for certain what's going on. I've talked with Casica. She's as much in the dark as you. Speak with her. Or if your pride prefers, I will." Her senior caught her eyes threateningly. "Don't you dare, Asla. Don't you dare interfere with this." "Or what?" Asla countered, her anger flashing. She repented instantly; this was no way to spar this woman. She held her hands before her.

"I'm sorry, Clarece," she retreated nimbly. "I won't interfere. But you can't continue hurting her like this, withholding yourself. I'm insulit. I read people the way you read books. A woman like Casica, this isn't a pride issue with her: tis an honor issue. You keep this up, and she'll feel she dishonors you by forcing your relationship. She'll interpret your silence as a desire to leave. And you don't want to leave...." The chief slave spun at the assertion.

"Maybe I do. Maybe I'm tired of being bound to people who treat me like—." "A slave?" her friend interrupted. "Clarece

Aerasa," Asla continued gently. "I know you've alot in your bowl right now. I don't think tis only this that's stirring it." The chime of Casica's clock spurred her to end. "Look. I don't know what it's like to be jealous. To feel jealousy, one must love, and I don't know love like that. But I do know resentment. I swill it every day. Tis poison, Rece. And if you're not careful, even if you stop drinking it, the harm's done; 'twill rot your life."

The chief slaveswoman glanced from the alpine eyes to her mittens. *The harm's already done,* she thought. She'd a lifetime of harm with little of it poured from her own flask. Still, Asla's words clung to her. It was true: she wasn't accustomed to such spiteful passion. But as true was the fact Clarece *liked* the way it felt. She liked the sense of power that came from transferring her rage to another—especially one more powerful than she. She had been born free. It was royals, like the princess, that had stripped her of life and bound her naked in a collar.

Clarece studied the healer's satchel. Living with Casica had warmed her like spring sun, and to her surprise, she'd found hope budding in her heart. And she hated it, now; hated how much she wanted to hope. She scraped her foot into the leather. What an idiot she'd been. Hope was a divine comedy. Loving a man, a farce. She'd been a fool to think she could live beyond herself.

An image of childhood mocked her. The men in the livery were starving her as often they did. This time they had tied her by the ankle to a post outside, like a dog, to keep her from scavenging. They laughed as she tried vainly to free herself with her crippled claws. After two days, they threw her meat.

Meat. She lunged for it like an animal. But they had thrown it just beyond her reach. The leash held her at bay as she clawed and strained for the food. She struggled against the tie until her ankle was bloodied and raw. She could still hear them jeering as, again and again, she grasped at what she could not attain.

Her claw went to her throat. She was slave. The world would afford her nothing. Well, it wouldn't take her pride. She would rather live in misery than yield to the humility of need.

"Will you promise me to at least consider speaking with Casica?" her friend was asking. "Will you do that, Rece?" The sapphire eyes of Silva scanned those of God's beauty. They beckoned her to peace. She spurned it. Asla lowered her gaze. She knew better than to push this woman. Leeway proved most effective. “Tis your choice, of course,” she ended.

Clarece was assessing the scar she had made on her mistra’s bag. Asla secured her dagger in her belt. “I won’t see you tonight,” she said, resuming an air of normalcy. “I’m in the city till the morrow.” She offered her friend a final look of invitation and then, pulling her dark cloak about her, turned for Casica’s garden door.

Clarece listened as her footfalls tempered the stony way.

XLII

It was morning but the new day shrouded itself in fog. Casica sighed, feeling as dismal as the day. A lamp lit the small dining table and the empty plates. Bastien was gone for the city. A new falconry opened in the market and he wished to view the birds. His invitation for her to join him fell limp. She needed to stay and talk with Clarece, she explained. The woman's anger and withdrawal ate at her like a tumor, covered her like the low gray sky.

Bastien had listened patiently to her concern but still couldn't understand it; Clarece was slave. And to express anger to an owner was inexcusable. She should dismiss her, he said. Casica smiled wanly at his words. For Bastien, everything could be answered with action. How could she explain to a man like him her affection for the enslaved woman? She couldn't. So instead, she promised to join him that evening.

She watched as he ran down the garden stairs and shook her head at his excitement, thinking how like a little boy he was. It had been so long since she had felt that. She missed that weightlessness of joy. For weeks now, all she had felt was a nameless guilt. Clarece's anger felt like heaven closed against her. Gladly she would confess her sin, but how could she? No amount of inquiry or pleading would open the slave's door. The hardness left the princess utterly bewildered. She glanced out the window toward heaven and asked, again, for wisdom. Then she sensed her.

Clarece stood at the doorway, her face gazing slavishly to the floor. Thank God for the collar around her neck; she resorted to it exclusively these past days, hiding behind it her heart as well her face. If ever she looked Casica in the eye, all her resolve would fail.

"Come in, Clarece," her mistra invited sadly. The slave offered her greeting kneel and proceeded to clear her owner's settings. Casica watched as she worked, distant and mechanical. She stacked the plates and moved to leave when her owner spoke. "Hold, please." The slave held, standing at attention, looking at the floor. The princess gazed at the floor herself, thoughtfully caressing her shalonn. All night she had considered what she must do. Clearly, Clarece hated her company, for what she may never know. And while the bondwoman might contentedly enough abandon the role of friendship for slave, the healer could not. She couldn't bear living like this with someone she so deeply loved.

Casica crossed her arms. If Clarece were a different woman, she could initiate the end of their association. As slave, she hadn't that freedom. Casica must give her the option. It seemed utterly senseless after all that had formed between them, but to continue this facade of relationship dishonored them both. And Casica would not dishonor; she would not bind Clarece like one of Bastien's birds. So she surrendered her pride and desire and determined to offer the slave freedom. Freedom to leave.

"Clarece," she began. "I haven't a clue what I've done, but tis clear I've dishonored you greatly. I've begged your forgiveness. I beg you again; share your heart so we may reconcile." Silence. "Will you not even acknowledge me?" The mittened hands fled into the brown vest. "You own me. I will do as you want, Mistra. How do you wish me acknowledge you?" Casica struck her thigh, frustrated.

"Since *when* do I own you, Clarece? If I owned you, you wouldn't treat me this way. You wouldn't *dare* show such contempt. Your treatment of me is that of an insulted woman. Why don't you continue as such and speak your mind?" Silence. The dark woman looked away. "I thought...I thought we were friends. Am I such a fool in my judgment?"

"I am slave," Clarece replied icily. "You are slave," her owner rejoined. "It seems you become slave whenever it serves you, whenever tis expedient for you to hide inside that collar." Silence. Casica's heart pounded against the sickening surge in her stomach. She felt all the world as though she were cutting out her heart, but she must ask. "Clarece, please. Look at me."

The slave hesitated as her emotions she gathered into an orderly clutch. When she did meet the dark eyes of her mistra, her own were as moist with dread as they were hard with resolve. If the princess had known her in the past, she would have recognized the expression. It was the same Clarece wore when she approached the flogging post.

"Will you never wish us reconciled?" the healer asked one final time. The slave looked through her. Casica winced. "You pierce my heart," she whispered. Her tears flowed freely now. "Clarece, do you wish to leave me?" *No!* Clarece thought, but the image of Casica holding Poul's face in her hands cut her like a whip. "Yes," she heard herself say.

It was Casica who now was struck. She felt the rejection bleed into her body. Her ears burned at the shame of it. She allowed the impact to cut as deeply as it needed. She would not harm herself further by pretending she wasn't affected.

Clarece cringed at the sight of her lady's defeat. The hands that had so kindly blessed hers covered the lovely face. At that moment, the slave thought to abandon her siege on her mistra's heart, to run into it instead and beg forgiveness; but she was tired of groveling, tired of being made the fool. She would rather die outside the wall than humble herself to love.

Casica looked up finally. The pain all but silenced her. "Alright," she managed. "I'll speak this day with Dolca." The words invoked a searing sense of abandonment. She felt alone and did what she was prone to do at such a time. She bolted. "Please find Sergeant Poul, if you will. Tell him to ready Rigel for me."

Clarece knelt. She then stood and turned as a slave does to walk quickly to the door, anxious to escape her confusion. She did not see her former friend drop to her knees to pray....

Clarece fumed in the gray, cold air. Its dampness sliced through her blouse. Blast! She should have fetched her cloak before making this trek. She pawed at the gravel and scowled. Perhaps it was better she didn't have her cover. Something about feeling miserable in the flesh fortified her soulish misery. Never in her life would she have done what she just did, cut and break such a loving person. But she had. And as she walked, Clarece talked herself into a frenzy, trying desperately to kill any sense of loss.

Poul, to his misfortune, worked in the stables. He hummed happily to himself as he polished his saddle to a glowing sheen. "Clarece!" he smiled, excited at the presence of the one he loved. The slave stopped short at the sight of him and lowered her face. "Sergeant Poul," she replied officially. "The princess asks that you saddle Rigel for her." Poul stared, confused. They were alone; she should look at him in such a setting, yet here she was cold as the day. "Of course," he answered cautiously. "Shall I saddle Leharen also?"

"No," the voice instructed. "I will not be joining her." *Ever again,* Clarece thought. Suddenly, Asla's words broke into her armor. *Where's Poul in your equation?* she had asked. *Frappin right,* the slave thought now. Where indeed. She felt within a powerful explosion and wished suddenly to lay her hands upon the man she'd never touched in a most unaffectionate and uncharitable manner. She turned against the urge and moved to leave. A body blocked her way.

"What's wrong, Clarece?" the body asked, concerned. She moved to pass it. He blocked her again. "I've nothing to say to you, Sergeant," she jabbed. "Let me pass." "Nothing to say to me? You're saying alot right now. What the deuce is wrong?" *What the deuce is wrong?* she thought, screaming. *You blasted—*. "Is something wrong with your mistra?" he asked, panicked.

"My *mistra*," Clarece snarled, giving way now to her rage. What did she care what he thought? She wouldn't see him again after this day. She looked up at him. "My mistra?" she yelled quietly. "Your *lover*, you mean! Well, she isn't my concern anymore. You can have her all to yourself."

Poul's eyes squinted in bewilderment. "What the?! My *lover*?" he blurted, suddenly aware of their surroundings. "Come with me," he ordered. "You can come with yourself," she spat, "or better yet come with her. She's on her way!" A blur of anger and fear swept the sergeant like it did in battle. He responded as he did then—with action. He caught Clarece's arm and led her forcefully through the building. She acquiesced, anticipating the opportunity to strike him anyway she could.

They left the stable and walked a quarter hour into the wood behind it. Fog shielded them in the isolated place. She jerked her arm free of his grasp. "You *bastard*!" Clarece spit. "You lying, bastard!" Poul's face reddened with insult. "What the *devil* are you talking about?!" "What the devil? I'm talking about you—you and Casica!" "Me and Casica?" he demanded. "What do you mean?"

"What do I mean? I *saw* you, Poul! I saw you with her in blades." The man reeled with confusion as she prowled the grass. "I've been such a fool!" she was saying. "God! How did I not see it sooner? That's how you knew her name. That's why she fights like you! And the notes, all those notes she's sent me with! What were you—lovers in Cassica?" *Oh, my God,* he realized silently. His voice calmed immediately. "Clarece, by my honor...."

"Your *honor*? A *slave* has more honor than you! I thought...." The truth subdued her. "I thought you loved me. I thought you...." She faltered, dropping her head, defeated. She was such a fool. What would a man like him ever want with a reclace like her? Of course he would have a woman like Casica. She was the sun....

"Clarece," Poul said quickly, approaching her. She turned from him. "I'm sorry. I can explain." "Don't Poul," she whispered, shaking her head. All rage was spent. Only the ragged bag of reality remained. "You needn't explain. You're in love with a powerful and beautiful woman. You needn't apologize for that."

"I don't apologize," he said, turning her gently to himself. She met his gaze. "I *am* in love with a powerful and beautiful woman. But tis not Casica Elespoir." She squinted, questioningly. "Tis you, Clarece. I'm in love with you." Slowly, the woman backed away from his confession, her mind straining at the task of understanding.

"How can you say that?" she wept. "I'm not like you. I've given up all men for you. I cannot share my heart." "Tis not like that," he injected. He paused debating within himself. She had given him permission, had released him from her father's order. He nodded to himself. He would entrust to her his life. "Clarece," he explained, "I do love Casica. And, yes, we knew each other before. I grew up with her. You see..." he presented himself, extending his hands, "I'm Cassican. My name is K'net. Netilous. I'm her cousin."

The woman stood, transfixed. Cocking her head suspiciously, she studied his blonde hair, his fair skin, his blue eyes—and tried to force upon herself the illusion of a dark Poul. For an instant she considered she might be going mad. The juxtaposition scraped across her reasoning; frustration boiled from the wound.

"Cassican, my arse! What happened? You fell into a vat of bleach? Nepa! Not only do you play me for a fool, you think me an idiot, too!" "No!" cried K'net. "I'm telling the truth: I'm Cassican! Berea—you remember Berea? She made me this way! Honestly!" "'Honestly?' I don't think you've the capacity for honesty!" The exasperation on his face challenged her. She might be wrong. "So you're her cousin?" she asked challengingly. "Yes!" "If you're her cousin, what happened the day she broke her arm?"

K'net blinked. She knew that story? "It was my fault. I was mad at her for beating me at arrows, so I loosened her horse's cinch. She fell and tore out her arm. I thought K'eran was going to kill me." Her expression changed. "It was he who sent me here, Clarece," he continued, encouraged. "Ahead as her altage. Even M'Yat didn't know I was here until the night you sent me to find her." He approached her now. "All those notes? Just excuses for us to see one another. I've wanted to tell you about me so many times. But I was bound by an oath. But Cass wouldn't have it. That day in the blades room? She released me to tell you."

The slavewoman glanced from his eyes, fearful of the truth. "So you befriended me as a way to her," she quietly surmised. "No," he said, taking her hands. "I've never used you, Clarece. I didn't know who you were until later." His eyes embraced hers. "I fell in love in with you that day when you sang to my horse."

They were a breath apart. She gazed into the face that seemed as Byzanthian as her own. But it wasn't.... "Netilous," she breathed. "What is the meaning of your name?" He smiled at his name in her voice. "'A quiver filled'." She laughed lightly in his eyes and rested there. It didn't matter if she were a fool, if she were mad. Singing to his horse. He loved her. His mouth lowered for her own.

His horse! Scads! The horror of what she'd done fell on her.

"*Rigel!*" she exclaimed breaking away from him. "Idiot! I'm such a frappin idiot!" She paced the ground, fretting with her vest, unfastening it and worrying with the hooks. What had she done to Casica? she mused. *Scads!* Forget Casica! What had she done to herself? She turned to him, explaining.

"I did something awful Poul—Netilous—whoever you are! I didn't *know*. Asla told me to ask. Stupid! I was so jealous. I told her to transfer me." "*Transfer* you?" "Yes. She's giving me to Dolca. What have I *done*? She must feel...I need go, Netilous! I've got to stop her." He nodded and taking her by the hand, jogged with her from the woods.

The couple ran eleven steps on the path when a voice from behind snagged them. "Sergeant!" K'net froze in his tracks. His companion dropped to her knees. "Sir!" he spun, saluting. It was Macartus the Elder with his son. The two returned from a ride to exercise the younger's recuperating legs. They studied Poul: his face was red with exertion; the woman still panted, her vest hanging, unfastened. The men grinned at each other knowingly.

"Well, Sergeant Poul," the commander observed, "so we've caught you at last! Been on maneuvers, have you?" The woman blushed in her neck. Poul looked about nervously. "Uh, I can explain, Sir." The younger Macartus laughed. "I *bet* you can! Laying down on the job like this!" He glanced at the cringing slave. "Or was it kneeling?" (Everyone knew how slaves did it.)

"Uh, yes, Sir," stammered Poul. Better to shame them both than have suspicion stirred. The father and son prolonged their enjoyment at the guard's expense. "Blast it, Sergeant," the father roared, "carry on!" The two rode away, laughing. Finally, after all these years, Poul caught. What a tale they would tell this evening in the great room.

Clarece rose. She could be gutted for this lie. But she wouldn't. She had helped save the son's life. And no one cared. It was Poul who would suffer greatly at the hands of his friends. The couple turned and laughed, relieved, at one another. "Kneeling?" she quipped, her eyes shining playfully. "Is that how you would want it, Netilous?" He gaped, shocked. "I need to go," she hurried. "I love you!"

He still stood, stunned, as she disappeared into the fog. Sergeant Poul crossed his arms happily, his mind tantalized with the most enticing imaginations.

XLIII

A quick glance in the stall revealed Rigel. She hadn't come. Scads! She might be with Dolca this very moment. This thought spurred her from the stable. Clarece clipped along the west path, half-kneeling along the way to the increasing traffic. The fog thinned, and it was through this gauze she saw her, or rather her shalonn, glowing intensely. *Strange,* thought the slave, dropping instantly to her knees for acceptance. Rarely did her mistra display her necklace.

She waited in the muddy path, listening as the woman she'd maligned approached. *Receive me, please! Please!* the slave begged silently. Never had Casica not received her, even when she didn't need her. She always stopped to greet her friend and offer the distinct touch of her hand. But this time, everything was different. For one, she wasn't hers to receive.

The familiar boots and hem of the familiar cloak brushed by her. Clarece winced at the rejection. She turned her head and called softly, "Princess, please!" The steps continued, unheeding. Clarece reached into herself and drew her ace, a card she'd kept hidden in propriety. "Casica!" She spoke it loudly enough to be heard, by the princess alone, she hoped, but it didn't matter. A strap of leather couldn't harm her more than she had, herself, already.

"Casica." The princess took two more steps and stopped, the name grappling her to the voice that spoke it. She dropped her head and sighed. Now, after all that can't be unsaid, she speaks her name. A prideful place in the royal drove her forward, but a better place drew her back. If Clarece were bleeding she wouldn't pass her. Wordlessly she approached and placed her hand on the slave's bowed head. Warmth filled them both. Clarece stood and with her face hid pled, "Please. May I go with you?"

Casica paused. Her hesitancy prompted the slave to risk her eyes. In Josquin's warm darkness was revealed a deep, pained sadness. The royal nodded. The two walked silently to the stables. Casica saddled Rigel. A young man saddled Leharen, wondering within himself why women would venture forth on such a day. Casica waited until her companion mounted then trotted her horse to the meadow. This was not an ocean kind of visit. She led them through the worsening fog and cold. The dreary weather bid the woodland creatures stay in their nests and dens. Even Rigel seemed subdued.

At a clearing, the princess stopped and reined 'round her horse. The slave paused only long enough to shiver some warmth and encouragement into her chilled body. Her breath steamed as she dropped from her saddle and kneeled. Wet grass christened the face she bowed to the ground. She had read of humbling oneself into dust and ashes; surely that was a warmer humiliation but she deserved this. Deserved any punishment given her this day.

"My lady," she began. "I have greatly wronged you and now humble myself before Your Highness." The boots and cloak dropped to the ground and approached her. Casica squatted before the slave. "Please, Clarece," she asked, defeated, "you don't have to do this." The blonde head lifted, cautiously. Something in her body prepared for a beating. She faced the dark woman and wept.

"I'm so sorry, Princess. I've so terribly treated you. I've harmed you as I have not an enemy. I...," she fretted with her mitten, "I didn't know. I only now know, but tis no excuse for what I've done to you. I acted a fool and severed myself from the kindest soul I have ever known." Casica shook her head, confused. "What are you talking about?"

A mitten wiped the sea eyes. "I mean...I was jealous. That's why I hurt you so." "Jealous? Of what?" "You and Poul. I thought you were lovers." Casica plopped to the ground at the absurdity. "Lovers?!"

"I saw you." Clarece grimaced at the shame of this all. "I saw you in the blades room. He knows your pet name. You fight like him. You blushed when I told you I loved him.... I didn't know, and I was too proud to ask and then it wasn't pride at all; twas just cruelty. I wanted to hurt you. And I knew the best way would be to slight you. I...." She lost her thoughts. Her mittens dropped in defeat. "I thought you were lovers."

Casica shook her head at the clarity of the situation. Of course she would have thought that. Asla had told Josquin enough of the illicit intrigues of the palace for her to understand Clarece's conclusion; even outside the palace it was common enough for women of rank to have discreetly bedded escorts. But still, how could someone who knew her as Clarece ever think her capable of betraying such a beloved friend? "Clarece," she began, her mind as foggy as the weather, "I swear. Poul and I are only...." She searched for a word. Her slave provided it. "Cousins."

Casica gaped. "You *know*?" "Yes," Clarece nodded, "but only just now. I was raking him over my coals when he told me. He said you gave him permission to tell." The Princess of Cassica poured herself into the grass. A wave of relief washed from her the nagging burden. Finally, her friend knew.

"Are you truly cousins, my lady?" Clarece was asking. Casica glanced at the secluded meadow. "Yes," she laughed, smiling. Clarece relaxed with her. "I never would have known. He's so... white." "Not in Cassica he wasn't. Look," her companion said, taking from her karosh the locket. She peeled past the first three panels to reveal the fourth. Clarece blinked at the portrait. There was Poul, with skin darker than even her lady's. He wore a beard but the eyes were the same, blue and playful.

"This is Netilous?" Clarece voiced. Casica nodded. "We call him K'net. The 'K' in the name indicates royalty." "Dear God," the slave breathed, "I'm in love with a Cassican royal." She returned the locket and stood. "He's your cousin," Clarece breathed, shutting her eyes against the knowledge. "I'm in love with the cousin of a Cassican princess. I must be mad."

"Well, if it's any consolation, he's only a minor royal," the princess was explaining, standing. "And he's only very distantly related to me. Prick his finger and he's lost all our shared blood. K'net's my father's (she counted on her fingers) fifth cousin's son—once removed. He only lived in the palace because my father liked his father so much, he agreed to nourish him. He's like a big brother, actually." "Big brother?" A nod. "He said he's your 'altage'. What's that? Your bodyguard?"

Casica considered the dangers that had befallen her: he'd better not be her bodyguard. "Not a guard—a guardian. An altage is someone who watches for you more than over you. They're meant to be an encouraging presence. The term is an athletic one. In racing, an altage is someone who runs beside you to keep you going." The student in Clarece smiled, pleased with the concept. "Your parents didn't want you to run this race alone." "No. They know I don't do well being...alone. Tis a lifelong weakness."

The princess looked away at her vulnerable confession. At once, the slave understood more fully, the target she had hit with her rejection of the young woman. It wasn't a royal or free or owner she had harmed; it was a woman, as she. "Casica." The brown eyes looked up in surprise. Twice in one day. Clarece kneeled again, not as a slave, but as a woman humbled by the awfulness of her act. She would kneel before God to ask his forgiveness later, but for now she would do so before His child.

"I have misjudged in thinking you betrayed me but that is not my sin. That was an error bred in an environment of which you are ignorant. My sin is that I intentionally harmed you in the cruelest way I knew. I know I've already brought judgment upon myself by the consequences of my actions; I'll be denied the presence of your person. But I ask you, will you forgive me for harming you so viciously?"

Casica took Clarece's hand and invited her stand, noticing how she trembled with cold. The healer removed her cloak and placed it on her friend, thinking her parents needn't have worried about providing an altage; God had done so fourteen years in advance. "I forgive you." The forgiven smiled greatly at both her release and the warmth of the cloak. "But I wonder, Clarece. How could you have thought I would betray your trust?"

Clarece shook her head. She wondered the same thing. "I don't know, Princess. I wasn't thinking a'tall. That's the problem. I seem to be thinking less and feeling more. Tis disorienting. I don't understand."

Josquin's memory brushed against Bastien's warning concerning Clarece and her cornballs. "I *understand*," she spoke within. *Knowledge is power. You have the pride of a royal and passion of a slave.* What she said aloud was, "Well, is there anything for which I need ask *your* forgiveness?" Clarece smirked to herself. "Yes. The sin of allowing me to act like a spoiled freewoman."

Casica shook her head. She wouldn't repent of that. "Does this mean you'll be addressing me by name now?" The slave now shook her head. "No, my lady. I'm certain my mistra, Dolca, would not approve." Her owner smiled broadly to herself. There was much to talk about. She began with this first piece of information. "I haven't met with Dolca."

Asla listened intently; it was late and the slaves should all be sleeping but one could never know. Clarece told of the day as softly as shone her lamp. "And then he tells me he's the cousin of…." She pointed up. The insulit gazed reverently above.

Unbelievable! He had cousins? "God?" she mouthed. Clarece tossed an exasperated look. *The insulit! If ever there were a more theologically confused people….* She pointed again and made a sweeping motion along her neck, like a necklace hanging. Asla's eyes grew even larger. "Casica?!" she yelled silently. A nod. The g'Helderleit shook her head. Her world was getting too queer.

The women finally settled for sleep, but for Clarece there was none. She lay under her purple cover restlessly, pondering her actions of the last few days, pondering more her motives and passions. She felt frighteningly out of control, and for a bound person that was a frightening thing indeed. But what fretted her most as she drifted finally to Asla's deep breaths was her personal punishment.

Netilous. For years she'd dreamed of being alone with him; and then when she'd been given the chance, she'd missed it. God had answered her prayer, but she was in no condition to enjoy it. Such was a riveting revelation. What good was the granting of a heart's desire if one's life weren't yet able to embrace it?

XLIV

The audience laughed excitedly. "And then," the storyteller concluded, "the good prince took the dark queen to his home, which looked very much like this one, and made her his wife. They had many children who looked very much like you...and they lived happily evermore."

There was a coda in the crowd of children and parents; then all erupted in applause. The tall woman with a band of silver about her throat bowed gracefully. "She always tells stories at the games," Bastien informed his companion. "They always enjoy it. Your slave knows how to weave a tale."

"Indeed," the dark princess agreed, clapping. "And tell me good prince, how does it feel to have as your former charge one of the most intelligent people in the kingdom?" Bastien frowned. "I've never considered it. But tis a good thing. As long as she doesn't become too smart for her class." They watched the slave gather the coins tossed at her feet into a leather bag. "What if she's in the wrong class to begin with?" Josquin countered.

Clarece's presence prevented Bastien's response. "Salute, chief slaveswoman!" he offered instead. "Once again you prove yourself the highlight of the children's day!" The slave kneeled humbly. "You are too kind, Master." "And what of your story?" he continued. "How many children do they have?" "As the stars, my lord," she replied, gazing slavishly to the ground. "The prince and his lady begin a new race, one with no end." Casica was still digesting Bastien's earlier comment on class. "And maybe no beginning if the good prince isn't careful," she breathed to herself.

"I see your people's treasury begins its recovery," she said aloud. "Indeed, Mistra! The games make all generous. But this is mere seed money. The true stake is wrestling. Tarrant is utterly unbeatable." "Utterly," Bastien agreed, gnawing his turkey leg. "Not even the soldiers conquer him. He's limited to five bouts only—being a slave, but still, he walks with respect." He glanced towards the east. "Come, Casica," he urged. "Let's to the swords. Poul will be competing." He dangled the leg for enticement. It worked.

"So we'll see you there, Clarece?" asked Casica, chewing. The slave's reddened face wasn't due entirely to sun. "You won't see me, my lady. I'll stand in back with the slaves but I'll be there." Casica grinned. "And you won't forget: I'd be greatly honored to have your kingdom back me in arrows." Her friend smiled. "As the coffers allow, Highness. But I believe your competition has already begun." The dark woman gulped her ale. "Only the appetizer. Tis the main course I want. I'll make it my dessert."

"Then bon appetite," her charge wished. She paused only long enough for the couple to depart then hurried to the wrestling pit....

Raina watched all with an awed amazement. So many people. Free people. Poor people. Rich people. Slave. Slaves with iron about their necks. Slaves with bronze. Children and adults in rags and all here on the castle lawn. What a wondrous day was this, day of the summer games! Color everywhere. And excitement. She drank with her eyes as one does from a stream. More was missed than received but all of her was satisfied. She nearly tripped as she walked with her mistra, swept as she was in the activity.

Dolca stopped to barter with the beef vendor. The child waited in her shadow, her eyes scanning the market at waist level. And there, she saw them. Girls, a score or so, sitting in a row. They sat in the sun and its rays lit their blondish hair. Faces, white as porcelain, looked blankly into the crowd. They dressed warmly for the day—cloaks covering some, woolen sleeves others. But it was a particular child that mesmerized Dolca's charge. She wore a simple brown tunic and simple black trousers. She had not as much hair as the others and it was drawn plainly into a pony's tail. She lured the young girl like music.

Dolca glanced anxiously to her feet. Raina was missing. “Over here!” a male voice announced. He’d been watching the royal’s girl closely. She didn’t seem to be a thief, but still, one could never tell about a slave. Dolca smiled, relieved, and walked to squat beside her child. “What do you think?” she asked.

Raina jumped, startled. It was her mistra. She glanced shyly away. Her hand went to the metal around her throat. “She’s slave...like me.” Dolca studied the doll. Its maker had sewn a gray strip of cloth about the neck to hide a seam. “Indeed,” she nodded. She looked at the other, finer toys and thought how they held no interest for the slavechild.

“Well,” the countess observed, “it seems to me, she looks lonely.” The blue green eyes fell to the ground. Their possessor knew, well, how loneliness felt. “What do you say to her coming home with us?” Instantly, the young girl lit. She looked into her owner’s face then quickly away. She could not speak. Dolca took the doll. “We can make her vests and pretty things,” she said offering the gift. Carefully, Raina received the slavegirl. She clutched her to her chest. “Thank you, mother,” she whispered, kneeling. “I’ll take *good* care of her.”

The merchant was laughing. “Here, slave,” he offered to Dolca’s coin. “A backing wrap. You’ll need your hands free for slaving, yes?” Raina took the strip of cloth from her owner and carefully tied her doll against her lower back. Backing children was a slave’s way. Except that this child, she would not lose in eight weeks. She ate her chicken as in a dream and skipped beside her owner to the acrobats....

There were more wayward men about her than wayward pets. The blonde woman acknowledged both sets of attendants with equal indifference as she flirted pleasantly with the game master. Her winnings accumulated: fruit, bread, a string of beads, a small knife. She now eyed greater, more distant prizes. She fingered the offered dagger seductively. The man watched with growing interest. He might be losing all his wares, but what he lost in property, he gained in pleasure.

“I see you have a jacket and cape,” she was saying. “How far for them?” Natter glanced behind him. This whore was good. He’d better make it impossibly far. “Thirty cubits,” he grinned. “Or...,” he continued, leaning towards her, “a distance considerably closer. Flesh to flesh?" A golden finger traced his nose and traversed over his lips to lodge in a dimpled chin.

"I'm not for hire today," she sighed, "and I'm afraid the rest the year, I'm completely booked. However...." She licked her finger and ran it across the blade. "I feel lucky." The man blinked. "It seems as though your blades have grown imbalanced, from use no doubt. If you don't mind, I'll use my own and you set the target at forty cubits."

Approving hoots filled the booth. The game master snorted. No one, not even an assassin, could hit a gourd at forty cubits. "As you wish, my lady." He stepped off the paces. Bets were quickly placed. Natter drove his stand in the dirt. The little gourd swung lazily in the breeze.

She waited only long enough for him to face her. He was about to challenge her when suddenly, a flash of metal flew past him and exploded into a burst of shell. Gourd innards splattered his tunic. The woman smiled sweetly amidst cheers and groans.

Natter brushed the slimy entrails from his shirt. Outdone by a whore. He'd remember her next year and forbid her play. What would she need with a cape and jacket anyway? he wondered, retrieving her dagger. With great reluctance he offered it and the clothing. "Tis been a pleasure," she crooned, "as I'm certain tis true for all your women." She kissed her finger and pressed it to his lips. He stared with the others as she disappeared into the throng.

She slipped through the crowds as inconspicuously as possible. And found them quickly. They stood huddled together, shivering even in the heat. It was a young boy and his baby sister. All morning they had begged. The boy glanced to the sky; it would grow evening soon and they must race for their hideaway. Darkness made them prey to everything darker.

They saw her approach and hoped. Earlier in the day, he had noticed her attention; perhaps she returned to give them alms. They fell to their knees. Asla studied the gaunt and filthy bodies. Something in her ached. She knew too well what it was like, this desperate survival. She squatted before them. "You've worked hard all day. You must be hungry." "Yes, my lady," the boy answered. His sister clutched his hand. "Where do you stay?" she asked quietly. "The culverts?" The boy met her eyes, frightened. How could she know that?

"Well, tis a good place except for rains, yes? And it's been raining alot. You know the cooper's shop? Not the one by the stables...tis the one by the gardeners, I mean." The boy nodded. "I know it." Asla glanced around them.

"Good. The owner, he's a friend of mine. Behind his shop is where he and his wife live. Under his back stairs, you'll find a loose board. It leads under his house. You'll be safer and drier there." She looked at the trembling girl. "Twill be better for your sister. I'll talk to Cooper. He's a kind man. He'll give you scraps and may have work for you. Now you replace that board when you get underneath and prop it up with the stone you'll find under the house. You understand?"

For once the child smiled. "I understand." Asla smiled in return. Her expression warmed them. "Now," she said, handing him the jacket and cape. "Here's food and warmth for you." She placed the beads around the girl's neck. "And beauty for you." She scanned the crowds. It would be jousting and melee soon. No one would notice their departure. "Tis a good time to leave. Go to Cooper's. I'll watch for you and check on you two nights from this." The boy did not know what to say. "Go now," she encouraged.

The boy grasped his sister's hand and began jogging down the path. They would soon reach the city and their new home. Asla stood and felt for the dagger in her belt. She turned back to the pair in time to see them pause. The little girl looked at the woman who must be an angel. She smiled shyly, as one not used to smiling, and offered a tentative wave of goodbye. The insulit swallowed her tears. She offered her palm a kiss and blew it to the child. Her brother pulled her along. They must hurry....

Batis beamed. He loved giving a show and this competition had been a glorious one. All his twelve opponents, downed within their third shot. He was good. He was best. He was Batis. He bowed to the wild cheering. Another year, champion of the summer points.

One voice wasn't cheering. Clarece stood with her fellow slaves, their treasury in her mitten. Tarrant had weighed the purse with a goodly number of bronze pieces. Each slave awarded themselves with drink and food and now waited with their leader to progress to the jousts. There, they would dine fully as a group;

no porridge this night! The chief slave hesitated. She said she would come, but where was she? Even now the crowd pocketed their winnings and moved to disperse.... A dark figure captured her sight.

"Lieutenant Batis!"

The man turned from handing his quiver to his assistant. *By God,* he thought. *What's this?* What it was passed through the crowd. It parted before her, fearful of touching the alien woman. "Hail to your shooting!" she was saying. "I've never seen such a display of accurate attack. But then, I think you're known for precise piercing."

The man squinted, suspicious at first, but then only disgusted. *Cassicans: what a loathsome lot,* he thought, viewing their queen. She looked a fitting figure of Cassican royalty. Clarece gaped in disbelief. Clearly, her owner had been enjoying the day. Her blouse hung half out of her waist. Her right boot yawned, untied. She bore a tankard of something in her right hand and wielded it clumsily as her speech. Even her steps were staggered. Casica gulped more of what she drank.

"Kai! What a day! Your people excel at every sort of sport, Lieutenant! I've never seen such a display of physical prowess. I honor you!" she toasted with an audible belch. "You know," she continued, "on my runty island land, *I* was known as something of an archer." Batis gave his full attention.

"Truly, Your Highness? That surprises me. You don't seem like the outdoor type." "Truly?" Casica bantered. "That surprises *me*, kind Batis. After all, you've seen what I can do outdoors. How are you feeling?" The man blushed with resentment. How he hated his indebtedness to this wench. "Well," he bowed and turned toward his attendant.

"A moment, Sir Soldier," Casica announced. "In the spirit of the day, would you honor me with a match?" The crowd murmured its surprise. The archer eyed his enemy. "You mean arrows?" Casica laughed. "Sharp in mind as you are with tips," she observed with her drink. "Of course, arrows! And to show my goodwill, I'll let you the first shot. But to show yours, allow me two. I haven't shot since leaving my infinitesimal island." She pointed to the farthest target. It stood a hundred ninety cubits hence.

"Your once to my twice at that target. Best shot wins." The crowd's murmurs turned to speech. Already odds were being laid and bets considered. Batis surveyed the situation. He glanced at the crowd; the prince was nowhere seen, embarrassed, no doubt, by the appearance of his woman. He rubbed his chin. He disdained entertaining the Cassican but wished greatly to shame her. Civility gilded his response.

"As you wish, Your Highness," he bowed. "'Twill be a rare honor to shoot against so lovely a target." Clarece glanced to Cullis. This was her cue. "Bet all," she instructed, softly. "*What*?" the slaveman exclaimed. "No woman has ever shot in the games! And look at her. She barely stands!" Clarece pressed the bag to him. "Bet it all! The blame falls to me!" Cullis looked to his comrades. They stood stunned as he. The chief had better know what she did. They'd almost ten pounds in their bag. He ran to the bookmakers.

The chief slave looked worriedly to her owner. Scads! She hoped she wasn't making a mistake. In front, Batis had already taken his bow and a single arrow. He paused a moment before his target. A good show should keep the audience in suspense, and since the outcome of this contest was assured, he should prolong the action.

Casica staggered slightly where she stood. An arrow boy stood beside her. She leaned against him for support. At the target, another boy waved the course clear. Batis offered one final look of disdain then raised his bow. For a sixth of a minute he aimed. And released. The arrow sailed through space and struck the eye full center. All cheered. The target boy raised a gold flag: perfect shot!

The lieutenant turned to his opponent. She was clapping her tankard. "Kai, good shot, Lieutenant!" she announced. "Kai, I wish I could shoot like that!" She nodded to the audience, applauding him further before handing her drink to the boy. He offered her an unstrung bow.

The princess stepped through, positioned the bow and strained. The bow bent but not nearly enough. She grimaced as she worked still harder. It wouldn't give. She turned sheepishly to the boy. Taking the loop in her teeth, she fought with both hands. Slowly, very slowly the wood surrendered. "Would you, please?" she managed between clinched teeth. The boy took the loop from her mouth and slot it.

Batis shook his head, contemptuous. Casica started to raise the bow. "A guard, my lady?" the boy offered. "What's that?" she asked. He held the leather piece. "A guard for your arm...." She peered at the leather, confused. "Oh, yes!" she spat. "I'm sorry. I'm as out of practice as I am of shape!" She slid the guard onto her right forearm. "Thank you."

He offered an arrow. She nocked it and squinted at the target. "Blast far," she mumbled and with her right hand, drew. Her arm strained against the tension and before she knew what happened, she released. The arrow flew wildly. The crowd gasped as the target boy scrambled and fell.

"Good, God!" Batis exclaimed. "*Scads!*" thought Clarece. "Kai!" the princess blurted. "Did I hit you?" she yelled. The boy rose to his feet. He had only tripped. "I can heal you if I hurt you!" she yelled again. He raised his hands high and bowed before the roaring crowd, relishing his moment of fame. Casica laughed with the others. "Thank God!" she grinned to her boy.

Clarece cringed before her people. They needn't say what they were thinking; she could feel it. "Another if you will, please," Casica was saying. She turned to Batis. "As I've said. Tis been a while." Again she set the arrow. This time there was little strain and even less aim. The arrow flew.

The air split with sound as Batis' shaft did with iron. Batis gaped. A split arrow. He turned to see the princess grinning. "Mere luck, Sir Lieutenant," she explained under the cheering crowd. Batis was growing nervous. He glanced at his attendant. That wasn't luck.

"Excellent shot, Princess," he bowed. "Perhaps. But not best," she replied. "We are at a tie, Lieutenant. What would you suggest?" She didn't give him time to answer. Josquin snapped her fingers. "I know! We'll shoot blind." The man stared. "Blind?" he asked. "Yes! Excellent idea!" she smiled, delighted with herself. "You know: blindfolded. What archer hasn't played that game with himself? One draw blindfolded. The closest to the eye wins."

The crowd cheered approval. Again odds were laid. Clarece moved to call in their winnings. "Let it ride," a voice instructed behind her. It was Poul. "What?" "Let it ride," he repeated. "But we've thirty pounds!" she answered under her breath. "So? Make it ninety! I know this trick. Trust me." The chief slaveswoman glanced at the sergeant and then to Cullis. “Let it ride,” she ordered. “What?! But we’ve—.” “Let it ride. All of it!” Cullis cursed and turned helplessly to his fellows. Another slave moved to intercept the bag. A large man stopped him; slowly, Tarrant shook his head. All grumbling ceased.

Someone produced a black scarf. Casica was propped on her bow. “We should make this interesting....” she suggested. “More interesting than blind shooting?” Batis countered. His hands were sweaty. “Yes!” Casica agreed. “Excellent idea! A bet between us!” With an arrow tip, she cleaned her teeth of turkey, contemplating. “Let’s see.... I’ve been told there are several orphanages in this region. Let’s play for the children of Byzanthia. The loser donates say...a thousand talents among them?” The people gasped.

“A thousand talents?!” Batis objected. “I’m a mere lieutenant... not royal as yourself!” Casica smiled pleasantly. “But of course you’re royal, Earl Batis. Your family owns estates to the north, do they not?” Batis bit his teeth. Few knew that. How did she? The answer stood silently, chewing another turkey leg. There was no more reason to hide. Bastien moved up front. He glowed with pride.

Earl Batis was wavering. One thousand talents: he could lose his inheritance. The dark woman played her card. “Come now, Earl,” she said softly. “You’re not afraid, are you?” The man jerked his head to the familiar words. She smiled challengingly. “Even a Cassican’s gold spends here. What say you?” The man was trapped. He could not withdraw and shame himself before his people. Already they were chanting, “Points! Points!” He nodded.

Batis memorized the target as the blindfold was tied on him. His attendant placed an arrow into his outstretched hand. His bow hand never moved. As she had said, he’d often played this game. All grew silent. Batis set the nock. He drew and waited. The target. He could see it in his mind. The crowd cheered his arrow on. It struck the target with a victorious thud. Eight rings in! The point was two rings outside the eye! The man shed the scarf with a yell, brandishing his bow like a spear. She could not best that, the Cassican! Of this, he was certain.

Casica stared, dumbfounded. Never had she seen such a shot. “Incredible, Earl Batis! Never have I seen such a blind shot!” The earl offered a smirk. “And now, Cassican, tis your turn.” “Well,” she said, studying the distant target, "I've been told, in so many words, that my people excel in shooting bull. Let's see how this gifting translates now."

The crowd laughed. Batis wasn't laughing. He ordered his assistant to put the blindfold on her. "Make it sure," he whispered. The attendant tripled the cloth and wrapped it around her face. He secured it tightly. "Satisfied?" she asked. "I wouldn't want to be accused of cheating." Batis viewed the cloth. "I'm satisfied," he answered, thinking to himself, *Satisfied you'll never even strike the pad.*

Casica turned to her boy and, curiously, asked for two arrows. She rolled them together in a peculiar fashion. Then turned to face the confused soldier. The blindfold studied him silently.

The hair on Batis' neck stood. A horrifying realization crept over the man as sweat: she was looking directly into his eyes. "Ironic, isn't it?" she said softly, no smile in her voice now. "The first time we met: I was blindfolded then, too." Batis went cold.

She said nothing more. To his face, she took both arrows and nocked them. She smiled at Batis in a decidedly unfriendly manner, and then, in fluid motion, spun, drew, and released. She saw what everyone did. Her twin points split the target—one in its eye and other just outside its ring.

Screams of excitement exploded first from a group in back. "We're rich!" the slaves were yelling to one another. Clarece felt dizzy from shock. A greater shock came. The fifth prince of Byzanthia burst to the competitor's side. He stripped her of the blindfold and spun her playfully around. As they laughed together, the cheers increased, rising, now, more for their happiness than for the shot.

Batis dropped his head. Something was suffocating him. She knew. Somehow, she knew. What he'd thought would never come to light had; and now he would pay dearly. In plain view of a hundred witnesses. One thousand talents. The man felt faint. "I'll send for the money!" Bastien was saying. "The orphaned thank you!"

Batis stared at the woman. Her dark eyes found his. For a moment they locked. And then she turned and departed with her prince.

XLV

She was shaking her head as she had a dozen times on the subject. "Of course," he was saying, "such a small island as your own couldn't accommodate such an imposing mount as Taborhan. See how it rises with impressive might." She stayed Rigel to gaze more intently upon the fog-cloaked peak.

"Indeed, my lord," Casica replied flatly, "its size would make many blush with envy. However, tis been my observation that a fixation on the size of one's domain is often an indication of some...lack...in the same's fruitfulness." Bastien gaped. She still gazed at the skyline and turned only to smile pleasantly. Her dark eyes were unreadable.

"Indeed," he mumbled to himself, spurring his horse to continue their trek. "So tell me, Princess, did you ever summit such an edifice?" She thought for a long moment. "To date, no. At least not anything so impressive. However, I would think it the anticipated journey of ascension that most entices me."

"The journey of ascension," he repeated. He smiled at scenes of such an experience. "Well, to my knowledge, no woman has ever attempted Taborhan. Would you be interested?" She looked fully at him. "Most certainly, great prince." Bastien grinned. She liked his grin. "Then we shall do it someday, if it pleases you." "How could it not?" Her expression challenged him.

Her expressed challenge changed to action. Playfully she bid Rigel run. Her companion yelled as he chased after her, but she would not be caught. Her mount seemed to increase speed with distance. She cleared a fallen tree and spun to face him. "You cheat, Cassican!" he panted, reining beside her. "Tis the only way one from such a small land can win, great lord!" "I doubt that!" he laughed. "I think you cheat for the fun of it!" She offered a sideward smile. "Perhaps," she confessed.

They walked together now. Taboran's fog was thickening, lowering to their level. Thunder rolled in the distance. The air was cooling. "This is a beautiful land," the princess commented finally, admiring the lush green grass. "It has a good spirit about it." Bastien agreed. "It's called the 'Softlands'—like a soft, rainy day." "Or a tender day," she added. She stopped and dropped to the earth.

Something about the motion intrigued Bastien. It didn't seem quite normal, the way she landed. His speculation ended with a new curiosity. The dark woman left her horse to survey the meadow. A single tree graced it. She walked towards it and paused. She was looking at something he couldn't see. Bastien dismounted as she knelt to the ground to scoop some dirt. He squatted beside her.

"I love the earth," she spoke softly. "Pobbles are made of it, as is our flesh." She smelled the rich soil and sighed. He smiled at her enjoyment. "Why are they called 'pobbles'?" he asked. "Is it for 'odd pebble'?"

"'Power pebble,'" She grinned. "Truly, I don't know...." She freed the dirt and dug her fingers into the earth. Her shalonn glowed, but to her disappointment, nothing happened. No stones, no light. "The ancient ones say that pobbles fill your land as ours. But they sleep, awaiting a healer to rest here."

Her expression confused him. "But you're a healer," he observed. "You rest here." Casica studied his face. "I rest in my bed. Not in the earth, not yet, anyway. At home, you can tell where a healer lies in death. The ground all around is green with brilliant life." Something in the young man winced.

"Well, then, these pobbles will have to wait." She nodded. "Yes, but," she continued, brightening, "in the meantime, God has filled your land with promise. You can feel it." You *can feel it,* the man thought, taking some dirt into his own hands. All he could do was smell. Casica watched with interest. "Here," she invited, "let me help you."

She cupped her hands under his own. A familiar sensation filled him but then something new. It was coming to life, the earth, either that or he was. Bastien gasped at the feeling. It was as if an eternal connection were being forged between them, him and the soil, like a stream meeting the ocean. It drew him unto itself—or himself. He couldn't tell. He was closing his eyes to sense it more when, suddenly, a flash of lightening bolted him into the present. Their horses fled before the thunder.

"Scads!" he exclaimed, grabbing his companion. They gained the tree just in time. The rain came upon them in sheets. Bastien winced at a second strike. "This might not be the wisest location," he observed, wryly. That's all he needed, her struck by lightning. She was laughing.

"Here," she instructed, "take my hands. You'll be safe." He complied. He might not be safe, but he was happy. "Josquins aren't affected by lightning," she was explaining over the rain. "What?" "Yes. Tis true. Three hundred forty-two years ago, the healer, Hamista? She was struck full in the forehead with a bolt of lightning. The ground all around her caught fire. Some rocks even melted, but she didn't even bear a burn mark." She frowned at the next thought. "Her eyebrows fell out though."

He laughed at the image and backed her against the tree's trunk. The rain was penetrating their cover but still, this felt safer. She drew him closer. "You'll get all wet." "That's the least of our worries," he replied, thinking of the horses. He turned to say something more. And froze.

Their eyes had fixed. Transfixed. Casica barely breathed, so lost was she in his blue pools, his touch, his body. She could feel his heat and through his hands felt something more. In response, her own body stirred. *Oh, God,* she thought, *please...please.* Her mouth parted in the silent prayer.

It was all he could see. Slowly, he lowered his mouth to hers. Their lips brushed. She expelled a soft breath as he kissed her.

In all her life, never had the woman known anything as that moment. Her body surged with the connection, as did her shalonn. But with her stones, this was another of a thousand such experiences; with her, the first. She closed her eyes and searched for him. He was waiting. Bastien thrilled at her desire. Her lips caressed his in a most curious manner. It was as no kiss he'd known before. The experience with the earth came to him. Her energy was washing him into herself. Light. She was light.

The light was moving, for her hands released his and traveled up his arms to his neck. They kissed more freely. He pulled her body close and in that instant, she stepped back. Her breaths were quick, as were his, but he didn't realize that. Nothing existed but her. She was gazing into him. He could not know all that was happening in her.

Casica swallowed hard and pursed her lips. "My eyebrows might fall out," she whispered. Bastien grinned. "More likely, I'll melt...." His brought his hand to her cheek. "I don't know about my being safe with a healer...." She moved his palm to her lips and kissed it. "Whatever harm I might bring, I can heal."

This time, he didn't grin. He sighed and drew her into his arms. For a long time they rested in their silent embrace, silent, the more, with the falling rain as its backdrop. Their canopy was surrendering. They were getting soaked. Neither cared.

Bastien looked around them. Evening was coming. "Tis a long walk home. We may have to stay the night." Josquin met his playful smile. "Another night...." She turned and looked away for something. "Rigel," she said quietly. Her shalonn conveyed the call to a wooded stand not far away. He reared his head and ran to his lady's voice. Bastien snorted at the sight of the white horse. "Pony...."

She was laughing. "May I give you a ride, Prince Bastien?" "You always do, Princess." Casica mounted and offered her hand. He took his place behind and she handed him the reins, wishing his arms around her. They began their journey.

It was as their first ride together...yet nothing like it. The soft lands rang with laughter....

Clarece was reliving a time when she'd stumbled onto a cat fight. The two queens separated at her presence but neither departed. They prowled, fuming, a few cubits from each other, fur rankled, tails swishing, growls deep in their throats. That's how she felt at this moment.

Asla sat not four cubits away, silent and resentful. It wasn't enough, the blonde mused, their unresolved argument of the morning; now her body antagonized her, too. Her last lay was rough on her, reinjuring neck muscles that never seemed to heal completely. She rubbed her hand; it tingled with numbness. She would massage herself but the soreness was out of reach. The young woman glanced at the clock. Only a half hour until she must leave for the city. She could not pray but she wished, wished desperately for the healer to return. She wouldn't bear the night's services with her neck the way it was. The rain further disheartened her; what an evening to slave in the city, hurting....

"I was getting concerned!" the large man with a pony tail called. "Xerxes's been returned an hour. And without his rider. I thought I would check your chamber before sending a party." The couple were still laughing. "We had a party all our own," Bastien announced. "Quite the fireworks...." "I can imagine, Sir Prince," his friend teased. Casica's expression wasn't lost on her cousin. Poul smiled broadly; it was so good to see.

"Princess," Bastien invited, "by your leave. I'll deposit you here at your door so you may warm in a steaming bath. I'll be your stableboy and care for Rigel." "You are gracious, Great Prince," she answered, accepting his hand. She hopped to the ground. Again the movement intrigued him. He couldn't put a word on it, what made it seem so peculiar.

She looked up at him. "I'll see you for supper?" "Of course," he nodded, extending his palm. She slid her own under it; their finger tips gently caught. It was a Cassican ritual of parting, and she wondered where he had learned it. The answer stood beside her. "I'll see you at the stable, Poul," Bastien announced and rode away. She still watched him when her cousin spoke.

"Good day, Cousin?" he asked in Cassican. "The best—so far," she winked. His smile softened. "It looks good on you." "What?" "Love."

The young woman blushed. "You think we've a chance, K'net? To make a good life?" The blue eyes she knew so well glistened. "I think it was destined." She smiled her gratitude and fought the impulse to embrace him. She settled for a blessing. "God's blessing upon you, dear cousin." "And upon you. And Casica...." K'net looked toward her garden door. "Send her my greeting."

The knowledge of what her cousin suffered pricked Casica's happiness. The one he loved was denied him. "I will." She watched as he turned and started down the path.

Casica jogged lightly towards her garden. Her shalonn burned with energy—and she had nowhere to spend it. She glanced about her. No one was present, she decided. No one would see....

The clock chimed. Only a quarter hour. Asla glared at the drink stand where her dagger lay. The cherry table was too beautiful to carve holes in, so she rubbed her frustration into her palm instead, glancing at the sofa where her senior read. Or acted to read. Her calm demeanor angered the blonde more. Why was it Clarece never showed all the fear that stalked within? Asla's shoulder protested a new spasm.

"You know, if you had hands, you might help me." Clarece lowered the book. "You keep my hands out of it," she said threateningly. "Oh, I don't have to, chief slaveswoman," Asla shot. "You do that all by yourself." Clarece burned with rage.

"That's enough, whore."

Her friend blinked, stunned. Never in their history had Clarece called her that. Pain flooded Asla's eyes before they dropped, searching about herself, lost. Her aching hand she clutched to her chest. Clarece recognized the gesture and something of its familiarity pricked her with remorse. How could she ever have said that?

"I'm so sorry, Asla," she began, "I didn't mean—." The insulit stood to leave. "I take that from everyone," she recovered, "but cursed if I'll take it from you." She slid the knife behind her into its sheath. Clarece jumped to her feet. "Asla, please," she begged, "that was cruel of me. Please, forgive...."

She froze.

Something, something very large dropped onto the landing. They had both seen it, the gray blur. Whatever it was fell from the sky—nothing came up the stairs, of that she was certain—and now it lurked, eerily, outside the door. The hair on Clarece's neck stood. Asla reached for her weapon; their eyes met on the common ground of terror.

The room exploded with thunder.

The thing outside burst through the door. Casica glanced ecstatically at her friends, raising her arms in a flourish of majesty. "I am the *Royal Mother*, Queen of Life!" she announced. "Greetings, dear friends!" Asla gaped. Clarece had gone white. Oblivious to all, the princess leaned against the door, sighing.

“God, what a day! Life. Tis a beautiful thing.” Clarece studied her owner in bewilderment. She was soaking, soaking wet. Mud covered her boots and splattered her clothing. Water dripped from her curling hair into her face. She glanced to the floor. It puddled with a muddy mess. Asla was studying, also, but from a different perspective. She squinted at the glowing woman.

“You’ve been kissed,” she diagnosed. The princess collapsed into a happy heap to the floor. “So I have, mighty g’Helderleit,” she confessed. “And I’m beyond all healing. The Blessed Prince has anointed me with the gracious fragrance of his lips.” Asla laughed kindly. What would it be like, she wondered, to know such innocence?

“If such is your response to his anointing,” she voiced, “imagine what it’ll be at the offering of his scepter.” Casica grinned. “I have,” she breathed, “but tis treasonous to possess such ere investment.” Asla’s eyes shone with happiness, then relief. She could feel it. The pain in her neck and shoulder evaporated. Her hand regained its feeling.

Casica leapt to her feet. “To the city?” she asked. The insulit nodded, grateful. “Well, before you leave—a toast!” She poured three glasses of wine and presented them to her companions. “To friendship,” she offered, “and to love and hope and to the One who brings it.” It had the effect of prayer, the women’s toast, and as such, the room’s tension dispersed. Asla gulped her drink and reached for her cape.

“Tis bitter,” Casica observed. “Take my cloak with you.” She wrapped the garment about her friend and added softly, “And wake me when you return. We’ll better treat that neck of yours, yes?” Asla nodded. “Thank you, Casica.” “You’re welcome, and...I send you off with news: your prince comes for you.” “Hathen?! Hathen’s coming?!” “Yes! Bastien says next month. For two weeks.”

The g’Helderleit beamed. “There *are* gods in heaven! Two weeks.” All in her lightened. There was strength to live this night. She opened the door, fortified. “Good night, Casica.” The princess nodded. “I’ll light a candle....” Asla paused before addressing the silent slave. “Good night, Sala.” Clarece’s eyes said all. “And to you, Sala....” Her friend smiled then slipped into the darkness. Clarece listened as her steps flowed down the stairs.

Casica closed the door and began shedding her boots. It wasn't wise to dirty the senior slave's floor. Except for the rain and ticking of the clock, the room was silent. Josquin took her place in the chair. Her wine warmed to her touch as did Clarece's with her will. The slave resumed her seat on the sofa. Her owner studied her but a moment.

"I have news for you, also, Clarece," she shared. "The one you love sends his heart." The slave focused on her mittens, feeling somewhat ashamed. Someone like she didn't deserve love. "He's kind," she said simply.

The healer watched the mittens fret with one another. "What's wrong?" A tear spotted the leather. "Oh...I don't know, Mistra. I don't know what's wrong with me. Asla and I had a fight and...." She closed her eyes against the word. "I called her something reprehensible. It was awful. I've never done that before. I don't know what's wrong with me." Casica's thoughts went to Raina's story. About a rockslide. Had Clarece's knowledge of her history begun an avalanche?

"And I'm afraid," the slave continued. "Jonas has gone missing three nights now. No one knows where. Last night a guard came looking for him." She looked anxiously to her owner. "I don't know what frightens me most: his absence, what he might be doing, or the thought they might interrogate us." Casica winced. Her friend was chewing her mitten. "I'm the leader," she explained softly. "They'd begin with me."

A door opened in the other chamber. Bastien was home. The slave jumped to her feet and kneeled. "I must to your supper, Mistra. By your leave." Casica nodded. She couldn't speak. Her mind was spinning, retching. Her dear friend tortured. She'd read all the laws concerning slavery: though royal, she'd be powerless to prevent it.

Casica touched her lips. They still warmed with pleasure. Something in the woman flared with resentment. She was tired. Tired of dealing with others' pain when so much happiness stood at her door. She wished to enter into it fully, unfettered by burden.

"Josquin?" Her heart leapt at his voice. It might break, so torn it was.

XLVI

She was a happy slave. That's what she had told the healer the night before. The little girl remembered her quiet evening with the dark princess. For a long time (so it seemed to her young mind) they had read together.

"The black horse pawed at the donkey. 'You cannot race with us along the mountain path. This path is for horses. You are not a horse. You are a donkey. A donkey cannot run with horses.' 'A donkey can race with horses,' the donkey cried. 'He can race as a donkey runs. He can run a race up the mountain.'

"The donkey ran up the mountain. He saw the horses running below him. They laughed at his hard way through the rocks. He could not run with them. A donkey could not run with horses. The black horse led the horses. He ran with great speed. They could not catch him. The donkey stumbled. A little rock raced down the mountain. It woke other rocks. They all raced together in a mighty rockslide...."

"What is a rockslide, Princess?" Raina asked. Casica frowned a moment. "You see how you like to stack your mistra's bobbins in a neat pile?" The girl nodded. "Imagine what would happen if you pulled one bobbin out of the bottom." Raina imagined. "They would all fall down," she ventured. "Exactly. A rockslide is like that. One rock moves above, or sometimes below, other rocks, and they all come sliding and rolling down. Tis a dangerous thing."

"Will the horses be killed?" the slave asked worriedly. The author was kind. They wouldn't, Casica knew. "I don't know," she voiced. "Let's find out." Raina resumed her story. "They all raced together in a mighty rockslide, rolling to the horses below. The horses saw the rocks. They stopped. They reared and ran together back as they had come. The rocks covered the path behind them. They were blocked from racing on. The black horse raced by himself. Or so he thought."

Raina now knew a new word. She must tell her mistra the morrow, she decided, as the healer handed her the strange fork that made music. The girl quieted. Gently, she struck the fork on her knee. She closed her eyes and held it as far as she could from her left ear. She moved it towards her and stopped when her ear knew its tone. Dark arms embraced her warmly.

"Look how much farther it is!" Josquin whispered. "Soon, you will hear well as an owl." The slave beamed. She was warm in her new vest. She was full with milk and porridge. She was held by the kind royal. And tomorrow, she would be home with her mistra. She looked to the brown eyes. They glowed with a secret joy.

"I'm a happy slave," Raina announced. Casica mirrored a smile of her own. "And I'm a happy healer." And so she was. As healing poured into her, Raina drifted asleep with her head in the josquin's lap. She never felt Casica carry her to her stall and tuck her in. The child's comforter warmed with more than down. A healer's touch could do many things, and Casica found herself spending her giftings more and more freely. Love was releasing her from restraint.

And so now the girl all but skipped down the hall towards her mistra. Already Raina had cut greenery and dusted, but she had needed to make water and returned to her pen to do so. She must hurry back to the countess. There were bobbins to thread. Her mind wandered from rockslides to bobbin slides when suddenly, before her slave's line, she saw it. A sight more terrifying than any imagination. The baroness.

At once, the child did as her mistra had instructed weeks before. She stopped and moved to the far side of the hall. There, against the cool wall, she knelt with her head down. "'Do not look,'" Mistra had said. "'Do not speak. Do not move. Let the baroness pass before you resume whatever it is you do.'" Raina waited, a rabbit before a wolf. The steps approached. She clinched her eyes against the sound. She never saw Muriel reach for her.

"You cursed shoat!" The girl winced as, brutally, the royal grasped her by the collar. She dragged the child across the hall and flung her against the wall. Terrors—past and anticipated seized the slave. She trembled at the woman's touch and familiar stench.

"You cursed little shoat!" Muriel growled, slapping Raina across the face. The girl cried out as, time and time again, the blows came. First to her face, then to her head, her ear. The ringing all but deafened her. "Look at you!" she was saying, the Terror. "You flop like a rag in my service but flow like a cape in Dolca's. You whelp! You tricked me! You make me a fool!" She grabbed the girl's fine vest and ripped it open.

Ice poured into Raina's body. She would kill her, she knew. The baroness would kill her this time. Muriel shook her violently. "You listen to me, whelp," she whispered ominously. "You heed my words. You think you're safe with that dog, Dolca? Well, you're not! You're *mine*—you hear? You'll always be mine! You're worthless and always will be. You hear me?"

Raina tried to nod, but she couldn't, so seized with fear was she. Muriel smirked at the effect. "Now," she said softly, comfortingly, "you tell your mistra who did this to you, shoat. You do that. And I will come for you and cut your throat and feed you to the moat. Understand?" The girl understood. The woman's laugh brought poison to Raina's breath. The steps walked away.

For a long time, the slave waited, motionless. Didn't move to wipe the hot liquid that flowed from her nose. Didn't speak. Dared not open her eyes. The throbbing in her ear made her wince, but she feared to move even for it, for the steps might return.

Finally, Raina opened her eyes. It was her vest she saw first. Naked threads gaped where fine buttons had been. Bright red colored where it shouldn't. She glanced about. There they were, the buttons, scattered on the floor. The hands that gathered the bright pieces still shook but obeyed like those of a marionette. They obeyed. She must obey. There were bobbins to thread....

Dolca barely registered the opening door. A knitting needle graced her ear. "Where have you been, Raina?" she asked into her loom, "I was growing concerned." No answer. "Raina?" Silence. The royal looked. Her slave stood trembling, eyes set into the tapestried floor.

"Please forgive me, Mistra," Raina was saying. "I spoiled my vest." Dolca blinked. It didn't seem real, what she was seeing. "My God...." She raced to the child and dropped to her knees. "Raina," she managed, studying the beaten face, the bloodied nose. "Child, what happened? Who did this to you?"

In answer, Raina offered her palm. Four brass buttons peeked up at Dolca. "I'm sorry, Mother. I'm sorry I broke them." Dumbly, Dolca reached for the offering. "Raina," she asked quietly. "Look at me." Blue-green eyes locked into hers. "Who did this to you?" The eyes wept. Raina shook her head. She could not speak the name. Realization flooded Dolca. "Muriel? Did Muriel do this?"

At once the dam burst. "She told me not to tell!" Raina wept uncontrollably. "She said she would finish me! I don't want to die. I don't want to die again!" Dolca drew her into a protective embrace. It was as that time so long ago. "Peace, Little One," she breathed, rocking her child comfortingly. "No one will harm you, you hear? You're safe with me now."

"My ear...." The countess looked up, frightened. "Tis hurting?" Raina nodded, fearfully. The healer would be angry, her hurting her ear again. Dolca squinted in thought; answers must wait. "Come," she said, standing with Raina in her arms. "We'll to the princess at once," she decided, never once considering what it might look like, a royal racing down the hall with a slave in her arms.

Casica wandered in musings, her quill scratching busily upon the letter. Across the sitting area lay Clarece in her customary post-tea posture, stretched full upon the sofa, snoring delicately, a book dozing beneath mittened hands. Both women jumped as Bastien's door burst open.

"Casica!"

Clarece gasped. There stood the Countess Dolca, a bloodied and teary Raina in her arms. The royal looked helplessly at the women. "Raina's hurt!" At once, Josquin took the child. A quick glance of her shalonn revealed all. Bruises, swelling...but no true injury. Her hand went to Raina's ear. It rang and hurt but otherwise, its healing remained. "She's alright, Dolca. She's bruised but only that." Dolca went limp with relief.

"Thank God," she breathed, running her hands through her hair. Her fingers found the knitting needle, still tucked behind her ear. She stared at it. “Muriel did this,” she told herself. Casica and Clarece glanced at one another. The rage was palatable. The needle snapped in Dolca’s hands. “Witch!” she declared, gripping the pieces. The countess remembered herself. “Excuse me, ladies,” she apologized. “Raina, stay here with the princess. I’ll be back.” The child watched fearfully as her owner spun to exit the room, depositing the broken needle on Casica’s dining table with violent force.

Clarece stood, wide-eyed as Raina. “She’s vexed,” the child wept. “She’s vexed at me.” “Yes,” the princess agreed, “your mistra is very angry, but not at you, Raina. Not you. Tis Muriel she’s angry with.” She caressed the young face comfortingly. Warmth and healing filled the child. “Now, you rest for a bit, yes?” the healer soothed. “Your mistra will speak with the baroness. Everything will be alright.” Raina nodded, sleepy.

Beside her, Clarece smoldered.

XLVII

She found her seated at her table, goblet in hand. The baroness didn't look up. "Blast you, Muriel!" Dolca demanded. "How dare you! How dare you touch another's slave!" In response, the goblet rose. Dolca's hand exploded, catapulting the vessel and its contents across the room. The metal rang loudly upon the marbled floor. Muriel tensed, fully expecting the next slap to cross her face. And while she did consider it, Dolca clenched her eyes to the pain in her hand, instead.

Never in life had she exhibited such rage, she thought, studying the cowering woman. The Baroness Muriel, wife of Baron Ramlan. Scenes, distant in time but intimate in person bobbed in Dolca's memory. Could this shadow woman be the same Muriel who swayed society's court two decades earlier? Before the war? Before the death of her son and husband?

The countess sat heavily at the table. Her voice still brimmed with indignation. "I ought to have you stocked. And I swear, if not for the grace of memory, I would." At these words, Muriel looked up. Memory. It was all she had. That and the numbing effects of wine; but no amount of that tyrannous god could bleed her dry of hatred. Nothing adequately numbed her soul. Dolca's eyes moistened at the defeated image.

"Look at you, Muriel," she observed quietly. "Our husbands were friends once, comrades in battle. And you, you were Ramlan's glory. He adorned himself with you like a garland about his life. But look at yourself now. Look at where your bitterness has taken you. Tis brittled your leaves."

As she spoke, Dolca knew it was not merely the baroness she addressed. She understood from whence her sympathy flowed. In Muriel she saw herself, had it not been for another's intervention, had God not surprised her with mercy. With grace. Dolca considered Muriel's tears and sighed. "You're killing yourself," she declared softly. "Your slavery is making you mad. There's a convent is Teristan. They can help you there. I'm a benefactress. I could send letters on your behalf." Muriel's hands trembled. "But if you won't have help," Dolca concluded, "I give you warning: if you so much as look at Raina again, I'll have you before the king."

There was nothing more to say. Dolca stood. She had taken three steps upon the rug that at one time Raina's blood had stained, when behind her, a weak voice wakened. "Would you, indeed, write letters?"

Clarece cleaned the face of her young charge. While the woman's actions were tender, their energy was not. Her task complete, the chief slaveswoman held the little slave silently; yet, there was nothing silent in her mind.

Casica could not read Clarece's thoughts, but she could feel them, rising like steam from a laborer's head in winter.... Tarrant's daughter. Property of a powerful royal. Attacked and harmed in a palace hallway. In broad daylight. And nothing, Clarece knew, nothing would happen as consequence. It mattered not Raina wore clothing fit for a daughter; her throat was bound by a piece of metal. Its presence unraveled everything else. She was slave. She was a not human.

Bastien's door opened again, this time calmly. Raina looked up attentively. It was her mother. "Raina," Dolca smiled, "how are you feeling?" The girl knelt in her owner's presence. Dolca received her. "Well, Mistra," she answered. "The healer says I'm well." "And your ear?" The slave nodded. "The bells have stopped." "Good," Dolca grinned. "Your head's not a belfry, is it? No bats inside. Only dreams." She looked to her hostess. "Thank you, Princess. Could you come to tea after supper? I wish speak with you." "Of course," Casica nodded. The countess bowed in acknowledgment then addressed her slave.

"And now, Raina. Do you wish to rest in your stall or do you want to come with me?" "I want to be with you." The woman glowed. "Then come. We'll mend your vest and clean it. 'Twill be good as new." Casica waited until Dolca and Raina's departure before addressing her friend. Clarece was scowling at her mittens.

"So. What's weaving in that loom of yours, Clarece? You're fit to be tied." The tall slave dug her boot into the floor. "I'm already tied, Mistra," she said more to herself than anyone. "And I'm confused." She faced her owner plainly. "You've a justice streak in you as conspicuous as your gold stones, yet you seem unmoved by what has happened." Casica blinked. "I'm not unmoved. But I am satisfied. Dolca's taken care of it." The blue eyes turned cold.

"Taken care of what? Nothing's changed. If Raina were one of Dolca's hounds, there'd be hell to pay. The baroness would be fined, if not stocked, and not for the countess' will. The magistrate would bring this action to court. But Raina," she snorted, "Raina is slave. Many notches below a dog. She's no rights, no recourse, no protection." "Dolca is her protection," Casica challenged. "Of course," replied Clarece sarcastically, "I *see* how she protects. Protection for slaves is mending. There's no preventing the tear; there's merely sewing after the harm is done."

Something in the princess stirred, indignant. "I don't know what transpired between Dolca and Muriel, Clarece, but I'm certain of this: Muriel won't harm Raina again." Clarece's laugh was bitter.

"Baroness Muriel? You think the baroness is the worst thing that can happen to Raina? What of the guard that decides to take her or some servant who wishes her "pay" for the fine clothes she wears? She is prey to anything and everything, and there's nothing some royal can do to stop it. There is nothing because Raina is slave. She is the not human. We slaves, we've no help because we are *not* at all."

The healer paused before replying, taken aback by the fury she witnessed. "You *are* human, Clarece Aerasa," she offered finally. "Tis not some law that accords humanity. Tis God."

"*God*," sneered Clarece. "God does nothing to save us. Nothing to free us. There are some who think that any salvation for slaves must come from slaves. There are some who suggest that to be considered human, we must act as human. We must fight for ourselves and do what cannot be ignored by the owner."

Casica felt cold. She crossed her arms and tasted her friend's words. Clarece skirted a deadly ledge. "Do what such acts, Clarece? Burning men in their beds?" The slave held her gaze threateningly. "You think slave did that?" "I don't know who did it," Casica challenged. "Do you?" For a moment, Clarece resisted. "It was not slave," she answered finally. "How can you know that?" pried Casica. "I know. But perhaps," Clarece's voice continued darkly, "perhaps it should have been."

The healer leaned into her warning. Her eyes burned. "Clarece Aerasa, you hear me: any such act of rebellion would be a futile gesture." The bound woman smirked. "'A futile gesture'," she repeated. "What is a slave's existence if not a pathetic farce of futile gestures? You cannot tell me you haven't thought how absurd they are, our little tricks. How we kneel before flesh as to God. How we cringe in the presence of the free as to the Eternal." Her mind spun a cynical web. "We stave off our hunger in dark, stone passages and conceive on our knees children we cannot keep with men we cannot have. We feed our lives on threats of death and polish signs of bondage like finery. You speak of futility. Futility defines us." She looked away to memory.

"When I was a young slave, just come to the palace, we had a man in our pen. Comadious was his name. He was a kind man. He used to give me extra portions at supper." Her eyes moistened. "One day, a falcon of his mastra escaped its cage. His mastra had twenty-nine falcons. Twenty-nine, but for the one, he required of Comadious everything. We were eating our supper, wondering where Comadious was, when he came.

"He arrived to our meal by two guards borne. When they tossed his body onto our table, his entrails poured out." She closed her eyes against the grisly scene. "I can still smell them. Still see them ooze onto the place where we dine every night." She turned to face her owner. "What was that if not a 'futile gesture'? We weren't that man's property. There was nothing he could do to us. But he made his mark. It was futile, perhaps, but I swear to you, Princess of Cassica, that *futile* gesture seared into our minds an impression that far outlasted the stains of Comadious' blood on our table."

Casica was aghast. The story cut off any response. And she would have dangled in her suspension had Clarece not voiced one final conviction. “No gesture is futile if it leaves a lasting impression. If it unsettles the peace of the established.” These words awakened in Casica what was royal.

Her hand reached into her vest. It found her kerchief. Without seeing it, she knew what she felt in its embroidered corner. A fleur d’lis with the crest of K’eran, King of Cassica. Actions empowered by such words as she had heard could topple a crown. Any crown. Evil or good. “Tis not the place of humans to uproot what is divinely sown,” she countered aloud. Clarece’s expression was unreadable. “You speak of the human. What of the not?”

In the next chamber, a door opened. It was Bastien, coming to visit Casica before they dined. The slave glanced at the sound. “I must to your meals, Mistra,” she said casually. Casica held her gaze. “We will speak more of this, Clarece.” The blue eyes of Silva hid. “There’s nothing more to be said,” the slave replied quietly. She kneeled before rising to disappear into the dark slave passage.

Casica propped against her dining table, her mind awash in turmoil. Curiously, she didn’t know what troubled her more. The content of their exchange or the realization it was held, almost entirely, in fluent Cassican....

About the Author

I have spent most of my life serving in a variety of educational and ministry settings. Along the way, I have observed and experienced, firsthand, the marvelous transformative power of Christ. My novels are based on the belief that real life is the greatest of all stories. The themes of your life, you will find woven into the lives of *The Cassican Chronicles.* It is my desire that as you enter the world of Clarece d'Casica, you will find inspiration to live more fully in freedom and hope.

My world is, currently, a mixture of writing, schooling, caretaking and farming. My husband, Kyle, and I live with our two children in beautiful rural Virginia.

I love hearing from my readers. Please contact me at
Martha@cassicanpress.com.

Thank you for reading and remember: horses dance....
Martha J. Vaught

Next in the *Cassican Chronicles* Series: *Asla, The Beauty of God*